D1068758

The Best

OF THE

Best American
Short Stories

1915–1950

The Best

OF THE

Best American

Short Stories

1915-1950

EDITED BY

MARTHA FOLEY

19 52

HOUGHTON MIFFLIN COMPANY BOSTON

The Riverside Press Cambridge

COPYRIGHT, 1952, BY HOUGHTON MIFFLIN COMPANY

ALL RIGHTS RESERVED INCLUDING THE RIGHT TO REPRODUCE
THIS BOOK OR PARTS THEREOF IN ANY FORM

"How the Devil Came Down Division Street," by Nelson Algren. Copyright, 1944, by *Harper's Bazaar.*
"I'm a Fool," by Sherwood Anderson. Copyright, 1923, by Sherwood Anderson.
"The Blue Sash," by Warren Beck. Copyright, 1938, by *Story Magazine.*
"Nothing Ever Breaks Except the Heart," by Kay Boyle. Copyright, 1941, by Kay Boyle.
"Horse Thief," by Erskine Caldwell. Copyright, 1933, by Condé Nast Publishers.
"Sex Education," by Dorothy Canfield. Copyright 1945, by Yale University Press.
"The Enormous Radio," by John Cheever. Copyright, 1947, by The New Yorker Magazine, Inc.
"The Wind and the Snow of Winter," by Walter Van Tilburg Clark. Copyright, 1944, by Yale University Press.
"Boys Will Be Boys," by Irvin S. Cobb. Copyright, 1917, by Irvin S. Cobb.
"Christ in Concrete," by Pietro Di Donato. Copyright, 1937, by *Esquire-Coronet.*
"Hand Upon the Waters," by William Faulkner. Copyright, 1939, by Curtis Publishing Company.
"My Old Man," by Ernest Hemingway. Copyright, 1928, by Scribners.
"The Peach Pit," by Paul Horgan. Copyright, 1942, by Paul Horgan.
"Haircut," by Ring Lardner. Copyright, 1929, by Scribners.
"Man On a Road," by Albert Maltz. Copyright, 1938, by Albert Maltz.
"Prince of Darkness," by J. F. Powers. Copyright, 1946 by J. F. Powers.
"Resurrection of a Life," by William Saroyan. Copyright, 1936, by The Modern Library, Inc.
"Search Through the Streets of the City," by Irwin Shaw. Copyright, 1941, by Irwin Shaw.
"The Interior Castle," by Jean Stafford. Copyright, 1946, by *Partisan Review.*
"How Beautiful With Shoes," by Wilbur Daniel Steele. Copyright, 1933, by Wilbur Daniel Steele.
"The Women on the Wall," by Wallace Stegner. Copyright, 1946, by Wallace Stegner.
"Dawn of Remembered Spring," by Jesse Stuart. Copyright, 1942, by Jesse Stuart.
"A Wife of Nashville," by Peter Taylor. Copyright, 1949, by The New Yorker Magazine, Inc.
"The Catbird Seat," by James Thurber. Copyright, 1942, by James Thurber.
"A Curtain of Green," by Eudora Welty. Copyright, 1938, by Eudora Welty.

813.508
B56/b

To
the memory of
EDWARD J. O'BRIEN

Acknowledgment

Grateful ACKNOWLEDGMENT for permission to reprint the stories in this volume is made to the following:

To the Editors of Condé Nast Publishers, Curtis Publishing Company, *Esquire-Coronet, Harper's Bazaar,* The Modern Library, Inc., The New Yorker Magazine, Inc., *Partisan Review,* Scribners, and Yale University Press; and to Nelson Algren, Sherwood Anderson, Warren Beck, Kay Boyle, Erskine Caldwell, Dorothy Canfield, John Cheever, Walter Van Tilburg Clark, Mrs. Irvin S. Cobb, Pietro Di Donato, William Faulkner, Ernest Hemingway, Paul Horgan, Ring Lardner, Albert Maltz, J. F. Powers, William Saroyan, Irwin Shaw, Jean Stafford, Wilbur Daniel Steele, Wallace Stegner, Jesse Stuart, Peter Taylor, James Thurber, and Eudora Welty.

Foreword

THE TWENTY-FIVE STORIES in this volume have been selected from the thirty-five annual volumes of *The Best American Short Stories* which have appeared since the late Edward J. O'Brien first established the series in 1915. Selecting only twenty-five stories from close to a thousand stories that were considered of such high literary excellence that they themselves had been chosen for reprinting from among thousands of other stories has been the most difficult task the present editor ever attempted.

In other words, and to continue the statistics, these stories represent a selection from more than fifty thousand short stories which have been published in America during that thirty-five-year period. Whether this selection does justice to such a terrific winnowing, only the reader can decide.

When I first began to read the volume in the series for this particular book, I had an abundance of paper and pencils ready to note major and minor literary trends. In editing the annual volumes I had been able to observe very definite changes and developments from year to year. But, if I were to be asked now what is the most observable over-all trend in the American short story since 1915, I simply could not answer.

It is true that there does seem to have been a growth out of a certain kind of naïve writing in many of the stories first reprinted in the series into a more fully realized art form. Otherwise, the variety of content and style has been so great that it is hopeless to try to determine any one overwhelming trend. A single fact is indisputable and that is that in no country on earth, at any period in history, have so many short stories been written and published as in the United States of America during the past thirty-five years.

The stories represent those written in the years following the First World War, during the blazing twenties, during the depression years and during the forties which yet have to receive a label. The latter decade, of course, has been divided between the Second World War years and the five years which followed the worst conflict in history.

In many of the stories which were reprinted from 1915 to 1920 a great emotionalism is apparent. Then for a while realism became predominant. In the thirties came, not so much what has been called the proletarian school of writing, as what might be called stories with the conversion ending. This is the kind of story in which the main character suddenly, at the very end, became aware that he should fight for the rights of labor, or that minority groups really were worth-while people in their own right.

The stories that appeared during the First World War were given over to the emotionalism mentioned before. A typical example is the tale of a musician sent out to sing to the Czar's troops while they are fighting the Austrians. He sings to the Russian soldiers of their homeland, of their little villages there, of the children at play and of the girls that were left behind. The effect on the Russians is not to make them want to fight harder, as was intended. Instead, as they listen to the singer, they throw down their arms, want no more to do with war and yearn only to return to the homes they had left. The story, of course, was not written as baldly as it has been told here and, with others in the same genre, has a tearful impact. It must have been a much simpler world then.

Stories of soldiers published during the Second World War show much more vivid reality and objectivity. They can horrify but they do not make the reader weep.

One of the reasons there are so many editors in the world is that they disagree with one another. Just as Edward J. O'Brien, if he were alive, undoubtedly would be astounded at some of the decisions I have made in those volumes I have edited, I have been surprised at some of his decisions, or rather omissions. One such omission is "Silent Snow, Secret Snow" by Conrad Aiken. Another is "The Devil and Daniel Webster" by Stephen Vincent Benet. If those stories had been printed in the series I would have chosen them for inclusion here.

The reader will also observe, alas, that one of our very finest writers, Willa Cather, is not included. Her stories appeared in yearly volumes of *The Best American Short Stories* but she left strict instructions with her literary executor that none of her stories, save two, were to be published again. Neither of the exceptions was reprinted in the anthology.

I always have liked the work of Wilbur Daniel Steele, but not until I read again many of his stories while preparing this work did I appreciate his real importance. He has been represented many times in the yearly collections and each of his stories remains magnificent. Unlike many famous writers, whose work was in the early volumes, he has never fluctuated in quality or compromised his values. I want to pay specific tribute to him.

Because of the limits placed upon this book, I have had to omit many stories I very much would have liked to include. I hope, however, that readers will understand that, although they may not be given a vast panoramic view of the tremendous number of fine short stories our country has produced since 1915, they are being afforded as choice a selection — ranging from such earlier writers as Theodore Dreiser and Ring Lardner down to such newer authors as John Cheever and Peter Taylor — as an editor who has done an awful lot of reading can devise.

MARTHA FOLEY

New York City

Contents

xi

The Best

OF THE

Best American
Short Stories

1915–1950

NELSON   ALGREN

How the Devil Came Down
Division Street

LAST SATURDAY EVENING there was a great argument in the
Polonia Bar. All the biggest drunks on Division were there, trying
to decide who the biggest drunk of them was. Symanksi said he was,
and Oljiec said he was, and Koncel said he was, and Czechowski said
he was.

Then Roman Orlov came in and the argument was decided. For
Poor Roman had been drunk so long, night and day, that when we
remember living men we almost forget Poor Roman, as though he
were no longer really among the living at all.

"The devil lives in a double-shot," Roman explains himself
obscurely. "I got a great worm inside. Gnaws and gnaws. Every day
I drown him and every day he gnaws. Help me drown the worm,
fellas."

So I bought Poor Roman a double-shot and asked him frankly how,
before he was thirty, he had become the biggest drunk on Division.

It took a long time, and many double-shots, for him to tell. But
tell it he did, between curses and sobs, and I tell it now as closely to

1

what he told as I can. Without the sobs, of course. And of course without any cursing.

When Roman was thirteen, it seems, the Orlovs moved into three stove-heated rooms in the rear of a lopsided tenement on Noble Street. Mama O. cooked in a Division Street restaurant by day and cooked in her own home by night.

Papa O. played an accordion for pennies in Division Street taverns by night and slept alone in the rooms by day.

There were two beds in the tiny flat, so nobody encouraged Papa O. to come home at all.

Because he was the oldest, Roman slept between the twins, on the bed set up in the front room, to keep the pair from fighting during the night as they did during the day. Every day, Teresa, who was eleven and could not learn her lessons as well as some of her classmates, slept with Mama O. in the windowless back bedroom; under a bleeding heart in a gilded oval frame.

If Papa O. got in before light, as happened occasionally early in the week, he crawled uncomplainingly under Roman's bed until Roman rose and got the twins, who were seven, up with him in time for Mass.

If Udo, who was something between a collie and a St. Bernard and as big as both, was already curled up beneath the front-room bed, Papa O. slugged him with the accordion in friendly reproach — and went on into the back bedroom to crawl under Mama O.'s bed. In such an event he slept under a bed all day. For he never crawled, even with daylight, into Mama O.'s bed. Empty or not. As though he did not feel himself worthy to sleep there even when she was gone.

It was as though, having given himself all night to his accordion, he must remain true to it during the day.

For all manner of strange things went on in Papa O.'s head, as even the twins had become aware. Things so strange that Teresa was made ashamed of them by her schoolmates, whenever they wanted someone to tease.

This, too, was why no one, not even the twins, paid Papa O. any heed when the family returned from Mass one Sunday forenoon and he told them someone had been knocking while they were away.

"Some*body* was by door," he insisted. "I say 'Hallo.' Was no*body*." He looked slyly about him at the children. "Who plays tricks by Papa?" he asked.

"Maybe was the Zolewitzes," Mama O. suggested indifferently. "Mama Z. comes perhaps to borrow."

That Sunday night it was cold in all the corners. Papa O. was gone to play for pennies and drinks, Mama O. was frying *pierogi,* the twins were in bed and Teresa was studying her catechism across the table from Roman, when someone knocked lightly twice.

To Roman it sounded like someone at the clothes closet door; but that was foolish to think, since the twins were in bed. Yet, when he opened the hall door, only a cold wind came into the room from the long gaslit passage.

Roman, being only thirteen, did not dare look behind the door. Far less to speak of the clothes closet.

All that night a light snow fell, while Roman O. lay wakeful fancying he saw it falling on darkened streets all over the mysterious earth, on the pointing rooftops of Old World cities, on mountain-high waves of the mid-Atlantic, and in the leaning eaves of Noble Street. He was just falling off to sleep when the knocking came again. Three times, like a measured warning. The boy stiffened under the covers, listening with his fear. Heard the hall door squeak softly, as though Papa O. were sneaking in. But Papa O. never knocked, and Papa O. never sneaked. Papa O. came home with the accordion banging against buildings all down Noble Street, jingling his pennies proudly, singing off-key bravely, mumbling and laughing and stumbling. Papa O. never knocked. He kicked the door in happily and shouted cheerfully, "What you say, all peoples? How's t'ings, everbody?" Papa O. pulled people out of bed and rattled pans and laughed at nothing and argued with unseen bartenders until somebody gave him sausage and eggs and coffee and bread and hung the accordion safely away.

Roman crept, barefooted, in the long underwear Mama O. had sewed on him in the early fall, to the hallway door.

The whole house slept. The windows were frosted and a thin line of ice had edged up under the front window and along the pane. The family slept. Roman shoved the door open gently. The tenement slept. Down the hall the single gas jet flickered feebly. No one. Nothing. The people slept.

Roman looked behind the door, shivering now with more than cold.

No one. Nothing. All night long.

He returned to bed and prayed quietly, until he heard Mama O. rise; waited till he knew she had the fire going in the big kitchen stove. Then, dressing with his back to the heat, he told Mama O. what he had heard. Mama O. said nothing.

Two mornings later, Papa O. came home without the accordion. It did not matter then to Mama O. whether he had sold it or lost it or loaned it: she knew it at last for a sign, she had felt the change coming, she said, in her blood. For she had dreamed a dream, all night, of a stranger waiting in the hall: a young man, drunken, leaning against the gaslit wall for support, with blood down the front of his shirt and on his hands. She knew, as all the Orlovs knew, that the unhappy dead return to warn or comfort, to plead or repent, to gain peace or to avenge.

That day, standing over steaming kettles, Mama O. went back in her mind to all those dear to her of earth who had died: the cousin drowned at sea, the brother returned from the war to die, the mother and father gone from their fields before she had married.

That night she knocked on Mama Zolewitz's door. Mama Z. sat silently, as though she had been expecting Mama O. for many evenings.

"Landlord doesn't like we should tell new tenants too soon," Mama Z. explained even before being told of the knocking, "so you shouldn't say it, I told. It was a young man lived in this place, in your very rooms. A strange young man, and good to look at. But sick, sick in the head from the drink. A sinner certainly. For here he lived with his lady without being wed, and she worked and he did not. That he did not work had little to do with what happened, and the drink had little to do. For it was being unwed that brought it on, at night, on the New Year. He returned from the taverns that night and beat her till her screams were a whimpering. Till her whimpering became nothing. A strong young man, like a bull, made violent by the drink. When the whimpering ceased, there was no sound at all. No sound until noon, when the police came with shouting.

"What was there to shout about? I could have them before they came. The young man had hanged himself in the bedroom closet. Thus it is that one sin leads to another and both were buried together. In unsanctified ground, with no priest near."

Mama O. grew pale. Her very clothes closet.

"It is nothing to worry," Mama Z. told her neighbor sagely, "he does not knock to do harm. He comes only to gain a little peace that good Christian prayer for him may give. Pray for the young man, Mama O. He wishes peace."

That night after supper the Orlovs gathered in prayer about the front-room stove, and Papa O. prayed also. For now that the accordion was gone, the tavern must do without him. When the prayer was done, he went to bed with Mama O. like a good husband, and the knocking did not come again.

Each night the Orlovs prayed for the poor young man. And each night Papa O. went to bed with Mama O. for lack of his accordion.

Mama O. knew then that the knocking had been a sign of good omen, and told the priest, and the priest blessed her for a Christian. He said it was the will of God that the Orlovs should redeem the young man by prayer and that Papa O. should have no accordion.

Papa O. stayed at home until, for lack of music, he became the best janitor in the 800 block on Noble Street. Mama Z. went to the priest and told of her part in the miracle of the poor young man, and the priest blessed Mama Z. also.

When the landlord learned that his house was no longer haunted, he brought the Orlovs gifts; and when the rent was late, he said nothing. So the priest blessed him equally, and in time the Orlovs paid no rent at all, but prayed for the landlord instead.

Teresa became the most important person in her class, for it became known that a miracle had been done in the Orlov home. Sister Mary Ursula said the child looked more like a little saint every day. And no other child in the room ever had her lessons as well as Teresa thereafter.

The twins sensed the miracle, and grew up to be fast friends, doing all things together, even to wearing the same clothes and reading the same catechism. Udo, too, knew that the home was blessed. For he received no more blows from the accordion.

Only one sad aspect shadowed this great and happy change: Poor Roman was left bedless. For with Papa O. home every night like a good husband, Teresa must sleep between the twins.

Thus it came about that the nights of Roman Orlov became fitful and restless, first under the front-room bed and then under the back-room bed. With the springs overhead squeaking half the night as likely as not. The nights of Roman's boyhood were thereafter passed beneath one bed or the other, with no bed of his own at all. Until, reaching his young manhood and his seventeenth year, he took at last to sleeping during the day in order to have no need for sleep at night.

And at night, as everyone knows, there is no place to go but the taverns.

So it was, being abroad with no place to go and the whole night to kill, that Roman took his father's place. He had no accordion for excuse — only lack of a bed. He came to think of the dawn, when the taverns closed and he must go home, as the bitterest hour of the day.

This is why he still calls the dawn the bitterest hour: he must go home though he has no home. Nor wife, nor family, nor hope, nor joy.

Is this a drunkard's tale or sober truth? I can only say he told it like the truth, drinking double-shots all the while. I only know that no one argues about who the biggest drunk on Division is if Roman O. is around.

I only know what Mama O. now tells, after many years and Papa O. in his grave and the twins scattered: that the young man who knocked was in truth the devil. For did she not give, without knowing what she did, a son in return for a husband?

"I'm drownin' the worm t'night," Poor Roman explains, talking to his double-shot. "Help me drown the worm t'night, fellas."

Does the devil live in a double-shot? Or is he the one who gnaws, all night, within?

SHERWOOD ANDERSON

I'm a Fool

I T WAS a hard jolt for me, one of the most bitterest I ever had to face. And it all came about through my own foolishness too. Even yet, sometimes, when I think of it, I want to cry or swear or kick myself. Perhaps, even now, after all this time, there will be a kind of satisfaction in making myself look cheap by telling of it.

It began at three o'clock one October afternoon as I sat in the grandstand at the fall trotting and pacing meet at Sandusky, Ohio.

To tell the truth, I felt a little foolish that I should be sitting in the grandstand at all. During the summer before I had left my home town with Harry Whitehead and, with a nigger named Burt, had taken a job as swipe with one of the two horses Harry was campaigning through the fall race meets that year. Mother cried and my sister Mildred, who wanted to get a job as a schoolteacher in our town that fall, stormed and scolded about the house all during the week I left. They both thought it something disgraceful that one of our family should take a place as a swipe with race horses. I've an idea Mildred thought my taking the place would stand in the way of her getting the job she'd been working so long for.

7

But after all I had to work and there was no other work to be got. A big lumbering fellow of nineteen couldn't just hang around the house and I had got too big to mow people's lawns and sell newspapers. Little chaps who could get next to people's sympathies by their sizes were always getting jobs away from me. There was one fellow who kept saying to everyone who wanted a lawn mowed or a cistern cleaned, that he was saving his money to work his way through college, and I used to lay awake nights thinking up ways to injure him without being found out. I kept thinking of wagons running over him and bricks falling on his head as he walked along the street. But never mind him.

I got the place with Harry and I liked Burt fine. We got along splendid together. He was a big nigger with a lazy sprawling body and soft kind eyes, and when it came to a fight he could hit like Jack Johnson. He had Bucephalus, a big black pacing stallion that could do 2.09 or 2.10 if he had to, and I had a little gelding named Doctor Fritz that never lost a race all fall when Harry wanted him to win.

We set out from home late in July in a boxcar with the two horses and after that, until late November, we kept moving along to the race meets and the fairs. It was a peachy time for me, I'll say that. Sometimes, now, I think that boys who are raised regular in houses, and never have a fine nigger like Burt for best friend, and go to high schools and college, and never steal anything or get drunk a little, or learn to swear from fellows who know how, or come walking up in front of a grandstand in their shirt sleeves and with dirty horsey pants on when the races are going on and the grandstand is full of people all dressed up — What's the use talking about it? Such fellows don't have nothing at all. They've never had no opportunity.

But I did. Burt taught me how to rub down a horse and put the bandages on after a race and steam a horse out and a lot of valuable things for any man to know. He could wrap a bandage on a horse's leg so smooth that if it had been the same color you would think it was his skin, and I guess he'd have been a big driver too and got to the top like Murphy and Walter Cox and the others if he hadn't been black.

Gee whizz, it was fun. You got to a county seat town maybe, say, on a Saturday or Sunday, and the fair began the next Tuesday and lasted until Friday afternoon. Doctor Fritz would be, say, in the 2.25

trot on Tuesday afternoon and on Thursday afternoon Bucephalus would knock 'em cold in the "free-for-all" pace. It left you a lot of time to hang around and listen to horse talk, and see Burt knock some yap cold that got too gay, and you'd find out about horses and men and pick up a lot of stuff you could use all the rest of your life if you had some sense and salted down what you heard and felt and saw.

And then at the end of the week when the race meet was over, and Harry had run home to tend up to his livery stable business, you and Burt hitched the two horses to carts and drove slow and steady across country to the place for the next meeting so as to not overheat the horses, etc., etc., you know.

Gee whizz, gosh amighty, the nice hickorynut and beechnut and oaks and other kinds of trees along the roads, all brown and red, and the good smells, and Burt singing a song that was called "Deep River," and the country girls at the windows of houses and everything. You can stick your colleges up your nose for all me. I guess I know where I got my education.

Why, one of those little burgs of towns you come to on the way, say now, on a Saturday afternoon, and Burt says, "Let's lay up here." And you did.

And you took the horses to a livery stable and fed them and you got your good clothes out of a box and put them on.

And the town was full of farmers gaping, because they could see you were race horse people, and the kids maybe never see a nigger before and was afraid and run away when the two of us walked down their main street.

And that was before prohibition and all that foolishness, and so you went into a saloon, the two of you, and all the yaps come and stood around, and there was always someone pretended he was horsey and knew things and spoke up and began asking questions, and all you did was to lie and lie all you could about what horses you had, and I said I owned them, and then some fellow said, "Will you have a drink of whiskey?" and Burt knocked his eye out the way he could say, offhand like, "Oh, well, all right, I'm agreeable to a little nip. I'll split a quart with you." Gee whizz.

But that isn't what I want to tell my story about. We got home late in November and I promised mother I'd quit the race horses for good. There's a lot of things you've got to promise a mother because she don't know any better.

And so, there not being any work in our town any more than when I left there to go to the races, I went off to Sandusky and got a pretty good place taking care of the horses for a man who owned a teaming and delivery and storage business there. It was a pretty good place with good eats and a day off each week and sleeping on a cot in the big barn, and mostly just shoveling in hay and oats to a lot of big good-natured skates of horses that couldn't have trotted a race with a toad. I wasn't dissatisfied and I could send money home.

And then, as I started to tell you, the fall races come to Sandusky and I got the day off and I went. I left the job at noon and had on my good clothes and my new brown derby hat I'd just bought the Saturday before, and a stand-up collar.

First of all I went downtown and walked about with the dudes. I've always thought to myself, Put up a good front, and so I did it. I had forty dollars in my pocket and so I went into the West House, a big hotel, and walked up to the cigar stand. "Give me three twenty-five cent cigars," I said. There was a lot of horse men and strangers and dressed-up people from other towns standing around in the lobby and in the bar, and I mingled amongst them. In the bar there was a fellow with a cane and a Windsor tie on, that it make me sick to look at him. I like a man to be a man and dress up, but not to go put on that kind of airs. So I pushed him aside, kind of rough, and had me a drink of whiskey. And then he looked at me as though he thought maybe he'd get gay, but he changed his mind and didn't say anything. And then I had another drink of whiskey, just to show him something, and went out and had a hack out to the races all to myself, and when I got there I bought myself the best seat I could get up in the grandstand, but didn't go in for any of these boxes. That's putting on too many airs.

And so there I was, sitting up in the grandstand as gay as you please and looking down on the swipes coming out with their horses and with their dirty horsey pants on and the horse blankets swung over their shoulders same as I had been doing all the year before. I liked one thing about the same as the other, sitting up there and feeling grand and being down there and looking up at the yaps and feeling grander and more important too. One thing's about as good as another if you take it just right. I've often said that.

Well, right in front of me, in the grandstand that day, there was a fellow with a couple of girls and they was about my age. The young fellow was a nice guy all right. He was the kind maybe that goes to college and then comes to be a lawyer or maybe a newspaper editor or something like that, but he wasn't stuck on himself. There are some of that kind are all right and he was one of the ones.

He had his sister with him and another girl and the sister looked around over his shoulder, accidental at first, not intending to start anything — she wasn't that kind — and her eyes and mine happened to meet.

You know how it is. Gee, she was a peach. She had on a soft dress, kind of a blue stuff and it looked carelessly made, but was well sewed and made and everything. I knew that much. I blushed when she looked right at me and so did she. She was the nicest girl I've ever seen in my life. She wasn't stuck on herself and she could talk proper grammar without being like a schoolteacher or something like that. What I mean is, she was O.K. I think maybe her father was well-to-do, but not rich to make her chesty because she was his daughter, as some are. Maybe he owned a drugstore or a dry-goods store in their home town, or something like that. She never told me and I never asked.

My own people are all O.K. too, when you come to that. My grandfather was Welsh and over in the old country, in Wales he was — but never mind that.

The first heat of the first race come off and the young fellow setting there with the two girls left them and went down to make a bet. I knew what he was up to, but he didn't talk big and noisy and let everyone around know he was a sport, as some do. He wasn't that kind. Well, he come back and I heard him tell the two girls what horse he'd bet on, and when the heat was trotted they all half got to their feet and acted in the excited, sweaty way people do when they've got money down on a race, and the horse they bet on is up there pretty close at the end, and they think maybe he'll come on with a rush, but he never does because he hasn't got the old juice in him, come right down to it.

And then, pretty soon, the horses came out for the 2.18 pace and there was a horse in it I knew. He was a horse Bob French had in his string, but Bob didn't own him. He was a horse owned by a Mr. Mathers down at Marietta, Ohio.

This Mr. Mathers had a lot of money and owned some coal mines or something, and he had a swell place out in the country, and he was stuck on race horses, but was a Presbyterian or something, and I think more than likely his wife was one, too, maybe a stiffer one than himself. So he never raced his horses hisself, and the story round the Ohio race tracks was that when one of his horses got ready to go to the races he turned him over to Bob French and pretended to his wife he was sold.

So Bob had the horses and he did pretty much as he pleased and you can't blame Bob, at least, I never did. Sometimes he was out to win and sometimes he wasn't. I never cared much about that when I was swiping a horse. What I did want to know was that my horse had the speed and could go out in front if you wanted him to.

And, as I'm telling you, there was Bob in this race with one of Mr. Mathers' horses, was named "About Ben Ahem" or something like that, and was fast as a streak. He was a gelding and had a mark of 2.21, but could step in .08 or .09.

Because when Burt and I were out, as I've told you, the year before, there was a nigger Burt knew, worked for Mr. Mathers, and we went out there one day when we didn't have no race on at the Marietta Fair and our boss Harry was gone home.

And so everyone was gone to the fair but just this one nigger, and he took us all through Mr. Mathers' swell house and he and Burt tapped a bottle of wine Mr. Mathers had hid in his bedroom, back in a closet, without his wife knowing, and he showed us this Ahem horse. Burt was always stuck on being a driver, but didn't have much chance to get to the top, being a nigger, and he and the other nigger gulped the whole bottle of wine and Burt got a little lit up.

So the nigger let Burt take this About Ben Ahem and step him a mile in a track Mr. Mathers had all to himself, right there on the farm. And Mr. Mathers had one child, a daughter, kinda sick and not very good looking, and she came home and we had to hustle and get About Ben Ahem stuck back in the barn.

I'm only telling you to get everything straight. At Sandusky, that afternoon I was at the fair, this young fellow with the two girls was fussed, being with the girls and losing his bet. You know how a fellow is that way. One of them was his girl and the other his sister. I had figured that out.

Gee whizz, I says to myself, I'm going to give him the dope.

He was mightily nice when I touched him on the shoulder. He and the girls were nice to me right from the start and clear to the end. I'm not blaming them.

And so he leaned back and I gave him the dope on About Ben Ahem. "Don't bet a cent on this first heat because he'll go like an oxen hitched to a plough, but when the first heat is over go right down and lay on your pile." That's what I told him.

Well, I never saw a fellow treat anyone sweller. There was a fat man sitting beside the little girl that had looked at me twice by this time, and I at her, and both blushing, and what did he do but have the nerve to turn and ask the fat man to get up and change places with me so I could set with his crowd.

Gee whizz, amighty. There I was. What a chump I was to go and get gay up there in the West House bar, and just because that dude was standing there with a cane and that kind of a necktie on, to go and get all balled up and drink that whiskey, just to show off.

Of course she would know, me setting right beside her and letting her smell of my breath. I could have kicked myself right down out of that grandstand and all around that race track and made a faster record than most of the skates of horses they had there that year.

Because that girl wasn't any mutt of a girl. What wouldn't I have give right then for a stick of chewing gum to chew, or a lozenger, or some licorice, or most anything. I was glad I had those twenty-five-cent cigars in my pocket, and right away I give that fellow one and lit one myself. Then that fat man got up and we changed places and there I was plunked right down beside her.

They introduced themselves, and the fellow's best girl he had with him was named Miss Elinor Woodbury, and her father was a manufacturer of barrels from a place called Tiffin, Ohio. And the fellow himself was named Wilbur Wessen and his sister was Miss Lucy Wessen.

I suppose it was their having such swell names got me off my trolley. A fellow, just because he has been a swipe with a race horse, and works taking care of horses for a man in the teaming, delivery and storage business, isn't any better or worse than any one else. I've often thought that, and said it, too.

But you know how a fellow is. There's something in that kind of nice clothes, and the kind of nice eyes she had, and the way she had looked at me, awhile before, over her brother's shoulder, and me looking back at her, and both of us blushing.

I couldn't show her up for a boob, could I?

I made a fool of myself, that's what I did. I said my name was Walter Mathers from Marietta, Ohio, and then I told all three of them the smashingest lie you ever heard. What I said was that my father owned the horse About Ben Ahem, and that he had let him out to this Bob French for racing purposes, because our family was proud and had never gone into racing that way, in our own name, I mean. Then I had got started and they were all leaning over and listening, and Miss Lucy Wessen's eyes were shining, and I went the whole hog.

I told about our place down at Marietta, and about the big stables and the grand brick house we had on a hill, up above the Ohio River, but I knew enough not to do it in no bragging way. What I did was to start things and then let them draw the rest out of me. I acted just as reluctant to tell as I could. Our family hasn't got any barrel factory, and, since I've known us, we've always been pretty poor, but not asking anything of anyone at that, and my grandfather, over in Wales — but never mind that.

We set there talking like we had known each other for years and years, and I went and told them that my father had been expecting maybe this Bob French wasn't on the square, and had sent me up to Sandusky on the sly to find out what I could.

And I bluffed it through I had found out all about the 2.18 pace in which About Ben Ahem was to start.

I said he would lose the first heat by pacing like a lame cow and then he would come back and skin 'em alive after that. And to back up what I said I took thirty dollars out of my pocket and handed it to Mr. Wilbur Wessen and asked him would he mind, after the first heat, to go down and place it on About Ben Ahem for whatever odds he could get. What I said was that I didn't want Bob French to see me and none of the swipes.

Sure enough the first heat come off and About Ben Ahem went off his stride, up the back stretch, and looked like a wooden horse or a sick one, and come in to be last. Then this Wilbur Wessen went down to the betting place under the grandstand and there I was with the two girls, and when that Miss Woodbury was looking the other way once, Lucy Wessen kinda, with her shoulder you know, kinda touched me. Not just tucking down, I don't mean. You know how a woman can do. They get close, but not getting gay either. You know what they do. Gee whizz.

And then they give me a jolt. What they had done when I didn't know, was to get together, and they had decided Wilbur Wessen would bet fifty dollars, and the two girls had gone and put in ten dollars each of their own money, too. I was sick then, but I was sicker later.

About the gelding, About Ben Ahem, and their winning their money, I wasn't worried a lot about that. It come out O.K. Ahem stepped the next three heats like a bushel of spoiled eggs going to market before they could be found out, and Wilbur Wessen had got nine to two for the money. There was something else eating at me.

Because Wilbur come back after he had bet the money, and after that he spent most of his time talking to that Miss Woodbury, and Lucy Wessen and I was left alone together like on a desert island. Gee, if I'd only been on the square or if there had been any way of getting myself on the square. There ain't any Walter Mathers, like I said to her and them, and there hasn't ever been one, but if there was, I bet I'd go to Marietta, Ohio, and shoot him tomorrow.

There I was, big boob that I am. Pretty soon the race was over, and Wilbur had gone down and collected our money, and we had a hack downtown, and he stood us a swell dinner at the West House, and a bottle of champagne beside.

And I was with that girl and she wasn't saying much, and I wasn't saying much either. One thing I know. She wasn't stuck on me because of the lie about my father being rich and all that. There's a way you know. . . . Craps amighty. There's a kind of girl you see just once in your life, and if you don't get busy and make hay then you're gone for good and all and might as well go jump off a bridge. They give you a look from inside of them somewhere, and it ain't no vamping, and what it means is — you want that girl to be your wife, and you want nice things around her like flowers and swell clothes, and you want her to have the kids you're going to have, and you want good music played and no ragtime. Gee whizz.

There's a place over near Sandusky, across a kind of bay, and it's called Cedar Point. And when we had had that dinner we went over to it in a launch, all by ourselves. Wilbur and Miss Lucy and that Miss Woodbury had to catch a ten o'clock train back to Tiffin, Ohio, because when you're out with girls like that you can't get careless and miss any trains and stay out all night like you can with some kinds of Janes.

And Wilbur blowed himself to the launch and it cost him fifteen cold plunks, but I wouldn't ever have knew if I hadn't listened. He wasn't no tin horn kind of a sport.

Over at the Cedar Point place we didn't stay around where there was a gang of common kind of cattle at all.

There was big dance halls and dining places for yaps, and there was a beach you could walk along and get where it was dark, and we went there.

She didn't talk hardly at all and neither did I, and I was thinking how glad I was my mother was all right, and always made us kids learn to eat with a fork at table and not swill soup and not be noisy and rough like a gang you see around a race track that way.

Then Wilbur and his girl went away up the beach and Lucy and I set down in a dark place where there was some roots of old trees the water had washed up, and after that, the time, till we had to go back in the launch and they had to catch their trains, wasn't nothing at all. It went like winking your eye.

Here's how it was. The place we were setting in was dark, like I said, and there was the roots from that old stump sticking up like arms, and there was a watery smell, and the night was like — as if you could put your hand out and feel it — so warm and soft and dark and sweet like a orange.

I most cried and I most swore and I most jumped up and danced, I was so mad and happy and sad.

When Wilbur come back from being alone with his girl, and she saw him coming, Lucy she says, "We got to go to the train now," and she was most crying, too, but she never knew nothing I knew, and she couldn't be so all busted up. And then, before Wilbur and Miss Woodbury got up to where she was, she put her face up and kissed me quick and put her head up against me and she was all quivering and — Gee whizz.

Sometimes I hope I have cancer and die. I guess you know what I mean. We went in the launch across the bay to the train like that, and it was dark too. She whispered and said it was like she and I could get out of the boat and walk on the water, and it sounded foolish, but I knew what she meant.

And then quick, we were right at the depot, and there was a big gang of yaps, the kind that goes to the fairs, and crowded and milling around like cattle, and how could I tell her? "It won't be long because you'll write and I'll write to you." That's all she said.

I got a chance like a hay barn afire. A swell chance I got.

And maybe she would write me, down at Marietta that way, and the letter would come back, and stamped on the front of it by the U.S.A. "There ain't any such guy," or something like that, whatever they stamp on a letter that way.

And me trying to pass myself off for a bigbug and a swell — to her, as decent a little body as God ever made. Craps amighty. A swell chance I got.

And then the train come in and she got on, and Wilbur Wessen come and shook hands with me and that Miss Woodbury was nice and bowed to me and I at her and the train went and I busted out and cried like a kid.

Gee, I could have run after that train and made Dan Patch look like a freight train after a wreck, but socks amighty, what was the use? Did you ever see such a fool?

I'll bet you what — if I had an arm broke right now or a train had run over my foot — I wouldn't go to no doctor at all. I'd go set down and let her hurt and hurt — that's what I'd do.

I'll bet you what — if I hadn't a drunk that booze I'd never been such a boob as to go tell such a lie — that couldn't never be made straight to a lady like her.

I wish I had that fellow right here that had on a Windsor tie and carried a cane. I'd smash him for fair. Gosh darn his eyes. He's a big fool — that's what he is.

And if I'm not another you just go find me one and I'll quit working and be a bum and give him my job. I don't care nothing for working and earning money and saving it for no such boob as myself.

WARREN BECK

"The Blue Sash"

I WAS ALL SET to go, and then this thing had to happen. I even had all my stuff packed in the car that morning. When I drove around to his apartment to pick him up, he was supposed to fling in his bags and hop right in for our little spin to the West Coast. Not that we were in any hurry to get to Los Angeles — we had a month before our jobs began out there — but we'd both saved up a little dough, and we proposed to wander along at our own sweet will squandering it, sampling the grandeurs of nature, especially the wine and women of all the sister states we could string onto our route without actually traveling in circles.

Maybe his having the money saved up was what made the difference. Having cash in hand to pay the bill leads to all kinds of foolishness, I've noticed. Maybe what really threw him was knowing he had enough to buy a marriage license and furniture for an apartment and get himself two or three new suits besides. And then too the Los Angeles job was just a leap in the dark, even if he did have friends in the outfit, whereas his job here was a sure thing, with pretty good prospects.

He was a salesman for a company that made some kind of heavy machinery. That's how we met. He used the planes quite a lot for business trips, and once when he was waiting around to see if the wind was going to let the ship get off the ground, he strayed into the hangar and watched me bossing the mechanics, and we got to talking. A few nights later we happened to meet, and he asked me to have a beer with him, and we talked some more. Well, we've done plenty of that since.

It may seem kind of funny that we got to be friends, he being a college graduate with a whitecollar job, but I guess we just took to each other. We both liked to drink and talk and "midnightum," as he always put it, and we hit it off that way. My dad used to say that talk is a three-legged race, a damned awkward nuisance and cause for stumbling unless the pair just naturally hit the same stride. Not that I'm setting myself up as the equal of a college graduate in every way. But I'm no untutored clod, either. My dad was a steeplejack, and he never worked except in fine weather, at twenty-five bucks a day or more, and he spent his leisure reading Robert Ingersoll and Mark Twain and expatiating on them and other violent subjects to anybody who would listen. He taught me to read, and he taught me to answer back, and I guess he taught me a lot of other things I'm not conscious of. He wouldn't have been surprised to see me out drinking beer and spieling night after night with a college graduate. Dad himself always said he wished he could have an evening's conversation with Teddy Roosevelt.

But about Bob — it couldn't have been the good job that kept him here. At one time he was ready to follow me in the matter of jobs. My thought was that if we went to L.A., it was not for better jobs, but for variety and adventure befitting young men of some vigor and curiosity. And on the other hand, for him, at odd moments, the thought was that if he stayed here in town, he'd settle down and marry Helen.

Many's the time we'd argued about it. Listen, pal, I'd say, you're not the kind of guy who likes to sit down in a booth and stay there all evening, eating all your pretzels out of one bowl — you're like me, you want to barge along. Isn't that the way it is with everything?

Look, he said once, that's because the beer is just about as bad one place as the next. But if you could find one place where everything was the best you'd ever had, wouldn't you stay there all evening?

Well, I told him, the beer isn't everything. Part of it is the going and coming here and there, getting around where things are different, having a change now and then — new faces and so forth.

And part of the time he agreed. We still had an old-fashioned evening together once in a while, and we still packed a lot into 'em. It came natural to us, and we kind of bucked each other up. Dames that fell in with us just once remembered us, and everybody in the bars kept an eye out for us because they liked to watch us roll by under full sail. But then he quit me altogether on these parties. When I began to turn up without him everybody was as surprised as if they'd seen a pair of Siamese twins sawed in two. All I could tell 'em was the shameful truth that he'd fallen for a girl.

Now and then I'd meet him when he was with Helen. If I had a dame, he and I would just say hello. If I was alone, he'd always call me over and buy me a beer and we'd talk awhile. That's the way it was the first time I met Helen. She was always nice to me too. She's a good girl; I'll say that for her. Pretty enough for the movies, and smart, too. She was all for him from the start — you could see that. And he was quite in favor of her too, in a different way from what I saw him show with the dames we used to chase. He and this Helen would talk like a game of ping-pong, where the ball flies back and forth and neither one misses, and most of the time I couldn't even see it. She had been to college too, and she could follow him when he was just a blur of dust to me. They'd try to take me along, but I'd just finish my beer and wish them a merry evening and leave them to their world. That always left me feeling lonesome, though, and I'd usually page the bars until I picked up a quick one, whatever she looked like.

I kept telling him he was in for it if he didn't watch his step. He just laughed at me.

No doubt you're a very hard gent, he says, and a great hand with monkey wrenches and bar babes, but don't try to tell me how to take care of myself.

I will try, I says. I'll more than try: I'll tell you. If you're man enough, you can take my advice. But if you don't, we'll know how much value to give all these large phrases of yours. I'll tell you how to save yourself, I says. Blow your job.

What? he says.

Come on, now, I told him, if you're out for a good time, you can't tie yourself down to a salary. I'll blow my job too. We'll take my car and make for Californy, exercising our manly instincts for fun along the way. Once in Los Angeles, we could line up something that would feed us while we investigated the customs and cuties of Aimee Mc-Pherson's diocese.

Just like that, he says, huh? A couple of conquering heroes, huh? Haven't you heard there's a depression?

Don't be vulgar, I says. As long as there's planes for me to doctor and monkey mechanics for me to boss, I live above that sort of thing.

If we barged into California like a couple of forty-niners who'd dropped behind with tire trouble, you know what we'd find to do? he says. Join a Townsend Club, that's all.

You see, I tell him. It's got you. You're worried about your job, your future, your prospects. You'll be a married man next thing you know.

Not at all, he says. That's not what's holding me back from this belated gold rush you propose. I just want to eat something besides beans, and smoke the first half of my own cigarette instead of the second half of somebody else's. I'm not denying there's merit in your scheme, but the least we could do would be to get some information in advance.

For instance, I says.

For instance, write what friends we have in L.A. and ask them whether there's a toe-hold for us, he says.

I took him up on that. Never let it be said, I answered him, that we failed to do the least we could do. We've been a very doing pair of men, and our sun is not yet set. And so I got some paper and envelopes right away, and we began writing notes to any people we knew out there, and I kidded him along until he'd turned out half a dozen.

But the more I thought about it next day, the more I agreed with him that the chances were against us. I was almost as surprised as he was when we both clicked. A couple of flier friends of mine found me a place practically as good as the one here, and one of his college buddies knew of a humble berth he could slip into when another guy's contract was up in three months.

Then of course we were into it all over again. He'd taken me up about the letters, and so at least he had to admit that his going was an open question. He wavered pro and con for the whole month. I thought this Helen must be putting the heat on him to do right by her, but he swore she was keeping out of it and said she wanted him to do what he really preferred. I could hardly believe it. Maybe there are some women like that, but I never knew one. But he swore that's the way she was.

Then something happened. Maybe everything I'd been needling into him began to take effect. Or maybe he and Helen had some kind of blow-up. I don't know for sure. He never told me. But he was dour as a wet cat for a week, and on my hands every evening, and then all of a sudden one night he says he'd go to California with me. He laid two more Scotches on top of what he already had, and we went out and telegraphed the joyful news that they could expect us in six weeks. That gave us the month for the trip, and two weeks to quit our jobs and voice our farewells around about the old haunts, which we did with our usual thoroughness.

All that two weeks he never said a word about changing his mind again and not going. In fact, he seemed quite determined, and when his friends kidded him about dropping a good job, he kidded them back about getting stuck in a rut like they were. He wasn't very cheerful, but you could have put that down partly to leaving the old town and job and everything — not just this Helen. Anyhow, if he was wavering, I never got a whiff of it. Maybe he wasn't. Maybe it hit him all in a minute that morning, the way he said it did. All that stuff about a blue sash. Jesus! It's enough to make a man's head swim.

It was like this. I pulled up at his apartment house ten minutes early, blew a tattoo on my horn, and bounded up the stairs to help him carry down his stuff. I found him with suitcases spread on the bed, bureau drawers standing open, and clothes all over the room.

All set? says I, just to show him I thought he wasn't so prompt.

No, he says, and goes ahead with what he's doing.

Then I see that he's not putting things into the cases, he's taking 'em out.

What the hell, I said.

I'm not going, he said, without looking up.

I didn't say anything. I walked over and sat down on the window sill. I looked out at the car, with my stuff in it. I lit a cigarete. I took one drag and then I threw the damned thing out the window. Still he didn't say anything. I was sore as hell for a minute. I wasn't going to let him know it, though. And pretty soon it dawned on me that he didn't have to go to California if he didn't want to and he had a right to change his mind if he wanted to. I lit another cigarette.

Listen, pal, I says. Just one word. Why?

He didn't look at me. He just went on tossing socks back into a drawer.

Maybe it's enough that I'm not going, he says. Maybe you don't really care to know why.

Did you think I was just asking out of politeness? I said.

Oh, I know, he said. I do owe you some kind of an excuse.

You needn't feel that way about it, I yelled at him.

You needn't either, he said, in a kind of sad voice. The only trouble is, I don't quite know how to explain it to you.

If you'll make it simple and use short words, maybe I can get it, I said.

Please don't be that way about it, he said. It's nothing against you. You ought to know that.

Oh, all right, I said. It's okay, whatever it is.

Well, he said, and then he stopped and straightened up and looked out the window as though he was trying to remember what he was going to say.

I'm out of cigarettes, I said.

He fumbled his out of his shirt pocket and threw 'em to me, and waited till I lit one and tossed him the pack.

Well, he said, I saw a girl in a blue sash.

And then he stopped.

Oh, so that's it, I said, and laughed, even if I didn't feel like it. You saw a girl in a blue sash. That makes it all perfectly clear.

I know, I know, he says. It doesn't make sense. But Jesus, he says, you got to try to make it make sense, don't you?

It all depends, I says.

He said nothing, and so I went on.

Just where did you see this girl in a blue sash, I says, in a dream?

No, he says. I didn't see her in a dream. I was awake. I was up too — it was about seven o'clock this A.M. — I was just finishing packing — and I looked out the window and there across the street went a girl in a blue sash. Anyhow, I guess you'd call it a sash. It was like a belt, but it was wider than a belt, and — well, she didn't need it on that dress, if you see what I mean. She was just wearing it for adornment, sort of, and that's why I call it a sash.

I follow you, I says. Adornment. A thing like this is just a flourish, kind of. Whereas a belt holds up your pants, and that's utility.

Quite, he says. Oh, quite.

Then he goes on with his unpacking without another word, as though he'd told me everything. I saw I'd have to get him back on the track again.

But I wonder about one thing, I says. Why should this girl be so all adorned with a blue sash walking down the street at seven o'clock in the morning?

I suppose she was on her way to work, he says. I suppose she's somebody's maid.

Don't laugh, boys, I says. Don't laugh, boys. She's somebody's maid.

He looked over at me for a second and scowled.

The way I feel right now, he says, you're too goddam bright for me. Just too goddam bright, or something. You don't exactly dazzle me, but you give me a pain in the head.

Mine's in the neck, I says.

I know, I know, he says, and he sat down on the bed and rumpled up his hair with both hands. You've got a right to be sore. I promised I'd make this trip with you, but —

That isn't it, I says. The promise is nothing. The trip is nothing. What gets me is seeing an old friend slipping into mental breakdown. A girl in a blue sash walked down the street, and you decide not to go to L.A. with me. Do you suppose if I was to hire somebody to drive a flock of white rats down the street the opposite way you'd pack up again and go?

At that he jumped up and went on taking his shirts out of his suitcase and piling them back into the bureau drawer. It was like he was piling up something between him and Los Angeles and piling up something between him and me. I felt like hell about it. I knew right then he was a good guy even if and when screwy. He finished putting the shirts back in the drawer. He looked kind of relieved, but he looked like he felt bad about it too.

Think nothing of it, I told him. Keep your shirts in your bureau drawer. L.A. can get along without you. And I guess I can find my way across the country alone.

Look, he says, it's no use explaining, but I got to try.

If it's about the girl in the blue sash, I says, don't bother. Every man has got to have some secrets.

Listen, he says, and try to think seriously for once. As I told you, this sash was a broad blue ribbon —

You can't imagine how funny that sounds to me, I told him.

What? he says.

A broad blue ribbon, I says. Where do they give out those ribbons? Do they walk the broads round a ring, or show 'em in cages?

He went right on. He never even smiled.

It was a kind of gay contrast to the pink dress she was wearing, he says. She was stepping right along, as if she felt dressed up. Maybe she was thinking somebody might notice the blue sash.

At seven o'clock in the A.M.? I asks.

Maybe she was thinking about wearing the blue sash that afternoon or evening, on her way back from work, he says.

Oh, says I, so maybe that's it. You think she's coming back the same way she went, right past your door. So that's why you're unpacking and settling down again in the same old convenient room, only one flight up and such a comfortable bed.

He made a face at me as if I was a bad smell and waved me down with his hand, but I went right on.

It seems to me, I says, that you're acting very impulsive. What do you know about this girl? Did you get a good look at her? How do you know you'll like what the blue ribbon is hung on?

Don't you ever think of anything else? he asks me.

Often, I says, I think of liquor, or sometimes maybe food, or now and then I think of the pleasures of our philosophical conversations, but mostly I stick to my specialty. You know what the French saying is, about every man having his own kind of gout.

Listen, stupid, he said, why should I change all my plans about going just so I can lurk at this window until a girl in a blue sash comes back and I can coax her up here. Why? Why?

Amen, amen, I says. In God's name, why? Why, when we're all set for a cross-country ride, with a chance to take our pick of all the prairie flowers, should you go nuts over one girl in a blue sash?

He ran his fingers through his hair and threw his arms up straight over his head.

Can't you get it through your skull that I'm not panting after her that way? he shouted at me. For one thing, she was kind of thick-ankled and heavy in the hips. And I never even saw her face. And besides, that wasn't what her blue sash made me think of. And most of all, I'm quite a little preoccupied just now with the idea of marrying Helen — if she'll have me.

Well, I says, this sure is a sudden shift in the subject of our little chat, but if that's what's worrying you — whether Helen will have you — why, be calm. My observation of women leads me to think that Helen will have you. And then you'll have her, and you'll both have each other, and neither one of you will have anything else.

Yes, yes, I know, he says. We've been all over that before. Only it happens that I've changed my opinion.

By that time I was kinda punch-drunk with it all, and hopeless, and I just let my tongue ramble on, just to fill in the bare spaces all around.

Listen, I says, was it this way? You looked at this girl's kinda thick ankles and her heavy backside, and you thought Helen wasn't so bad after all, huh?

God damn you, he says to me, shut up. And listen to me. I'm going to tell you all about this, even if your one-way mind can't grasp it. I've got to tell you, because you need it. Look, did you ever hear of the Ancient Mariner?

Would that be Noah? I asks.

No, it wouldn't be Noah, he says. The Ancient Mariner is in a poem —

How strange, then, says I, that I don't know him. I live with poetry. It is my consuming passion. Like to hear me recite?

This Ancient Mariner, he goes on, got the low-down on himself. He began to see what life was all about —

Always farsighted, these mariner guys, I put in.

Shut up, he says, and listen. The Ancient Mariner would get a hunch now and then that he ought to tell this or that man what he had found out, for the man's own good. That's how the poem begins — three men are going to a wedding feast, and the Ancient Mariner stops one of them.

You sure stop me, I says.

But I can't tell you anything, he says. No, it's no good trying. You've got to see it for yourself.

He sat down on the chair again and stared at the floor.

Come, come, I says, wasn't I promised the details about the case of the girl in the blue sash? It doesn't seem like much of a substitute for your esteemed company all the way to California, but it's something.

Listen, he says, in a kind of solemn way, I looked out of the window this morning and there she went, walking along kind of briskly, adorned in that blue sash, and I could see she wasn't much to look at, at least not her shape, and I knew she must be on her way to a day's hard work, and yet she had tried to fix herself up and make herself attractive —

Well, for God's sake, I said, is that your discovery for the morning? They all do that, all the time.

But why? he says. Not just to pick up a date for a good time. They're always hoping they'll find what every woman wants —

I've got it, I yelled.

Listen, he says. What they want is a husband and a home and children — something permanent. And they have a right to it, too.

They have a right to it? I says. How do you figure that?

Because that's the way things are, he says. There's got to be homes and children to keep the human race going. And the women want to do their part — they have an instinct for it — but they have to depend on the men.

I'll say they do, I says.

What I mean, he says, is that a man has to establish a home for a woman and give her and her children some protection and security — something permanent.

Yeh, I guess that's what a lot of 'em want, I says.

And here goes this girl I saw this morning, he says, walking along through a world of bums like you and me, wearing a blue sash for adornment, making the best of herself, and hoping for the best, and keeping her chin up. In a world of bums. In a world of heels like you and me. Women are in a tough spot, I tell you.

Maybe they are, I says. Maybe that's just the way it is, as you said. But that's something I don't care about. I didn't make the world, and it's not my business to run it. What I want to know is, are you going to marry Helen just because you feel sorry for her?

He looked straight at me for a minute, and then he smiled at me, a warm smile.

You're a smart guy, he says. That's a sensible question, he says. I've been asking myself that this morning. I wouldn't marry her out of pity — that would be condescending. That wouldn't do either one of us any good. No, I'm going to marry her because I love her.

The old, old story, I says. The sweetest ever told. And what do you get out of it, may I ask.

I get the feeling of being a man, he says, of playing my part. And I get the feeling of really knowing what love is — something two people build together that time can't tear down.

Well, I says, it may sound like the music of the spheres to you, but what I detect by way of principal tunes is the dull crash of the monthly grocery bill and the prolonged wail of a colicky baby. You once asked me did I know there was a depression on, and I now return you the question, practically good as new.

There have been depressions before, he says, and they haven't stopped the women. Remember that women have borne and raised their children on the edge of the frontier, if only there were men who were men enough to protect their families with a stockade and get them a little grain and wild game. We're all better off now. The depression is no excuse.

Not for a lineal descendant of Daniel Boone, I says, of course not. But I'm from one of the lesser breeds without the law.

Daniel Boone the hell, he says. On this issue every man writes his own coat of arms. The question is simply can he love a woman or can't he.

Can he love a woman? I answers.

Meaning, he says, can he marry and make a family and hold it up with his courage. I've just realized that that's what loving means. If a man really loves a woman, that's what he wants to do for her.

That all depends on how you look at it, I says.

That's how I look at it, he says.

So you're going to be married, I says.

Yeh, he says, and I've tried my best to tell you why.

Well, pal, I says, yours are profound thoughts, but I leave 'em with you, because I'm on my way to California, and you sure taught me one thing, not to look at any dames in blue sashes before I've had my morning coffee.

And so I walked out and leaves him sitting there looking at nothing as if he was trying to add up a lot of figures in his head.

I didn't go to Los Angeles. I didn't want to go without him. I haven't seen much of him since, though. We both got our old jobs back, and he still comes out to the airport. We've had a few beers together, too, now and then, but usually he's with Helen, and when I've been with him alone I could tell he was thinking about her, and about things he doesn't mention because he thinks I wouldn't understand.

He's going to be married next week.

It's taken a lot of the joy out of my life, I tell you. I don't know how to figure it any more. Sometimes it gives me the creeps to think what happened to him all at once. Just because he saw a girl in a blue sash. But then I tell myself nothing like that is going to happen to me.

KAY BOYLE

Nothing Ever Breaks
Except the Heart

PERHAPS you have been there, and you know the Avenida and the way the trees grow the length of it — palm trees and the foreign varieties of hawthorn and maple. Perhaps you've drunk iced coffee under a colored umbrella there, with your back turned to the traffic's noise and the sight of the horses and your face turned to the strips of green, fresh-watered grass. The trees make the long avenues of shade that flow like a dark stream through the city, and on the edges of them stagger the horses, knee-deep in burning, if imaginary sands. Perhaps you've walked up the avenue through the leafy jungle-dark toward where the American flag hangs, heavy with summer, on its white pole in this foreign city's air. Either children or tropical mirages of them must have run barefoot and scrofulous after you, asking for something as cool as money, and if you were there this summer, you must have seen Miss Del Monte eating ice cream at one of the tin tables under the trees.

Miss Del Monte used to buy all the American picture magazines there were, and she would sit there looking at them, so as not to think of the horses, with the carts they drew breaking their back and crippling their limbs beneath them, nor of the lather frothing under the harness that bound them irrevocably to man. Something was always doing it to her, taking the heart out of her breast and tearing it apart, and now she had come to the end. The first day she arrived she told this to Mr. McCloskey. She said, "You can have the horses and the children with pellagra. I'll take the mint juleps," and Mr. McCloskey stopped looking at the German and the Polish and the Czech and the Russian refugees for a moment and decided, without much interest in it, that she was probably the prettiest woman he had ever seen.

Perhaps you even know Mr. McCloskey — the set of his shoulders in his American businessman's suit, and the rather jaded look in his eyes, and the thick hair just beginning to go gray. He had a roll-top desk to himself, but he never sat down at it, because for eight hours a day he stood behind the elegant glass-topped counter in the airways office and told the roomful of foreigners, and Americans even, that they wouldn't be able to board a plane and go where they wanted to go for at least another month or two. Miss Del Monte went into the office in June, the first day she got to the city, and spun the propeller of the miniature plane with one finger as she waited there. She had left her stockings at the hotel because of the heat, and her arms and legs and her head were bare and cool enough looking; her nails were long and immaculately done, and her mouth was far too brilliant. Once you'd seen her, you watched for her everywhere you went: at the Tivoli Bar before dinner, or at the Casino, or dancing at the Palace or the Atlantico. But she was never anywhere like that. She was always in the airways office, talking to Mr. McCloskey or waiting to talk to Mr. McCloskey, smoking one cigarette after another and putting fresh lip rouge on from time to time.

"I'd like to get over by Saturday," Miss Del Monte had said to him the first day, and when she said it all the refugees sitting on the benches along the wall stopped breathing for a moment and looked at something that wasn't bitterness and hopelessness at last.

"Look," said Mr. McCloskey, making a gesture. "Everyone in this country's trying to get over." His eyes were haggard and his face was a little gaunt from the heat and the amount of talking he had to

do. There were three telephone calls waiting for him on three different desks and fifteen people at the counter where Miss Del Monte
stood. "It's either the language that's driving them out, or else it's
because they don't kill their bulls in the *corsos* here," he said.

"They broke my heart every Sunday afternoon in Spain," said Miss
Del Monte. "They dragged it out with the horses, and now I'm not
having any more." She took another cigarette and she said, "On
account my show's opening up, I'd like to get over by Saturday."

"Saturday!" a little man in a pongee suit behind her cried out,
and for a moment Miss Del Monte thought he had been stabbed. "I've
been three monce waiting here — three monce!" he said, and he held
up that number of fingers. He didn't speak English very well, but
he had diamonds on his hand.

That was the first day, and the second day, in the morning, they
were standing three-deep around the counter, so Miss Del Monte
gave it up after an hour and came back in the afternoon. When she
got opposite Mr. McCloskey at last, she lit a cigarette and looked at
him carefully and evenly. He must have been just over thirty, in spite
of the gray in his hair, and his shoulders would probably have looked
too broad for any chair he sat in.

"I'm not prepared for summer," she said. "Monday's the latest
I can wait. I haven't a single sharkskin to put on."

"Do you know Mr. Sumner Welles?" said Mr. McCloskey, and for
the first time Miss Del Monte saw the madness in his eyes. "Have
you influential friends in Washington?" he asked, and Miss Del
Monte shook her head. "Then perhaps I can help you out," he said,
and he walked rather handsomely to his desk, passing Mr. Concachina
at the counter on his way.

Mr. Concachina was native, and his head was bald, and his mind
was going. "I'm just now speaking four different languages at the same
time to five different parties, Mr. McCloskey," he said, and there was
sweat on his forehead. "I tell you, I can't do it much longer. I'm at
the breaking point."

"You've been saying that for a year and a half," said Mr. Mc-
Closkey. He was looking among the other papers for the typewritten
list of names. "But nothing ever breaks, nothing," he said, and he
repeated it vaguely. "Nothing ever breaks," and he held the list in

one hand while he said "Hello there" into one of the three telephones. When he came back to the counter, he looked at Miss Del Monte. "We have a very nice opening for the seventeenth of November," he said.

This went on for a week or more, and then, one Monday morning, Miss Del Monte felt she was getting somewhere at last. She was on her fourth cigarette, and she had combed back her hair and put fresh lipstick on her mouth, and she looked more beautiful than ever.

"Just a minute," said Mr. McCloskey, studying the list. "How old are you? How much do you weigh?"

"A hundred and fifteen," said Miss Del Monte quickly. "I'm twenty-four, but I feel a lot older."

Mr. McCloskey pondered for a moment, and then he said, "Did you ever think of trying a boat, Miss Del Monte?"

"A boat? Do you mean a boat?" she said.

"Yes," said Mr. McCloskey. He looked at her and moved his hand in a swaying motion. "You'd be surprised. You might like a boat."

Mr. Concachina, a little way down the counter, had a telephone receiver in one hand and a fountain pen in the other, and he was writing something down. But still he had time enough to look up at Miss Del Monte. "You know about Pola Negri?" he said, and then he spoke the other language into the mouthpiece. "Well, Pola Negri got fed up," he said, after a moment. "She went out of here in a huff this morning. She's going to take a boat."

"I'd just as soon go out of here in a huff as in what I have on," said Miss Del Monte evenly. "I'm sure it would be cooler."

"It ought to be awfully cool on shipboard," Mr. McCloskey said.

It was never Mr. McCloskey's intention to start going out in the evening with Miss Del Monte, but by the second week he had got so accustomed to seeing her around that it seemed the natural thing to find her on the Avenida one evening after dinner and walk back and forth with her beneath the trees. She carried a guidebook in one hand, with a cablegram marking a page in it, and she said she'd just had a double whiskey-and-soda.

"It breaks my heart to talk shop," she said, "but my show's opening on the first of September."

"It can't if you're not there," said Mr. McCloskey. Behind them, in the fountains, illuminated water lilies with iron stems and china petals floated monstrously through the night, and the bookstalls, each one shaped like a book, and the leather tooled across the back, were open.

"If I stay much longer, I'll be right in time for the summer season," said Miss Del Monte. "It says so in the guidebook on page twenty-three. It says there are always balls and processions, varinos exhibitions, gymkhanas, and firelarks. However they want to spell it, I'd give up the varinos exhibitions any day if I could see a gymkhana or a firelark."

"You probably will without a bit of trouble if you have another double whiskey," said Mr. McCloskey, but Miss Del Monte said she'd rather hear a *fado* sung.

Mr. McCloskey had never been to a *fado* café before, but Miss Del Monte seemed quite familiar with the back street where one was. The lights were still on when they walked in and took a table, and all the men in their pongee suits and their white silk shoes turned to watch Miss Del Monte go past. The only other women there were the female fado singers, with their Spanish-looking shawls on their shoulders, sitting there rather grimly at separate tables, some with their fathers keeping an eye on them and some with their entrepreneurs, either sitting silent or writing out *fados* while they waited for their turn to come. In a minute the lights went out, and two guitar players mounted a little platform and sat down on the chairs that were placed on opposite sides of it and tuned their instruments up. No one looked very pleased about it, not even when the fado singer himself ran quickly up the steps in his patent-leather shoes and stood in the spotlight between the two guitarists on the platform's boards. He was a short, evil-looking man in a black suit, and his hair was wavy and very well greased, and he kept his hands in his trousers pockets all the time.

"If he takes his hands out of his pockets, he isn't a *fado* singer," said Miss Del Monte, and although the man hadn't yet started to sing, someone behind her hissed.

Presently the singer announced the title of the *fado* and added that this was the first time it had been sung in public, for it was about a stabbing that had occurred near the fish market that day. But when he opened his mouth he might just as well have been telling them all what he thought of them, one minute facing half of the room with his neck going red, and then one minute berating the other half with the veins in his forehead beginning to swell. He said the same words over and over to them, so that there could be no mistake, breaking the rhythm savagely and throwing it in their faces while the throbbing of the guitars wove steadily and systematically upward and, finding no foothold, wove steadily and carefully down again.

When he was done, the lights sprang up all over, and the applause scattered about him, and Miss Del Monte lit another cigarette.

"Did you find this in the guidebook?" Mr. McCloskey asked. He removed the crockery jug from its pail of ice and poured the green wine out.

"Don't be absurd," said Miss Del Monte. "This is neither a bewildering panorama nor a rendezvous of the élite, nor is it an imposing terrace overlooking the sea."

"It might be a gymkhana," said Mr. McCloskey, and he took another drink of wine.

The second night they went out together, again to one of the back-street cafes, Miss Del Monte explained to him further about the *fado*. She said the better ones were either patriotic or heroic, and these had been handed down from generation to generation. The ones they sat writing out quickly at the tables were only the personal ones she told him.

"You simply have to sense which kind it is," she said.

This time it was a girl who sang first, standing up on the platform between the two seated guitarists, with the fringe of the black Spanish shawl hanging just below her knees. Her throat was bare and broad, and her face was primitive under the *maquillage,* and it was only the feet that had nothing to do with the rest. She wore pink stockings, and her feet were as small as mice and twisted like mice in the traps of the open-toed, cork-soled shoes she had on. She began her statement of fact with her teeth showing white in her mouth, and her voice was husky. She said it beautifully, repeating it first to one side of the room and then to the other, with her hands clasped on her stomach, holding the shawl.

"This is a personal one," said Miss Del Monte in a whisper to Mr. McCloskey.

"I'd be interested to know," said Mr. McCloskey rather wearily, "if she makes any mention of Mr. Sumner Welles."

"It's something she read in the paper," said Miss Del Monte. "It's about a girl whose fiancé kills her sister because she takes the bracelets he'd given the other one and wears them to go out dancing with another man. He couldn't stand it."

Mr. McCloskey filled their glasses up again. "Miss Del Monte," he said, "I don't know how your public's getting on without you."

It may have been later in the summer, perhaps it was in July, that Mr. McCloskey took her across on the ferry to have dinner on the other shore. They were probably sitting on the open part of the ferry's deck when Mr. McCloskey said, "She's over there." He didn't look toward the city's delicately starred hills but off into the darkness. "The only thing in life I care about is over there," he said, and as he spoke the strung lights of the battleship and the cutter went running past.

He said it again, after they had left the ferry and left the taxi and were walking down through the grass to the river's edge. The moon had risen now, and everything was as brilliantly lit as if by daylight, and although no explanation had been asked for or given as to why they had come here, and why they went down through the night-drenched grass to where the bright stream of water lay, still it seemed, and singularly without question, the one thing left for them to do.

"She's out there, tethered on the water," Mr. McCloskey said. "The plane," he said, a little impatiently, because Miss Del Monte didn't seem to be able to understand English any more. "She's out there. You can see her just to the left of the jetty." They stood on a foot-path at the water's edge, where a half-dozen dories, white-flanked and rocking empty on the tide, were chained up to the shore. "We can row out to her," he said, and Miss Del Monte stepped into the boat that he held steady with his foot and sat down on the cross seat, doing it slowly and without wonder, like one hynotized.

Mr. McCloskey followed her in and fitted the oars in their grooves and then pushed off from shore. The water was smooth, and the light and the dark moved clearly in broken pieces on it, first light and then dark around them as the oars dipped softly in the night. Every now and then he turned partway in his seat and let the oars feather while he looked ahead at the suave, enormous body of the plane.

"I love her," he said. "I love her," and Miss Del Monte couldn't think of the right thing to say. As they drew nearer he pulled hard and in silence on one oar so as to bring them up against the wing.

"Have you ever piloted one?" Miss Del Monte asked, and Mr. McCloskey didn't say anything for a little while. They were riding close to the plane and he had pulled the oars in, and, until the water began drying on them, the splays of them looked as bright as glass.

"That's what's the matter with me," he said after a moment. "I used to be one. I used to fly them across." He did not move from his seat, but he raised one hand and ran it along the hard, sweet, sloping, metallic breast. "I didn't have what it takes," he said, and his voice was bitter to hear. "Or, rather, I gave away what it takes. I had it. I had it." The dory gyrated slowly and without direction near the marvelously still body of the plane. "One or two whiskeys too much every now and then, and jitters," he said. "Single whiskeys when I was tired and double ones to get me out of whatever trouble I happened to be in. Jitters," he said. "So now I'm just good enough to stand up all day behind a counter and tell them what day the company's going to let them fly."

When Miss Del Monte got to the airways office the next morning, there was one Frenchwoman talking faster and better than the others, leaning across to Mr. McCloskey, with her hand in the black fish-net glove closed sharply on his arm. She was telling him, in French, that she knew Mr. Sumner Welles and that she'd been to school with Eve Curie, and Mr. McCloskey stood there looking at her with a rather faded, hopeless look around his eyes.

ERSKINE CALDWELL

Horse Thief

I DIDN'T steal Lud Moseley's calico horse.

People all over have been trying to make me out a thief, but anybody who knows me will tell you that I've never been in trouble like this before in all my life. Mr. John Turner will tell you all about me. I've worked for him, off and on, for I don't know exactly how many years. I reckon I've worked for him just about all my life, since I was a boy. Mr. John knows I wouldn't steal a horse. That's why I say I didn't steal Lud Moseley's, like he swore I did. I didn't grow up just to turn out to be a horse thief.

Night before last, Mr. John told me to ride his mare, Betsy. I said I wanted to go off a little way after something, and he told me to go ahead and ride Betsy, like I have been doing every Sunday night for going on two years now. Mr. John told me to take the Texas saddle, but I told him I didn't care about riding saddle. I like to ride with a bridle and reins, and nothing else. That's the best way to ride, anyway. And where I was going I didn't want to have a squeaking saddle under me. I wasn't up to no mischief; it was just a little private

39

business of my own that nobody has got a right to call me down about. I nearly always rode saddle Sunday nights, but night before last was Thursday night, and that's why I didn't take a saddle when I went.

Mr. John Turner will tell you I'm not the kind to go off and get into trouble. Ask Mr. John about me. He has known me all my life, and I've never given him or anybody else trouble.

When I took Betsy out of the stable that night after supper, Mr. John came out to the barnyard and asked me over again if I didn't want to take the Texas saddle. That mare, Betsy, is a little rawboned, but I didn't mind that. I told Mr. John I'd just as leave ride bareback. He said it was all right with him, if I wanted to get sawn in two, and for me to go ahead and do like I pleased about it. He was standing right there all the time, rubbing Betsy's mane, and trying to find out where I was going, without coming right out and asking me. But he knew all the time where I was going, because he knows all about me. I reckon he just wanted to have a laugh at me, but he couldn't do that if I didn't let on where I was headed. So he told me it was all right to ride his mare without a saddle, if I didn't want to be bothered with one, and I opened the gate and rode off down the road toward Bishop's crossroads.

That was night before last — Thursday night. It was a little after dark then, but I could see Mr. John standing at the barnyard gate, leaning on it a little, and watching me ride off. I'd been plowing that day, over in the new ground, and I was dog-tired. That's one reason why I didn't gallop off like I always did on Sunday nights. I rode away slow, letting Betsy take her own good time, because I wasn't in such a big hurry. I had about two hours' time to kill, and only a little over three miles to go. That's why I went off like that.

Everybody knows I've been going to see Lud Moseley's youngest girl, Naomi. I was going to see her again that night. But I couldn't show up there till about nine-thirty. That's why I wasn't in such a big hurry to get away from home. Lud Moseley wouldn't let me come to see her but once a week, on Sunday nights, and night before last was Thursday. I'd been there to see her three or four times before on Thursday nights, that Lud Moseley didn't know about. Naomi told me to come to see her on Thursday nights; that's why I had been going there when Lud Moseley said I couldn't come to his house but once a week. Naomi told me to come, anyway; and she had been coming out to the swing under the trees in the front yard to meet me.

I haven't got a thing in the world against Lud Moseley. Mr. John Turner will tell you I haven't. I don't especially like him, and he knows why. Once a week isn't enough to go to see a girl you like a lot, like I do Naomi. And I reckon she likes me a little, or she wouldn't tell me to come to see her on Thursday nights, when Lud Moseley told me not to come. Lud Moseley thinks if I go to see her more than once a week that maybe we'll take it into our heads to get married without letting him catch on. That's why he said I couldn't come to his house but once a week, on Sunday nights.

He's fixing now to have me sent to the penitentiary for twenty years for stealing his calico horse, Lightfoot. I reckon he knows I didn't steal the horse, but he figures he's got a good chance to put me out of the way till he can get Naomi married to somebody else. That's the way I figure it out; because everybody knows I'm not a horse thief. Mr. John Turner will tell you that about me. Mr. John knows me better than that. I've worked for him so long he even tried to make me out as one of the family, but I won't let him do that.

So night before last, Thursday night, I rode off from home, bareback, on Betsy. I killed a little time down at the creek, about a mile down the road, and when I looked at my watch again, it was nine o'clock sharp. I got on Betsy and rode off toward Lud Moseley's place. Everything was still and quiet around the house and barn; it was just about his bedtime. I rode right up to the barnyard gate, like I always did on Thursday nights. I could see a light up in Naomi's room, where she slept with her older sister, Mary Lee. We had always figured on Mary Lee being out with somebody, or else being ready to go to sleep by nine-thirty. When I looked up at their window, I could see Naomi lying across her bed, and Mary Lee was standing beside her talking to her about something. That looked bad, because when Mary Lee tried to make Naomi undress and go to bed before she did, it always meant that it would take Naomi another hour or more to get out of the room. She had to wait till Mary Lee was asleep, and then she had to get up and dress in the dark before she could come down to the frontyard and meet me in the swing under the trees.

I sat there on Betsy for ten or fifteen minutes, waiting to see how

Naomi was going to come out with her sister. After a while I saw her get up and start to undress. I knew right away that that meant waiting another hour or longer for her to be able to come and meet me. The moon was coming up, and it was as bright as day out there in the barnyard. I'd been in the habit of opening the gate and turning Betsy loose in the yard, but I was scared to do it night before last. If Lud Moseley should get up for a drink of water or something and look out toward the barn and see a horse standing there, he would either think it was one of his and come out to lock it in the stalls, or else he would catch on it was me out there. So I opened the barn door and led Betsy inside and put her in the first empty stall I could find in the dark. I was scared to strike a light, because I didn't know but what Lud Moseley would be looking out the window and see the flare of the match. I put Betsy in the stall, closed the door, and came back outside to wait for Naomi to get a chance to come out and meet me at the swing in the yard.

It was about twelve-thirty or one when I got ready to leave for home. The moon had been clouded, and it was darker than everything in the barn. I couldn't see my hand in front of me, it was that dark. I was scared to strike a light that time, too, and I felt my way in and opened the stall door and stepped inside to lead out Betsy. I couldn't see a thing, and when I found her neck, I thought she had slipped her bridle like she was always doing when she had to stand too long to suit her. I was afraid to try to ride her home without a lead of some kind, because I was scared she might shy in the barnyard and start to tearing around out there and wake up Lud Moseley. I felt around on the ground for the bridle, but I couldn't find it anywhere. Then I went back to the stall door and felt on it, and there was a halter hanging up. I slipped it over her head and let her out. It was still so dark I couldn't see a thing, and I had to feel my way outside and through the barnyard gate. When I got to the road, I threw a leg over her, and started for home without wasting any more time. I thought she trotted a little funny, because she had a swaying swing that made me slide from side to side, and I didn't have a saddle pommel to hold on to. But I got home all right and slipped the halter off and put her in her stall. It was around one o'clock in the morning then.

The next morning after breakfast when I was getting ready to catch the mules and gear them up to start plowing in the new ground, Lud Moseley and three or four other men, including the sheriff, came riding up the road from town and hitched at the rack. Mr. John came out and slapped the sheriff on the back and told him a funny story. They carried on like that for nearly half an hour, and then the sheriff asked Mr. John where I was. Mr. John told him I was getting ready to go off to the new ground, where we had planted a crop of corn that spring, and then the sheriff said he had a warrant for me. Mr. John asked him what for, and the sheriff told him it was for stealing Lud Moseley's calico horse. Mr. John laughed at him, because he thought it was just a joke, but the sheriff pulled out the paper and showed it to him. Mr. John still wouldn't believe it, and he told them there was a mixup somewhere, because he told them, I wouldn't steal a horse. Mr. John knows I'm not a horse thief. I've never never been in any kind of trouble before in all my life.

They brought me to town right away and put me in the cell room at the sheriff's house. I knew I hadn't stole Lud Moseley's horse, and I wasn't scared a bit about it. But right after they brought me to town, they all rode back and the sheriff looked in the barn and found Lud Moseley's calico horse, Lightfoot, in Betsy's stall. Mr. John said things were all mixed up because he knew he didn't steal the horse, and he knew I wouldn't do it. But the horse was there, the calico one, Lightfoot, and the halter was hanging on the stall door. After that they went back to Lud Moseley's and measured my foot tracks in the barnyard, and then they found Betsy's bridle. Lud Moseley said I had rode Mr. John's mare over there, turned her loose, and put the bridle on his Lightfoot and rode him off. The stall door was not locked, and it wasn't broken down. It looks like I forgot to shut it tight when I put Betsey in it, because she got out and come home sometime that night.

Lud Moseley says he's going to send me away for twenty years where I won't have a chance to worry him over his youngest daughter, Naomi. He wants her to marry a widowed farmer over beyond Bishop's crossroads who runs twenty plows, and who's got a big white house with fifteen rooms in it. Mr. John Turner says he'll hire the best lawyer in town to take my case, but it don't look like it will do much good, because my footprints are all over Lud Moseley's barnyard, and his Lightfoot was in Mr. John's stable. I reckon I could worm out of it someway, if I made up my mind to do it. But I don't like to do things like that. It would put Naomi in a bad way, because if I said I was there seeing her, and had put Betsy in the stall to keep her quiet, and took Lightfoot out by mistake in the dark when I got ready to leave — well, it would just look bad, that's all. She would have to say she was in the habit of slipping out to see me after everybody had gone to sleep, on Thursday nights, and it would just look bad all around. She might take it into her head some day that she'd rather marry somebody else than me, and by that time she'd have a bad name for having been mixed up with me — and sneaking out of the house.

Naomi knows I'm no horse thief. She knows how it all happened — that I rode Lud Moseley's calico horse, Lightfoot, off by mistake in the dark, and left the stall door unfastened, and Betsy got out and came home.

Lud Moseley has been telling people all around the courthouse as how he is going to send me away for twenty years, so he can get Naomi married to that widowed farmer who runs twenty plows. Lud Moseley is right proud of it, it looks like, because he's got me cornered in a trap, and maybe he will get me sent away sure enough before Naomi gets a chance to say what she knows is true. But somehow, I don't know if she'll say it if she does get a chance. Everybody knows I'm nothing but a hired man at Mr. John Turner's, and I've been thinking that maybe Naomi might not come to tell what she knows, after all.

I'd come right out and explain to the sheriff how the mixup happened, but I sort of hate to mention Naomi's name in the mess. If it had been a Sunday night, instead of night before last, a Thursday, I could — well, it would just sound too bad, that's all.

If Naomi comes to town and tells what she knows, I won't say a word to stop her, because that'll mean she's willing to say it and marry me; but if she stays at home, and lets Lud Moseley and that widowed farmer send me away for twenty years, I'll just have to go, that's all. I always told Naomi I'd do anything in the world for her, and I reckon this will be that time when I've got to prove whether I'm a man of my word, or not.

DOROTHY CANFIELD

Sex Education

IT WAS three times — but at intervals of many years — that I heard my Aunt Minnie tell about an experience of her girlhood that had made a never-to-be-forgotten impression on her. The first time she was in her thirties, still young. But she had then been married for ten years, so that to my group of friends, all in the early teens, she seemed quite of another generation.

The day she told us the story, we had been idling on one end of her porch as we made casual plans for a picnic supper in the woods. Darning stockings at the other end, she paid no attention to us until one of the girls said, "Let's take blankets and sleep out there. It'd be fun."

"No," Aunt Minnie broke in sharply, "you mustn't do that."

"Oh, for goodness sakes, why not!" said one of the younger girls, rebelliously. "The boys are always doing it. Why can't we, just once?"

Aunt Minnie laid down her sewing. "Come here, girls," she said,

"I want you should hear something that happened to me when I was your age."

Her voice had a special quality which, perhaps, young people of today would not recognize. But we did. We knew from experience that it was the dark voice grownups used when they were going to say something about sex.

Yet at first what she had to say was like any dull family anecdote. She had been ill when she was fifteen; and afterwards she was run down, thin, with no appetite. Her folks thought a change of air would do her good, and sent her from Vermont out to Ohio — or was it Illinois? I don't remember. Anyway, one of those places where the corn grows high. Her mother's Cousin Ella lived there, keeping house for her son-in-law.

The son-in-law was the minister of the village church. His wife had died some years before, leaving him a young widower with two little girls and a baby boy. He had been a normally personable man then, but the next summer, on the Fourth of July when he was trying to set off some fireworks to amuse his children, an imperfectly manufactured rocket had burst in his face. The explosion had left one side of his face badly scarred. Aunt Minnie made us see it, as she still saw it, in horrid detail — the stiffened, scarlet scar tissue distorting one cheek, the lower lip turned so far out at one corner that the moist red mucous-membrane lining always showed, one lower eyelid hanging loose, and watering.

After the accident, his face had been a long time healing. It was then that his wife's elderly mother had gone to keep house and take care of the children. When he was well enough to be about again, he found his position as pastor of the little church waiting for him. The farmers and village people in his congregation, moved by his misfortune, by his faithful service and by his unblemished character, said they would rather have Mr. Fairchild, even with his scarred face, than any other minister. He was a good preacher, Aunt Minnie told us, "and the way he prayed was kind of exciting. I'd never known a preacher, not to live in the same house with him, before. And when he was in the pulpit, with everybody looking up at him, I felt the way his children did, kind of proud to think we had just eaten breakfast at the same table. I liked to call him 'Cousin Malcolm' before folks. One side of his face was all right, anyhow. You could see from that he *had* been a good-looking man. In fact, probably one of those ministers that all the women — " Aunt Minnie paused, drew her lips together, and looked at us uncertainly.

Then she went back to the story as it happened — as it happened that first time I heard her tell it. "I thought he was a saint. Everybody out there did. That was all *they* knew. Of course, it made a person sick to look at that awful scar — the drooling corner of his mouth was the worst. He tried to keep that side of his face turned away from folks. But you always knew it was there. That was what kept him from marrying again, so Cousin Ella said. I heard her say lots of times that he knew no woman would touch any man who looked the way he did, not with a ten-foot pole.

"Well, the change of air did do me good. I got my appetite back, and ate a lot and played outdoors a lot with my cousins. They were younger than I (I had my sixteenth birthday there) but I still liked to play games. I got taller and laid on some weight. Cousin Ella used to say I grew as fast as the corn did. Their house stood at the edge of the village. Beyond it was one of those big cornfields they have out West. At the time when I first got there, the stalks were only up to a person's knee. You could see over their tops. But it grew like lightning, and before long, it was the way thick woods are here, way over your head, the stalks growing so close together it was dark under them.

"Cousin Ella told us youngsters that it was lots worse for getting lost in than woods, because there weren't any landmarks in it. One spot in a cornfield looked just like any other. 'You children keep out of it,' she used to tell us almost every day '*especially you girls*. It's no place for a decent girl. You could easy get so far from the house nobody could hear you if you hollered. There are plenty of men in this town that wouldn't like anything better than — ' she never said what.

"In spite of what she said, my little cousins and I had figured out that if we went across one corner of the field, it would be a short cut to the village, and sometimes, without letting on to Cousin Ella, we'd go that way. After the corn got really tall, the farmer stopped cultivating, and we soon beat down a path in the loose dirt. The minute you were inside the field it was dark. You felt as if you were miles from anywhere. It sort of scared you. But in no time the path turned and brought you out on the far end of Main Street. Your breath was coming fast, maybe, but that was what made you like to do it.

"One day I missed the turn. Maybe I didn't keep my mind on it. Maybe it had rained and blurred the tramped-down look of the path. I don't know what. All of a sudden, I knew I was lost. And the minute I knew that, I began to run, just as hard as I could run. I couldn't help it, any more than you can help snatching your hand off a hot stove. I didn't know what I was scared of, I didn't even know I *was* running, till my heart was pounding so hard I had to stop.

"The minute I stood still, I could hear Cousin Ella saying, 'There are plenty of men in this town that wouldn't like anything better than — ' I didn't know, not really, what she meant. But I knew she meant something horrible. I opened my mouth to scream. But I put both hands over my mouth to keep the scream in. If I made any noise, one of those men would hear me. I thought I heard one just behind me, and whirled around. And then I thought another one had tiptoed up behind me, the other way, and I spun around so fast I almost fell over. I stuffed my hands hard against my mouth. And then — I couldn't help it — I ran again — but my legs were shaking so I soon had to stop. There I stood, scared to move for fear of rustling the corn and letting the men know where I was. My hair had come down, all over my face. I kept pushing it back and looking around, quick, to make sure one of the men hadn't found out where I was. Then I thought I saw a man coming toward me, and I ran away from him — and fell down, and burst some of the buttons off my dress, and was sick to my stomach — and thought I heard a man close to me and got up and staggered around, knocking into the corn because I couldn't even see where I was going.

"And then, off to one side, I saw Cousin Malcolm. Not a man — The minister. He was standing still, one hand up to his face, thinking. He hadn't heard me.

"I was so *terrible* glad to see him, instead of one of those men, I ran as fast as I could and just flung myself on him, to make myself feel how safe I was." . . .

Aunt Minnie had become strangely agitated. Her hands were shaking, her face was crimson. She frightened us. We could not look away from her. As we waited for her to go on, I felt little spasms twitch at the muscles inside my body — "And what do you think that *saint,* that holy minister of the Gospel, did to an innocent child who clung to him for safety? The most terrible look came into his eyes — you girls are too young to know what he looked like. But once you're married, you'll find out. He grabbed hold of me — that dreadful face of his was *right on mine* — and began clawing the clothes off my back."

She stopped for a moment, panting. We were too frightened to speak. She went on: "He had torn my dress right down to the waist before I — then I *did* scream — all I could — and pulled away from him so hard I almost fell down, and ran and all of a sudden I came out of the corn, right in the backyard of the Fairchild house. The children were staring at the corn, and Cousin Ella ran out of the kitchen door. They had heard me screaming. Cousin Ella shrieked out, 'What is it? What happened? Did a man scare you?' And I said, 'Yes, yes, yes, a man — I ran — !' And then I fainted away. I must have. The next thing I knew I was on the sofa in the living room and Cousin Ella was slapping my face with a wet towel."

She had to wet her lips with her tongue before she could go on. Her face was gray now. "There! that's the kind of thing girls' folks ought to tell them about — so they'll know what men are like."

She finished her story as if she were dismissing us. We wanted to go away, but we were too horrified to stir. Finally, one of the youngest girls asked in a low trembling voice, "Aunt Minnie, did you tell on him?"

"No, I was ashamed to," she said briefly. "They sent me home the next day, anyhow. Nobody ever said a word to me about it. And I never did either. Till now." . . .

By what gets printed in some of the modern child-psychology books, you would think that girls to whom such a story had been told would never develop normally. Yet, as far as I can remember what happened to the girls in that group, we all grew up about like anybody. Most of us married, some happily, some not so well. We kept house. We learned — more or less — how to live with our

husbands; we had children and struggled to bring them up right —
we went forward into life just as if we had never been warned not to.

Perhaps, young as we were that day, we had already had enough
experience of life so that we were not quite blank paper for Aunt
Minnie's frightening story. Whether we thought of it then or not,
we couldn't have failed to see that at this very time Aunt Minnie had
been married for ten years or more, comfortably and well married,
too. Against what she tried by that story to brand into our minds,
stood the cheerful homelife in that house, the good-natured, kind,
hard-working husband, and the children — the three rough-and-
tumble, nice little boys, so adored by their parents, and the sweet
girl baby who died, of whom they could never speak without tears.
It was such actual contact with adult life that probably kept generation after generation of girls from being scared by tales like Aunt
Minnie's into a neurotic horror of living. . . .

Of course, since Aunt Minnie was so much older than we, her boys
grew up to be adolescents and young men while our children were
still little enough so that our worries over them were nothing more
serious than whooping cough and trying to get them to make their
own beds. Two of our aunt's three boys followed, without losing
their footing, the narrow path which leads across adolescence into
normal adult life. But the middle one, Jake, repeatedly fell off into
the morass. "Girl trouble," as the succinct family phrase put it. He
was one of those boys who have "charm," whatever we mean by that,
and he was always being snatched at by girls who would be "all
wrong" for him to marry. And once, at nineteen, he ran away from
home, whether with one of these girls or not we never heard, for
through all her ups and downs with this son, Aunt Minnie tried
fiercely to protect him from scandal that might cloud his later life.

Her husband had to stay on his job to earn the family living. She
was the one who went to find Jake. When it was gossiped around
that Jake was in "bad company" his mother drew some money from
the family savings-bank account, and silent, white-cheeked, took the
train to the city where rumor said he had gone.

Some weeks later he came back with her. With no girl. She had
cleared him of that entanglement. As of others, which followed,
later. Her troubles seemed over when, at a "suitable" age, he fell in

love with a "suitable" girl, married her and took her to live in our shire town, sixteen miles away, where he had a good position. Jake was always bright enough.

Sometimes, idly, people speculated as to what Aunt Minnie had seen that time she went after her runaway son, wondering where her search for him had taken her — very queer places for Aunt Minnie to be in, we imagined. And how could such an ignorant home-keeping woman ever have known what to say to an errant wilful boy to set him straight?

Well, of course, we reflected, watching her later struggles with Jake's erratic ways, she certainly could not have remained ignorant, after seeing over and over what she probably had; after talking with Jake about the things which, a good many times, must have come up with desperate openness between them.

She kept her own counsel. We never knew anything definite about the facts of those experiences of hers. But one day she told a group of us — all then married women — something which gave us a notion about what she had learned from them. . . .

We were hastily making a layette for a not especialy welcome baby in a poor family. In those days, our town had no such thing as a district-nursing service. Aunt Minnie, a vigorous woman of fifty-five, had come in to help. As we sewed, we talked, of course; and because our daughters were near or in their teens, we were comparing notes, about the bewildering responsibility of bringing up girls.

After a while, Aunt Minnie remarked: "Well, I hope you teach your girls some *sense*. From what I read, I know you're great on telling them 'the facts,' facts we never heard of when we were girls. Like as not, some facts I don't know now. But knowing the facts isn't going to do them any more good than *not* knowing the facts ever did, unless they have some sense taught them, too."

"What do you mean, Aunt Minnie?" one of us asked her uncertainly.

She reflected, threading a needle: "Well, I don't know but what the best way to tell you what I mean, is to tell you about something that happened to me, forty years ago. I've never said anything about it before. But I've thought about it a good deal. Maybe — "

She had hardly begun when I recognized the story — her visit to her Cousin Ella's midwestern home, the widower with his scarred face and saintly reputation and, very vividly, her getting lost in the great cornfield. I knew every word she was going to say — to the very end, I thought.

But no, I did not. Not at all.

She broke off, suddenly, to exclaim with impatience: "Wasn't I the big ninny? But not so big a ninny as that old cousin of mine. I could wring her neck for getting me in such a state. Only she didn't know any better, herself. That was the way they brought young people up in those days, scaring them out of their wits about the awfulness of getting lost, but not telling them a thing about how *not* to get lost. Or how to act, if they did.

"If I had had the sense I was born with, I'd have known that running my legs off in a zigzag was the worst thing I could do. I couldn't have been more than a few feet from the path when I noticed I wasn't on it. My tracks in the loose ploughed dirt must have been perfectly plain. If I'd h' stood still, and collected my wits, I could have looked down to see which way my footsteps went and just walked back over them to the path and gone on about my business.

"Now I ask you, if I'd been told how to do that, wouldn't it have been a lot better protection for me — if protection was what my cousin thought she wanted to give me — than to scare me so at the idea of being lost that I turned deef-dumb-and-blind when I thought I was?

"And anyhow that patch of corn wasn't as big as she let on. And she knew it wasn't. It was no more than a big field in a farming country. I was a well-grown girl of sixteen, as tall as I am now. If I couldn't have found the path, I could have just walked along one line of cornstalks — *straight* — and I'd have come out somewhere in ten minutes. Fifteen at the most. Maybe not just where I wanted to go. But all right, safe, where decent folks were living."

She paused, as if she had finished. But at the inquiring blankness in our faces, she went on: "Well now, why isn't teaching girls — and boys, too, for the Lord's sake don't forget they need it as much as the girls — about this man-and-woman business, something like that? If you give them the idea — no matter whether it's *as* you tell them the facts, or as you *don't* tell them the facts, that it is such a terribly scary thing that if they take a step into it, something's likely to happen to them so awful that you're ashamed to tell them what — well, they'll lose their heads and run around like crazy things, first time they take one step away from the path.

"For they'll be trying out the paths, all right. You can't keep them from it. And a good thing, too. How else are they going to find out what it's like. Boys' and girls' going together is a path across one corner of growing up. And when they go together, they're likely to get off the path some. Seems to me, it's up to their folks to bring them up so, when they do, they don't start screaming and running in circles, but stand still, right where they are, and get their breath and figure out how to get back.

"And, anyhow, you don't tell 'em the truth about sex" (I was astonished to hear her use the actual word, tabu to women of her generation) "if they get the idea from you that it's all there is to living. It's not. If you don't get to where you want to go in it, well, there's a lot of landscape all around it a person can have a good time in.

"D'you know, I believe one thing that gives girls and boys the wrong idea is the way folks *look!* My old cousin's face, I can see her now, it was red as a rooster's comb when she was telling me about men in that cornfield. I believe now she kind of *liked* to talk about it!"

(Oh, Aunt Minnie — and yours! I thought.)

Someone asked, "But how *did* you get out, Aunt Minnie?"

She shook her head, laid down her sewing. "More foolishness. That minister my mother's cousin was keeping house for — her son-in-law — I caught sight of him, down along one of the aisles of cornstalks, looking down at the ground, thinking, the way he often did. And I was so glad to see him I rushed right up to him, and flung my arms around his neck and hugged him. He hadn't heard me coming. He gave a great start, put one arm around me and turned his face full towards me — I suppose for just a second he had forgotten how awful one side of it was. His expression, his eyes — well, you're all married women, you know how he looked, the way any able-bodied man thirty-six-or-seven, who'd been married and begotten children, would look — for a minute, anyhow, if a full-blooded girl of sixteen, who ought to have known better, flung herself at him without any warning, her hair tumbling down, her dress half-unbuttoned, and hugged him with all her might.

"I was what they called innocent in those days. That is, I knew just as little about what men are like as my folks could manage I should. But I was old enough to know all right what that look meant. And it gave me a start. But, of course, the real thing of it was that dreadful scar of his, so close to my face — that wet corner of his mouth, his eye drawn down with the red inside of the lower eyelid showing —

"It turned me so sick, I pulled away with all my might, so fast that I ripped one sleeve nearly loose, and let out a screech like a wildcat. And ran. Did I run! And in a minute, I was through the corn and had come out in the backyard of the house. I hadn't been more than a few feet from it, probably, any of the time. And then I fainted away. Girls were always fainting away; it was the way our corset strings were pulled tight, I suppose, and then — oh, a lot of fuss.

"But anyhow," she finished, picking up her work and going on, setting neat, firm stitches with steady hands, "there's one thing, I never told anybody it was Cousin Malcolm I had met in the cornfield. I told my old cousin that 'a man had scared me.' And nobody said anything more about it to me, not ever. That was the way they did in those days. They thought if they didn't let on about something, maybe it wouldn't have happened. I was sent back to Vermont right away, and Cousin Malcolm went on being minister of the church.

"I've always been," said Aunt Minnie moderately, "kind of proud that I didn't go and ruin a man's life for just one second's slip-up. If you could have called it that. For it *would* have ruined him. You know how hard as stone people are about other folks' let-downs. If I'd have told, not one person in that town would have had any charity. Not one would have tried to understand. One slip, *once,* and they'd have pushed him down in the mud. If I had told, I'd have felt pretty bad about it, later — when I came to have more sense. But I declare, I can't see how I came to have the decency, dumb as I was then, to know that it wouldn't be fair." . . .

It was not long after this talk that Aunt Minnie's elderly husband died, mourned by her, by all of us. She lived alone then. It was peaceful October weather for her, in which she kept a firm roundness of face and figure, as quiet-living countrywomen often do, on into her late sixties.

But then Jake, the boy who had had girl trouble, had wife trouble. We heard he had taken to running after a young girl, or was it that she was running after him? It was something serious. For his nice wife left him and came back with the children to live with her mother in our town. Poor Aunt Minnie used to go to see her for long talks which made them both cry. And she went to keep house for Jake, for months at a time.

She grew old, during those years. When finally she (or something) managed to get the marriage mended so that Jake's wife relented and went back to live with him, there was no trace left of her pleasant brisk freshness. She was stooped and slow-footed and shrunken. We, her kinspeople, although we would have given our lives for any one of our own children, wondered whether Jake was worth what it had cost his mother to — well, steady him, or reform him. Or perhaps just understand him. Whatever it took.

She came of a long-lived family and was able to go on keeping house for herself well into her eighties. Of course, we and the other neighbors stepped in often to make sure she was all right. Mostly, during those brief calls, the talk turned on nothing more vital than her geraniums. But one midwinter afternoon, sitting with her in front of her cozy stove, I chanced to speak in rather hasty blame of someone who had, I thought, acted badly. To my surprise this brought from her the story about the cornfield which she had evidently quite forgotten telling me, twice before.

This time she told it almost dreamily, swaying to and fro in her rocking chair, her eyes fixed on the long slope of snow outside her window. When she came to the encounter with the minister she said, looking away from the distance and back into my eyes: "I know now that I had been, all along, kind of *interested* in him, the way any girl as old as I was would be in any youngish man living in the same house with her. And a minister, too. They have to have the gift of gab so much more than most men, women get to thinking they are more alive than men who can't talk so well. I *thought* the reason I threw my arms around him was because I had been so scared. And I certainly had been scared, by my own cousin's horrible talk about the cornfield being full of men waiting to grab girls. But that wasn't all the reason I flung myself at Malcolm Fairchild and hugged him. I know that now. Why in the world shouldn't I have been taught *some* notion of it then? 'Twould do girls good to know that they are just like everybody else — human nature *and* sex, all mixed up together. I didn't have to hug him. I wouldn't have, if he'd been dirty or fat and old, or chewed tobacco."

I stirred in my chair, ready to say, "But it's not so simple as all that to tell girls — " and she hastily answered my unspoken protest. "I know, I know, most of it can't be put into words. There just aren't any words to say something that's so both-ways-at-once all the time as this man-and-woman business. But look here, you know as well as I do that there are lots more ways than in words to teach young folks what you want 'em to know."

The old woman stopped her swaying rocker to peer far back into the past with honest eyes. "What was in my mind back there in the cornfield — partly, anyhow — was what had been there all the time I was living in the same house with Cousin Malcolm — that he had long straight legs, and broad shoulders, and lots of curly brown hair, and was nice and flat in front, and that one side of his face was good-looking. But most of all, that he and I were really alone, for the first time, without anybody to see us.

"I suppose, if it hadn't been for that dreadful scar, he'd have drawn me up, tight, and — most any man would — kissed me. I know how I must have looked, all red and hot and my hair down and my dress open. And, used as he was to big cornfields, he probably never dreamed that the reason I looked that way was because I was scared to be by myself in one. He may have thought — you know what he may have thought.

"Well — if his face had been like anybody's, when he looked at me the way he did, the way a man does look at a woman he wants to have, it would have scared me — some. I'd have cried, maybe. And probably he'd have kissed me again. You know how such things go. I might have come out of the cornfield halfway engaged to marry him. Why not? I was old enough, as people thought then. That would have been Nature. That was probably what he thought of, in that first instant.

"But what did I do? I had one look at his poor horrible face, and started back as though I'd stepped on a snake. And screamed and ran.

"What do you suppose *he* felt, left there in the corn? He must have been sure that I would tell everybody he had attacked me. He probably thought that when he came out and went back to the village he'd already be in disgrace and put out of the pulpit.

"But the worst must have been to find out, so rough, so plain from the way I acted — as if somebody had hit him with an ax — the way he would look to any woman he might try to get close to.

"That must have been — " she drew a long breath — "well, pretty hard on him."

After a silence, she murmured pityingly, "Poor man!"

JOHN CHEEVER

The Enormous Radio

JIM AND IRENE WESTCOTT were the kind of people who seem
to strike that satisfactory average of income, endeavor, and respect-
ability that is reached by the statistical reports in college alumni bul-
letins. They were the parents of two young children, they had been
married nine years, they lived on the twelfth floor of an apartment
house in the East Seventies between Fifth and Madison Avenues, they
went to the theatre on an average of 10.3 times a year, and they hoped
someday to live in Westchester. Irene Westcott was a pleasant, rather
plain girl with soft brown hair and a wide, fine forehead upon which
nothing at all had been written, and in the cold weather she wore a
coat of fitch skins dyed to resemble mink. You could not say that Jim
Westcott, at thirty-seven, looked younger than he was, but you could
at least say of him that he seemed to feel younger. He wore his
graying hair cut very short, he dressed in the kind of clothes his class
had worn at Andover, and his manner was earnest, vehement, and
intentionally naïve. The Westcotts differed from their friends, their
classmates, and their neighbors only in an interest they shared in

58

serious music. They went to a great many concerts — although they seldom mentioned this to anyone — and they spent a good deal of time listening to music on the radio.

Their radio was an old instrument, sensitive, unpredictable, and beyond repair. Neither of them understood the mechanics of radio — or of any of the other appliances that surrounded them — and when the instrument faltered, Jim would strike the side of the cabinet with his hand. This sometimes helped. One Sunday afternoon, in the middle of a Schubert quartet, the music faded away altogether. Jim struck the cabinet repeatedly, but there was no response; the Schubert was lost to them forever. He promised to buy Irene a new radio, and on Monday when he came home from work he told her that he had got one. He refused to describe it, and said it would be a surprise for her when it came.

The radio was delivered at the kitchen door the following afternoon, and with the assistance of her maid and the handy man Irene uncrated it and brought it into the living room. She was struck at once with the physical ugliness of the large gumwood cabinet. Irene was proud of her living room, she had chosen its furnishings and colors as carefully as she chose her clothes, and now it seemed to her that the new radio stood among her intimate possessions like an aggressive intruder. She was confounded by the number of dials and switches on the instrument panel, and she studied them thoroughly before she put the plug into a wall socket and turned the radio on. The dials flooded with a malevolent green light, and in the distance she heard the music of a piano quintet. The quintet was in the distance for only an instant; it bore down upon her with a speed greater than light and filled the apartment with the noise of music amplified so mightily that it knocked a china ornament from a table to the floor. She rushed to the instrument and reduced the volume. The violent forces that were snared in the ugly gumwood cabinet made her uneasy. Her children came home from school then, and she took them to the Park. It was not until later in the afternoon that she was able to return to the radio.

The maid had given the children their suppers and was supervising their baths when Irene turned on the radio, reduced the volume, and sat down to listen to a Mozart quintet that she knew and enjoyed.

The music came through clearly. The new instrument had much purer tone, she thought, than the old one. She decided that tone was most important and that she could conceal the cabinet behind a sofa. But as soon as she had made her peace with the radio, the interference began. A crackling sound like the noise of a burning powder fuse began to accompany the singing of the strings. Beyond the music, there was a rustling that reminded Irene unpleasantly of the sea, and as the quintet progressed, these noises were joined by many others. She tried all the dials and switches but nothing dimmed the interference, and she sat down, disappointed and bewildered, and tried to trace the flight of the melody. The elevator shaft in her building ran beside the living-room wall, and it was the noise of the elevator that gave her a clue to the character of the static. The rattling of the elevator cables and the opening and closing of the elevator doors were reproduced in her loudspeaker, and, realizing that the radio was sensitive to electrical currents of all sorts, she began to discern through the Mozart the ringing of telephone bells, the dialing of phones, and the lamentation of a vacuum cleaner. By listening more carefully, she was able to distinguish doorbells, elevator bells, electric razors, and Waring mixers, whose sounds had been picked up from the apartments that surrounded hers and transmitted through her loudspeaker. The powerful and ugly instrument, with its mistaken sensitivity to discord, was more than she could hope to master, so she turned the thing off and went into the nursery to see her children.

When Jim Westcott came home that night, he went to the radio confidently and worked the controls. He had the same sort of experience Irene had had. A man was speaking on the station Jim had chosen, and his voice swung instantly from the distance into a force so powerful that it shook the apartment. Jim turned the volume control and reduced the voice. Then, a minute or two later, the interference began. The ringing of telephones and doorbells set in, joined by the rasp of the elevator doors and the whir of cooking appliances. The character of the noise had changed since Irene had tried the radio earlier; the last of the electric razors was being unplugged, the vacuum cleaners had all been returned to their closets, and the static reflected that change in pace that overtakes the city after the sun goes down. He fiddled with the knobs but couldn't get rid of the noises, so he turned the radio off and told Irene that in the morning he'd call the people who had sold it to him and give them hell.

The following afternoon, when Irene returned to the apartment from a luncheon date, the maid told her that a man had come and fixed the radio. Irene went into the living room before she took off her hat or her furs and tried the instrument. From the loudspeaker came a recording of the "Missouri Waltz." It reminded her of the thin, scratchy music from an old-fashioned phonograph that she sometimes heard across the lake where she spent her summers. She waited until the waltz had finished, expecting an explanation of the recording, but there was none. The music was followed by silence, and then the plaintive and scratchy record was repeated. She turned the dial and got a satisfactory burst of Caucasian music — the thump of bare feet in the dust and the rattle of coin jewelry — but in the background she could hear the ringing of bells and a confusion of voices. Her children came home from school then, and she turned off the radio and went to the nursery.

When Jim came home that night, he was tired, and he took a bath and changed his clothes. Then he joined Irene in the living room. He had just turned on the radio when the maid announced dinner, so he left it on, and he and Irene went to the table.

Jim was too tired to make even a pretense of sociability, and there was nothing about the dinner to hold Irene's interest, so her attention wandered from the food to the deposits of silver polish on the candlesticks and from there to the music in the other room. She listened for a few moments to a Chopin prelude and then was surprised to hear a man's voice break in. "For Christ's sake, Kathy," he said, "do you always have to play the piano when I get home?" The music stopped abruptly. "It's the only chance I have," a woman said. "I'm at the office all day." "So am I," the man said. He added something obscene about an upright piano, and slammed a door. The passionate and melancholy music began again.

"Did you hear that?" Irene asked.

"What?" Jim was eating his dessert.

"The radio. A man said something while the music was still going on — something dirty."

"It's probably a play."

"I don't think it *is* a play," Irene asid.

They left the table and took their coffee into the living room. Irene asked Jim to try another station. He turned the knob. "Have you seen my garters?" a man asked. "Button me up," a woman said. "Have you seen my garters?" the man said again. "Just button me up and I'll find your garters," the woman said. Jim shifted to another station. "I wish you wouldn't leave apple cores in the ashtrays," a man said. "I hate the smell."

"This is strange," Jim said.

"Isn't it?" Irene said.

Jim turned the knob again. " 'On the coast of Coromandel where the early pumpkins blow,' " a woman with a pronounced English accent said, " 'in the middle of the woods lived the Yonghy-Bonghy-Bo. Two old chairs, and half a candle, one old jug without a handle . . . ' "

"My God!" Irene cried. "That's the Sweeneys' nurse."

" 'These were all his worldly goods,' " the British voice continued.

"Turn that thing off," Irene said. "Maybe they can hear *us*." Jim switched the radio off. "That was Miss Armstrong, the Sweeneys' nurse," Irene said. "She must be reading to the little girl. They live in 17-B. I've talked with Miss Armstrong in the Park. I knew her voice very well. We must be getting other people's apartments."

"That's impossible," Jim said.

"Well, that was the Sweeneys' nurse," Irene said hotly. "I know her voice. I know it very well. I'm wondering if they can hear us."

Jim turned the switch. First from a distance and then nearer, nearer, as if borne on the wind, came the pure accents of the Sweeneys' nurse again: " 'Lady Jingly! Lady Jingly!' " she said, " 'Sitting where the pumpkins blow, will you come and be my wife,' said the Yonghy-Bonghy-Bo . . . "

Jim went over to the radio and said "Hello" loudly into the speaker.

" 'I am tired of living singly,' " the nurse went on, " 'on this coast so wild and shingly, I'm a-weary of my life; if you'll come and be my wife, quite serene would be my life . . . ' "

"I guess she can't hear us," Irene said. "Try something else."

Jim turned to another station, and the living room was filled with the uproar of a cocktail party that had overshot its mark. Someone was playing the piano and singing the Whiffenpoof Song, and the voices that surrounded the piano were vehement and happy. "Eat some more sandwiches," a woman shrieked. There were screams of laughter and a dish of some sort crashed to the floor.

"Those must be the Hutchinsons, in 15-B," Irene said. "I knew they were giving a party this afternoon. I saw her in the liquor store. Isn't this too divine? Try something else. See if you can get those people in 18-C."

The Westcotts overheard that evening a monologue on salmon fishing in Canada, a bridge game, running comments on home movies of what had apparently been a fortnight at Sea Island, and a bitter family quarrel about an overdraft at the bank. They turned off the radio at midnight and went to bed, weak with laughter. Sometime in the night, their son began to call for a glass of water and Irene got one and took it to his room. It was very early. All the lights in the neighborhood were extinguished, and from the boy's window she could see the empty street. She went into the living room and tried the radio. There was some faint coughing, a moan, and then a man spoke. "Are you all right, darling?" he asked. "Yes," a woman said wearily. "Yes, I'm all right, I guess," and then she added with great feeling, "But, you know, Charlie, I don't feel like myself any more. Sometimes there are about fifteen or twenty minutes in the week when I feel like myself. I don't like to go to another doctor, because the doctor's bills are so awful already, but I just don't feel like myself, Charlie. I just never feel like myself." They were not young, Irene thought. She guessed from the timbre of their voices that they were middle-aged. The restrained melancholy of the dialogue and the draft from the bedroom window made her shiver, and she went back to bed.

The following morning, Irene cooked breakfast for the family — the maid didn't come up from her room in the basement until ten — braided her daughter's hair, and waited at the door until her children and her husband had been carried away in the elevator. Then she went into the living room and tried the radio. "I don't want to go to school," a child screamed. "I hate school. I won't go to school. I hate school." "You will go to school," an enraged woman said. "We paid eight hundred dollars to get you into that school and you'll go if it kills you." The next number on the dial produced the worn record of the "Missouri Waltz." Irene shifted the control and invaded the privacy of several breakfast tables. She overheard demonstrations of indigestion, carnal love, abysmal vanity, faith, and despair. Irene's life was nearly as simple and sheltered as it appeared to be, and the forthright and sometimes brutal language that came from the loudspeaker that morning astonished and troubled her. She continued to listen until her maid came in. Then she turned off the radio quickly, since this insight, she realized, was a furtive one.

Irene had a luncheon date with a friend that day, and she left her apartment at a little after twelve. There were a number of women in the elevator when it stopped at her floor. She stared at their handsome and impassive faces, their furs, and the cloth flowers in their hats. Which one of them had been to Sea Island, she wondered. Which one had overdrawn her bank account? The elevator stopped at the tenth floor and a woman with a pair of Skye terriers joined them. Her hair was rigged high on her head and she wore a mink cape. She was humming the "Missouri Waltz."

Irene had two Martinis at lunch, and she looked searchingly at her friend and wondered what her secrets were. They had intended to go shopping after lunch, but Irene excused herself and went home. She told the maid that she was not to be disturbed; then she went into the living room, closed the doors, and switched on the radio. She heard in the course of the afternoon, the halting conversation of a woman entertaining her aunt, the hysterical conclusion of a luncheon party, and a hostess briefing her maid about some cocktail guests. "Don't give the best Scotch to anyone who hasn't white hair," the hostess said. "See if you can get rid of that liver paste before you pass those hot things, and could you lend me five dollars? I want to tip the elevator man."

As the afternoon waned, the conversations increased in intensity. From where Irene sat, she could see the open sky above Central Park. There were hundreds of clouds in the sky, as though the south wind had broken the winter into pieces and were blowing it north, and on her radio she could hear the arrival of cocktail guests and the return of children and businessmen from their schools and offices. "I found a good-sized diamond on the bathroom floor this morning," a woman said. "It must have fallen out of that bracelet Mrs. Dunston was wearing last night." "We'll sell it," a man said. "Take it down to the jeweller on Madison Avenue and sell it. Mrs. Dunston won't know the difference, and we could use a couple of hundred bucks. . . ." " 'Oranges and lemons, say the bells of St. Clement's,' " the Sweeneys' nurse sang. " 'Half-pence and farthings, say the bells of St. Martin's. When will you pay me? say the bells at old Bailey . . .' " "It's not a hat," a woman cried, and at her back roared a cocktail party. "It's not a hat, it's a love affair. That's what Walter Florell said. He said it's not a hat, it's a love affair," and then, in a lower voice, the same woman added, "Talk to somebody, for Christ's sake, honey, talk to somebody. If she catches you standing here not talking to anybody, she'll take us off her invitation list, and I love these parties."

The Westcotts were going out for dinner that night, and when Jim came home Irene was dressing. She seemed sad and vague, and he brought her a drink. They were dining with friends in the neighborhood, and they walked to where they were going. The sky was broad and filled with light. It was one of those splendid spring evenings that excite memory and desire, and the air that touched their hands and faces felt very soft. A Salvation Army band was on the corner playing "Jesus Is Sweeter." Irene drew on her husband's arm and held him there for a minute, to hear the music. "They're really such nice people, aren't they?" she said. "They have such nice faces. Actually, they're so much nicer than a lot of the people we know." She took a bill from her purse and walked over and dropped it into the tambourine. There was in her face, when she returned to her husband, a look of radiant melancholy that he was not familiar with. And her conduct at the dinner party that night seemed strange to him, too. She interrupted her hostess rudely and stared at the people across the table from her with an intensity for which she would have punished her children.

It was still mild when they walked home from the party, and Irene looked up at the spring stars. " 'How far that little candle throws its beams,' " she exclaimed. " 'So shines a good deed in a naughty world.' " She waited that night until Jim had fallen asleep, and then went into the living room and turned on the radio.

Jim came home at about six the next night. Emma, the maid, let him in, and he had taken off his hat and was taking off his coat when Irene ran into the hall. Her face was shining with tears and her hair was disordered. "Go up to 16-C, Jim!" she screamed. "Don't take off your coat. Go up to 16-C. Mr. Osborn's beating his wife. They've been quarreling since four o'clock, and now he's hitting her. Go up there and stop him."

From the radio in the living room, Jim heard screams, obscenities, and thuds. "You know you don't have to listen to this sort of thing," he said. He strode into the living room and turned the switch. "It's indecent," he said. "It's like looking in windows. You know you don't have to listen to this sort of thing. You can turn it off."

"Oh, it's so terrible, it's so dreadful," Irene was sobbing. "I've been listening all day, and it's so depressing."

"Well, if it's so depressing, why do you listen to it? I bought this damned radio to give you some pleasure," he said. "I paid a great deal of money for it. I thought it might make you happy. I wanted to make you happy."

"Don't, don't, don't, don't quarrel with me," she moaned, and laid her head on his shoulder. "All the others have been quarreling all day. Everybody's been quarreling. They're all worried about money. Mrs. Hutchinson's mother is dying of cancer in Florida and they don't have enough money to send her to the Mayo Clinic. At least, Mr. Hutchinson says they don't have enough money. And some woman in this building is having an affair with the superintendent — with that hideous superintendent. It's too disgusting. And Mrs. Melville has heart trouble and Mr. Hendricks is going to lose his job in April and Mrs. Hendricks is horrid about the whole thing and that girl who plays the 'Missouri Waltz' is a whore, a common whore, and the elevator man has tuberculosis and Mr. Osborn has been beating Mrs. Osborn." She wailed, she trembled with grief and checked the stream of tears down her face with the heel of her palm.

"Well, why do you have to listen?" Jim asked again. "Why do you have to listen to this stuff if it makes you so miserable?"

"Oh, don't don't don't," she cried. "Life is too terrible, too sordid and awful. But we've never been like that, have we, darling? Have we? I mean we've always been good and decent and loving to one another, haven't we? And we have two children, two beautiful children. Our lives aren't sordid, are they, darling? Are they?" She flung her arms around his neck and drew his face down to hers. "We're happy, aren't we, darling? We are happy, aren't we?"

"Of course we're happy," he said tiredly. He began to surrender his resentment. "Of course we're happy. I'll have that damned radio fixed or taken away tomorrow." He stroked her soft hair. "My poor girl," he said.

"You love me, don't you?" she asked. "And we're not hypercritical or worried about money or dishonest, are we?"

"No, darling," he said.

A man came in the morning and fixed the radio. Irene turned it on cautiously and was happy to hear a California-wine commercial and a recording of Beethoven's Ninth Symphony, including Schiller's "Ode to Joy." She kept the radio on all day and nothing untoward came from the speaker.

A Spanish suite was being played when Jim came home. "Is everything all right?" he asked. His face was pale, she thought. They had some cocktails and went into dinner to the "Anvil Chorus" from *Il Trovatore.* This was followed by Debussy's "La Mer."

"I paid the bill for the radio today," Jim said. "It cost four hundred dollars. I hope you'll get some enjoyment out of it."

"Oh, I'm sure I will," Irene said.

"Four hundred dollars is a good deal more than I can afford," he went on. "I wanted to get something that you'd enjoy. It's the last extravagance we'll be able to indulge in this year. I see that you haven't paid your clothing bills yet. I saw them on your dressing table." He looked directly at her. "Why did you tell me you'd paid them? Why did you lie to me?"

"I just didn't want you to worry, Jim," she said. She drank some water. "I'll be able to pay my bills out of this month's allowance. There were the slipcovers last month, and that party."

"You've got to learn to handle the money I give you a little more intelligently, Irene," he said. "You've got to understand that we won't have as much money this year as we had last. I had a very sobering talk with Mitchell today. No one is buying anything. We're spending all our time promoting new issues, and you know how long that takes. I'm not getting any younger, you know. I'm thirty-seven. My hair will be gray next year. I haven't done as well as I'd hoped to do. And I don't suppose things will get any better."

"Yes, dear," she said.

"We've got to start cutting down," Jim said. "We've got to think of the children. To be perfectly frank with you, I worry about money a great deal. I'm not at all sure of the future. No one is. If anything should happen to me, there's the insurance, but that wouldn't go very far today. I've worked awfully hard to give you and the children a comfortable life," he said bitterly. "I don't like to see all of my energies, all of my youth, wasted in fur coats and radios and slipcovers and—"

"Please, Jim," she said. "Please. They'll hear us."

"*Who'll* hear us? Emma can't hear us."

"The radio."

"Oh, I'm sick!" he shouted. "I'm sick to death of your apprehensiveness. The radio can't hear us. Nobody can hear us. And what if they can hear us? Who cares?"

Irene got up from the table and went into the living room. Jim went to the door and shouted at her from there. "Why are you so Christly all of a sudden? What's turned you overnight into a convent girl? You stole your mother's jewelry before they probated her will. You never gave your sister a cent of that money that was intended for her— not even when she needed it. You made Grace Howland's life miserable, and where was all your piety and your virtue when you went to that abortionist? I'll never forget how cool you were. You packed your bag and went off to have that child murdered as if you were going to Nassau. If you'd had any reasons, if you'd had any good reasons—"

Irene stood for a minute before the hideous cabinet, disgraced and sickened, but she held her hand on the switch before she extinguished the music and the voices, hoping that the instrument might speak to her kindly, that she might hear the Sweeneys' nurse. Jim continued to shout at her from the door. The voice on the radio was suave and noncommittal. "An early-morning railroad disaster in Tokyo," the loudspeaker said, "killed twenty-nine people. A fire in a Catholic hospital near Buffalo for the care of blind children was extinguished early this morning by nuns. The temperature is forty-seven. The humidity is eighty-nine."

WALTER VAN TILBURG CLARK

The Wind and the Snow
of Winter

IT WAS NEAR sunset when Mike Braneen came onto the last
pitch of the old wagon road which had led into Gold Rock from the
east since the Comstock days. The road was just two ruts in the hard
earth, with sagebrush growing between them, and was full of steep
pitches and sharp turns. From the summit it descended even more
steeply into Gold Rock in a series of short switchbacks down the
slope of the canyon. There was a paved highway on the other side
of the pass now, but Mike never used that. Cars coming from behind
made him uneasy, so that he couldn't follow his own thoughts long,
but had to keep turning around every few minutes, to see that his
burro, Annie, was staying out on the shoulder of the road, where she
would be safe. Mike didn't like cars anyway, and on the old road he
could forget about them, and feel more like himself. He could forget
about Annie too, except when the light, quick tapping of her hoofs
behind him stopped. Even then he didn't really break his thoughts.
It was more as if the tapping were another sound from his own inner
machinery, and when it stopped, he stopped too, and turned around to

see what she was doing. When he began to walk ahead again at the same slow, unvarying pace, his arms scarcely swinging at all, his body bent a little forward from the waist, he would not be aware that there had been any interruption of the memory or the story that was going on in his head. Mike did not like to have his stories interrupted except by an idea of his own, something to do with prospecting, or the arrival of his story at an actual memory which warmed him to closer recollection or led into a new and more attractive story.

An intense, golden light, almost liquid, fanned out from the peaks above him and reached eastward under the gray sky, and the snow which occasionally swarmed across this light was fine and dry. Such little squalls had been going on all day, and still there was nothing like real snow down, but only a fine powder which the wind swept along until it caught under the brush, leaving the ground bare. Yet Mike Braneen was not deceived. This was not just a flurrying day; it was the beginning of winter. If not tonight, then tomorrow, or the next day, the snow would begin which shut off the mountains, so that a man might as well be on a great plain for all he could see, perhaps even the snow which blinded a man at once and blanketed the desert in an hour. Fifty-two years in this country had made Mike Braneen sure about such things, although he didn't give much thought to them, but only to what he had to do because of them. Three nights before, he had been awakened by a change in the wind. It was no longer a wind born in the near mountains, cold with night and altitude, but a wind from far places, full of a damp chill which got through his blankets and into his bones. The stars had still been clear and close above the dark humps of the mountains, and overhead the constellations had moved slowly in full panoply, unbroken by any invisible lower darkness; yet he had lain there half awake for a few minutes, hearing the new wind beat the brush around him, hearing Annie stirring restlessly and thumping in her hobble. He had thought drowsily, Smells like winter this time, and then, It's held off a long time this year, pretty near the end of December. Then he had gone back to sleep, mildly happy because the change meant he would be going back to Gold Rock. Gold Rock was the other half of Mike Braneen's life. When the smell of winter came, he always started back for Gold Rock. From March or April until the smell of winter, he wandered slowly about among the mountains, anywhere between the White Pines and the Virginias, with only his burro for company. Then there would come the change, and they would head back for Gold Rock.

Mike had travelled with a good many burros during that time, eighteen or twenty, he thought, although he was not sure. He could not remember them all, but only those he had had first, when he was a young man and always thought most about seeing women when he got back to Gold Rock, or those with something queer about them, like Baldy, who'd had a great, pale patch, like a bald spot, on one side of his belly, or those who'd had something queer happen to them, like Maria. He could remember just how it had been that night. He could remember it as if it were last night. It had been in Hamilton. He had felt unhappy, because he could remember Hamilton when the whole hollow was full of people and buildings, and everything was new and active. He had gone to sleep in the hollow shell of the Wells Fargo Building, hearing an old iron shutter banging against the wall in the wind. In the morning, Maria had been gone. He had followed the scuffing track she made on account of her loose hobble, and it had led far up the old snow-gullied road to Treasure Hill, and then ended at one of the black shafts that opened like mouths right at the edge of the road. A man remembered a thing like that. There weren't many burros that foolish. But burros with nothing particular about them were hard to remember — especially those he'd had in the last twenty years or so, when he had gradually stopped feeling so personal about them, and had begun to call all the jennies Annie and all the burros Jack.

The clicking of the little hoofs behind him stopped, and Mike stopped too, and turned around. Annie was pulling at a line of yellow grass along the edge of the road.

"Come on, Maria," Mike said patiently. The burro at once stopped pulling at the dead grass and came on up towards him, her small black nose working, the ends of the grass standing out on each side of it like whiskers. Mike began to climb again, ahead of her.

It was a long time since he had been caught by a winter, too. He could not remember how long. All the beginnings ran together in his mind, as if they were all the beginning of one winter so far back that he had almost forgotten it. He could still remember clearly, though, the winter he had stayed out on purpose, clear into January.

He had been a young man then, thirty-five or forty or forty-five, somewhere in there. He would have to stop and try to bring back a whole string of memories about what had happened just before, in order to remember just how old he had been, and it wasn't worth the trouble. Besides, sometimes even that system didn't work. It would lead him into an old camp where he had been a number of times, and the dates would get mixed up. It was impossible to remember any other way; because all his comings and goings had been so much alike. He had been young, anyhow, and not much afraid of anything except running out of water in the wrong place; not even afraid of the winter. He had stayed out because he'd thought he had a good thing, and he had wanted to prove it. He could remember how it felt to be out in the clear winter weather on the mountains; the piñon trees and the junipers weighted down with feathery snow, and making sharp, blue shadows on the white slopes. The hills had made blue shadows on one another too, and in the still air his pick had made the beginning of a sound like a bell's. He knew he had been young, because he could remember taking a day off now and then, just to go tramping around those hills, up and down the white and through the blue shadows, on a kind of holiday. He had pretended to his common sense that he was seriously prospecting, and had carried his hammer, and even his drill along, but he had really just been gallivanting, playing colt. Maybe he had been even younger than thirty-five, though he could still be stirred a little, for that matter, by the memory of the kind of weather which had sent him gallivanting. High-blue weather, he called it. There were two kinds of high-blue weather, besides the winter kind, which didn't set him off very often, spring and fall. In the spring it would have a soft, puffy wind and soft, puffy white clouds which made separate shadows that travelled silently across hills that looked soft too. In the fall it would be still, and there would be no clouds at all in the blue, but there would be something in the golden air and the soft, steady sunlight on the mountains that made a man as uneasy as the spring blowing, though in a different way, more sad and not so excited. In the spring high-blue, a man had been likely to think about women he had slept with, or wanted to sleep with, or imaginary women made up with the help of news-paper pictures of actresses or young society matrons, or of the old oil paintings in the Lucky Boy Saloon, which showed pale, almost naked women against dark, sumptuous backgrounds — women with long hair or braided hair, calm, virtuous faces, small hands and feet, and ponderous limbs, breasts, and buttocks. In the fall high-blue, though it had been much longer since he had seen a woman, or heard a woman's voice, he was more likely to think about old friends, men, or places he had heard about, or places he hadn't seen for a long time. He himself thought most often about Goldfield the way he had last seen it in the summer in 1912. That was as far south as Mike had ever been in Nevada. Since then, he had never been south of Tonopah. When the high-blue weather was past, though, and the season worked toward winter, he began to think about Gold Rock. There were only three or four winters out of the fifty-two when he hadn't gone home to Gold Rock, to his old room at Mrs. Wright's, up on Fourth Street, and to his meals in the dining room at the International House, and to the Lucky Boy, where he could talk to Tom Connover and his other friends, and play cards, or have a drink to hold in his hand while he sat and remembered.

This journey had seemed a little different from most, though. It had started the same as usual, but as he had come across the two vast valleys, and through the pass in the low range between them, he hadn't felt quite the same. He'd felt younger and more awake, it seemed to him, and yet, in a way, older too, suddenly older. He had been sure that there was plenty of time, and yet he had been a little afraid of getting caught in the storm. He had kept looking ahead to see if the mountains on the horizon were still clearly outlined, or if they had been cut off by a lowering of the clouds. He had thought more than once, how bad it would be to get caught out there when the real snow began, and he had been disturbed by the first flakes. It had seemed hard to him to have to walk so far, too. He had kept thinking about distance. Also the snowy cold had searched out the regions of his body where old injuries had healed. He had taken off his left mitten a good many times, to blow on the fingers which had been frosted the year he was sixty-three, so that now it didn't take much cold to turn them white and stiffen them. The queer tingling, partly like an itch and partly like a pain, in the patch on his back that had been burned in that old powder blast, was sharper than he could remember its ever having been before. The rheumatism in his joints, which was so old a companion that it usually made him feel no more than tight-knit and stiff, and the place where his leg had been broken and torn when that ladder broke in '97 ached, and had a pulse he could count. All this made him believe that he was walking more slowly than usual, although nothing, probably not even a deliberate attempt, could actually have changed his pace. Sometimes he even thought, with a moment of fear, that he was getting tired.

On the other hand, he felt unusually clear and strong in his mind. He remembered things with a clarity which was like living them again — nearly all of them events from many years back, from the time when he had been really active and fearless and every burro had had its own name. Some of these events, like the night he had spent in Eureka with the little, brown-haired whore, a night in the fall in 1888 or '89, somewhere in there, he had not once thought of for years. Now he could remember even her name. Armandy she had called herself: a funny name. They all picked names for their business, of course, romantic names like Cecily or Rosamunde or Belle or Claire, or hard names like Diamond Gert or Horseshoe Sal, or names that were pinned on them, like Indian Kate or Roman Mary, but Armandy was different.

He could remember Armandy as if he were with her now, not the way she had behaved in bed; he couldn't remember anything particular about that. In fact, he couldn't be sure that he remembered anything particular about that at all. There were others he could remember more clearly for the way they had behaved in bed, women he had been with more often. He had been with Armandy only that one night. He remembered little things about being with her, things that made it seem good to think of being with her again. Armandy had a room upstairs in a hotel. They could hear a piano playing in a club across the street. He could hear the tune, and it was one he knew, although he didn't know its name. It was a gay tune that went on and on the same, but still it sounded sad when you heard it through the hotel window, with the lights from the bars and hotels shining on the street, and the people coming and going through the lights, and then, beyond the lights, the darkness where the mountains were. Armandy wore a white silk dress with a high waist, and a locket on a gold chain. The dress made her look very brown and like a young girl.

She used a white powder on her face, that smelled like violets, but this could not hide her brownness. The locket was heart-shaped, and it opened to show a cameo of a man's hand holding a woman's hand very gently, just their fingers laid out long together, and the thumbs holding, the way they were sometimes on tombstones. There were two little gold initials on each hand, but Armandy would never tell what they stood for, or even if the locket was really her own. He stood in the window, looking down at the club from which the piano music was coming, and Armandy stood beside him, with her shoulders against his arm, and a glass of wine in her hand. He could see the toe of her white satin slipper showing from under the edge of her skirt. Her big hat, loaded with black and white plumes, lay on the dresser behind him. His own leather coat, with the sheepskin lining, lay across the foot of the bed. It was a big bed, with a knobby brass foot and head. There was one oil lamp burning in the chandelier in the middle of the room. Armandy was soft-spoken, gentle, and a little fearful, always looking at him to see what he was thinking. He stood with his arms folded. His arms felt big and strong upon his heavily muscled chest. He stood there, pretending to be in no hurry, but really thinking eagerly about what he would do with Armandy, who had something about her which tempted him to be cruel. He stood there, with his chin down into his heavy dark beard, and watched a man come riding down the middle of the street from the west. The horse was a fine black, which lifted its head and feet with pride. The man sat very straight, with a high rein, and something about his clothes and hat made him appear to be in uniform, although it wasn't a uniform he was wearing. The man also saluted friends upon the sidewalks like an officer, bending his head just slightly, and touching his hat instead of lifting it. Mike Braneen asked Armandy who the man was, and then felt angry because she could tell him, and because he was an important man who owned a mine that was in bonanza. He mocked the airs with which the man rode, and his princely greetings. He mocked the man cleverly, and Armandy laughed and repeated what he said, and made him drink a little of her wine as a reward. Mike had been drinking whisky, and he did not like wine anyway, but this was not the moment in which to refuse such an invitation.

Old Mike remembered all this, which had been completely forgotten for years. He could not remember what he and Armandy had said, but he remembered everything else, and he felt very lonesome for Armandy, and for the room with the red, figured carpet and the brass chandelier with oil lamps in it, and the open window with the long tune coming up through it, and the young summer night outside on the mountains. This loneliness was so much more intense than his familiar loneliness that it made him feel very young. Memories like this had come up again and again during these three days. It was like beginning life over again. It had tricked him into thinking, more than once, next summer I'll make the strike, and this time I'll put it into something safe for the rest of my life, and stop this fool wandering around while I've still got some time left — a way of thinking which he had really stopped a long time before.

It was getting darker rapidly in the pass. When a gust of wind brought the snow against Mike's face so hard that he noticed the flakes felt larger, he looked up. The light was still there, although the fire was dying out of it, and the snow swarmed across it more thickly. Mike remembered God. He did not think anything exact. He did not think about his own relationship to God. He merely felt the idea as a comforting presence. He'd always had a feeling about God whenever he looked at a sunset, especially a sunset which came through under a stormy sky. It had been the strongest feeling left in him until these memories like the one about Armandy had begun. Even in this last pass, his strange fear of the storm had come on him again a couple of times, but now that he had looked at the light and thought of God, it was gone. In a few minutes he would come to the summit and look down into his lighted city. He felt happily hurried by this anticipation.

He would take the burro down and stable her in John Hammersmith's shed, where he always kept her. He would spread fresh straw for her, and see that the shed was tight against the wind and snow, and get a measure of grain for her from John. Then he would go up to Mrs. Wright's house at the top of Fourth Street, and leave his things in the same room he always had, the one in front, which looked down over the roofs and chimneys of his city, and across at the east wall of the canyon, from which the sun rose late. He would trim his beard with Mrs. Wright's shears, and shave the upper part of his cheeks. He would bathe out of the blue bowl and pitcher, and wipe himself with the towel with yellow flowers on it, and dress in the good dark suit and the good black shoes with the gleaming box toes, and the good black hat which he had left in the chest in his room. In this way he would perform the ceremony which ended the life of the desert and began the life of Gold Rock. Then he would go down to the International House, and greet Arthur Morris in the gleaming bar, and go into the dining room and eat the best supper they had, with fresh meat and vegetables, and new-made pie, and two cups of hot clear coffee. He would be served by the plump blonde waitress who always joked with him, and gave him many little extra things with his first supper, including the drink which Arthur Morris always sent in from the bar.

At this point Mike Braneen stumbled in his mind, and his anticipation wavered. He would not be sure that the plump blonde waitress would serve him. For a moment he saw her in a long skirt, and the dining room of the International House, behind her, had potted palms standing in the corners, and was full of the laughter and loud, manly talk of many customers who wore high vests and mustaches and beards. These men leaned back from tables covered with empty dishes. They patted their tight vests and lighted expensive cigars. He knew all their faces. If he were to walk down the aisle between the tables on his side, they would all speak to him. But he also seemed to remember the dining room with only a few tables, with oil-cloth on them instead of linen, and with moody young men sitting at them in their work clothes — strangers who worked for the high-way department, or were just passing through, or talked mining in terms which he did not understand or which made him angry.

No, it would not be the plump blonde waitress. He did not know who it would be. It didn't matter. After supper he would go up Canyon Street under the arcade to the Lucky Boy Saloon, and there it would be the same as ever. There would be the laurel wreaths on the frosted glass panels of the doors, and the old sign upon the window, the sign that was older than Tom Connover, almost as old as Mike Breen himself. He would open the door and see the bottles and the white women in the paintings, and the card table in the back corner and the big stove and the chairs along the wall. Tom would look around from his place behind the bar.

"Well, now," he would roar, "look who's here, boys."

"Now will you believe it's winter?" he would roar at them.

Some of them would be the younger men, of course, and there might even be a few strangers, but this would only add to the dignity of his reception, and there would also be his friends. There would be Henry Bray with the gray walrus mustache, and Mark Wilton and Pat Gallagher. They would all welcome him loudly.

"Mike, how are you anyway?" Tom would roar, leaning across the bar to shake hands with his big, heavy, soft hand with the diamond ring on it.

"And what'll it be, Mike? The same?" he'd ask, as if Mike had been in there no longer ago than the night before.

Mike would play that game too. "The same," he would say.

Then he would really be back in Gold Rock: never mind the plump blonde waitress.

Mike came to the summit of the old road and stopped and looked down. For a moment he felt lost again, as he had when he'd thought about the plump blonde waitress. He had expected Canyon Street to look much brighter. He had expected a lot of orange windows close together on the other side of the canyon. Instead there were only a few scattered lights across the darkness, and they were white. They made no communal glow upon the steep slope, but gave out only single, white needles of light, which pierced the darkness secretly and lonesomely, as if nothing could ever pass from one house to another over there. Canyon Street was very dark, too. There it went, the street he loved, steeply down into the bottom of the canyon, and down its length there were only the few street lights, more than a block apart, swinging in the wind and darting about that cold, small light. The snow whirled and swooped under the nearest street light below.

"You are getting to be an old fool," Mike Braneen said out loud to himself, and felt better. This was the way Gold Rock was now, of course, and he loved it all the better. It was a place that grew old with a man, that was going to die sometime, too. There could be an understanding with it.

He worked his way slowly down into Canyon Street, with Annie slipping and checking behind him. Slowly, with the blown snow behind them, they came to the first built-in block, and passed the first dim light showing through a smudged window under the arcade.

They passed the dark places after it, and the second light. Then Mike Braneen stopped in the middle of the street, and Annie stopped beside him, pulling her rump in and turning her head away from the snow. A highway truck, coming down from the head of the canyon, had to get way over into the wrong side of the street to pass them. The driver leaned out as he went by, and yelled, "Pull over, Pop. You're in town now."

Mike Braneen didn't hear him. He was staring at the Lucky Boy. The Lucky Boy was dark, and there were boards nailed across the big window that had shown the sign. At last Mike went over onto the board walk to look more closely. Annie followed him, but stopped at the edge of the walk and scratched her neck against a post of the arcade. There was the other sign, hanging crossways under the arcade, and even in that gloom Mike could see that it said Lucky Boy and had a Jack of Diamonds painted on it. There was no mistake. The Lucky Boy sign, and others like it under the arcade, creaked and rattled in the wind.

There were footsteps coming along the boards. The boards sounded hollow, and sometimes one of them rattled. Mike Braneen looked down slowly from the sign and peered at the approaching figure. It was a man wearing a sheepskin coat with the collar turned up round his head. He was walking quickly, like a man who knew where he was going, and why, and where he had been. Mike almost let him pass. Then he spoke.

"Say, fella —"

He even reached out a hand as if to catch hold of the man's sleeve, though he didn't touch it. The man stopped, and asked impatiently, "Yeah?" and Mike let the hand down again slowly.

"Well, what is it?" the man asked.

"I don't want anything," Mike said. "I got plenty."

"O.K., O.K.," the man said. "What's the matter?"

Mike moved his hand towards the Lucky Boy. "It's closed," he said.

"I see it is, Dad," the man said. He laughed a little. He didn't seem to be in quite so much of a hurry now.

"How long has it been closed?" Mike asked.

"Since about June, I guess," the man said. "Old Tom Connover, the guy that ran it, died last June."

Mike waited for a moment. "Tom died?" he asked.

"Yup. I guess he'd just kept it open out of love of the the place any-way. There hasn't been any real business for years. Nobody cared to keep it open after him."

The man started to move on, but then he waited, peering, trying to see Mike better.

"This June?" Mike asked finally.

"Yup. This last June."

"Oh," Mike said. Then he just stood there. He wasn't thinking anything. There didn't seem to be anything to think.

"You knew him?" the man asked.

"Thirty years," Mike said. "No, more'n that," he said, and started to figure out how long he had known Tom Connover, but lost it, and said, as if it would do just as well, "He was a lot younger than I am, though."

"Hey," said the man, coming closer, and peering again. "You're Mike Braneen, aren't you?"

"Yes," Mike said.

"Gee, I didn't recognize you at first. I'm sorry."

"That's all right," Mike said. He didn't know who the man was, or what he was sorry about.

He turned his head slowly, and looked out into the street. The snow was coming down heavily now. The street was all white. He saw Annie with her head and shoulders in under the arcade, but the snow settling on her rump.

"Well, I guess I'd better get Molly under cover," he said. He moved toward the burro a step, but then halted.

"Say, fella —"

The man had started on, but he turned back. He had to wait for Mike to speak.

"I guess this about Tom's mixed me up."

"Sure," the man said. "It's tough, an old friend like that."

"Where do I turn to get to Mrs. Wright's place?"

"Mrs. Wright?"

"Mrs. William Wright," Mike said. "Her husband used to be a foreman in the Aztec. Got killed in the fire."

"Oh," the man said. He didn't say anything more, but just stood there, looking at the shadowy bulk of old Mike.

"She's not dead, too, is she?" Mike asked slowly.

"Yeah, I'm afraid she is, Mr. Braneen," the man said.

"Look," he said more cheerfully. "It's Mrs. Branley's house you want right now, isn't it? Place where you stayed last winter?"

Finally Mike said, "Yeah. Yeah, I guess it is."

"I'm going up that way. I'll walk up with you," the man said.

After they had started, Mike thought that he ought to take the burro down to John Hammersmith's first, but he was afraid to ask about it. They walked on down Canyon Street, with Annie walking along beside them in the gutter. At the first side street they turned right and began to climb the steep hill toward another of the little street lights dancing over a crossing. There was no sidewalk here, and Annie followed right at their heels. That one street light was the only light showing up ahead.

When they were halfway up to the light, Mike asked, "She die this summer, too?"

The man turned his body half around, so that he could hear inside his collar.

"What?"

"Did she die this summer, too?"

"Who?"

"Mrs. Wright," Mike said.

The man looked at him, trying to see his face as they came up towards the light. Then he turned back again, and his voice was muffled by the collar.

"No, she died quite a while ago, Mr. Braneen."

"Oh," Mike said finally.

They came up onto the crossing under the light, and the snow-laden wind whirled around them again. They passed under the light, and their three lengthening shadows before them were obscured by the innumerable tiny shadows of the flakes.

Boys Will Be Boys

W HEN Judge Priest, on this particular morning, came puffing into his chambers at the courthouse, looking, with his broad beam and in his costume of flappy, loose white ducks, a good deal like an old-fashioned full-rigger with all sails set, his black shadow, Jeff Poindexter, had already finished the job of putting the quarters to rights for the day. The cedar water bucket had been properly replenished; the jagged flange of a fifteen-cent chunk of ice protruded above the rim of the bucket; and alongside, on the appointed nail, hung the gourd dipper that the master always used. The floor had been swept, except, of course, in the corners and underneath things; there were evidences, in streaky scrolls of fine grit particles upon various flat surfaces, that a dusting brush had been more or less sparingly employed. A spray of trumpet flowers, plucked from the vine that grew outside the window, had been draped over the framed steel engraving of President Davis and his Cabinet upon the wall; and on top of the big square desk in the middle of the room, where a small section of cleared green-blotter space formed an oasis in a dry and arid desert of cluttered law journals and dusty documents, the morning's mail rested in a little heap.

Having placed his old cotton umbrella in a corner, having removed his coat and hung it upon a peg behind the hall door, and having seen to it that a palm-leaf fan was in arm's reach should he require it, the Judge, in his billowy white shirt, sat down at his desk and gave his attention to his letters. There was an invitation from the Hylan B. Gracy Camp of Confederate Veterans of Eddyburg, asking him to deliver the chief oration at the annual reunion, to be held at Mineral Springs on the twelfth day of the following month; an official notice from the clerk of the Court of Appeals concerning the affirmation of a judgment that had been handed down by Judge Priest at the preceding term of his own court; a bill for five pounds of a special brand of smoking tobacco; a notice of a lodge meeting — altogether quite a sizable batch of mail.

At the bottom of the pile he came upon a long envelope addressed to him by his title, instead of by his name, and bearing on its upper right-hand corner several foreign-looking stamps; they were British stamps, he saw, on closer examination.

To the best of his recollection it had been a good long time since Judge Priest had had a communication by post from overseas. He adjusted his steel-bowed spectacles, ripped the wrapper with care, and shook out the contents. There appeared to be several inclosures; in fact, there were several — a sheaf of printed forms, a document with seals attached, and a letter that covered two sheets of paper with typewritten lines. To the letter the recipient gave consideration first. Before he reached the end of the opening paragraph he uttered a profound grunt of surprise; his reading of the rest was frequently punctuated by small exclamations, his face meantime puckering up in interested lines. At the conclusion, when he came to the signature, he indulged himself in a soft, low whistle. He read the letter all through again, and after that he examined the forms and the document which had accompanied it.

Chuckling under his breath, he wriggled himself free from the snug embrace of his chair arms and waddled out of his own office and down the long, bare, empty hall to the office of Sheriff Giles Birdsong. Within, that competent functionary, Deputy Sheriff Breck

Quarles, sat at ease in his shirt sleeves, engaged, with the smaller blade of his pocketknife, in performing upon his fingernails an operation that combined the fine deftness of the manicure with the less delicate art of the farrier. At the sight of the Judge in the open doorway he hastily withdrew from a tabletop, where they rested, a pair of long, thin legs, and rose.

"Mornin', Breck," said Judge Priest to the other's salutation. "No, thank you, son. I won't come in; but I've got a little job for you. I wisht, ef you ain't too busy, that you'd step down the street and see ef you can't find Peep O'Day fur me and fetch him back here with you. It won't take you long, will it?"

"No, suh — not very." Mr. Quarles reached for his hat and snuggled his shoulder holster back inside his unbuttoned waistcoat. "He'll most likely be down round Gafford's stable. Whut's Old Peep been doin', Judge — gettin' himself in contempt of court or somethin'?" He grinned, asking the question with the air of one making a little joke.

"No," vouchsafed the Judge; "he ain't done nothin'. But he's about to have somethin' of a highly onusual nature done to him. You jest tell him I'm wishful to see him right away — that'll be sufficient, I reckin."

Without making further explanation, Judge Priest returned to his chambers and for the third time read the letter from foreign parts. Court was not in session, and the hour was early and the weather was hot; nobody interrupted him. Perhaps fifteen minutes passed. Mr. Quarles poked his head in at the door.

"I found him, suh," the deputy stated. "He's outside here in the hall."

"Much obliged to you, son," said Judge Priest. "Send him on in, will you, please?"

The head was withdrawn; its owner lingered out of sight of His Honor, but within earshot. It was hard to figure the presiding judge of the First Judicial District of the State of Kentucky as having business with Peep O'Day; and, though Mr. Quarles was no eavesdropper, still he felt a pardonable curiosity in whatsoever might transpire. As he feigned an absorbed interest in a tax notice, which was pasted on a blackboard just outside the office door, there entered the presence of the Judge a man who seemingly was but a few years younger than the Judge himself — a man who looked to be somewhere between sixty-five and seventy. There is a look that you may have seen in the eyes of ownerless but well-intentioned dogs — dogs that, expecting kicks as their daily portion, are humbly grateful for kind words and stray bones; dogs that are fairly yearning to be adopted by somebody — by anybody — being prepared to give to such a benefactor a most faithful doglike devotion in return.

This look, which is fairly common among masterless and homeless dogs, is rare among humans; still, once in a while you do find it there too. The man who now timidly shuffled himself across the threshold of Judge Priest's office had such a look out of his eyes. He had a long, simple face, partly inclosed in gray whiskers. Four dollars would have been a sufficient price to pay for the garments he stood in, including the wrecked hat he held in his hands and the broken, misshaped shoes on his feet. A purchaser who gave more than four dollars for the whole in its present state of decrepitude would have been but a poor hand at bargaining.

The man who wore this outfit coughed in an embarrassed fashion and halted, fumbling his ruinous hat in his hands.

"Howdy do?" said Judge Priest heartily. "Come in!"

The owner diffidently advanced himself a yard or two.

"Excuse me, suh," he said apologetically, "but this-here Breck Quarles he come after me and he said ez how you wanted to see me. 'Twas him ez brung me here, suh."

Faintly underlying the drawl of the speaker was just a suspicion — a mere trace, as you might say — of a labial softness that belongs solely and exclusively to the children, and in a diminishing degree to the grandchildren, of native-born sons and daughters of a certain small green isle in the sea. It was not so much a suggestion of a brogue as it was the suggestion of the ghost of a brogue; a brogue almost extinguished, almost obliterated, and yet persisting through the generations — south of Ireland struggling beneath south of Mason and Dixon's Line.

"Yes," said the Judge; "that's right. I do want to see you." The tone was one that he might employ in addressing a bashful child. "Set down there and make yourself at home."

The newcomer obeyed to the extent of perching himself on the extreme forward edge of a chair. His feet shuffled uneasily where they were drawn up against the cross rung of the chair.

The Judge reared well back, studying his visitor over the tops of his glasses with rather a quizzical look. In one hand he balanced the large envelope which had come to him that morning.

"Seems to me I heard somewheres, years back, that your regular Christian name was Paul — is that right?"

"Shorely is, suh," assented the ragged man, surprised and plainly grateful that one holding a supremely high position in the community should vouchsafe to remember a fact relating to so inconsequent an atom as himself. "But I ain't heared it fur so long I come mighty nigh furgittin' it sometimes, myself. You see, Judge Priest, when I wasn't nothin' but jest a shaver folks started in to callin' me Peep — on account of my last name bein O'Day, I reckin. They been callin' me so ever since. Fust off, 'twas Little Peep, and then just plain Peep; and now it's got to be Old Peep. But my real entitled name is Paul, jest like you said Judge — Paul Felix O'Day."

"Uh-huh! And wasn't your father's name Philip and your mother's name Katherine Dwyer O'Day?"

"To the best of my recollection that's partly so, too, suh. They both of 'em up and died when I was a baby, long before I could remember anything a-tall. But they always told me my paw's name was Phil, or Philip. Only my maw's name wasn't Kath — Kath — wasn't whut you jest now called it, Judge. It was plain Kate."

"Kate or Katherine — it makes no great difference," explained Judge Priest. "I reckin the record is straight this fur. And now think hard and see ef you kin ever remember hearin' of an uncle named Daniel O'Day — your father's brother."

The answer was a shake of the tousled head.

"I don't know nothin' about my people. I only jest know they come over frum some place with a funny name in the Old Country before I was born. The onliest kin I ever had over here was that there no-'count triflin' nephew of mine — Perce Dwyer — him that uster hang around this town. I reckin you call him to mind, Judge?"

The old Judge nodded before continuing:

"All the same, I reckin there ain't no manner of doubt but whut you had an uncle of the name of Daniel. All the evidences would seem to p'int the way. Accordin' to the proofs, this-here Uncle Daniel of yours lived in a little town called Kilmare, in Ireland." He glanced at one of the papers that lay on his desktop, then added in a casual tone: "Tell me, Peep, whut are you doin' now fur a livin'?"

The object of this examination grinned a faint grin of extenuation.

"Well, suh, I'm knockin' about, doin' the best I kin — which ain't much. I help out round Gafford's liver' stable, and Pete Gafford he lets me sleep in a little room behind the feed room, and his wife she gives me my vittles. Oncet in a while I git a chancet to do odd jobs fur folks round town — cuttin' weeds and splittin' stove wood and packin' in coal, and sech ez that."

"Not much money in it, is there?"

"No, suh; not much. Folks is more prone to offer me old clothes than they are to pay me in cash. Still, I manage to git along. I don't live very fancy; but, then, I don't starve, and that's more'n some kin say."

"Peep, whut was the most money you ever had in your life — at one time?"

Peep scratched with a freckled hand at his thatch of faded whitish hair to stimulate recollection.

"I reckin not more'n six bits at any one time, suh. Seems like I've sorter got the knack of livin' without money."

"Well, Peep, sech bein' the case, whut would you say ef I was to tell you that you're a rich man?"

The answer came slowly:

"I reckin, suh, ef it didn't sound disrespectful, I'd say you was prankin' with me — makin' fun of me, suh."

Judge Priest bent forward in his chair.

"I'm not prankin' with you. It's my pleasant duty to inform you that at this moment you are the rightful owner of eight thousand pounds."

"Pounds of whut, Judge?" The tone expressed a heavy incredulity.

"Why, pounds in money."

Outside, in the hall, with one ear held conveniently near the crack in the door, Deputy Sheriff Quarles gave a violent start; and then, at once, was torn between a desire to stay and hear more and an urge to hurry forth and spread the unbelievable tidings. After the briefest of struggles the latter inclination won; this news was too marvelously good to keep; surely a harbinger and a herald were needed to spread it broadcast .

Mr. Quarles tiptoed rapidly down the hall. When he reached the sidewalk the volunteer bearer of a miraculous tale fairly ran. As for the man who sat facing the Judge, he merely stared in a dull bewilderment.

"Judge," he said at length, "eight thousand pounds of money oughter make a powerful big pile, oughten it?"

"It wouldn't weigh quite that much ef you put it on the scales," explained His Honor painstakingly. "I mean pounds sterlin' — English money. Near ez I kin figger offhand, it comes in our money to somewheres between thirty-five and forty thousand dollars — nearer forty than thirty-five. And it's yours, Peep — every red cent of it."

"Excuse me, suh, and not meanin' to contradict you, or nothin' like that; but I reckin there must be some mistake. Why, Judge, I don't scursely know anybody that's ez wealthy ez all that, let alone anybody that'd give me sech a lot of money."

"Listen, Peep: This-here letter I'm holdin' in my hand came to me by today's mail — jest a little spell ago. It's frum Ireland — frum the town of Kilmare, where your people come frum. It was sent to me by a firm of barristers in that town — lawyers, we'd call 'em. In this letter they ask me to find you and tell you what's happened. It seems, from whut they write, that your uncle, by name Daniel O'Day, died not very long ago without issue — that is to say, without leavin' any children of his own, and without makin' any will.

"It appears he had eight thousand pounds saved up. Ever since he died those lawyers and some other folks over there in Ireland have been tryin' to find out who that money should go to. They learnt in some way that your father and your mother settled in this town a mighty long time ago, and that they died here and left one son, which is you. All the rest of the family over there in Ireland have already died out, it seems; that natchelly makes you the next of kin and the heir at law, which means that all your uncle's money comes direct to you.

"So, Peep, you're a wealthy man in your own name. That's the news

I had to tell you. Allow me to congratulate you on your good fortune."

The beneficiary rose to his feet, seeming not to see the hand the old Judge had extended across the desktop toward him. On his face, of a sudden, was a queer, eager look. It was as though he foresaw the coming true of long-cherished and heretofore unattainable visions.

"Have you got it here, suh?"

He glanced about him as though expecting to see a bulky bundle. Judge Priest smiled.

"Oh, no; they didn't send it along with the letter — that wouldn't be regular. There's quite a lot of things to be done fust. There'll be some proofs to be got up and sworn to before a man called a British consul; and likely there'll be a lot of papers that you'll have to sign; and then all the papers and the proofs and things will be sent across the ocean. And, after some fees are paid out over there — why, then you will git your inheritance."

The rapt look faded from the strained face, leaving it downcast. "I'm afeared, then, I won't be able to claim that-there money," he said forlornly.

"Why not?"

"Because I don't know how to sign my own name. Raised the way I was, I never got no book learnin'. I can't neither read nor write."

Compassion shadowed the Judge's chubby face; and compassion was in his voice as he made answer:

"You don't need to worry about that part of it. You can make your mark — just a cross mark on the paper, with witnesses present — like this."

He took up a pen, dipped it in the inkwell, and illustrated his meaning.

"Yes, suh; I'm glad it kin be done thataway. I always wisht I knowed how to read big print and spell my own name out. I ast a feller oncet to write my name out fur me in plain letters on a piece of paper. I was aimin' to learn to copy it off; but I showed it to one of the hands at the liver' stable and he busted out laughin'. And then I come to find out this-here feller had tricked me fur to make game of me. He hadn't wrote my name out a-tall — he'd wrote some dirty words instid. So after that I give up tryin' to educate myself. That was several years back and I ain't tried sence. Now I reckin I'm too old to learn. . . . I wonder, suh — I wonder ef it'll be very long before that there money gits here and I begin to have the spendin' of it?"

"Makin' plans already?"

"Yes, suh," O'Day answered truthfully; "I am." He was silent for a moment, his eyes on the floor; then timidly he advanced the thought that had come to him. "I reckin, suh, it wouldn't be no more'n fair and proper ef I divided my money with you to pay you back fur all this trouble you're fixin' to take on my account. Would — would half of it be enough? The other half oughter last me fur what uses I'll make of it."

"I know you mean well and I'm much obliged to you fur your offer," stated Judge Priest, smiling a little; "but it wouldn't be fittin' or proper fur me to tech a cent of your money. There'll be some court dues and some lawyers' fees, and sech, to pay over there in Ireland; but after that's settled up everything comes direct to you. It's goin' to be a pleasure to me to help you arrange these-here details that you don't understand — a pleasure and not a burden."

He considered the figure before him.

"Now, here's another thing, Peep; I judge it's hardly fittin' fur a man of substance to go on livin' the way you've had to live durin' your life. Ef you don't mind my offerin' you a little advice I would suggest that you go right down to Felsburg Brothers when you leave here and git yourself fitted out with some suitable clothin'. And you'd better go to Max Biederman's, too, and order a better pair of shoes fur yourself than them you've got on. Tell 'em I sent you and that I guarantee the payment of your bills. Though I reckin that'll hardly be necessary — when the news of your good luck gits noised round I misdoubt whether there's any firm in our entire city that wouldn't be glad to have you on their books fur a stiddy customer.

"And, also, ef I was you I'd arrange to git me regular board and lodgin's somewheres around town. You see, Peep, comin' into a property entails consider'ble many responsibilities right frum the start."

"Yes, suh," assented the legatee obediently. "I'll do jest ez you say, Judge Priest, about the clothes and the shoes, and all that; but — but, ef you don't mind, I'd like to go on livin' at Gafford's. Pete

Gafford's been mighty good to me — him and his wife both; and I wouldn't like fur 'em to think I was gittin' stuck-up jest because I've had this-here streak of luck come to me. Mebbe, seein' ez how things has changed with me, they'd be willin' to take me in fur a table boarder at their house; but I shorely would hate to give up livin' in that there little room behind the feed room at the liver' stable. I don't know ez I could ever find any place that would seem ez homelike to me ez whut it is."

"Suit yourself about that," said Judge Priest heartily. "I don't know but whut you've got the proper notion about it after all."

"Yes, suh. Them Gaffords have been purty nigh the only real true friends I ever had that I could count on." He hesitated a moment. "I reckin — I reckin, suh, it'll be a right smart while, won't it, before that money gits here frum all the way acrost the ocean?"

"Why, yes; I imagine it will. Was you figurin' on investin' a little of it now?"

"Yes, suh; I was."

"About how much did you think of spendin' fur a beginnin'?"

O'Day squinted his eyes, his lips moving in silent calculation.

"Well, suh," he said at length, "I could use ez much ez a silver dollar. But, of course, sence —"

"That sounds kind of moderate to me," broke in Judge Priest. He shoved a pudgy hand into a pocket of his white trousers. "I reckin this detail kin be arranged. Here, Peep" — he extended his hand — "here's your dollar." Then, as the other drew back, stammering a refusal, he hastily added: "No, no, no; go ahead and take it — it's yours. I'm jest advancin' it to you out of whut'll be comin' to you shortly.

"I'll tell you whut: Until sech time ez you are in position to draw on your own funds you jest drap in here to see me when you're in need of cash, and I'll try to let you have whut you require — in reason. I'll keep a proper reckinin' of whut you git and you kin pay me back ez soon ez your inheritance is put into your hands.

"One thing more," he added as the heir, having thanked him, was making his grateful adieu at the threshold. "Now that you're wealthy, or about to be so, I kind of imagine quite a passel of fellers will suddenly discover themselves strangely and affectionately drawed toward you. You're liable to find out you've always had more true and devoted friends in this community than whut you ever imagined to be the case before.

"Now, friendship is a mighty fine thing, takin' it by and large; but it kin be overdone. It's barely possible that some of this-here new crop of your well-wishers and admirers will be makin' little business propositions to you — desirin' to have you go partners with 'em in business, or to sell you desirable pieces of real estate; or even to let you loan 'em various sums of money. I wouldn't be surprised but whut a number of sech chances will be comin' your way durin' the next few days, and frum then on. Ef sech should be the case I would suggest to you that, before committin' yourself to anybody or anything, you tell 'em that I'm sort of actin' as your unofficial adviser in money matters, and that they should come to me and outline their little schemes in person. Do you git my general drift?"

"Yes, suh," said Peep. "I won't furgit; and thank you ag'in, Judge, specially fur lettin' me have this dollar ahead of time."

He shambled out with the coin in his hand; and on his face was again the look of one who sees before him the immediate fulfillment of a delectable dream.

With lines of sympathy and amusement cross-hatched at the outer corners of his eyelids, Judge Priest, rising and stepping to his door, watched the retreating figure of the town's newest and strangest capitalist disappear down the wide front steps of the courthouse.

Presently he went back to his chair and sat down, tugging at his short chin beard.

"I wonder now," said he, meditatively addressing the emptiness of the room, "I wonder whut a man sixty-odd-year-old is goin' to do with the furst whole dollar he ever had in his life!"

It was characteristic of our circuit judge that he should have voiced his curiosity aloud. Talking to himself when he was alone was one of his habits. Also, it was characteristic of him that he had refrained from betraying his inquisitiveness to his late caller. Similar motives of delicacy had kept him from following the other man to watch the sequence.

However, at second hand, the details very shortly reached him. They were brought by no less a person than Deputy Sheriff Quarles, who, some twenty minutes or possibly half an hour later, obtruded himself upon Judge Priest's presence.

"Judge," began Mr. Quarles, "you'd never in the world guess whut Old Peep O'Day done with his first piece of money he got his hands on out of that-there forty thousand pounds of silver dollars he's come into from his uncle's estate."

The old man slanted a keen glance in Mr. Quarles' direction.

"Tell me, son," he asked softly, "how did you come to hear the glad tidin's so promptly?"

"Me?" said Mr. Quarles innocently. "Why, Judge Priest, the word is all over this part of town by this time. Why, I reckin twenty-five or fifty people must 'a' been watchin' Old Peep to see how he was goin' to act when he come out of this courthouse."

"Well, well, well!" murmured the Judge blandly. "Good news travels almost ez fast sometimes ez whut bad news does — don't it, now? Well, son, I give up the riddle. Tell me jest whut our elderly friend did do with the first installment of his inheritance."

"Well, suh, he turned south here at the gate and went down the street, a-lookin' neither to the right nor the left. He looked to me like a man in a trance, almost. He keeps right on through Legal Row till he comes to Franklin Street, and then he goes up Franklin to B. Weil & Son's confectionery store; and there he turns in. I happened to be followin' 'long behind him, with a few others — with several others, in fact — and we-all sort of slowed up in passin' and looked in at the door; and that's how I come to be in a position to see what happened.

"Old Peep, he marches in jest like I'm tellin' it to you, suh; and Mr. B. Weil comes to wait on him, and he starts in buyin'. He buys hisself a five-cent bag of gumdrops; and a five-cent bag of jelly beans; and a ten-cent bag of mixed candies — kisses and candy mottoes, and sech ez them, you know; and a sack of fresh-roasted peanuts — a big sack, it was, fifteen-cent size; and two prize boxes; and some gingersnaps — ten cents' worth; and a coconut; and half a dozen red bananas; and a half a dozen more of the plain yaller ones. Altogether I figger he spent a even dollar; in fact, I seen him hand Mr. Weil a dollar, and I didn't see him gittin' no change back out of it.

"Then he comes out of the store, with all these things stuck in his pockets and stacked up in his arms till he looks sort of like some new kind of a summertime Santy Klaws; and he sets down on a goods box at the edge of the pavement, with his feet in the gutter, and starts in eatin' all them things.

"First, he takes a bite off a yaller banana and then off a red banana, and then a mouthful of peanuts; and then maybe some mixed candies — not sayin' a word to nobody, but jest natchelly eatin' his fool head off. A young chap that's clerkin' in Bagby's grocery, next door, steps up to him and speaks to him, meanin', I suppose, to ast him is it true he's wealthy. And Old Peep, he says to him, 'Please don't come botherin' me now, sonny — I'm busy ketchin' up,' he says; and keeps right on a-munchin' and a-chewin' like all possessed.

"That ain't all of it, neither, Judge — not by a long shot it ain't! Purty soon Old Peep looks round him at the little crowd that's gathered. He didn't seem to pay no heed to the grown-up people standin' there; but he sees a couple of boys about ten years old in the crowd, and he beckons to them to come to him, and he makes room fur them alongside him on the box and divides up his knickknacks with them.

"When I left there to come on back here he had no less'n six kids squattered round him, includin' one little nigger boy; and between 'em all they'd jest finished up the last of the bananas and peanuts and the candy and the gingersnaps, and was fixin' to take turns drinkin' the milk out of the coconut. I s'pose they've got it all cracked out of the shell and et up by now — the coconut, I mean. Judge, you oughter stepped down into Franklin Street and taken a look at the picture whilst there was still time. You never seen such a funny sight in all your days, I'll bet!"

"I reckin 'would be too late to be startin' now," said Judge Priest. "I'm right sorry I missed it. . . . Busy ketchin' up, huh? Yes; I reckin he is. . . . Tell me, son, whut did you make out of the way Peep O'Day acted?"

"Why, suh," stated Mr. Quarles, "to my mind, Judge, there ain't no manner of doubt but whut prosperity has went to his head and turned it. He acted to me like a plum' distracted idiot. A grown man with forty thousand pounds of solid money settin' on the side of a gutter eatin' jimcracks with a passel of dirty little boys! Kin you figure it out any other way, Judge — except that his mind is gone?"

"I don't set myself up to be a specialist in mental disorders, son," said Judge Priest softly; "but sence you ask me the question, I should say, speakin' offhand, that it looks to me more ez ef the heart was the organ that was mainly affected. And possibly" — he added this last with a dry little smile — "and possibly, by now, the stomach also."

Whether or not Mr. Quarles was correct in his psychopathic diagnosis, he certainly had been right when he told Judge Priest that the word was already all over the business district. It had spread fast and was still spreading; it spread to beat the wireless, traveling as it did by that mouth-to-ear method of communication which is so amazingly swift and generally so tremendously incorrect. Persons who could not credit the tale at all nevertheless lost no time in giving to it a yet wider circulation; so that, as though borne on the wind, it moved in every direction, like ripples on a pond; and with each time of retelling the size of the legacy grew.

The *Daily Evening News,* appearing on the streets at 5 P.M., confirmed the tale; though by its account the fortune was reduced to a sum far below the gorgeously exaggerated estimates of most of the earlier narrators. Between breakfast and suppertime Poop O'Day's position in the common estimation of his fellow citizens underwent a radical and revolutionary change. He ceased — automatically, as it were — to be a town character; he became, by universal consent, a town notable, whose every act and every word would thereafter be subjected to close scrutiny and closer analysis.

The next morning the nation at large had opportunity to know of the great good fortune that had befallen Paul Felix O'Day, for the story had been wired to the city papers by the local correspondents of the same; and the press associations had picked up a stickful of the story and sped it broadcast over leased wires. Many who until that day had never heard of the fortunate man, or, indeed, of the place where he lived, at once manifested a concern in his well-being.

Certain firms of investment brokers in New York and Chicago

promptly added a new name to what vulgarly they called their "sucker" lists. Dealers in mining stocks, in oil stocks, in all kinds of attractive stocks, showed interest; in circular form samples of the most optimistic and alluring literature the world has ever known were consigned to the post, addressed to Mr. P. F. O'Day, such-and-such a town, such-and-such a state, care of general delivery.

Various lonesome ladies in various lonesome places lost no time in sitting themselves down and inditing congratulatory letters; object matrimony. Some of these were single ladies; others had been widowed, either by death or request. Various other persons of both sexes, residing here, there, and elsewhere in our country suddenly remembered that they, too, were descended from the O'Days of Ireland, and wrote on forthwith to claim proud and fond relationship with the particular O'Day who had come into money.

It was a remarkable circumstance, which speedily developed, that one man should have so many distant cousins scattered over the Union, and a thing equally noteworthy that practically all these kinspeople, through no fault of their own, should at the present moment be in such straitened circumstances and in such dire need of temporary assistance of a financial nature. Ticker and printer's ink, operating in conjunction, certainly did their work mighty well; even so, several days were to elapse before the news reached one who, of all those who read it, had most cause to feel a profound personal sensation in the intelligence.

This delay, however, was nowise to be blamed upon the tardiness of the newspapers; it was occasioned by the fact that the person referred to was for the moment well out of contact with the active currents of world affairs, he being confined in a workhouse at Evansville, Indiana.

As soon as he had rallied from the shock this individual set about making plans to put himself in direct touch with the inheritor. He had ample time in which to frame and shape his campaign, inasmuch as there remained for him yet to serve nearly eight long and painfully tedious weeks of a three-months vagrancy sentence. Unlike most of those now manifesting their interest, he did not write a letter; but he dreamed dreams that made him forget the annoyances of a ball and chain fast on his ankle and piles of stubborn stones to be cracked up into fine bits with a heavy hammer.

We are getting ahead of our narrative, though — days ahead of it. The chronological sequence of events properly dates from the morning following the morning when Peep O'Day, having been abruptly translated from the masses of the penniless to the classes of the wealthy, had forthwith embarked upon the gastronomic orgy so graphically detailed by Deputy Sheriff Quarles.

On that next day more eyes probably than had been trained in Peep O'Day's direction in all the unremarked and unremarkable days of his life put together were focused upon him. Persons who theretofore had regarded his existence — if indeed they gave it a thought — as one of the utterly trivial and inconsequential incidents of the cosmic scheme were moved to speak to him, to clasp his hand, and, in numerous instances, to express a hearty satisfaction over his altered circumstances. To all these, whether they were moved by mere neighborly good will, or perchance were inspired by impulses of selfishness, the old man exhibited a mien of aloofness and embarrassment.

This diffidence or this suspicion — or this whatever it was — protected him from those who might entertain covetous and ulterior designs upon his inheritance even better than though he had been brusque and rude; while those who sought to question him regarding his plans for the future drew from him only mumbled and evasive replies, which left them as deeply in the dark as they had been before. Altogether, in his intercourse with adults he appeared shy and very ill at ease.

It was noted, though, that early in the forenoon he attached to him perhaps half a dozen urchins, of whom the oldest could scarcely have been more than twelve or thirteen years of age; and that these youngsters remained his companions throughout the day. Likewise the events of that day were such as to confirm a majority of the observers in practically the same belief that had been voiced by Mr. Quarles — namely, that whatever scanty brains Peep O'Day might have ever had were now completely addled by the stroke of luck that had befallen him.

In fairness to all — to O'Day and to the town critics who sat in judgment upon his behavior — it should be stated that his conduct at the very outset was not entirely devoid of evidences of sanity. With his troupe of ragged juveniles trailing behind him, he first visited

Felsburg Brothers' Emporium to exchange his old and disreputable costume for a wardrobe that, in accordance with Judge Priest's recommendation, he had ordered on the afternoon previous, and which had since been undergoing certain necessary alterations.

With his meager frame incased in new black woolens, and wearing, as an incongruous added touch, the most brilliant of neckties, a necktie of the shade of a pomegranate blossom, he presently issued from Felsburg Brothers' and entered M. Biederman's shoe store, two doors below. Here Mr. Biederman fitted him with shoes, and in addition noted down a further order, which the purchaser did not give until after he had conferred earnestly with the members of his youthful entourage.

Those watching this scene from a distance saw — and perhaps marveled at the sight — that already, between these small boys, on the one part, and this old man, on the other, a perfect understanding appeared to have been established.

After leaving Biederman's, and tagged by his small escorts, O'Day went straight to the courthouse and, upon knocking at the door, was admitted to Judge Priest's private chambers, the boys meantime waiting outside in the hall. When he came forth he showed them something he held in his hand and told them something; whereupon all of them burst into excited and joyous whoops.

It was at that point that O'Day, by the common verdict of most grown-up onlookers, began to betray the vagaries of a disordered intellect. Not that his reason had not been under suspicion already, as a result of his freakish excess in the matter of B. Weil & Son's wares on the preceding day; but the relapse that now followed, as nearly everybody agreed, was even more pronounced, even more symptomatic than the earlier attack of aberration.

In brief, this was what happened: To begin with, Mr. Virgil Overall, who dealt in lands and houses and sold insurance of all the commoner varieties on the side, had stalked O'Day to this point and was lying in wait for him as he came out of the courthouse into the Public Square, being anxious to describe to him some especially desirable bargains, in both improved and unimproved realty; also, Mr. Overall was prepared to book him for life, accident, and health policies on the spot.

So pleased was Mr. Overall at having distanced his professional rivals in the hunt that he dribbled at the mouth. But the warmth of his disappointment and indignation dried up the salivary founts instantly when the prospective patron declined to listen to him at all and, breaking free from Mr. Overall's detaining clasp, hurried on into Legal Row, with his small convoys trotting along ahead and alongside him.

At the door of the Blue Goose Saloon and Short Order Restaurant its proprietor, by name Link Iserman, was lurking, as it were, in ambush. He hailed the approaching O'Day most cordially; he inquired in a warm voice regarding O'Day's health; and then, with a rare burst of generosity, he invited, nay urged, O'Day to step inside and have something on the house — wines, ales, liquors, or cigars; it was all one to Mr. Iserman. The other merely shook his head and, without a word of thanks for the offer, passed on as though bent upon an important mission.

Mark how the proofs were accumulating: The man had disdained the company of men of approximately his own age or thereabout; he had refused an opportunity to partake of refreshment suitable to his years; and now he stepped into the Bon Ton toy store and bought for cash — most inconceivable of accquisitions! — a little wagon that was painted bright red and bore on its sides, in circled letters, the name Comet.

His next stop was made at Bishop & Bryan's grocery, where, with the aid of his youthful compatriots, he first discriminatingly selected, and then purchased on credit, and finally loaded into the wagon, such purchases as a dozen bottles of soda pop, assorted flavors; cheese, crackers — soda and animal; sponge cakes with weatherproof pink icing on them; fruits of the season; cove oysters; a bottle of pepper sauce; and a quantity of the extra large-sized bright green cucumber pickles known to the trade as the Fancy Jumbo Brand, Prime Selected.

Presently the astounding spectacle was presented of two small boys, with string bridles on their arms, drawing the wagon through our town and out of it into the country, with Peep O'Day in the rôle of teamster walking alongside the laden wagon. He was holding the lines in his hands and shouting orders at his team, who showed a colty inclination to shy at objects, to kick up their heels without provo-

cation, and at intervals to try to run away. Eight or ten small boys —
for by now the troupe had grown in number and in volume of noise —
trailed along, keeping step with their elderly patron and advising him
shrilly regarding the management of his refractory span.

As it turned out, the destination of this preposterous procession was
Bradshaw's Grove, where the entire party spent the day picknicking
in the woods and, as reported by several reliable witnesses, playing
games. It was not so strange that holidaying boys should play games;
the amazing feature of the performance was that Peep O'Day, a man
old enough to be grandfather to any of them, played with them, being
by turns an Indian chief, a robber baron, and the driver of a stage-
coach attacked by Wild Western desperadoes.

When he returned to town at dusk, drawing his little red wagon
behind him, his new suit was rumpled into many wrinkles and
marked by dust and grass stains; his flame-colored tie was twisted
under one ear; his new straw hat was mashed quite out of shape; and
in his eyes was a light that sundry citizens, on meeting him, could
only interpret for a spark struck from the inner fires of madness.

Days that came after this, on through the midsummer, were, with
variations, but repetitions of the day I have just described. Each
morning Peep O'Day would go to either the courthouse or Judge
Priest's home to turn over to the Judge the unopened mail which had
been delivered to him at Gafford's stables; then he would secure from
the Judge a loan of money against his inheritance. Generally the
amount of his daily borrowing was a dollar; rarely was it so much
as two dollars; and only once was it more than two dollars.

By nightfall the sum would have been expended upon perfectly
useless and absolutely childish devices. It might be that he would
buy toy pistols and paper caps for himself and his following of
urchins; or that his whim would lead him to expend all the money in
tin flutes. In one case the group he so incongruously headed would be
for that one day a gang of make-believe banditti; in another, they
would constitute themselves a fife-and-drum corps — with barrel tops
for the drums — and would march through the streets, where scan-
dalized adults stood in their tracks to watch them go by, they all the
while making weird sounds, which with them passed for music.

Or again, the available cash resources would be invested in prov-

ender; and then there would be an outing in the woods. Under Peep
O'Day's captaincy his chosen band of youngsters picked dewberries;
they went swimming together in Guthrie's Gravel Pit, out by the old
Fair Grounds, where his spare naked shanks contrasted strongly with
their plump freckled legs as all of them splashed through the shallows,
making for deep water. Under his leadership they stole watermelons
from Mr. Dick Bell's patch, afterward eating their spoils in thickets of
grapevines along the banks of Perkins' Creek.

It was felt that mental befuddlement and mortal folly could reach
no greater heights — or no lower depths — than on a certain hour
of a certain day, along toward the end of August, when O'Day came
forth from his quarters in Gafford's stables, wearing a pair of boots
that M. Biederman's establishment had turned out to his order and
his measure — not such boots as a sensible man might be expected to
wear, but boots that were exaggerated and monstrous counterfeits of
the red-topped, scroll-fronted, brass-toed, stub-heeled, squeaky-soled
bootees that small boys of an earlier generation possessed.

Very proudly and seemingly unconscious of, at least oblivious to,
the derisive remarks that the appearance of these new belongings
drew from many persons, the owner went clumping about in them,
with the rumply legs of his trousers tucked down in them,
and ballooning up and out over the tops in folds which overlapped
from his knee joints halfway down his attenuated calves.

As Deputy Sheriff Quarles said, the combination was a sight fit
to make a horse laugh. It may be that small boys have a lesser sense
of humor than horses have, for certainly the boys who were the old
man's invariable shadows did not laugh at him, or at his boots either.
Between the whiskered senior and his small comrades there existed a
freemasonry that made them all sense a thing beyond the ken of most
of their elders. Perhaps this was because the elders, being blind in
their superior wisdom, saw neither this thing nor the communion that
flourished. They saw only the farcical joke. But His Honor, Judge
Priest, to cite a conspicuous exception, seemed not to see the lamen-
table comedy of it.

Indeed, it seemed to some almost as if Judge Priest were aiding
and abetting the befogged O'Day in his demented enterprises, his
peculiar excursions, and his weird purchases. If he did not actually

encourage him in these constant exhibitions of witlessness, certainly there were no evidences available to show that he sought to dissuade O'Day from his strange course.

At the end of a fortnight one citizen, in whom patience had ceased to be a virtue and to whose nature, long-continued silence on any public topic was intolerable, felt it his duty to speak to the Judge upon the subject. This gentleman — his name was S. P. Escott — held with many that, for the good name of the community, steps should be taken to abate the infantile, futile activities of the besotted legatee.

Afterward Mr. Escott, giving a partial account of the conversation with Judge Priest to certain of his friends, showed unfeigned annoyance at the outcome.

"I claim that old man's not fittin' to be runnin' a court any longer," he stated bitterly. "He's too old and peevish — that's what ails him! For one, I'm certainly never goin' to vote fur him again. Why, it's gettin' to be ez much ez a man's life is worth to stop that-there spiteful old crank in the street and put a civil question to him — that's whut's the matter!"

"What happened, S. P.?" inquired someone.

"Why, here's what happened!" exclaimed the aggrieved Mr. Escott. "I hadn't any more than started in to tell him the whole town was talkin' about the way that daffy Old Peep O'Day was carryin' on, and that somethin' had oughter be done about it, and didn't he think it was beholdin' on him ez circuit judge to do somethin' right away, sech ez havin' O'Day tuck up and tried fur a lunatic, and that I fur one was ready and willin' to testify to the crazy things I'd seen done with my own eyes — when he cut in on me and jez ez good ez told me to my own face that ef I'd quit tendin' to other people's business I'd mebbe have more business of my own to tend to.

"Think of that, gentlemen! A circuit judge bemeanin' a citizen and a taxpayer" — he checked himself slightly — "anyhow, a citizen, thataway! It shows he can't be rational his ownself. Personally I claim Old Priest is failin' mentally — he must be! And ef anybody kin be found to run against him at the next election you gentlemen jest watch and see who gits my vote!"

Having uttered this threat with deep and significant emphasis, Mr. Escott, still muttering, turned and entered the front gate of his boarding house. It was not exactly his boarding house; his wife ran it. But Mr. Escott lived there and voted from there.

But the apogee of Peep O'Day's carnival of weird vagaries of deportment came at the end of two months — two months in which each day the man furnished cumulative and piled-up material for derisive and jocular comment on the part of a very considerable proportion of his fellow townsmen.

Three occurrences of a widely dissimilar nature, yet all closely interrelated to the main issue, marked the climax of the man's new rôle in his new career. The first of these was the arrival of his legacy; the second was a one-ring circus; and the third and last was a nephew.

In the form of sundry bills of exchange the estate left by the late Daniel O'Day, of the town of Kilmare, in the island of Ireland, was on a certain afternoon delivered over into Judge Priest's hands, and by him, in turn, handed to the rightful owner, after which sundry indebtednesses, representing the total of the old Judge's day-to-day cash advances to O'Day, were liquidated.

The ceremony of deducting this sum took place at the Planters' Bank, whither the two had journeyed in company from the courthouse. Having, with the aid of the paying teller, instructed O'Day in the technical details requisite to the drawing of personal checks, Judge Priest went home and had his bag packed, and left for Reelfoot Lake to spend a week fishing. As a consequence he missed the remaining two events, following immediately thereafter.

The circus was no great shakes of a circus; no grand, glittering, gorgeous, glorious pageant of education and entertainment, traveling on its own special trains; no vast tented city of world's wonders and world's champions, heralded for weeks and weeks in advance of its coming by dead walls emblazoned with the finest examples of the lithographer's art, and by half-page advertisements in the *Daily Evening News.* On the contrary, it was a shabby little wagon show, which, coming overland on short notice, rolled into town under horse-power, and set up its ragged and dusty canvases on the vacant lot across from Yeiser's Drugstore.

Compared with the street parade of any of its great and famous rivals, the street parade of this circus was a meager and disappointing thing. Why, there was only one elephant, a dwarfish and debilitated-looking creature, worn mangy and slick on its various angles, like the cover of an old-fashioned haircloth trunk; and obviously most of the closed cages were weather-beaten stake wagons in disguise. Nevertheless, there was a sizable turnout of people for the afternoon performance. After all, a circus was a circus.

Moreover, this particular circus was marked at the afternoon performance by happenings of a nature most decidedly unusual. At one o'clock the doors were opened; at one-ten the eyes of the proprietor were made glad and his heart was uplifted within him by the sight of a strange procession, drawing nearer and nearer across the scuffed turf of the Common, and heading in the direction of the red ticket wagon.

At the head of the procession marched Peep O'Day — only, of course, the proprietor didn't know it was Peep O'Day — a queer figure in his rumpled black clothes and his red-topped, brass-toed boots, and with one hand holding fast to the string of a captive toy balloon. Behind him, in an uneven jostling formation, followed many small boys and some small girls. A census of the ranks would have developed that here were included practically all the juvenile white population who otherwise, through a lack of funds, would have been denied the opportunity to patronize this circus, or, in fact, any circus.

Each member of the joyous company was likewise the bearer of a toy balloon — red, yellow, blue, green, or purple, as the case might be. Over the line of heads the taut rubbery globes rode on their tethers, nodding and twisting like so many big iridescent bubbles; and half a block away, at the edge of the lot, a balloon vender, whose entire stock had been disposed of in one splendid transaction, now stood, empty-handed but full-pocketed, marveling at the stroke of luck that enabled him to take an afternoon off and rest his voice.

Out of a seemingly bottomless exchequer Peep O'Day bought tickets of admission for all. But this was only the beginning. Once inside the tent he procured accommodations in the reserved-seat section for himself and those who accompanied him. From such superior points of vantage the whole crew of them witnessed the performance, from the thrilling grand entry, with spangled ladies and gentlemen riding two by two on broad-backed steeds, to the tumbling-bout introducing the full strength of the company, which came at the end.

They munched fresh-roasted peanuts and balls of sugar-coated popcorn, slightly rancid, until they munched no longer with zest but merely mechanically. They drank pink lemonade to an extent that threatened absolute depletion of the fluid contents of both barrels in the refreshment stand out in the menagerie tent. They whooped their unbridled approval when the wild Indian chief, after shooting down a stuffed coon with a bow and arrow from somewhere up near the top of the center pole while balancing himself jauntily erect from the haunches of a coursing white charger, suddenly flung off his feathered headdress, his wig, and his fringed leather garments, and revealed himself in pink fleshings as the principal bareback rider.

They screamed in a chorus of delight when the funny old clown, who had been forcibly deprived of three tin flutes in rapid succession, now produced yet a fourth from the seemingly inexhaustible depths of his baggy white pants — a flute with a string and a bent pin attached to it — and, secretly affixing the pin in the tail of the cross ringmaster's coat, was thereafter enabled to toot sharp blasts at frequent intervals, much to the chagrin of the ringmaster, who seemed utterly unable to discover the whereabouts of the instrument dangling behind him.

But no one among them whooped louder or laughed longer than their elderly and bewhiskered friend, who sat among them, paying the bills. As his guests they stayed for the concert; and, following this, they partonized the side show in a body. They had been almost the first upon the scene; assuredly they were the last of the audience to quit it.

Indeed, before they trailed their confrère away from the spot, the sun was nearly down; and at scores of supper tables all over town the tale of poor old Peep O'Day's latest exhibition of freakishness was being retailed, with elaborations, to interested auditors. Estimates of the sum probably expended by him in this crowning extravagance ranged well up into the hundreds of dollars.

As for the object of these speculations, he was destined not to eat any supper at all that night. Something happened that so upset him as to make him forget the meal altogether. It began to happen when he reached the modest home of P. Gafford, adjoining the Gafford stables, on Locust Street, and found sitting on the lowermost step of the porch a young man of untidy and unshaved aspect, who hailed him affectionately as Uncle Paul, and who showed deep annoyance and acute distress upon being rebuffed with chill words.

It is possible that the strain of serving a three-months sentence, on the technical charge of vagrancy, in a workhouse somewhere in Indiana, had affected the young man's nerves. His ankle bones still ached where the ball and chain had been hitched; on his palms the blisters induced by the uncongenial use of a sledgehammer on a rock pile had hardly as yet turned to calluses. So it is only fair to presume that his nervous system felt the stress of his recent confining experiences also.

Almost tearfully he pleaded with Peep O'Day to remember the ties of blood that bound them; repeatedly he pointed out that he was the only known kinsman of the other in all the world, and therefore had more reason than any other living being to expect kindness and generosity at his uncle's hands. He spoke socialistically of the advisability of an equal division; failing to make any impression here he mentioned the subject of a loan — at first hopefully, but finally despairingly.

When he was done Peep O'Day, in a perfectly colorless and unsympathetic voice, bade him good-bye — not good night but good-bye! And, going inside the house, he closed the door behind him, leaving his newly returned relative outside and quite alone.

At this the young man uttered violent language; but, since there was nobody present to hear him, it is likely he found small satisfaction in his profanity, rich though it may have been in metaphor and variety. So presently he betook himself off, going straight to the office in Legal Row of H. B. Sublette, Attorney-at-Law.

From the circumstance that he found Mr. Sublette in, though it was long past that gentleman's office hours, and, moreover, found Mr. Sublette waiting in an expectant and attentive attitude, it might have been adduced by one skilled in the trick of putting two and two together that the pair of them had reached a prior understanding sometime during the day; and that the visit of the young man to the Gafford home and his speeches there had all been parts of a scheme planned out at a prior conference.

Be this as it may, so soon as Mr. Sublette had heard his caller's version of the meeting upon the porch he lost no time in taking certain legal steps. That very night, on behalf of his client, denominated in the documents as Percival Dwyer, Esquire, he prepared a petition addressed to the circuit judge of the district, setting forth that, inasmuch as Paul Felix O'Day had by divers acts shown himself to be of unsound mind, now, therefore, came his nephew and next of kin praying that a committtee or curator be appointed to take over the estate of the said Paul Felix O'Day, and administer the same in accordance with the orders of the court until such time as the said Paul Felix O'Day should recover his reason, or should pass from this life, and so forth and so on; not to mention whereases in great number and aforesaids abounding throughout the text in the utmost profusion.

On the following morning the papers were filed with Circuit Clerk Milam. That vigilant barrister, Mr. Sublette, brought them in person to the courthouse before nine o'clock, he having the interests of his client at heart and perhaps also visions of a large contingent fee in his mind. No retainer had been paid. The state of Mr. Dwyer's finances — or, rather, the absence of any finances — had precluded the performance of that customary detail; but to Mr. Sublette's experienced mind the prospects of future increment seemed large.

Accordingly, he was all for prompt action. Formally he said he wished to go on record as demanding for his principal a speedy hearing of the issue, with a view to preventing the defendant named in the pleadings from dissipating any more of the estate lately bequeathed to him and now fully in his possession — or words to that effect.

Mr. Milam felt justified in getting into communication with Judge Priest over the long-distance phone; and the Judge, cutting short his vacation and leaving uncaught vast numbers of bass and perch in Reelfoot Lake, came home, arriving late that night.

Next morning, having issued divers orders in connection with the impending litigation, he sent a messenger to find Peep O'Day and to direct O'Day to come to the courthouse for a personal interview.

Shortly thereafter a scene that had occurred some two months earlier, with His Honor's private chamber for a setting, was substantially duplicated: there was the same cast of two, the same stage properties, the same atmosphere of untidy tidiness. And, as before, the dialogue was in Judge Priest's hands. He led and his fellow character followed his leads.

"Peep," he was saying, "you understand, don't you, that this-here fragrant nephew of yours that's turned up from nowheres in particular is fixin' to git ready to try to prove that you are feeble-minded? And, on top of that, that he's goin' to ask that a committee be app'inted fur you — in other words, that somebody or other shall be named by the court, meanin' me, to take charge of your property and control the spendin' of it frum now on?"

"Yes, suh," stated O'Day. "Pete Gafford he set down with me and made hit all clear to me, yestiddy evenin', after they'd done served the papers on me."

"All right, then. Now I'm goin' to fix the hearin' fur tomorrow mornin' at ten. The other side is askin' fur a quick decision; and I rather figger they're entitled to it. Is that agreeable to you?"

"Whutever you say, Judge."

"Well, have you retained a lawyer to represent your interests in court? That's the main question that I sent fur you to ast you."

"Do I need a lawyer, Judge?"

"Well, there have been times when I regarded lawyers ez bein' superfluous," stated Judge Priest dryly. "Still, in most cases litigants do have 'em round when the case is bein' heard."

"I don't know ez I need any lawyer to he'p me say whut I've got to say," said O'Day. "Judge, you ain't never ast me no questions about the way I've been carryin' on sence I come into this-here money; but I reckin mebbe this is ez good a time ez any to tell you jest why I've been actin' the way I've done. You see, suh — "

"Hold on!" broke in Judge Priest. "Up to now, ez my friend, it would 'a' been perfectly proper fur you to give me your confidences ef you were minded so to do; but now I reckin you'd better not. You see, I'm the judge that's got to decide whether you are a responsible person — whether you're mentally capable of handlin' your own financial affairs, or whether you ain't. So you'd better wait and make your statement in your own behalf to me whilst I'm settin' on the bench. I'll see that you git an opportunity to do so and I'll listen to it; and I'll give it all the consideration it's deservin' of.

"And, on second thought, p'raps it would only be a waste of time and money fur you to go hirin' a lawyer specially to represent you. Under the law it's my duty, in sech a case ez this here one is, to app'int a member of the bar to serve durin' the proceedin's ez your guardian *ad litem.*

"You don't need to be startled," he added, as O'Day flinched at the sound in his ears of these strange and fearsome words. "A guardian *ad litem* is simply a lawyer that tends to your affairs till the case is settled one way or the other. Ef you had a dozen lawyers I'd have to app'int him jest the same. So you don't need to worry about that part of it.

"That's all. You kin go now ef you want to. Only, ef I was you, I wouldn't draw out any more money frum the bank 'twixt now and the time when I make my decision."

All things considered, it was an unusual assemblage that Judge Priest regarded over the top rims of his glasses as he sat facing it in his broad armchair, with the flat top of the bench intervening between him and the gathering. Not often, even in the case of exciting murder trials, had the old courtroom held a larger crowd; certainly never had it held so many boys. Boys, and boys exclusively, filled the back rows of benches downstairs. More boys packed the narrow, shelf-like balcony that spanned the chamber across its far end — mainly small boys, barefooted, sunburned, freckle-faced, shock-headed boys. And, for boys, they were strangely silent and strangely attentive.

The petitioner sat with his counsel, Mr Sublette. The petitioner had been newly shaved, and from some mysterious source had been equipped with a neat wardrobe. Plainly he was endeavoring to wear a look of virtue, which was a difficult undertaking, as you would understand had you known the petitioner.

The defending party to the action was seated across the room, touching elbows with old Colonel Farrell, dean of the local bar and its most florid orator.

"The court will designate Colonel Horatio Farrell as guardian *ad litem* for the defendant during these proceedings," Judge Priest had stated a few minutes earlier, using the formal and grammatical language he reserved exclusively for his courtroom.

At once old Colonel Farrell had hitched his chair up alongside O'Day; had asked him several questions in a tone inaudible to those about them, had listened to the whispered answers of O'Day, and then had nodded his huge, curly white dome of a head, as though amply satisfied with the responses.

Let us skip the preliminaries. True, they seemed to interest the audience; here, though, they would be tedious reading. Likewise, in touching upon the opening and outlining address of Attorney-at-Law Sublette let us, for the sake of time and space, be very much briefer than Mr. Sublette was. For our present purposes, I deem it sufficient to say that in all his professional career Mr. Sublette was never more eloquent, never more forceful, never more vehement in his allegations, and never more convinced — as he himself stated, not once but repeatedly — of his ability to prove the facts he alleged by competent and unbiased testimony. These facts, he pointed out, were common knowledge to the community, nevertheless, he stood prepared to buttress them with the evidence of reputable witnesses, given under oath.

Mr. Sublette, having unwound at length, now wound up. He sat down, perspiring freely and through the perspiration radiating confidence in his contentions, confidence in the result, and, most of all, unbound confidence in Mr. Sublette.

Now Colonel Farrell was standing up to address the court. Under the cloak of a theatrical presence and a large, orotund manner, and behind a Ciceronian command of sonorous language, the Colonel carried concealed a shrewd old brain. It was as though a skilled marksman lurked in ambush amid a tangle of luxuriant foliage. In this particular instance, moreover, it is barely possible that the Colonel was acting on a cue, privily conveyed to him before the court opened.

"May it please Your Honor," he began, "I have just conferred with the defendant here; and, acting in the capacity of his guardian *ad litem,* I have advised him to waive an opening address by counsel. Indeed, the defendant has no counsel. Furthermore, the defendant, also acting upon my advice, will present no witnesses in his own behalf. But, with Your Honor's permission, the defendant will now make a personal statement; and thereafter he will rest content, leaving the final arbitrament of the issue to Your Honor's discretion."

"I object!" exclaimed Mr. Sublette briskly.

"On what ground does the learned counsel object?" inquired Judge Priest.

"On the grounds that, since the mental competence of this man is concerned — since it is our contention that he is patently and plainly a victim of senility, an individual prematurely in his dotage — any utterances by him will be of no value whatsoever in aiding the conscience and intelligence of the court to arrive at a fair and just conclusion regarding the defendant's mental condition."

Mr. Sublette excelled in the use of big words; there was no doubt about that.

"The objection is overruled," said Judge Priest. He nodded in the direction of O'Day and Colonel Farrell. "The Court will hear the defendant. He is not to be interrupted while making his statement. The defendant may proceed."

Without further urging, O'Day stood up, a tall, slabsided rack of a man, with his long arms dangling at his sides, half facing Judge Priest and half facing his nephew and his nephew's lawyer. Without hesitation he began to speak. And this was what he said:

"There's mebbe some here ez knows about how I was raised and fetched up. My paw and my maw died when I was jest only a baby; so I was brung up out here at the old county porehouse ez a pauper. I can't remember the time when I didn't have to work for my board and keep, and work hard. While other boys was goin' to school and playin' hooky, and goin' in washin' in the creek, and playin' games, and all sech ez that, I had to work. I never done no playin' round in my whole life — not till here jest recently, anyway.

"But I always craved to play round some. I didn't never say nothin' about it to nobody after I growed up, 'cause I figgered it out they wouldn't understand and mebbe'd laugh at me; but all these years, ever sence I left that-there porehouse, I've had a hankerin' here inside of me" — he lifted one hand and touched his breast — "I've had a hankerin' to be a boy and do all the things a boy does; to do the things I was chiseled out of doin' whilst I was of a suitable age to be doin' 'em. I call to mind that I uster dream in my sleep about doin' 'em; but the dream never come true — not till jest here lately. It didn't have no chancet to come true — not till then.

"So, when this money come to me so sudden and unbeknownst-like I said to myself that I was goin' to make that-there dream come true; and I started out fur to do it. And I done it! And I reckin that's the cause of my bein' here today, accused of bein' feeble-minded. But, even so, I don't regret it none. Ef it was all to do over ag'in, I'd do it jest the very same way.

"Why, I never knowed whut it was, till here two months or so ago, to have my fill of bananas and candy and gingersnaps, and all sech knickknacks ez them. All my life I've been cravin' secretly to own a pair of red-topped boots with brass toes on 'em, like I used to see other boys wearin' in the wintertime when I was out younder at that porehouse wearin' an old pair of somebody else's cast-off shoes — mebbe a man's shoes, with rags wropped round my feet to keep the snow frum comin' through the cracks in 'em, and to keep 'em from slippin' right spang off my feet. I got three toes frostbit oncet durin' a cold spell, wearin' them kind of shoes. But here the other week I found myself able to buy me some red-top boots with brass toes on 'em. So I had 'em made to order and I'm wearin' 'em now. I wear 'em reg'lar even ef it is summertime. I take a heap of pleasure out of 'em. And also, all my life long I've been wantin' to go to a circus. But not till three days ago I didn't never git no chancet to go to one.

"That gentleman yonder — Mister Sublette — he 'lowed jest now that I was leadin' a lot of boys in this-here town into bad habits. He said that I was learnin' 'em nobody knowed whut devilment. And he spoke of my havin' egged 'em on to steal watermelons frum Mister Bell's watermelon patch out here three miles frum town, on the Marshville gravel road. You-all heared whut he jest now said about that.

"I don't mean no offense and I beg his pardon fur contradictin' him right out before everybody here in the big courthouse; but, mister, you're wrong. I don't lead these-here boys astray that I've been runnin' round with. They're mighty nice clean boys, all of 'em. Some of 'em are mighty near ez pore ez whut I uster be; but there ain't no real harm in any of 'em. We git along together fine — me and them. And, without no preachin', nor nothin' like that, I've done my best these weeks we've been frolikin' and projectin' round together to keep 'em frum growin' up to do mean things. I use chawin' tobacco myself; but I've told 'em, I don't know how many times, that ef they chaw it'll stunt 'em in their growth. And I've got several of 'em that was smokin' cigarettes on the sly to promise me they'd quit. So I don't figger ez I've done them boys any real harm by goin' round with 'em. And I believe ef you was to ast 'em they'd all tell you the same, suh.

"Now about them watermelons: Sence this gentleman has brung them watermelons up, I'm goin' to tell you-all the truth about that too."

He cast a quick, furtive look, almost a guilty look, over his shoulder toward the rear of the courtroom before he went on:

"Them watermelons wasn't really stole at all. I seen Mister Dick Bell beforehand and arranged with him to pay him in full fur whutever damage mout be done. But, you see, I knowed watermelons tasted sweeter to a boy ef he thaught he'd hooked 'em out of a patch; so I never let on to my little pardners yonder that I'd the same ez paid Mister Bell in advance fur the melons we snuck out of his patch and et in the woods. They've all been thinkin' up till now that we really hooked them watermelons. But ef that was wrong I'm sorry fur it.

"Mister Sublette, you jest now said that I was fritterin' away my property on vain foolishment. Them was the words you used — 'fritterin'' and 'vain foolishment.' Mebbe you're right, suh, about the fritterin' part; but ef spendin' money in a certain way gives a man ez much pleasure ez it's give me these last two months, and ef the money is his'n by rights, I figger it can't be so very foolish; though it may 'pear so to some.

"Excusin' these-here clothes I've got on and these-here boots, which ain't paid fur yet, but is charged up to me on Felsburg Brothers' books and Mister M. Biederman's books, I didn't spend only a dollar a day, or mebbe two dollars, and once three dollars in a single day out of whut was comin' to me. The Judge here, he let me have that out of his own pocket; and I paid him back. And that was all I did spend till here three days ago when that-there circus come to town. I reckin I did spend a right smart then.

"My money had come frum the old country only the day before; so I went to the bank and they writ out one of them pieces of paper which is called a check, and I signed it — with my mark; and they give me the money I wanted — an even two hundred dollars. And part of that-there money I used to pay fur circus tickets fur all the little boys and little girls I could find in this town that couldn't 'a' got to the circus no other way. Some of 'em are settin' back there behind you-all now — some of the boys, I mean; I don't see none of the little girls.

"There was several of 'em told me at the time they hadn't never seen a circus — not in their whole lives. Fur that matter, I hadn't, neither; but I didn't want no pore child in this town to grow up to be ez old ez I am without havin' been to at least one circus. So I taken 'em all in and paid all the bills; and when night come there wasn't but 'bout nine dollars left out of the whole two hundred that I'd started out with in the mornin'. But I don't begredge spendin' it. It looked to me like it was money well invested. They all seemed to enjoy it; and I know I done so.

"There may be bigger circuses'n whut that one was; but I don't see how a circus could 'a' been any better than this-here one I'm tellin' about, ef it was ten times ez big. I don't regret the investment and I don't aim to lie about it now. Mister Sublette, I'd do the same thing over ag'in ef the chance should come, lawsuit or no lawsuit. Ef you should win this-here case mebbe I wouldn't have no second chance.

"Ef some gentleman is app'inted ez a commitee to handle my money it's likely he wouldn't look at the thing the same way I do; and it's likely he wouldn't let me have so much money all in one lump to spend takin' a passel of little shavers that ain't no kin to me to the circus and to the side show, besides lettin' 'em stay fur the grand concert or after show, and all. But I done it once; and I've got it to remember and think about in my own mind ez long ez I live.

"I'm 'bout finished now. There's jest one thing more I'd like to say, and that is this: Mister Sublette he said a minute ago that I was in my second childhood. Meanin' no offense, suh, but you was wrong there too. The way I look at it, a man can't be in his second childhood without he's had his first childhood; and I was cheated plum' out of mine. I'm more'n sixty years old, ez near ez I kin figger; but I'm tryin' to be a boy before it's too late."

He paused a moment and looked round him.

"The way I look at it, Judge Priest, suh, and you-all, every man that grows up, no matter how old he may git to be, is entitled to 'a' been a boy oncet in his lifetime. I — I reckin that's all."

He sat down and dropped his eyes upon the floor, as though ashamed that his temerity should have carried him so far. There was a strange little hush filling the courtroom. It was Judge Priest who broke it.

"The court," he said, "has by the words just spoken by this man been sufficiently advised as to the sanity of the man himself. The court cares to hear nothing more from either side on this subject. The petition is dismissed."

Very probably these last words may have been as so much Greek to the juvenile members of the audience; possibly, though, they were made aware of the meaning of them by the look upon the face of Nephew Percival Dwyer and the look upon the face of Nephew Percival Dwyer's attorney. At any rate, His Honor hardly had uttered the last syllable of his decision before, from the rear of the courtroom and from the gallery above, there arose a shrill, vehement, sincere sound of yelling — exultant, triumphant, and deafening. It continued for upward of a minute before the small disturbers remembered where they were and reduced themselves to a state of comparative quiet.

For reasons best known to himself, Judge Priest, who ordinarily stickled for order and decorum in his courtroom, made no effort to quell the outburst or to have it quelled — not even when a considerable number of the adults present joined in it, having first cleared their throats of a slight huskiness that had come upon them, severally and generally.

Presently the Judge rapped for quiet — and got it. It was apparent that he had more to say; and all there hearkened to hear what it might be.

"I have just this to add," quoth His Honor. "It is the official judgment of this court that the late defendant, being entirely sane, is competent to manage his own affairs after his preferences.

"And it is the private opinion of this court that not only is the late defendant sane but that he is the sanest man in this entire jurisdiction. Mister Clerk, this court stands adjourned."

Coming down the three short steps from the raised platform of the bench, Judge Priest beckoned to Sheriff Giles Birdsong, who, at the tail of the departing crowd, was shepherding its last exuberant members through the doorway.

"Giles," said Judge Priest in an undertone, when the worthy sheriff had drawn near, "the circuit clerk tells me there's an indictment for malicious mischief ag'in this-here Perce Dwyer knockin' round amongst the records somewheres — an indictment the grand jury returned several sessions back, but which was never pressed, owin' to the sudden departure frum our midst of the person in question.

"I wonder if it would be too much trouble fur you to sort of drap a hint in the ear of the young man or his lawyer that the said indictment is apt to be revived, and that the said Dwyer is liable to be tuck into custody by you and lodged in the county jail sometime during the ensuin' forty-eight hours — without he should see his way clear durin' the meantime to get clean out of this city, county, and state! Would it?"

"Trouble? No, suh! It won't be no trouble to me," said Mr. Birdsong promptly. "Why, it'll be more of a pleasure, Judge."

And so it was.

Except for one small added and purely incidental circumstance, our narrative is ended. That same afternoon Judge Priest sat on the front porch of his old white house out on Clay Street, waiting for Jeff Poindexter to summon him to supper. Peep O'Day opened the front gate and came up the graveled walk between the twin rows of silver-leaf poplars. The Judge, rising to greet his visitor, met him at the top step.

"Come in," bade the Judge heartily, "and set down a spell and rest your face and hands."

"No, suh; much obliged, but I ain't got only a minute to stay," said O'Day. "I jest come out here, suh, to thank you fur whut you done today on my account in the big courthouse, and — and to make you a little kind of a present."

"It's all right to thank me," said Judge Priest, "but I couldn't accept any reward fur renderin' a decision in accordance with the plain facts."

" 'Tain't no gift of money, or nothin' like that," O'Day hastened to explain. "Really, suh, it don't amount to nothin' at all, scursely.

But a little while ago I happened to be in Mr. B. Weil & Son's store, doin' a little tradin', and I run acrost a new kind of knickknack, which it seemed like to me it was about the best thing I ever tasted in my whole life. So, on the chancet, suh, that you might have a sweet tooth, too, I taken the liberty of bringin' you a sack of 'em and — and — and here they are, suh; three flavors — strawberry, lemon, and vanilly."

Suddenly overcome with confusion, he dislodged a large-sized paper bag from his side coat pocket and thrust it into Judge Priest's hands; then, backing away, he turned and clumped down the graveled path in great and embarrassed haste.

Judge Priest opened the bag and peered down into it.

It contained a sticky, sugary dozen of flattened confections, each molded round a short length of wooden splinter. These sirupy articles, which have since come into quite general use, are known, I believe, as all-day suckers.

When Judge Priest looked up again, Peep O'Day was outside the gate, clumping down the uneven sidewalk of Clay Street with long strides of his booted legs. Half a dozen small boys, who, it was evident, had remained hidden during the ceremony of presentation, now mysteriously appeared and were accompanying the departing donor, half trotting to keep up with him.

PIETRO DI DONATO

Christ in Concrete

MARCH whistled stinging snow against the brick walls and up the gaunt girders. Geremio, the foreman, swung his arms about, and gaffed the men on.

Old Nick, the "Lean," stood up from over a dust-flying brick pile, and tapped the side of his nose.

"Master Geremio, the devil himself could not break his tail any harder than we here."

Burly Vincenzo of the walrus mustache, and known as the "Snout-nose," let fall the chute door of the concrete hopper and sang over in the Lean's direction: "Mari-Annina's belly and the burning night will make of me once more a milk-mouthed stripling lad. . . ."

The Lean loaded his wheelbarrow and spat furiously. "Sons of two-legged dogs . . . despised of even the devil himself! Work! Sure! For America beautiful will eat you and spit your bones into the earth's hole! Work!" And with that his wiry frame pitched the barrow violently over the rough floor.

Snoutnose waved his head to and fro and with mock pathos wailed, "Sing on, oh guitar of mine. . . ."

Short, cheery-faced Joe Chiappa, the scaffoldman, paused with hatchet in hand and tenpenny spike sticking out from small dicelike teeth to tell the Lean as he went by, in a voice that all could hear, "Ah, father of countless chicks, the old age is a carrion!"

Geremio chuckled and called to him: "Hey, little Joe, who are you to talk? You and big-titted Cola can't even hatch an egg, whereas the Lean has just to turn the doorknob of his bedroom and old Philomena becomes a balloon!"

Coarse throats tickled and mouths opened wide in laughter.

Mike, the "Barrel-mouth," pretended he was talking to himself and yelled out in his best English . . . he was always speaking English while the rest carried on in their native Italian: "I don't know myself, but somebody whose gotta bigga buncha keeds and he alla times talka from somebody elsa!"

Geremio knew it was meant for him and he laughed. "On the tomb of Saint Pimplelegs, this little boy my wife is giving me next week shall be the last! Eight hungry little Christians to feed is enough for any man."

Joe Chiappa nodded to the rest. "Sure, Master Geremio had a telephone call from the next bambino. Yes, it told him it had a little bell there instead of a rose bush. . . . It even told him its name!"

"Laugh, laugh all of you," returned Geremio, "but I tell you that all my kids must be boys so that they some day will be big American builders. And then I'll help him to put the gold away in the basements for safekeeping!"

A great din of riveting shattered the talk among the fast-moving men. Geremio added a handful of "honest" tobacco to his corncob, puffed strongly, and cupped his hands around the bowl for a bit of warmth. The chill day caused him to shiver, and he thought to himself, Yes, the day is cold, cold . . . but who am I to complain when the good Christ himself was crucified?

Pushing the job is all right (when has it been otherwise in my life?) but this job frightens me. I feel the building wants to tell me something; just as one Christian to another. I don't like this. Mr. Murdin tells me, "Push it up!" That's all he knows. I keep telling him that the underpinning should be doubled and the old material removed from the floors, but he keeps the inspector drunk and . . . "Hey, Ashes-ass! Get away from under that pilaster! Don't pull the old work. Push it away from you or you'll have a nice present for Easter if the wall falls on you!" . . . Well, with the help of God I'll see this job through. It's not my first, nor the. . . . "Hey, Patsy number two! Put more cement in that concrete we're putting up a building, not an Easter cake!"

Patsy hurled his shovel to the floor and gesticulated madly. "The padrone Jurdin-sa tells me, 'Too much, too much! Lil' bit is plenty!' And you tell me I'm stingy! The rotten building can fall after I leave!"

Six floors below, the contractor called: "Hey, Geremio! Is your gang of dagos dead?"

Geremio cautioned to the men: "On your toes, boys. If he writes out slips, someone won't have big eels on the Easter table."

The Lean cursed that "the padrone could take the job and shove it . . . !"

Curly-headed Sandino, the roguish, pigeon-toed scaffoldman, spat a clod of tobacco juice and hummed to his own music.

. . . "Yes, certainly yes to your face, master padrone . . . and behind, this to you and all your kind!"

The day, like all days, came to an end. Calloused and bruised bodies sighed, and numb legs shuffled towards shabby railroad flats. . . .

"Ah, *bella casa mia.* Where my little freshets of blood, and my good woman await me. Home where my broken back will not ache so. Home where midst the monkey chatter of my *piccolinos* I will float off to blessed slumber with my feet on the chair and the head on the wife's soft full breast."

These great childhearted ones leave each other without words or ceremony, and as they ride and walk home, a great pride swells the breast. . . .

"Blessings to Thee, oh Jesus. I have fought winds and cold. Hand to hand I have locked dumb stones in place and the great building rises. I have earned a bit of bread for me and mine."

The mad day's brutal conflict is forgiven, and strained limbs prostrate themselves so that swollen veins can send the yearning blood coursing and pulsating deliciously as though the body mountained leaping streams.

The job alone remained behind . . . and yet, they too, having left the bigger part of their lives with it. The cold ghastly beast, the Job, stood stark, the eerie March wind wrapping it in sharp shadows of falling dusk.

That night was a crowning point in the life of Geremio. He bought a house! Twenty years he had helped to mold the New World. And now he was to have a house of his own! What mattered that it was no more than a wooden shack? It was his own!

He had proudly signed his name and helped Annunziata to make her x on the wonderful contract that proved them owners. And she was happy to think that her next child, soon to come, would be born under their own rooftree. She heard the church chimes, and cried to the children: "Children, to bed! It is near midnight. And remember, shut-mouth to the *paesanos!* Or they will send the evil eye to our new home even before we put foot."

The children scampered off to the icy yellow bedroom where three slept in one bed and three in the other. Coltishly and friskily they kicked about under the covers; their black iron-cotton stockings not removed . . . what! and freeze the peanut-little toes?

Said Annunziata, "The children are so happy, Geremio; let them be, for even I would a Tarantella dance." And with that she turned blushing. He wanted to take her on her word. She patted his hands, kissed them, and whispered, "Our children will dance for us . . . in the American style some day."

Geremio cleared his throat and wanted to sing. "Yes, with joy I could sing in a richer feeling than the great Caruso." He babbled little old-country couplets and circled the room until the tenant below tapped the ceiling.

Annunziata whispered: "Geremio, to bed and rest. Tomorrow is a day for great things . . . and the day on which our Lord died for us."

The children were now hard asleep. Heads under the cover, over . . . moist noses whistling, and little damp legs entwined.

In bed Geremio and Annunziata clung closely to each other. They mumbled figures and dates until fatigue stilled their thoughts. And with chubby Johnnie clutching fast his bottle and warmed between them . . . life breathed heavily, and dreams entertained in far, far worlds, the nation-builder's brood.

But Geremio and Annunziata remained for a while staring into darkness, silently.

"Geremio?"

"Yes?"

"This job you are now working . . ."

"So?"

"You always used to tell me about what happened on the jobs . . . who was jealous, and who praised. . . ."

"You should know by now that all work is the same. . . ."

"Geremio. The month you have been on this job, you have not spoken a word about the work. . . . And I have felt that I am walking into a dream. Is the work dangerous? Why don't you answer . . . ?"

Job loomed up damp, shivery gray. Its giant members waiting.

Builders quietly donned their coarse robes, and waited.

Geremio's whistle rolled back into his pocket and the symphony of struggle began.

Trowel rang through brick and slashed mortar rivets were machine-gunned fast with angry grind Patsy number one check Patsy number two check the Lean three check Vincenzo four steel bellowed back at hammer donkey engines coughed purple Ashes-ass Pietro fifteen chisel point intoned stone thin steel whirred and wailed through wood liquid stone flowed with dull rasp through iron veins and hoist screamed through space Carmine the Fat twenty-four and Giacomo Sangini check. . . . The multitudinous voices of a civilization rose from the surroundings and melded with the efforts of the Job.

To the intent ear, Nation was voicing her growing pains, but, hands that create are attached to warm hearts and not to calculating minds. The Lean as he fought his burden on looked forward to only one goal, the end. The barrow he pushed, he did not love. The stones that brutalized his palms, he did not love. The great Good Job, he did not love. He felt a searing bitterness and a fathomless consternation at the queer consciousness that inflicted the ever mounting weight of structure that he HAD TO! HAD TO! raise above his shoulders! When, when and where would the last stone be? Never . . . did he bear his toil with the rhythm of song! Never . . . did his gasping heart knead the heavy mortar with lilting melody! A voice within him spoke in wordless language.

The language of worn oppression and the despair of realizing that his life had been left on brick piles. And always, there had been hunger and her bastard, the fear of hunger.

Murdin bore down upon Geremio from behind and shouted: "Goddamnit Geremio, if you're givin' the men two hours off today with pay, why the hell are they draggin' their tails? And why don't you turn that skinny old Nick loose, and put a young wop in his place?"

"Now, listen-a to me, Mister Murdin —"

"Don't give me that! And bear in mind that there are plenty of good barefoot men in the streets who'll jump for a day's pay!"

"Padrone — padrone, the underpinning gotta be make safe and —"

"Lissenyawopbastard! If you don't like it, you know what you can do!"

And with that he swung swaggering away.

The men had heard, and those who hadn't knew instinctively.

The new home, the coming baby, and his whole background, kept the fire from Geremio's mouth and bowed his head. "Annunziata speaks of scouring the ashcans for the children's bread in case I didn't want to work on a job where . . . But am I not a man, to feed my own with these hands? Ah, but day will end and no boss in the world can then rob me of the joy of my home!"

Murdin paused for a moment before descending the ladder.

Geremio caught his meaning and jumped to, nervously directing the rush of work. . . . No longer Geremio, but a machinelike entity.

The men were transformed into single, silent, beasts. Snoutnose steamed through ragged mustache whip lashing sand into mixer Ashes-ass dragged under four-by-twelve beam Lean clawed wall knots jumping in jaws masonry crumbled dust billowed thundered choked. . . .

At noon, Geremio drank his wine from an old-fashioned magnesia bottle and munched a great pepper sandwich . . . no meat on Good Friday. Said one, "Are some of us to be laid off? Easter is upon us and communion dresses are needed and . . ."

That, while Geremio was dreaming of the new house and the joys he could almost taste. Said he: "Worry not. You should know Geremio." It then all came out. He regaled them with his wonderful joy of the new house. He praised his wife and children one by one. They listened respectfully and returned him well wishes and blessings. He went on and on. . . . "Paul made a radio — all by himself mind you! One can hear Barney Google and many American songs! How proud he."

The ascent to labor was made, and as they trod the ladder, heads turned and eyes communed with the mute flames of the brazier whose warmth they were leaving, not with willing heart, and in that fleeting moment the breast wanted so, so much to speak, of hungers that never reached the tongue.

About an hour later, Geremio, called over to Pietro: "Pietro, see if Mister Murdin is in the shanty and tell him I must see him! I will convince him that the work must not go on like this . . . just for the sake of a little more profit!"

Pietro came up soon. "The padrone is not coming up. He was drinking from a large bottle of whiskey and cursed in American words that if you did not carry out his orders — "

Geremio turned away disconcerted, stared dumbly at the structure and mechanically listed in his mind's eye the various violations of construction safety. An uneasy sensation hollowed him. The Lean brought down an old piece of wall and the structure palsied. Geremio's heart broke loose and out thumped the floor's vibrations, a rapid wave of heat swept him and left a chill touch in its wake. He looked about to the men, a bit frightened. They seemed usual, lifesize, and moved about with the methodical deftness that made the moment then appear no different than the task of toil had ever been.

Snoutnose's voice boomed into him. "Master Geremio, the concrete is rea—dy!"

"Oh, yes, yes, Vincenz." And he walked gingerly toward the chute, but, not without leaving behind some part of his strength, sending out his soul to wrestle with the limbs of Job, who threatened in stiff silence. He talked and joked with Snoutnose. Nothing said anything, nor seemed wrong. Yet a vague uneasiness was to him as certain as the foggy murk that floated about Job's stone and steel.

"Shall I let the concrete down now, Master Geremio?"

"Well, let me see — no, hold it a minute. Hey, Sandino! Tighten the chute cables!"

Snoutnose straightened, looked about, and instinctively rubbed the sore small of his spine. "Ah," sighed he, "all the men feel as I — yes, I can tell. They are tired but happy that today is Good Friday and we quit at three o'clock . . ." And he swelled in human ecstasy at the anticipation of food, drink, and the hairy flesh-tingling warmth of wife, and then, extravagant rest. In truth, they all felt as Snoutnose, although perhaps with variations on the theme.

It was the Lean only who had lived, and felt otherwise. His soul, accompanied with time, had shredded itself in the physical war to keep the physical alive. Perhaps he no longer had a soul, and the corpse continued from momentum. May he not be the Slave, working on from the birth of Man — He of whom it was said, "It was not for Him to reason"? And probably He who, never asking, taking, nor wanting, created God and the creatables? Nevertheless, there existed in the Lean a sense of oppression suffered, so vast that the seas of time could never wash it away.

Geremio gazed about and was conscious of seeming to understand many things. He marveled at the strange feeling which permitted him to sense the familiarity of life. And yet — all appeared unreal, a dream pungent and nostalgic. Life, dream, reality, unreality, spiraling ever about each other. "Ha," he chuckled, "how and from where do these thoughts come?"

Snoutnose had his hand on the hopper latch and was awaiting the word from Geremio. "Did you say something, Master Geremio?"

"Why, yes, Vincenz, I was thinking — funny! A — yes, what is the time — yes, that is what I was thinking."

"My American can of tomatoes says ten minutes from two o'clock. It won't be long now, Master Geremio."

Geremio smiled. "No, about an hour . . . and then, home."

"Oh, but first we stop at Mulberry Street, to buy their biggest eels, and the other finger-licking stuffs."

Geremio was looking far off, and for a moment happiness came to his heart without words, a warm hand stealing over. Snoutnose's words sang to him pleasantly, and he nodded.

"And Master Geremio, we ought really to buy the seafruits with the shells — you know, for the much needed steam they put into the — "

He flushed despite himself and continued. "It is true, I know it — especially the juicy clams . . . uhmn, my mouth waters like a pump."

Geremio drew on his unlit pipe and smiled acquiescence. The men around him were moving to their tasks silently, feeling of their fatigue, but absorbed in contemplations the very same as Snoutnose's. The noise of labor seemed not to be noise, and as Geremio looked about, life settled over him a gray concert — gray forms, atmosphere, and gray notes. . . . Yes, his off-tone world felt so near, and familiar.

"Five minutes from two," swished through Snoutnose's mustache.

Geremio automatically took out his watch, rewound, and set it. Sandino had done with the cables. The tone and movement of the scene seemed to Geremio strange, differently strange, and yet, a dream familiar from a timeless date. His hand went up in motion to Vincenzo. The molten stone gurgled low, and then with heightening rasp. His eyes followed the stone-cementy pudding, and to his ears there was no other sound than its flow. From over the roofs somewhere, the tinny voice of Barney Google whined its way, hooked into his consciousness and kept itself a revolving record beneath his skull-plate.

"Ah, yes, Barney Google, my son's wonderful radio machine . . . wonderful Paul." His train of thought quickly took in his family, home and hopes. And with hope came fear. Something within asked, Is it not possible to breathe God's air without fear dominating with the pall of unemployment? And the terror of production for Boss, Boss and Job? To rebel is to love all of the very little. To be obedient is to choke. Oh, dear Lord, guide my path.

Just then, the floor lurched and swayed under his feet. The slipping of the underpinning below rumbled up through the undetermined floors.

Was he faint or dizzy? Was it part of the dreamy afternoon? He put his hands in front of him and stepped back, and looked up wildly. "No! No!"

The men poised stricken. Their throats wanted to cry out and scream but didn't dare. For a moment they were a petrified and straining pageant. Then the bottom of their world gave way. The building shuddered violently, her supports burst with the crackling slap of wooden gunfire. The floor vomited upward. Geremio clutched at the air and shrieked agonizingly. "Brother, what have we done. Ahhh-h, children of ours!" With the speed of light, balance went sickenly awry and frozen men went flying explosively. Job tore down upon them madly. Walls, floors, beams became whirling, solid, splintering waves crashing with detonations that ground man and material in bonds of death.

The strongly shaped body that slept with Annunziata nights and was perfect in all the limitless physical quantities, thudded as a worthless sack amongst the giant debris that crushed fragile flesh and bone with centrifugal intensity.

Darkness blotted out his terror and the resistless form twisted, catapulted insanely in its directionless flight, and shot down neatly and deliberately between the empty wooden forms of a foundation wall pilaster in upright position, his blue swollen face pressed against the form and his arms outstretched, caught securely through the meat by the thin round bars of reinforcing steel.

The huge concrete hopper that was sustained by an independent structure of thick timber, wavered a breath or so, its heavy concrete rolling uneasily until a great sixteen-inch wall caught it squarely with all the terrific verdict of its dead weight and impelled it downward through joists, beams and masonry until it stopped short, arrested by two girders, an arm's length above Geremio's head; the gray concrete gushing from the hopper mouth, and sealing up the mute figure.

Giacomo had been thrown clear of the building and dropped six floors to the street gutter, where he lay writhing.

The Lean had evinced no emotion. When the walls descended, he did not move. He lowered his head. One minute later he was hanging in mid-air, his chin on his chest, his eyes tearing loose from their sockets, a green foam bubbling from his mouth and his body spasming, suspended by the shreds left of his mashed arms pinned between a wall and a girder.

A two-by-four hooked little Joe Chiappa up under the back of his jumper and swung him around in a circle to meet a careening I-beam. In the flash that he lifted his frozen cherubic face, its shearing edge sliced through the top of his skull.

When Snoutnose cried beseechingly, "Saint Michael!" blackness enveloped him. He came to in a world of horror. A steady stream, warm, thick, and sickening as hot wine bathed his face and clogged his nose, mouth and eyes. The nauseous syrup that pumped over his face clotted his mustache red and drained into his mouth. He gulped for air, and swallowed the rich liquid scarlet. As he breathed, the pain shocked him to oppressive semi-consciousness. The air was wormingly alive with cries, screams, moans and dust, and his crushed chest seared him with a thousand fires. He couldn't see, nor breathe enough to cry. His right hand moved to his face and wiped at the gelatinizing substance, but it kept coming on, and a heartbreaking moan wavered about him, not far. He wiped his eyes in subconscious despair. Where was he? What kind of a dream was he having? Perhaps he wouldn't wake up in time for work, and then what? But how queer; his stomach beating him, his chest on fire, he sees nothing but dull red, only one hand moving about, and a moaning in his face!

The sound and clamor of the rescue squads called to him from far off.

Ah, yes, he's dreaming in bed, and far out in the streets, engines are going to a fire. Oh poor devils! Suppose his house were on fire? With the children scattered about in the rooms he could not remember! He must do his utmost to break out of this dream! He's swimming under water, not able to raise his head and get to the air. He must get back to consciousness to save his children!

He swam frantically with his one right hand, and then felt a face beneath its touch. A face! It's Angelina alongside of him! Thank God, he's awake! He tapped her face. It moved. It felt cold, bristly and wet. "It moves so. What is this?" His fingers slithered about grisly sharp bones and in a gluey, stringy, hollow mass, yielding as wet macaroni. Gray light brought sight, and hysteria punctured his heart. A girder lay across his chest, his right hand clutched a grotesque human mask, and suspended almost on top of him was the twitching, faceless body of Joe Chiappa. Vincenzo fainted with an inarticulate sigh. His fingers loosed and the bodyless-headless face dropped and fitted to the side of his face while the drippings above came slower and slower.

The rescue men cleaved grimly with pick and axe.

Geremio came to with a start . . . far from their efforts. His brain told him instantly what had happened and where he was. He shouted wildly. "Save me! Save me! I'm being buried alive!"

He paused exhausted. His genitals convulsed. The cold steel rod upon which they were impaled froze his spine. He shouted louder and louder. "Save me! I am hurt badly! I can be saved, I can — save me before it's too late!" But the cries went no farther than his own ears. The icy wet concrete reached his chin. His heart was appalled. "In a few seconds I shall be entombed. If I can only breathe, they will reach me. Surely they will!" His face was quickly covered, its flesh yielding to the solid, sharp-cut stones. "Air! Air!" screamed his lungs as he was completely sealed. Savagely, he bit into the wooden form pressed upon his mouth. An eighth of an inch of its surface splintered off. Oh, if he could only hold out long enough to bite even the smallest hole through to air! He must! There can be no other way! He is responsible for his family! He cannot leave them like this! He didn't want to die! This could not be the answer to life! He had bitten halfway through when his teeth snapped off to the gums in the uneven conflict. The pressure of the concrete was such, and its effectiveness so thorough, that the wooden splinters, stumps of teeth, and blood never left the choking mouth.

Why couldn't he go any farther?

Air! Quick! He dug his lower jaw into the little hollowed space and gnashed in choking agonized fury. "Why doesn't it go through? Mother of Christ, why doesn't it give? Can there be a notch, or two-by-four stud behind it? Sweet Jesu! No! No! Make it give. . . . Air! Air!"

He pushed the bone-bare jaw maniacally; it splintered, cracked, and a jagged fleshless edge cut through the form, opening a small hole to air. With a desperate burst the long-prisoned air blew an opening through the shredded mouth and whistled back greedily a gasp of fresh air. He tried to breathe, but it was impossible. The heavy concrete was settling immutably, and its rich cement-laten grout ran into his pierced face. His lungs would not expand, and were crushing in tighter and tighter under the settling concrete.

"Mother mine — mother of Jesu-Annunziata — children of mine — dear, dear, for mercy, Jesu-Guiseppe e 'Maria," his blue-foamed tongue called. It then distorted in a shuddering coil and mad blood vomited forth. Chills and fire played through him and his tortured tongue stuttered, "Mercy, blessed Father — salvation, most kind Father — Savior — Savior of His children help me — adored Savior — I kiss Your feet eternally — you are my God of infinite mercy — Hail Mary divine Virgin — Our Father who art in heaven hallowed be thy — name — our Father — my Father," and the agony excruciated with never-ending mount, "our Father — Jesu, Jesu, soon Jesu, hurry dear Jesu Jesu! Je-sssu . . . !'" His mangled voice trebled hideously, and hung in jerky whimperings.

The unfeeling concrete was drying fast, and shrinking into monolithic density. The pressure temporarily desensitized sensation; leaving him petrified, numb and substanceless. Only the brain remained miraculously alive.

"Can this be death? It is all too strangely clear. I see nothing nor feel nothing, my body and senses are no more, my mind speaks as it never did before. Am I or am I not Geremio? But I am Geremio! Can I be in the other world? I never was in any other world except the one I knew of; that of toil, hardship, prayer . . . of my wife who awaits with child for me, of my children and the first home I was to own. Where did I begin in this world? Where do I leave off? Why? I recall only a baffled life of cruelty from every direction. And hope was always as painful as fear, the fear of displeasing, displeasing the people and ideas whom I could never understand; laws, policemen, priests, bosses, and a rag with colors waving on a stick. I never did anything to these things. But what have I done with my life? Yes, my life! No one else's! Mine — mine — MINE — Geremio! It is clear. I was born hungry, and have always been hungry for free-

dom — life! I married and ran away to America so as not to kill
and be killed in Tripoli for things they call 'God and Country.' I've
never known the freedom I wanted in my heart. There was always
an arm upraised to hit at me. What have I done to them? I did
not want to make them toil for me. I did not raise my arm to them.
In my life I could never breathe, and now without air, my mind
breathes clearly for me. Wait! There has been a terrible mistake!
A cruel crime! The world is not right! Murderers! Thieves! You
have hurt me and my kind, and have taken my life from me! I have
long felt it — yes, yes, yes, they have cheated me with flags, signs, and
fear. . . . I say you can't take my life! Vincenz! Chiappa! Nick!
Men! Do you hear me? We must follow the desires within us for
the world has been taken from us; we, who made the world! Life!"

Feeling returned to the destroyed form.

"Ahhh-h, I am not dead yet. I knew it — you have not done with
me. Torture away! I cannot believe you, God and Country, no
longer!" His body was fast breaking under the concrete's closing
wrack. Blood vessels burst like mashed flower stems. He screamed.
"Show yourself now, Jesu! Now is the time! Save me! Why don't
you come! Are you there! I cannot stand it — ohhh, why do you let
it happen — it is bestial — where are you! Hurry, hurry, hurry! You
do not come! You make me suffer, and what have I done? Come,
come — come now — now save me, save me now! Now, now, now!
If you are God, save me!"

The stricken blood surged through a weltering maze of useless pipes
and exploded forth from his squelched eyes and formless nose, ears
and mouth, seeking life in the indifferent stone.

"Aie —aie, aie — devils and saints — beasts! Where are you —
quick, quick, it is death and I am cheated — cheat—ed! Do you hear,
you whoring bastards who own the world? Ohhh-ohhh aie aie —
hahahaha!" His bones cracked mutely and his sanity went sailing distorted in the limbo of the subconscious.

With the throbbing tones of an organ in the hollow background,
the fighting brain disintegrated and the memories of a baffled lifetime sought outlet.

He moaned the simple songs of barefoot childhood, scenes flashed desperately on and off in disassociated reflex, and words and parts of words came pitifully high and low from his inaudible lips, the hysterical mind sang cringingly and breathlessly, "Jesu my Lord my God my all Jesu my Lord my God my all Jesu my Lord my God my all Jesu my Lord my God my all," and on as the whirling tempo screamed now far, now near, and came in soul-sickening waves as the concrete slowly contracted and squeezed his skull out of shape.

WILLIAM FAULKNER

Hand upon the Waters

T HE TWO MEN followed the path where it ran between the river and the dense wall of cypress and cane and gum and brier. One of them carried a gunnysack which had been washed and looked as if it had been ironed too. The other was a youth, less than twenty, by his face. The river was low, at mid-July level.

"He ought to been catching fish in this water," the youth said.

"If he happened to feel like fishing," the one with the sack said. "Him and Joe run that line when Lonnie feels like it, not when the fish are biting."

Presently the ground rose to a cleared point almost like a headland. Upon it sat a conical hut with a pointed roof, built partly of mildewed canvas and odd-shaped boards and partly of oil tins hammered out flat. A rusted stovepipe projected crazily above it, there was a meager woodpile and an axe, and a bunch of cane poles leaned against it. Then they saw, on the earth before the open door, a dozen or so short lengths of cord just cut from a spool near-by, and a rusted can half full of heavy fishhooks, some of which had already been bent onto the cords. But there was nobody there.

"The boat's gone," the man with the sack said. "So he ain't gone to the store." Then he discovered that the youth had gone on, and he drew in his breath and was just about to shout when suddenly a man rushed out of the undergrowth and stopped, facing him and making an urgent whimpering sound — a man not large, but with tremendous arms and shoulders; an adult, yet with something childlike about him, about the way he moved, barefoot, in battered overalls and with the urgent eyes of the deaf and dumb.

"Hi, Joe," the man with the sack said, raising his voice as people will with those who they know cannot understand them. "Where's Lonnie?" He held up the sack. "Got some fish?"

But the other only stared at him, making that rapid whimpering. Then he turned and scuttled on up the path where the youth had disappeared, who, at that moment, shouted: "Just look at this line!"

The older one followed. The youth was leaning eagerly out over the water beside a tree from which a light cotton rope slanted tautly downward into the water. The deaf-and-dumb man stood just behind him, still whimpering and lifting his feet rapidly in turn, though before the older man reached him he turned and scuttled back past him, toward the hut. At this stage of the river the line should have been clear of the water, stretching from bank to bank, between the two trees, with only the hooks on the dependent cords submerged. But now it slanted into the water from either end, with a heavy downstream sag, and even the older man could feel movement on it.

"It's big as a man!" the youth cried.

"Yonder's his boat," the older man said. The youth saw it, too — across the stream and below them, floated into a willow clump inside a point. "Cross and get it, and we'll see how big this fish is."

The youth stepped out of his shoes and overalls and removed his shirt and waded out and began to swim, holding straight across to let the current carry him down to the skiff, and got the skiff and paddled back, standing erect in it and staring eagerly upstream toward the heavy sag of the line, near the center of which the water, from time to time, rolled heavily with submerged movement. He brought the skiff in below the older man, who, at that moment, discovered the deaf-and-dumb man just behind him again, still making the rapid and urgent sound and trying to enter the skiff.

"Get back!" the older man said, pushing the other back with his arm. "Get back, Joe!"

"Hurry up!" the youth said, staring eagerly toward the submerged line, where, as he watched, something rolled sluggishly to the surface, then sank again. "There's something on there, or there ain't a hog in Georgia. It's big as a man too!"

The older one stepped into the skiff. He still held the rope, and he drew the skiff, hand over hand, along the line itself.

Suddenly, from the bank of the river behind them, the deaf-and-dumb man began to make an actual sound. It was quite loud.

II

"Inquest?" Stevens said.

"Lonnie Grinnup." The coroner was an old country doctor. "Two fellows found him drowned on his own trotline this morning."

"No!" Stevens said. "Poor damned feeb. I'll come out." As county attorney he had no business there, even if it had not been an accident. He knew it. He was going to look at the dead man's face for a sentimental reason. What was now Yoknapatawpha County had been founded, not by one pioneer, but by three simultaneous ones. They came together on horseback, through the Cumberland Gap from the Carolinas, when Jefferson was still a Chickasaw Agency post, and bought land in the Indian patent and established families and flourished and vanished, so that now, a hundred years afterward, there was in all the county they helped to found but one representative of the three names.

This was Stevens, because the last of the Holston family had died before the end of the last century, and the Louis Grenier, whose dead face Stevens was driving eight miles in the heat of a July afternoon to look at, had never even known he was Louis Grenier. He could not even spell the Lonnie Grinnup he called himself — an orphan, too, like Stevens, a man a little under medium size and somewhere in his middle thirties, whom the whole county knew — the face which was almost delicate when you looked at it again, equable, constant, always cheerful, with an invariable fuzz of soft golden beard which had never known a razor, and light-colored peaceful eyes — "touched," they said, but whatever it was had touched him lightly, taking not very much away that need be missed — living, year in and year out, in the hovel he had built himself of an old tent and a few mismatched boards and flattened oil tins, with the deaf-and-dumb orphan he had taken into his hut ten years ago and clothed and fed and raised, and who had not even grown mentally as far as he himself had.

Actually his hut and trotline and fish trap were in almost the exact center of the thousand and more acres his ancestors had once owned. But he never knew it.

Stevens believed he would not have cared, would have declined to accept the idea that any one man could or should own that much of the earth which belongs to all, to every man for his use and pleasure — in his own case, that thirty or forty square feet where his hut sat and the span of river across which his trotline stretched, where anyone was welcome at any time, whether he was there or not, to use his gear and eat his food as long as there was food.

And at times he would wedge his door shut against prowling animals and with his deaf-and-dumb companion he would appear without warning or invitation at houses or cabins ten and fifteen miles away, where he would remain for weeks, pleasant, equable, demanding nothing and without servility, sleeping wherever it was convenient for his hosts to have him sleep — in the hay of lofts, or in beds in family or company rooms, while the deaf-and-dumb youth lay on the porch or the ground just outside, where he could hear him who was brother and father both, breathing. It was one sound out of all the voiceless earth. He was infallibly aware of it.

It was early afternoon. The distances were blue with heat. Then across the long flat where the highway began to parallel the river bottom, Stevens saw the store. By ordinary it would have been deserted, but now he could already see clotted about it the topless and battered cars, the saddled horses and mules and the wagons, the riders and drivers of which he knew by name. Better still, they knew him, voting for him year after year and calling him by his given name even though they did not quite understand him, just as they did not understand the Harvard Phi Beta Kappa key on his watch chain. He drew in beside the coroner's car.

Apparently it was not to be in the store, but in the grist mill beside it, before the open door of which the clean Saturday overalls and shirts and the bared heads and the sunburned necks striped with the white razor lines of Saturday neck shaves were densest and quietest. They made way for him to enter. There was a table and three chairs where the coroner and two witnesses sat.

Stevens noticed a man of about forty holding a clean gunnysack, folded and refolded until it resembled a book, and a youth whose face wore an expression of weary yet indomitable amazement. The body lay under a quilt on the low platform to which the silent mill was bolted. He crossed to it and raised the corner of the quilt and looked at the face and lowered the quilt and turned, already on his way back to town, and then he did not go back to town. He moved over among the men who stood along the wall, their hats in their hands, and listened to the two witnesses — it was the youth telling it in his amazed, spent, incredulous voice — finish describing the finding of the body. He watched the coroner sign the certificate and return the pen to his pocket, and he knew he was not going back to town.

"I reckon that's all," the coroner said. He glanced toward the door. "All right, Ike," he said. "You can take him now."

Stevens moved aside with the others and watched the four men cross toward the quilt. "You going to take him, Ike?" he said.

The eldest of the four glanced back at him for a moment. "Yes. He had his burying money with Mitchell at the store."

"You, and Pose, and Matthew, and Jim Blake," Stevens said.

This time the other glanced back at him almost with surprise, almost impatiently.

"We can make up the difference," he said.

"I'll help," Stevens said.

"I thank you," the other said. "We got enough."

Then the coroner was among them, speaking testily: "All right, boys. Give them room."

With the others, Stevens moved out into the air, the afternoon again. There was a wagon backed up to the door now which had not been there before. Its tail gate was open, the bed was filled with straw, and with the others Stevens stood bareheaded and watched the four men emerge from the shed, carrying the quilt-wrapped bundle, and approach the wagon. Three or four others moved forward to help, and Stevens moved, too, and touched the youth's shoulder, seeing again that expression of spent and incredulous wild amazement.

"You went and got the boat before you knew anything was wrong," he said.

"That's right," the youth said. He spoke quietly enough at first. "I swum over and got the boat and rowed back. I knowed something was on the line. I could see it swagged — "

"You mean you swam the boat back," Stevens said.

" — down into the — Sir?"

"You swam the boat back. You swam over and got it and swam it back."

"No, sir! I rowed the boat back. I rowed it straight back across! I never suspected nothing! I could see them fish — "

"What with?" Stevens said. The youth glared at him. "What did you row it back with?"

"With the oar! I picked up the oar and rowed it right back, and all the time I could see them flopping around in the water. They didn't want to let go! They held on to him even after we hauled him up, still eating him! Fish were! I knowed turtles would, but these were fish! Eating him! Of course it was fish we thought was there! It was! I won't never eat another one! Never!"

It had not seemed long, yet the afternoon had gone somewhere, taking some of the heat with it. Again in his car, his hand on the switch, Stevens sat looking at the wagon, now about to depart. And it's not right, he thought. It don't add. Something more that I missed, didn't see. Or something that hasn't happened yet.

The wagon was now moving, crossing the dusty banquette toward the highroad, with two men on the seat and the other two on saddled mules beside it. Steven's hand turned the switch; the car was already in gear. It passed the wagon, already going fast.

A mile down the road he turned into a dirt lane, back toward the hills. It began to rise, the sun intermittent now, for in places among the ridges sunset had already come. Presently the road forked. In the V of the fork stood a church, white-painted and steepleless, beside an unfenced straggle of cheap marble headstones and other graves outlined only by rows of inverted glass jars and crockery and broken brick.

He did not hesitate. He drove up beside the church and turned and stopped the car facing the fork and the road over which he had just come where it curved away and vanished. Because of the curve, he could hear the wagon for some time before he saw it, then he heard the truck. It was coming down out of the hills behind him, fast, sweeping into sight, already slowing — a cab, a shallow bed with a tarpaulin spread over it.

It drew out of the road at the fork and stopped; then he could hear the wagon again, and then he saw it and the two riders come around the curve in the dusk, and there was a man standing in the road beside the truck now, and Stevens recognized him: Tyler Ballenbaugh — a farmer, married and with a family and a reputation for self-sufficiency and violence, who had been born in the county and went out West and returned, bringing with him, like an effluvium, rumors of sums he had won gambling, who had married and bought land and no longer gambled at cards, but on certain years would mortgage his own crop and buy or sell cotton futures with the money — standing in the road beside the wagon, tall in the dusk, talking to the men in the wagon without raising his voice or making any gesture. Then there was another man beside him, in a white shirt, whom Stevens did not recognize or look at again.

His hand dropped to the switch; again the car was in motion with the sound of the engine. He turned the headlights on and dropped rapidly down out of the churchyard and into the road and up behind the wagon as the man in the white shirt leaped onto the running

board, shouting at him, and Stevens recognized him too: a younger
brother of Ballenbaugh's, who had gone to Memphis years ago,
where it was understood he had been a hired armed guard during a
textile strike, but who, for the last two or three years, had been at
his brother's, hiding, it was said, not from the police, but from some
of his Memphis friends or later business associates. From time to
time his name made one in reported brawls and fights at country
dances and picnics. He was subdued and thrown into jail once by
two officers in Jefferson, where, on Saturdays, drunk, he would brag
about his past exploits or curse his present luck and the older brother
who made him work about the farm.

"Who in hell you spying on?" he shouted.

"Boyd," the other Ballenbaugh said. He did not even raise his
voice. "Get back in the truck." He had not moved — a big somber-
faced man who stared at Stevens out of pale, cold, absolutely expressionless eyes. "Howdy, Gavin," he said.

"Howdy, Tyler," Stevens said. "You going to take Lonnie?"

"Does anybody here object?"

"I don't," Stevens said, getting out of the car. "I'll help you swap
him."

Then he got back into the car. The wagon moved on. The truck
backed and turned, already gaining speed; the two faces fled past —
the one which Stevens saw now was not truculent, but frightened; the
other, in which there was nothing at all save the still, cold, pale eyes.
The cracked tail lamp vanished over the hill. That was an Okatoba
County license number, he thought.

Lonnie Grinnup was buried the next afternoon, from Tyler Ballenbaugh's house.

Stevens was not there. "Joe wasn't there, either, I suppose," he
said. "Lonnie's dummy."

"No. He wasn't there, either. The folks that went in to Lonnie's
camp on Sunday morning to look at that trotline said that he was
still there, hunting for Lonnie. But he wasn't at the burying. When
he finds Lonnie this time, he can lie down by him, but he won't hear
him breathing."

"No," Stevens said.

III

He was in Mottstown, the seat of Okatoba County, on that afternoon. And although it was Sunday, and although he would not know until he found it just what he was looking for, he found it before dark — the agent for the company which, eleven years ago, had issued to Lonnie Grinnup a five-thousand-dollar policy, with double indemnity for accidental death, on his life, with Tyler Ballenbaugh as beneficiary.

It was quite correct. The examining doctor had never seen Lonnie Grinnup before, but he had known Tyler Ballenbaugh for years, and Lonnie had made his mark on the application and Ballenbaugh had paid the first premium and kept them up ever since.

There had been no particular secrecy about it other than transacting the business in another town, and Stevens realized that even that was not unduly strange.

Okatoba County was just across the river, three miles from where Ballenbaugh lived, and Stevens knew of more men than Ballenbaugh who owned land in one county and bought their cars and trucks and banked their money in another, obeying the country-bred man's inherent, possibly atavistic, faint distrust, perhaps, not of men in white collars, but of paving and electricity.

"Then I'm not to notify the company yet?" the agent asked.

"No. I want you to accept the claim when he comes in to file it, explain to him it will take a week or so to settle it, wait three days and send him word to come in to your office to see you at nine o'clock or ten o'clock the next morning; don't tell him why, what for. Then telephone me at Jefferson when you know he has got the message."

Early the next morning, about daybreak, the heat wave broke. He lay in bed watching and listening to the crash and glare of lightning and the rain's loud fury, thinking of the drumming of it and the fierce channeling of clay-colored water across Lonnie Grinnup's raw and kinless grave in the barren hill beside the steepleless church, and of the sound it would make, above the turmoil of the rising river, on the tin-and-canvas hut where the deaf-and-dumb youth probably still waited for him to come home, knowing that something had happened, but not how, not why. Not how, Stevens thought. They fooled him someway. They didn't even bother to tie him up. They just fooled him.

On Wednesday night he received a telephone message from the Mottstown agent that Tyler Ballenbaugh had filed his claim.

"All right," Stevens said. "Send him the message Monday, to come in Tuesday. And let me know when you know he has got it." He put the phone down. I am playing stud poker with a man who has proved himself a gambler, which I have not, he thought. But at least I have forced him to draw a card. And he knows who is in the pot with him.

So when the second message came, on the following Monday afternoon, he knew only what he himself was going to do. He had thought once of asking the sheriff for a deputy, or of taking some friend with him. But even a friend would not believe that what I have is a hole card, he told himself, even though I do: that one man, even an amateur at murder, might be satisfied that he had cleaned up after himself. But when there are two of them, neither one is going to be satisfied that the other has left no ravelings.

So he went alone. He owned a pistol. He looked at it and put it back into its drawer. At least nobody is going to shoot me with that, he told himself. He left town just after dusk.

This time he passed the store, dark at the roadside. When he reached the lane into which he had turned nine days ago, this time he turned to the right and drove on for a quarter of a mile and turned into a littered yard, his headlights full upon a dark cabin. He did not turn them off. He walked full in the yellow beam, toward the cabin, shouting: "Nate! Nate!"

After a moment a Negro voice answered, though no light showed.

"I'm going in to Mr. Lonnie Grinnup's camp. If I'm not back by daylight, you better go up to the store and tell them."

There was no answer. Then a woman's voice said: "You come on away from that door!" The man's voice murmured something.

"I can't help it!" the woman cried. "You come away and let them white folks alone!"

So there are others besides me, Stevens thought, thinking how quite often almost always, there is in Negroes an instinct, not for evil, but to recognize evil at once when it exists. He went back to the car and snapped off the lights and took his flashlight from the seat.

He found the truck. In the close-held beam of the light he read again the license number which he had watched nine days ago flee over the hill. He snapped off the light and put it into his pocket.

Twenty minutes later he realized he need not have worried about the light. He was in the path, between the black wall of jungle and the river, he saw the faint glow inside the canvas wall of the hut and he could already hear the two voices — the one cold, level, and steady, the other harsh and high. He stumbled over the woodpile and then over something else and found the door and flung it back and entered the devastation of the dead man's house — the shuck mattresses dragged out of the woden bunks, the overturned stove and scattered cooking vessels — where Tyler Ballenbaugh stood facing him with a pistol and the younger one stood half-crouched above an overturned box.

"Stand back, Gavin," Ballenbaugh said.

"Stand back yourself, Tyler," Stevens said. "You're too late."

The younger one stood up. Stevens saw recognition come into his face. "Well, by —" he said.

"Is it all up, Gavin?" Ballenbaugh said. "Don't lie to me."

"Enough," Stevens said. "Put your pistol down, Tyler."

"Hell," the younger one said. He began to move; Stevens saw his eyes go swiftly from him to the door behind him. "He's lying. There ain't anybody with him. He's just spying around like he was the other day, putting his nose into business he's going to wish he had kept it out of. Because this time it's going to get bit off."

He was moving toward Stevens, stooping a little, his arms held slightly away from his sides.

"Boyd!" Tyler said. The other continued to approach Stevens, not smiling, but with a queer light, a glitter, in his face. "Boyd!" Tyler said. Then he moved, too, with astonishing speed, and overtook the younger and with one sweep of his arm hurled him back into the bunk. They faced each other — the one cold, still, expressionless, the pistol held before him aimed at nothing, the other half-crouched, snarling.

"What the hell you going to do? Let him take us back to town like two damn sheep?"

"That's for me to decide," Tyler said. He looked at Stevens. "I never intended this, Gavin. I insured his life, kept the premiums paid — yes. But it was good business: if he had outlived me, I wouldn't have had any use for the money, and if I had outlived him, I would have collected on my judgment. There was no secret about it. It was done in open daylight. Anybody could have found out about it. Maybe he told about it. I never told him not to. And who's to say against it anyway? I always fed him when he came to my house, he always stayed as long as he wanted to, come when he wanted to. But I never intended this."

Suddenly the younger one began to laugh, half-crouched against the bunk where the other had flung him. "So that's the tune," he said. "That's the way it's going." Then it was not laughter any more, though the transition was so slight or perhaps so swift as to be imperceptible. He was standing now, leaning forward a little, facing his brother. "I never insured him for five thousand dollars! I wasn't going to get — "

"Hush," Tyler said.

"— five thousand dollars when they found him dead on that — "

Tyler walked steadily to the other and slapped him in two motions, palm and back, of the same hand, the pistol still held before him in the other.

"I said hush, Boyd," he sad. He looked at Stevens again. "I never intended this. I don't want that money now, even if they were going to pay it, because this is not the way I aimed for it to be. Not the way I bet. What are you going to do?"

"Do you need to ask that? I want an indictment for murder."

"And then prove it!" the younger one snarled. "Try and prove it! I never insured his life for — "

"Hush," Tyler said. He spoke almost gently, looking at Stevens with the pale eyes in which there was absolutely nothing. "You can't do that. It's a good name. Has been. Maybe nobody's done much for it yet, but nobody's hurt it bad yet, up to now. I have owed no man, I have taken nothing that was not mine. You musn't do that, Gavin."

"I musn't do anything else, Tyler."

The other looked at him. Stevens heard him draw a long breath and expel it. But his face did not change at all. "You want your eye for an eye and tooth for a tooth."

"Justice wants it. Maybe Lonnie Grinnup wants it. Wouldn't you?"

For a moment longer the other looked at him. Then Ballenbaugh turned and made a quiet gesture at his brother and another toward Stevens, quiet and peremptory.

Then they were out of the hut, standing in the light from the door; a breeze came up from somewhere and rustled in the leaves overhead and died away, ceased.

At first Stevens did not know what Ballenbaugh was about. He watched in mounting surprise as Ballenbaugh turned to face his brother, his hand extended, speaking in a voice which was actually harsh now: "This is the end of the row. I was afraid from that night when you came home and told me. I should have raised you better, but I didn't. Here. Stand up and finish it."

"Look out, Tyler!" Stevens said. "Don't do that!"

"Keep out of this, Gavin. If it's meat for meat you want, you will get it." He still faced his brother, he did not even glance at Stevens. "Here," he said. "Take it and stand up."

Then it was too late. Stevens saw the younger one spring back. He saw Tyler take a step forward and he seemed to hear in the other's voice the surprise, the disbelief, then the realization of the mistake. "Drop the pistol, Boyd," he said. "Drop it."

"So you want it back, do you?" the younger said. "I come to you that night and told you you were worth five thousand dollars as soon as somebody happened to look on that trotline, and asked you to give me ten dollars, and you turned me down. Ten dollars, and you wouldn't. Sure you can have it. Take it." It flashed, low against his side; the orange fire lanced downward again as the other fell.

Now it's my turn, Stevens thought. They faced each other: he heard again that brief wind come from somewhere and shake the leaves overhead and fall still.

"Run while you can, Boyd," he said. "You've done enough. Run, now."

"Sure I'll run. You do all your worrying about me now, because in a minute you won't have any worries. I'll run all right, after I've said a word to smart guys that come sticking their noses where they'll wish to hell they hadn't — "

Now he's going to shoot, Stevens thought, and he sprang. For an instant he had the illusion of watching himself springing, reflected somehow by the faint light from the river, that luminousness which water gives back to the dark, in the air above Boyd Ballenbaugh's head. Then he knew it was not himself he saw, it had not been wind he heard, as the creature, the shape which had no tongue and needed none, which had been waiting nine days now for Lonnie Grinnup to come home, dropped toward the murderer's back with its hands already extended and its body curved and rigid with silent and deadly purpose.

He was in the tree, Stevens thought. The pistol glared. He saw the flash, but he heard no sound.

IV

He was sitting on the veranda with his neat surgeon's bandage after supper when the sheriff of the county came up the walk — a big man, too, pleasant, affable, with eyes even paler and colder and more expressionless than Tyler Ballenbaugh's.

"It won't take but a minute," he said, "or I wouldn't have bothered you."

"How bothered me?" Stevens said.

The sheriff lowered one thigh to the veranda rail. "Head feel all right?"

"Feels all right," Stevens said.

"That's good. I reckon you heard where we found Boyd."

Stevens looked back at him just as blankly. "I may have," he said pleasantly. "Haven't remembered much today but a headache."

"You told us where to look. You were conscious when I got there. You were trying to give Tyler water. You told us to look on that trotline."

"Did I? Well, well, what won't a man say, drunk or out of his head? Sometimes he's right too."

"You were. We looked on the line, and there was Boyd hung on one of the hooks, dead, just like Lonnie Grinnup was. And Tyler Ballenbaugh with a broken leg and another bullet in his shoulder, and you with a crease in your skull you could hide a cigar in. How did he get on that trotline, Gavin?"

"I don't know," Stevens said.

"All right. I'm not sheriff now. How did Boyd get on that trotline?"

"I don't know."

The sheriff looked at him; they looked at each other. "Is that what you answer any friend that asks?"

"Yes. Because I was shot, you see. I don't know."

The sheriff took a cigar from his pocket and looked at it for a time. "Joe — that deaf-and-dumb boy Lonnie raised — seems to have gone away at last. He was still around there last Sunday, but nobody has seen him since. He could have stayed. Nobody would have bothered him."

"Maybe he missed Lonnie too much to stay," Stevens said.

"Maybe he missed Lonnie." The sheriff rose. He bit the end from the cigar and lit it. "Did that bullet cause you to forget this too? Just what made you suspect something was wrong? What was it the rest of us seem to have missed?"

"It was that paddle," Stevens said.

"Paddle?"

"Didn't you ever run a trotline, a trotline right at your camp? You don't paddle, you pull the boat hand over hand along the line itself from one hook to the next. Lonnie never did use his paddle; he even kept the skiff tied to the same tree his trotline was fastened to, and the paddle stayed in his house. If you had ever been there, you would have seen it. But the paddle was in the skiff when that boy found it."

My Old Man

I GUESS looking at it, now, my old man was cut out for a fat guy, one of those regular little roly-poly fat guys you see around, but he sure never got that way, except a little toward the last, and then it wasn't his fault, he was riding over the jumps only and he could afford to carry plenty of weight then. I remember the way he'd pull on a rubber shirt over a couple of jerseys and a big sweat shirt over that, and get me to run with him in the forenoon in the hot sun. He'd have, maybe, taken a trial trip with one of Razzo's skins early in the morning after just getting in from Torino at four o'clock in the morning and beating it out to the stables in a cab and then with the dew all over everything and the sun just starting to get going, I'd help him pull off his boots and he'd get into a pair of sneakers and all these sweaters and we'd start out.

"Come on, kid," he'd say, stepping up and down on his toes in front of the jock's dressing room, "let's get moving."

Then we'd start off jogging around the infield once, maybe, with him ahead, running nice, and then turn out the gate and along one

of those roads with all the trees along both sides of them that run out
from San Siro. I'd go ahead of him when we hit the road and I could
run pretty stout and I'd look around and he'd be jogging easy just
behind me and after a little while I'd look around again and he'd
begun to sweat. Sweating heavy and he'd just be dogging it along
with his eyes on my back, but when he'd catch me looking at him
he'd grin and say, "Sweating plenty?" When my old man grinned,
nobody could help but grin too. We'd keep right on running out
toward the mountains and then my old man would yell, "Hey, Joe!"
and I'd look back and he'd be sitting under a tree with a towel he'd
had around his waist wrapped around his neck.

I'd come back and sit down beside him and he'd pull a rope out of
his pocket and start skiping rope out in the sun with the sweat pouring off his face and him skipping rope out in the white dust with the
rope going cloppetty, cloppetty, clop, clop, clop, and the sun hotter,
and him working harder up and down a patch of the road. Say, it
was a treat to see my old man skip rope, too. He could whirr it fast
or lop it slow and fancy. Say, you ought to have seen wops look at
us sometimes, when they'd come by, going into town walking along
with big white steers hauling the cart. They sure looked as though
they thought the old man was nuts. He'd start the rope whirring till
they'd stop dead still and watch him, then give the steers a cluck
and a poke with the goad and get going again.

When I'd sit watching him working out in the hot sun I sure felt
fond of him. He sure was fun and he done his work so hard and he'd
finish up with a regular whirring that'd drive the sweat out of his
face like water and then sling the rope at the tree and come over
and sit down with me and lean back against the tree with the towel
and a sweater wrapped around his neck.

"Sure is hell keeping it down, Joe," he'd say and lean back and
shut his eyes and breathe long and deep, "it ain't like when you're a
kid." Then he'd get up before he started to cool and we'd jog along
back to the stables. That's the way it was keeping down to weight.
He was worried all the time. Most jocks can just about ride off all
they want to. A jock loses about a kilo every time he rides, but my
old man was sort of dried out and he couldn't keep down his kilos
without all that running.

I remember once at San Siro, Regoli, a little wop, that was riding for Buzoni, came out across the paddock going to the bar for something cool; and flicking his boots with his whip, after he'd just weighed in and my old man had just weighed in too, and came out with the saddle under his arm looking red-faced and tired and too big for his silks and he stood there looking at young Regoli standing up to the outdoors bar, cool and kid-looking, and I says, "What's the matter, Dad?" 'cause I thought maybe Regoli had bumped him or something and he just looked at Regoli and said, "Oh, to hell with it," and went on to the dressing room.

Well, it would have been all right, maybe, if we'd stayed in Milan and ridden at Milan and Torino, 'cause if there ever were any easy courses, it's those two. "Pianola, Joe," my old man said when he dismounted in the winning stall after what the wops thought was a hell of a steeplechase. I asked him once. "This course rides itself. It's the pace yo're going at, that makes riding the jumps dangerous, Joe. We ain't going any pace here, and they ain't any really bad jumps either. But it's the pace always — not the jumps that makes the trouble."

San Siro was the swellest course I'd ever seen but the old man said it was a dog's life. Going back and forth between Mirafiore and San Siro and riding just about every day in the week with a train ride every other night.

I was nuts about the horses, too. There's something about it, when they come out and go up the track to the post. Sort of dancy and tight looking with the jock keeping a tight hold on them and maybe easing off a little and letting them run a little going up. Then once they were at the barrier it got me worse than anything. Especially at San Siro with that big green infield and the mountains way off and the fat wop starter with his big whip and the jocks fiddling them around and then the barrier snapping up and that bell going off and them all getting off in a bunch and then commencing to string out. You know the way a bunch of skins get off. If you're up in the stand with a pair of glasses all you see is them plunging off and then that bell goes off and it seems like it rings for a thousand years and then they come sweeping round the turn. There wasn't ever anything like it for me.

But my old man said one day, in the dressing room, when he was getting into his street clothes, "None of these things are horses, Joe. They'd kill that bunch of skates for their hides and hoofs up at Paris." That was the day he'd won the Premio Commercio with Lantorna shooting her out of the field the last hundred meters like pulling a cork out of a bottle.

It was right after the Premio Commercio that we pulled out and left Italy. My old man and Holbrook and a fat wop in a straw hat that kept wiping his face with a handkerchief were having an argument at a table in the Galleria. They were all talking French and the two of them were after my old man about something. Finally he didn't say anything any more but just sat there and looked at Holbrook, and the two of them kept after him, first one talking and then the other, and the fat wop always butting in on Holbrook.

"You go out and buy me a *Sportsman,* will you, Joe?" my old man said, and handed me a couple of soldi without looking away from Holbrook.

So I went out of the Galleria and walked over to in front of the Scala and bought a paper, and came back and stood a little way away because I didn't want to butt in and my old man was sitting back in his chair looking down at his coffee and fooling with a spoon and Holbrook and the big wop were standing and the big wop was wiping his face and shaking his head. And I came up and my old man acted just as though the two of them weren't standing there and said, "Want an ice, Joe?" Holbrook looked down at my old man and said slow and careful, "You son of a b——," and he and the fat wop went out through the tables.

My old man sat there and sort of smiled at me, but his face was white and he looked sick as hell and I was scared and felt sick inside because I knew something had happened and I didn't see how anybody could call my old man a son of a b——, and get away with it. My old man opened up the *Sportsman* and studied the handicaps for a while and then he said, "You got to take a lot of things in this world, Joe." And three days later we left Milan for good on the Turin train for Paris, after an auction sale out in front of Turner's stables of everything we couldn't get into a trunk and a suitcase.

We got into Paris early in the morning in a long, dirty station the old man told me was the Gare de Lyon. Paris was an awful big town after Milan. Seems like in Milan everybody is going somewhere and all the trams run somewhere and there ain't any sort of a mixup, but Paris is all balled up and they never do straighten it out. I got to like it, though, part of it, anyway, and say it's got the best race courses in the world. Seems as though that were the thing that keeps it all going and about the only thing you can figure on is that every day the buses will be going out to whatever track they're running at, going right out through everything to the track. I never really got to know Paris well, because I just came in about once or twice a week with the old man from Maisons and he always sat at the Café de la Paix on the Opéra side with the rest of the gang from Maisons and I guess that's one of the busiest parts of the town. But, say, it is funny that a big town like Paris wouldn't have a Galleria, isn't it?

Well, we went out to live at Maisons-Lafitte, where just about everybody lives except the gang at Chantilly, with a Mrs. Meyers that runs a boardinghouse. Maisons is about the swellest place to live I've ever seen in all my life. The town ain't so much, but there's a lake and a swell forest that we used to go off bumming in all day, a couple of us kids, and my old man made me a slingshot and we got a lot of things with it but the best one was a magpie. Young Dick Atkinson shot a rabbit with it one day and we put it under a tree and were all sitting around and Dick had some cigarettes and all of a sudden the rabbit jumped up and beat it into the brush and we chased it but we couldn't find it. Gee, we had fun at Maisons. Mrs. Meyers used to give me lunch in the morning and I'd be gone all day. I learned to talk French quick. It's an easy language.

As soon as we got to Maisons, my old man wrote to Milan for his license and he was pretty worried till it came. He used to sit around the Café de Paris in Maisons with the gang, there were lots of guys he'd known when he rode up at Paris, before the war, lived at Maisons, and there's a lot of time to sit around because the work around a racing stable, for the jocks, that is, is all cleaned up by nine o'clock in the morning. They take the first batch of skins out to gallop them at five-thirty in the morning and they work the second lot at eight o'clock. That means getting up early all right and going to bed early, too. If a jock's riding for somebody too, he can't go boozing around because the trainer always has an eye on him if he's a kid and if he ain't a kid he's always got an eye on himself. So mostly if a jock ain't working he sits around the Café de Paris with the gang and they can all sit around about two or three hours in front of some drink like vermouth and seltz and they talk and tell stories and shoot pool and it's sort of like a club or the Galleria in Milan. Only it ain't really like the Galleria because there everybody is going by all the time and there's everybody around at the tables.

Well, my old man got his license all right. They sent it through to him without a word and he rode a couple of times. Amiens, up country and that sort of thing, but he didn't seem to get any engagement. Everybody liked him and whenever I'd come in to the Café in the forenoon I'd find somebody drinking with him because my old man wasn't tight like most of these jockeys that have got the first dollar they made riding at the World's Fair in St. Louis in nineteen ought four. That's what my old man would say when he'd kid George Burns. But it seemed like everybody steered clear of giving my old man any mounts.

We went out to wherever they were running every day with the car from Maisons and that was the most fun of all. I was glad when the horses came back from Deauville and the summer. Even though it meant no more bumming in the woods, 'cause then we'd ride to Enghien or Tremblay or St. Cloud and watch them from the trainers' and jockeys' stand. I sure learned about racing from going out with that gang and the fun of it was going every day.

I remember once out at St. Cloud. It was a big two hundred thousand franc race with seven entries and Kzar a big favorite. I went around to the paddock to see the horses with my old man and you never saw such horses. This Kzar is a great big yellow horse that looks like just nothing but run. I never saw such a horse. He was being led around the paddocks with his head down and when he went by me I felt all hollow inside he was so beautiful. There never was such a wonderful, lean, running built horse. And he went around the paddock putting his feet just so and quiet and careful and moving easy like he knew just what he had to do and not jerking and standing up on his legs and getting wild eyed like you see these selling platers with a shot of dope in them. The crowd was so thick I couldn't see him again except just his legs going by and some yellow and my old man started out through the crowd and I followed him over to the jocks' dressing room back in the trees and there was a big crowd around there, too, but the man at the door in a derby nodded to my old man and we got in and everybody was sitting around and getting dressed and pulling shirts over their heads and pulling boots on and it all smelled hot and sweaty and linimenty and outside was the crowd looking in.

The old man went over and sat down beside George Gardner that was getting into his pants and said, "What's the dope, George?" just in an ordinary tone of voice 'cause there ain't any use him feeling around because George either can tell him or he can't tell him.

"He won't win," George says very low, leaning over and buttoning the bottoms of his pants.

"Who will?" my old man says, leaning over close so nobody can hear.

"Kircubbin," George says, "and if he does, save me a couple of tickets."

My old man says something in a regular voice to George and George says, "Don't ever bet on anything, I tell you," kidding like, and we beat it out and through all the crowd that was looking in over to the 100 franc mutuel machine. But I knew something big was up because George is Kzar's jockey. On the way he gets one of the yellow odds-sheets with the starting prices on and Kzar is only paying 5 for 10, Cefisidote is next at 3 to 1 and fifth down the list this Kircubbin at 8 to 1. My old man bets five thousand on Kircubbin to win and puts on a thousand to place and we went around back of the grandstand to go up the stairs and get a place to watch the race.

We were jammed in tight and first a man in a long coat with a gray tall hat and a whip folded up in his hand came out and then one after another the horses, with the jocks up and a stable boy holding the bridle on each side and walking along, followed the old guy. That big yellow horse Kzar came first. He didn't look so big when you first looked at him until you saw the length of his legs and the whole way he's built and the way he moves. Gosh, I never saw such a horse. George Gardner was riding him and they moved along slow, back of the old guy in the gray tall hat that walked along like he was the ring master in a circus. Back of Kzar, moving along smooth and yellow in the sun, was a good looking black with a nice head with Tommy Archibald riding him; and after the black was a string of five more horses all moving along slow in a procession past the grandstand and the pesage. My old man said the black was Kircubbin and I took a good look at him and he was a nice looking horse, all right, but nothing like Kzar.

Everybody cheered Kzar when he went by and he sure was one swell-looking horse. The procession of them went around on the other side past the pelouse and then back to the near end of the course and the circus master had the stable boys turn them loose one after another so they could gallop by the stands on their way up to the post and let everybody have a good look at them. They weren't at the post hardly any time at all when the gong started and you could see them way off across the infield all in a bunch starting on the first swing like a lot of little toy horses. I was watching them through the glasses and Kzar was running well back, with one of the bays making the pace. They swept down and around and came pounding past and Kzar was way back when they passed us and this Kircubbin horse in front and going smooth. Gee, it's awful when they go by you and then you have to watch them go farther away and get smaller and smaller and then all bunched up on the turns and then come around towards into the stretch and you feel like swearing and goddamming worse and worse. Finally they made the last turn and came into the straightaway with this Kircubbin horse way out in front. Everybody was looking funny and saying "Kzar" in a sort of a sick way and them pounding nearer down the stretch, and then something came out of the pack right into my glasses like a horse-headed yellow streak and everybody began to yell "Kzar" as though they were crazy. Kzar came on faster than I'd ever seen anything in my life and pulled up on Kircubbin that was going fast as any black horse could go with the jock flogging hell out of him with the gad and they were right dead neck and neck for a second but Kzar seemed going about twice as fast with those great jumps and that head out — but it was while they were neck and neck that they passed the winning post and when the numbers went up in the slots the first one was 2 and that meant Kircubbin had won.

I felt all trembly and funny inside, and then we were all jammed in with the people going downstairs to stand in front of the board where they'd post what Kircubbin paid. Honest, watching the race I'd forgot how much my old man had bet on Kircubbin. I'd wanted Kzar to win so damned bad. But now it was all over it was swell to know we had the winner.

"Wasn't it a swell race, Dad?" I said to him.

He looked at me sort of funny with his derby on the back of his head. "George Gardner's a swell jockey, all right," he said. "It sure took a great jock to keep that Kzar horse from winning."

Of course I knew it was funny all the time. But my old man saying that right out like that sure took the kick all out of it for me and I didn't get the real kick back again ever, even when they posted the numbers up on the board and the bell rang to pay off and we saw that Kircubbin paid 67.50 for 10. All round people were saying, "Poor Kzar! Poor Kzar!" And I thought, I wish I were a jockey and could have rode him instead of that son of a b——. And that was funny, thinking of George Gardner as a son of a b—— because I'd always liked him and besides he'd given us the winner, but I guess that's what he is, all right.

My old man had a big lot of money after that race and he took to coming into Paris oftener. If they raced at Tremblay he'd have them drop him in town on their way back to Maisons, and he and I'd sit out in front of the Café de la Paix and watch the people go by. It's funny sitting there. There's streams of people going by and all sorts of guys come up and want to sell you things, and I loved to sit there with my old man. That was when we'd have the most fun. Guys would come by selling funny rabbits that jumped if you squeezed a bulb and they'd come up to us and my old man would kid with them. He could talk French just like English and all those kind of guys knew him 'cause you can always tell a jockey — and then we always sat at the same table and they got used to seeing us there. There were guys selling matrimonial papers and girls selling rubber eggs that when you squeezed them a rooster came out of them and one old wormy-looking guy that went by with postcards of Paris, showing them to everybody, and, of course, nobody ever bought any, and then he would come back and show the under side of the pack and they would all be smutty postcards and lots of people would dig down and buy them.

Gee, I remember the funny people that used to go by. Girls around suppertime looking for somebody to take them out to eat and they'd speak to my old man and he'd make some joke at them in French and they'd pat me on the head and go on. Once there was an American woman sitting with her kid daughter at the next table to us and they were both eating ices and I kept looking at the girl and she was awfully good-looking and I smiled at her and she smiled at me but that was all that ever came of it because I looked for her mother and her every day and I made up ways that I was going to speak to her and I wondered if I got to know if her mother would let me take her out to Auteuil or Tremblay but I never saw either of them again. Anyway, I guess it wouldn't have been any good, anyway, because looking back on it I remember the way I thought out would be best to speak to her was to say, "Pardon me, but perhaps I can give you a winner at Enghien today?" and, after all, maybe she would have thought I was a tout instead of really trying to give her a winner.

We'd sit at the Café de la Paix, my old man and me, and we had a big drag with the waiter because my old man drank whisky and it cost five francs, and that meant a good tip when the saucers were counted up. My old man was drinking more than I'd ever seen him, but he wasn't riding at all now and besides he said that whisky kept his weight down. But I noticed he was putting it on, all right, just the same. He'd busted away from his old gang out at Maisons and seemed to like just sitting around on the boulevard with me. But he was dropping money every day at the track. He'd feel sort of doleful after the last race, if he'd lost on the day, until we'd get to our table and he'd have his first whisky and then he'd be fine.

He'd be reading the *Paris-Sport* and he'd look over at me and say, "Where's your girl, Joe?" to kid me on account I had told him about the girl that day at the next table. And I'd get red, but I liked being kidded about her. It gave me a good feeling. "Keep your eye peeled for her, Joe," he'd say, "she'll be back."

He'd ask me questions about things and some of the things I'd say he'd laugh. And then he'd get started talking about things. About riding down in Egypt, or at St. Moritz on the ice before my mother died, and about during the war when they had regular races down in the south of France without any purses, or betting or crowd or anything just to keep the breed up. Regular races with the jocks riding hell out of the horses. Gee, I could listen to my old man talk by the hour, especially when he'd had a couple or so of drinks. He'd tell me about when he was a boy in Kentucky and going coon hunting, and the old days in the States before everything went on the bum there. And he'd say, "Joe, when we've got a decent stake, you're going back there to the States and go to school."

"What've I got to go back there to go to school for when everything's on the bum there?" I'd ask him.

"That's different," he'd say and get the waiter over and pay the pile of saucers and we'd get a taxi to the Gare St. Lazare and get on the train out to Maisons.

One day at Auteuil, after a selling steeplechase, my old man bought in the winner for 30,000 francs. He had to bid a little to get him but the stable let the horse go finally and my old man had his permit and his colors in a week. Gee, I felt proud when my old man was an owner. He fixed it up for stable space with Charles Drake and cut out coming in to Paris, and started his running and sweating out again, and him and I were the whole stable gang. Our horse's name was Gilford, he was Irish bred and a nice, sweet jumper. My old man figured that training him and riding him, himself, he was a good investment. I was proud of everything and I thought Gilford was as good a horse as Kzar. He was a good, solid jumper, a bay, with plenty of speed on the flat, if you asked him for it, and he was a nice looking horse, too.

Gee, I was fond of him. The first time he started with my old man up, he finished third in a 2500 meter hurdle race and when my old man got off him, all sweating and happy in the place stall, and went in to weigh, I felt as proud of him as though it was the first race he'd ever placed in. You see, when a guy ain't been riding for a long time, you can't make yourself really believe that he has ever rode. The whole thing was different now, 'cause down in Milan, even big races never seemed to make any difference to my old man, if he won he wasn't ever excited or anything, and now it was so I couldn't hardly sleep the night before a race and I knew my old man was excited, too, even if he didn't show it. Riding for yourself makes an awful difference.

Second time Gilford and my old man started was a rainy Sunday at Auteuil, in the Prix du Marat, a 4500 meter steeplechase. As soon as he'd gone out I beat it up in the stand with the new glasses my old man had bought for me to watch them. They started way over at the far end of the course and there was some trouble at the barrier. Something with goggle blinders on was making a great fuss and rearing around and busted the barrier once, but I could see my old man in our black jacket, with a white cross and a black cap, sitting up on Gilford, and patting him with his hand. Then they were off in a jump and out of sight behind the trees and the gong going for dear life and the pari-mutuel wickets rattling down. Gosh, I was so excited, I was afraid to look at them, but I fixed the glasses on the place where they would come out back of the trees and then out they came with the old black jacket going third and they all sailing over the jump like birds. Then they went out of sight again and then they came pounding out and down the hill and all going nice and sweet and easy and taking the fence smooth in a bunch, and moving away from us all solid. Looked as though you could walk across on their backs they were all so bunched and going so smooth. Then they bellied over the big double Bullfinch and something came down. I couldn't see who it was, but in a minute the horse was up and galloping free and the field, all bunched still, sweeping around the long left turn into the straightaway. They jumped the stone wall and came jammed down the stretch toward the big water jump right in front of the stands. I saw them coming and hollered at my old man as he went by, and he was leading by about a length and riding way out, and light as a monkey, and they were racing for the water jump. They took off over the big hedge of the water jump in a pack and then there was a crash, and two horses pulled sideways out of it, and kept on going and three others were piled up. I coulln't see my old man anywhere. One horse kneed himself up and the jock had hold of the bridle and mounted and went slamming on after the place money. The other horse was up and away by himself, jerking his head and galloping with the bridle rein hanging and the jock staggered over to one side of the track against the fence. Then Gilford rolled over to one side off my old man and got up and started to run on three legs with his off hoof dangling and there was my old man laying there on the grass flat out with his face up and blood all over the side of his head. I ran down the stand and bumped into a jam of people and got to the rail and a cop grabbed me and held me and two big stretcher bearers were going out after my old man and around on the other side of the course I saw three horses, strung way out, coming out of the trees and taking the jump.

My old man was dead when they brought him in and while a doctor was listening to his heart with a thing plugged in his ears, I heard a shot up the track that meant they'd killed Gilford. I lay down beside my old man, when they carried the stretcher into the hospital room, and hung on to the stretcher and cried and cried, and he looked so white and gone and so awfully dead, and I couldn't help feeling that if my old man was dead maybe they didn't need to have shot Gilford. His hoof might have got well. I don't know. I loved my old man so much.

Then a couple of guys came in and one of them patted me on the back and then went over and looked at my old man and then pulled a sheet off the cot and spread it over him; and the other was telephoning in French for them to send the ambulance to take him out to Maisons. And I couldn't stop crying, crying and choking, sort of, and George Gardner came in and sat down beside me on the floor and put his arm around me and says, "Come on, Joe, old boy. Get up and we'll go out and wait for the ambulance."

George and I went out to the gate and I was trying to stop bawling and George wiped off my face with his handkerchief and we were standing back a little ways while the crowd was going out of the gate and a couple of guys stopped near us while we were waiting for the crowd to get through the gate and one of them was counting a bunch of mutuel tickets and he said, "Well, Butler got his, all right."

The other guy said, "I don't give a good goddam if he did, the crook. He had it coming to him on the stuff he's pulled."

"I'll say he had," said the other guy, and tore the bunch of tickets in two.

And George Gardner looked at me to see if I'd heard and I had all right and he said, "Don't you listen to what those bums said, Joe. Your old man was one swell guy."

But I don't know. Seems like when they get started they don't leave a guy nothing.

PAUL HORGAN

The Peach Stone

As THEY all knew, the drive would take them about four hours, all the way to Weed, where *she* came from. They knew the way from travelling it so often, first in the old car, and now in the new one; new to them, that is, for they'd bought it second hand, last year, when they were down in Roswell to celebrate their tenth wedding anniversary. They still thought of themselves as a young couple, and *he* certainly did crazy things now and then, and always laughed her out of it when she was cross at the money going where it did, instead of where it ought to go. But there was so much droll orneriness in him when he did things like that that she couldn't stay mad, hadn't the heart; and the harder up they got, the more she loved him, and the little ranch he'd taken her to in the rolling plains just below the mountains.

This was a day in spring, rather hot, and the mountain was that melting blue that reminded you of something you could touch, like a china bowl. Over the sandy brown of the earth there was coming a green shadow. The air struck cool and deep in their breasts. *He* came from Texas, as a boy, and had lived here in New Mexico ever since. The word *home* always gave *her* a picture of unpainted, mouse-brown wooden houses in a little cluster by the rocky edge of the last mountain-step — the town of Weed, where Jodey Powers met and married her ten years ago.

They were heading back that way today.

Jodey was driving, squinting at the light. It never seemed so bright as now, before noon, as they went up the valley. He had a rangy look at the wheel of the light blue Chevvie — a bony man, but still fuzzed over with some look of a cub about him, perhaps the way he moved his limbs, a slight appealing clumsiness, that drew on thoughtless strength. On a rough road, he flopped and swayed at the wheel as if he were on a bony horse that galloped a little sidewise. His skin was red-brown from the sun. He had pale blue eyes, edged with dark lashes. *She* used to say he "turned them on" her, as if they were lights. He was wearing his suit, brown-striped, and a fresh blue shirt, too big at the neck. But he looked well dressed. But he would have looked that way naked, too, for he communicated his physical essence through any covering. It was what spoke out from him to anyone who encountered him. Until Cleotha married him, it had given him a time, all right, he used to reflect.

Next to him in the front seat of the sedan was Buddy, their nine-year-old-boy, who turned his head to stare at them both, his father and mother.

She was in back.

On the seat beside her was a wooden box, sandpapered, but not painted. Over it lay a baby's coverlet of pale yellow flannel with cross-stitched flowers down the middle in a band of bright colors. The mother didn't touch the box except when the car lurched or the tires danced over corrugated places in the gravel highway. Then she steadied it, and kept it from creeping on the seat cushions. In the box was coffined the body of their dead child, a two-year-old girl. They were on their way to Weed to bury it there.

In the other corner of the back seat sat Miss Latcher, the teacher. They rode in silence, and Miss Latcher breathed deeply of the spring day, as they all did, and she kept summoning to her aid the fruits of her learning. She felt this was a time to be intelligent, and not to give way to feelings.

The child was burned to death yesterday, playing behind the adobe chickenhouse at the edge of the arroyo out back, where the fence always caught the tumbleweeds. Yesterday, in a twist of wind, a few sparks from the kitchen chimney fell in the dry tumbleweeds and set them ablaze. Jodey had always meant to clear the weeds out: never seemed to get to it: told Cleotha he'd get to it next Saturday morning, before going down to Roswell: but Saturdays went by, and the wind and the sand drove the weeds into a barrier at the fence, and they would look at it every day without noticing, so habitual had the sight become. And so for many a spring morning, the little girl had played out there, behind the gray stucco house, whose adobe bricks showed through in one or two places.

The car had something loose; they believed it was the left rear fender: it chattered and wrangled over the gravel road.

Last night Cleotha stopped her weeping.

Today something happened; it came over her as they started out of the ranch lane, which curved up toward the highway. She looked as if she were trying to see something beyond the edge of Jodey's head and past the windshield.

Of course, she had sight in her eyes; she could not refuse to look at the world. As the car drove up the valley that morning, she saw in two ways — one, as she remembered the familiar sights of this region where she lived; the other, as if for the first time she were really seeing, and not simply looking. Her heart began to beat faster as they drove. It seemed to knock at her breast as if to come forth and hurry ahead of her along the sunlighted lanes of the life after today. She remembered thinking that her head might be a little giddy, what with the sorrow in her eyes so bright and slowly shining. But it didn't matter what did it. Ready never to look at anyone or anything again, she kept still; and through the window, which had a meandering crack in it like a river on a map, all that she looked upon seemed dear to her. . . .

Jodey could only drive. He watched the road as if he expected it to rise up and smite them all over into the canyon, where the trees twinkled and flashed with bright drops of light on their new varnished leaves. Jodey watched the road and said to himself that if it thought it could turn him over or make him scrape the rocks along the near side of the hill they were going around, if it thought for one minute that he was not master of this car, this road, this journey, why, it was just crazy. The wheels spraying the gravel across the surface of the road travelled on outward from his legs; his muscles were tight and felt tired as if he were running instead of riding. He tried to *think,* but he could not; that is, nothing came about that he would speak to her of, and he believed that she sat there, leaning forward, waiting for him to say something to her.

But this he could not do, and he speeded up a little, and his jaw made hard knots where he bit on his own rage; and he saw a lump of something coming in the road, and it aroused a positive passion in him. He aimed directly for it, and charged it fast, and hit it. The car shuddered and skidded, jolting them. Miss Latcher took a sharp breath inward, and put out her hand to touch someone, but did not reach anyone. Jodey looked for a second into the rear-view mirror above him, expecting something; but his wife was looking out of the window beside her, and if he could believe his eyes, she was smiling, holding her mouth with her fingers pinched up in a little claw.

The blood came up from under his shirt, he turned dark, and a sting came across his eyes.

He couldn't explain why he had done a thing like that to her, as if it were she he was enraged with, instead of himself.

He wanted to stop the car and get out and go around to the back door on the other side, and open it, and take her hands, bring her out to stand before him in the road, and hang his arms around her until she would be locked upon him. This made a picture that he indulged like a dream, while the car ran on, and he made no change, but drove as before. . . .

The little boy, Buddy, regarded their faces, again, and again, as if to see in their eyes what had happened to them.

He felt the separateness of the three.

He was frightened by their appearance of indifference to each other. His father had a hot and drowsy look, as if he had just come out of bed. There was something in his father's face which made it impossible for Buddy to say anything. He turned around and looked at his mother, but she was gazing out the window, and did not see him; and until she should see him, he had no way of speaking to her, if not with his words, then with his eyes, but if she should happen to look at him, why, he would wait to see what she looked *like,* and if she *did,* why, then he would smile at her, because he loved her, but he would have to know first if she was still his mother, and if everything was all right, and things weren't blown to smithereens — *bla-a-ash! wh-o-o-m!* — the way the dynamite did when the highway came past their ranch house, and the men worked out there for months, and whole hillsides came down at a time. All summer long, that was, always something to see. The world, the family, he, between his father and mother, was safe.

He silently begged her to face towards him. There was no security until she should do so.

"Mumma?"

But he said it to himself, and she did not hear him this time, and it seemed intelligent to him to turn around, make a game of it (the way things often were worked out), and face the front, watch the road, delay as long as he possibly could bear to, and *then* turn around again, and *this* time, why, she would probably be looking at him all the time, and it would *be:* it would simply *be.*

So he obediently watched the road, the white gravel ribbon passing under their wheels as steadily as time.

He was a sturdy little boy, and there was a silver nap of child's dust on his face, over his plum-red cheeks. He smelled something like a raw potato that has just been pared. The sun crowned him with a ring of light on his dark hair. . . .

What Cleotha was afraid to do was break the spell by saying anything or looking at any of them. This was *vision,* it was all she could think; never had anything looked so in all her life; everything made her heart lift, when she had believed this morning, after the night, that it would never lift again. There wasn't anything to compare her grief to. She couldn't t hink of anything to answer the death of her tiny child with. In her first hours of hardly believing what had happened, she had felt her own flesh and tried to imagine how it would have been if she could have borne the fire instead of the child. But all she got out of that was a longing avowal to herself of how gladly she would have borne it. Jodey had lain beside her, and she clung to his hand until she heard how he breathed off to sleep. Then she had let him go, and had wept at what seemed faithless in him. She had wanted his mind beside her then. It seemed to her that the last degree of her grief was the compassion she had had to bestow upon him while he slept.

But she had found this resource within her, and from that time on, her weeping had stopped.

It was like a wedding of pride and duty within her. There was nothing she could not find within herself, if she had to, now, she believed.

And so this morning, getting on toward noon, as they rode up the valley, climbing all the way, until they would find the road to turn off on, which would take them higher and higher before they dropped down toward Weed on the other side, she welcomed the sights of that dusty trip. Even if she had spoken her vision aloud, it would not have made sense to the others.

Look at that orchard of peach trees, she thought. I never saw such color as this year; the trees are like lamps, with the light coming from within. It must be the sunlight shining from the other side, and, of course, the petals are very thin, like the loveliest silk; so any light that shines upon them will pierce right through them and glow on this side. But they are so bright! When I was a girl at home, up to Weed, I remember we had an orchard of peach trees, but the blossoms were always a deeper pink than down here in the valley.

My! I used to catch them up by the handful, and I believed when I was a girl that if I crushed them and tied them in a handkerchief and carried the handkerchief in my bosom, I would come to smell like peach blossoms and have the same high pink in my face, and the girls I knew said that if I took a peach *stone* and held it *long enough* in my hand, it would *sprout;* and I dreamed of this one time, though, of course, I knew it was nonsense; but that was how children thought and talked in those days — we all used to pretend that *nothing* was impossible, if you simply did it hard enough and long enough.

But nobody wanted to hold a peach stone in their hand until it *sprouted,* to find out, and we used to laugh about it, but I think we believed it. I think I believed it.

It seemed to me, in between my *sensible* thoughts, a thing that any women could probably do. It seemed to me like a parable in the Bible. I could preach you a sermon about it this day.

I believe I see a tree down there in that next orchard which is dead; it has old black sprigs, and it looks twisted by rheumatism. There is one little shoot of leaves up on the top branch, and that is all. No, it is not dead, it is aged, it can no longer put forth blossoms in a swarm like pink butterflies; but there is that one little swarm of green leaves — it is just about the prettiest thing I've seen all day, and I thank God for it, for if there's anything I love, it is to see something growing. . . .

Miss Latcher had on her cloth gloves now, which she had taken from her blue cloth bag a little while back. The little winds that tracked through the moving car sought her out and chilled her nose, and the tips of her ears, and her long fingers, about which she had several times gone to visit various doctors. They had always told her not to worry, if her fingers seemed cold, and her hands moist. It was just a nervous condition, nothing to take very seriously; a good hand lotion might help the sensation, and in any case, some kind of digital exercise was a good thing — did she perhaps play the piano. It always seemed to her that doctors never *paid any attention* to her.

Her first name was Arleen, and she always considered this a very pretty name, prettier than Cleotha; and she believed that there was such a thing as an *Arleen look,* and if you wanted to know what it was, simply look at her. She had a long face, and pale hair; her skin was white, and her eyes were light blue. She was wonderfully clean, and used no cosmetics. She was a girl from "around here," but she had gone away to college, to study for her career, and what she had known as a child was displaced by what she had heard in classrooms. And she had to admit it: people *here* and *away* were not much alike. The men were different. She couldn't imagine marrying a rancher and "sacrificing" everything she had learned in college.

This poor little thing in the other corner of the car, for instance: she seemed dazed by what had happened to her — all she could do evidently was sit and stare out the window. And that man in front, simply driving, without a word. What did they have? What was their life like? They hardly had good clothes to drive to Roswell in, when they had to go to the doctor, or on some social errand.

But I must not think uncharitably, she reflected, and sat in an attitude of sustained sympathy, with her face composed in Arleenish interest and tact. The assumption of a proper aspect of grief and feeling produced the most curious effect within her, and by her attitude of concern she was suddenly reminded of the thing that always made her feel like weeping, though of course, she never did, but when she stopped and *thought* —

Like that painting at college, in the long hallway leading from the Physical Education lecture hall to the stairway down to the girls' gym: an enormous picture depicting the Agony of the Christian Martyrs, in ancient Rome. There were some days when she simply couldn't look at it; and there were others when she would pause and see those maidens with their tearful faces raised in calm prowess, and in them, she would find herself — they were all Arleens; and after she would leave the picture she would proceed in her imagination to the arena, and there she would know with exquisite sorrow and pain the ordeals of two thousand years ago, instead of those of her own lifetime. She thought of the picture now, and traded its remote sorrows for those of today until she had sincerely forgotten the mother and the father and the little brother of the dead child with whom she was riding up the spring-turning valley, where noon was warming the dust that arose from the gravelled highway. It was white dust, and it settled over them in an enriching film, ever so finely. . . .

Jodey Powers had a fantastic scheme that he used to think about for taking and baling tumbleweed and make a salable fuel out of it. First, you'd compress it — probably down at the cotton compress in Roswell — where a loose bale was wheeled in under the great power-drop, and when the nigger at the handle gave her a yank, down came the weight, and packed the bale into a little thing, and then they let the steam exhaust go, and the press sighed once or twice, and just seemed to *lie* there, while the men ran wires through the gratings of the press and tied them tight. Then up came the weight, and out came the bale.

If he did that to enough bales of tumbleweed, he believed he'd get rich. Burn? It burned like a house afire. It had oil in it, somehow, and the thing to do was to get it in shape for use as a fuel. Imagine all the tumbleweed that blew around the State of New Mexico in the fall, and sometimes all winter. In the winter, the weeds were black and brittle. They cracked when they blew against fence posts, and if one lodged there, then another one caught at its thorny lace; and next time it blew, and the sand came trailing, and the tumbleweeds rolled, they'd pile up at the same fence and build out, locked together against the wires. The wind drew through them, and the sand dropped around them. Soon there was a solid-looking but airy bank of tumbleweeds built right to the top of the fence, in a long windward slope; and the next time the wind blew, and the weeds came, they would roll up the little hill of brittle twigs and leap off the other side of the fence, for all the world like horses taking a jump, and go galloping ahead of the wind across the next pasture on the plains, a black and witchy procession.

If there was an arroyo, they gathered there. They backed up in the miniature canyons of dirt-walled watercourses, which were dry except when it rained hard up in the hills. Out behind the house, the arroyo had filled up with tumbleweeds; and in November, when it blew so hard and so cold, but without bringing any snow, some of the tumbleweeds had climbd out and scattered, and a few had tangled at the back fence, looking like rusted barbed wire. Then there came a few more; all winter the bank grew. Many times he'd planned to get out back there and clear them away, just e-e-ease them off away from the fence posts, so's not to catch the wood up, and then set a match to the whole thing, and in five minutes, have it all cleared off. If he did like one thing, it was a neat place.

How Cleotha laughed at him sometimes when he said that, because she knew that as likely as not he would forget to clear the weeds away. And if he'd said it once he'd said it a thousand times, that he was going to gather up that pile of scrap iron from the front yard, and haul it to Roswell, and sell it — old car parts, and the fenders off a truck that had turned over up on the highway, which he'd salvaged with the aid of the driver.

But the rusting iron was still there, and he had actually come to have a feeling of fondness for it. If someone were to appear one night and silently make off with it, he'd be aroused the next day, and demand to know who had robbed him: for it was dear junk, just through lying around and belonging to him. What was his was part of him, even that heap of fenders that rubbed off on your clothes with a rusty powder, like a caterpillar fur.

But even by thinking hard about all such matters, treading upon the fringe of what had happened yesterday, he was unable to make it all seem long ago, and a matter of custom and even of indifference. There was no getting away from it — if anybody was to blame for the terrible moments of yesterdy afternoon, when the wind scattered a few sparks from the chimney of the kitchen stove, why he was.

Jodey Powers never claimed to himself or anybody else that he was any *better* man than another. But everything he knew and hoped for, every reassurance his body had had from other people, and the children he had begotten, had been knowledge to him he was *as good* a man as any.

And of this knowledge he was now bereft.

If he had been alone in his barrenness, he could have solaced himself with heroic stupidities. He could have produced out of himself abominations, with the amplitude of biblical despair. But he wasn't alone; there they sat; there was Buddy beside him, and Clee in back, even the teacher, Arleen — even to her he owed some return of courage.

All he could do was drive the damned car, and keep *thinking* about it.

He wished he could think of something to say, or else that Clee would.

But they continued in silence, and he believed that it was one of his making. . . .

The reverie of Arleen Latcher made her almost ill, from the sad, sweet experiences she had entered into with those people so long ago. How wonderful it was to have such a rich life, just looking up things! — And the most wonderful thing of all was that even if they were beautiful, and wore semitransparent garments that fell to the ground in graceful folds, the maidens were all pure. It made her eyes swim to think how innocent they went to their death. Could anything be more beautiful, and reassuring, than this? Far, far better. Far better those hungry lions, than the touch of lustful men. Her breath left her for a moment, and she closed her eyes, and what threatened her with real feeling — the presence of the Powers family in the faded blue sedan climbing through the valley sunlight toward the turn-off that led to the mountain road — was gone. Life's breath on her cheek was not so close. Oh, others had suffered. She could suffer.

"All that pass by clap their hands at thee: they hiss and wag their heads at the daughter of Jerusalem — "

This image made her wince, as if she herself had been hissed and wagged at. Everything she knew made it possible for her to see herself as a proud and threatened virgin of Bible times, which were more real to her than many of the years she had lived through. Yet must not Jerusalem have sat in country like this with its sandy hills, the frosty stars that were so bright at night, the simple Mexicans riding their burros as if to the Holy Gates? We often do not see our very selves, she would reflect, gazing ardently at the unreal creature which the name Arleen brought to life in her mind.

On her cheeks there had appeared two islands of color, as if she had a fever. What she strove to save by her anguished retreats into the memories of the last days of the Roman Empire was surely crumbling away from her. She said to herself that she must not give way to it, and that she was just wrought up; the fact that she really *didn't* feel anything — in fact, it was a pity that she *couldn't* take that little Mrs. Powers in her arms, and comfort her, just *let* her go ahead and cry, and see if it wouldn't probably help some. But Miss Latcher was aware that she felt nothing that related to the Powers family and their trouble.

Anxiously she searched her heart again, and wooed back the sacrifice of the tribe of heavenly Arleens marching so certainly toward the lions. But they did not answer her call to mind, and she folded her cloth-gloved hands and pressed them together, and begged of herself that she might think of some way to comfort Mrs. Powers; for if she could do that, it might fill her own empty heart until it became a cup that would run over. . . .

Cleotha knew Buddy wanted her to see him; but though her heart turned toward him, as it always must, no matter what he asked of her, she was this time afraid to do it because if she ever lost the serenity of her sight now she might never recover it this day; and the heaviest trouble was still before her.

So she contented herself with Buddy's look as it reached her from the side of her eye. She glimpsed his head and neck, like a young cat's, the wide bones behind the ears, and the smooth but visible cords of his nape, a sight of him that always made her want to laugh because it was so pathetic. When she caressed him she often fondled those strenuous hollows behind his ears. Heaven only knew, she would think, what went on within the shell of that topknot! She would pray between her words and feelings that those unseen thoughts in the boy's head were ones that would never trouble him. She was often amazed at things in him which she recognized as being like herself; and at those of Buddy's qualities which came from some alien source, she suffered pangs of doubt and fear. He was so young to be a stranger to her!

The car went around the curve that hugged the rocky fall of a hill; and on the other side of it, a green quilt of alfalfa lay sparkling darkly in the light. Beyond that, to the right of the road, the land levelled out, and on a sort of platform of swept earth stood a two-room hut of adobe. It had a few stones cemented against the near corner, to give it strength. Clee had seen it a hundred times — the place where that old man Melendez lived, and where his wife had died a few years ago. He was said to be simple-minded and claimed he was a hundred years old. In the past, riding by here, she had more or less delicately made a point of looking the other way. It often distressed her to think of such a helpless old man, too feeble to do anything but crawl out when the sun was bright and the wall was warm, and sit there, with his milky gaze resting on the hills he had known since he was born, and had never left. Somebody came to feed him once a day, and see if he was clean enough to keep his health. As long as she could remember, there'd been some kind of dog at the house. The old man had sons and grandsons and great-grandsons — you might say a whole orchard of them, sprung from this one tree that was dying, but that still held a handful of green days in its ancient veins.

Before the car had quite gone by, she had seen him. The sun was bright, and the wall must have been warm, warm enough to give his shoulders and back a reflection of the heat which was all he could feel. He sat there on his weathered board bench, his hands on his branch of apple tree that was smooth and shiny from use as a cane, His house door was open, and a deep tunnel of shade lay within the sagged box of the opening. Cleotha leaned forward to see him, as if to look at him were one of her duties today. She saw his jaw moving up and down, not chewing, but just opening and closing. In the wind and flash of the car going by, she could not hear him; but from his closed eyes, and his moving mouth, and the way his head was raised, she wouldn't have been surprised if she had heard him singing. He was singing some thread of song, and it made her smile to imagine what kind of noise it made, a wisp of voice.

She was perplexed by a feeling of joyful fullness in her breast, at the sight of the very same old witless sire from whom in the past she had turned away her eyes out of delicacy and disgust.

The last thing she saw as they went by was his dog, who came around the corner of the house with a caracole. He was a mongrel puppy, partly hound — a comedian by nature. He came prancing outrageously up to the old man's knees, and invited his response, which he did not get. But as if his master were as great a wag as he, he hurled himself backward, pretending to throw himself recklessly into pieces. Everything on him flopped and was flung by his idiotic energy. It was easy to imagine, watching the puppy-fool, that the sunlight had entered him as it had entered the old man. Cleotha was reached by the hilarity of the hound, and when he tripped over himself and plowed the ground with his flapping jowls, she wanted to laugh out loud.

But they were past the place, and she winked back the merriment in her eyes, and she knew that it was something she could never have told the others about. What it stood for, in her, they would come to know in other ways, as she loved them. . . .

Jodey was glad of one thing. He had telephoned from Hondo last night, and everything was to be ready at Weed. They would drive right up the hill to the family burial ground. They wouldn't have to wait for anything. He was glad, too, that the wind wasn't blowing.

It always made his heart sink when the wind rose on the plains and began to change the sky with the color of dust.

Yesterday: it was all he could see, however hard he was *thinking* about everything else.

He'd been on his horse, coming back down the pasture that rose up behind the house across the arroyo, nothing particular in mind — except to make a joke with himself about how far along the peaches would get before the frost killed them all, *snap,* in a single night, like that — when he saw the column of smoke rising from the tumbleweeds by the fence. Now who could've lighted them, he reflected, following the black smoke up on its billows into the sky. There was just enough wind idling across the long front of the hill to bend the smoke and trail it away at an angle, toward the blue.

The hillside, the fire, the wind, the column of smoke.

Oh my God! And the next minute he was tearing down the hill as fast as his horse could take him, and the fire — he could see the flames now — the fire was like a bank of yellow rags blowing violently and torn in the air, rag after tearing up from the ground. Cleotha was there, and in a moment, so was he, but they were too late. The baby was unconscious. They took her up and hurried to the house, the back way where the screen door was standing open with its spring trailing on the ground. When they got inside where it seemed so dark and cool, they held the child between them, fearing to lay her down. They called for Buddy, but he was still at school up the road, and would not be home until the orange school bus stopped by their mailbox out front at the highway after four o'clock. The fire poured in cracking tumult through the weeds. In ten minutes they were only little airy lifts of ash off the ground. Everything was black. There were three fence posts still afire; the wires were hot. The child was dead. They let her down on their large bed.

He could remember every word Clee had said to him. They were not many, and they shamed him, in his heart, because he couldn't say a thing. He comforted her, and held her while she wept. But if he had spoken then, or now, riding in the car, all he could have talked about was the image of the blowing rags of yellow fire, and blue, blue, plaster blue behind the above, sky and mountains. But he believed that she knew why he seemed so short with her. He hoped earnestly that she knew. He might just be wrong. She might be blaming him, and keeping so still because it was more proper, now, to *be* still than full of reproaches.

But of the future, he was entirely uncertain; and he drove, and came to the turn-off, and they started winding in back among the sandhills that lifted them toward the rocky slopes of the mountains. Up and up they went; the air was so clear and thin that they felt transported, and across the valleys that dropped between the grand shoulders of the pine-haired slopes, the air looked as if it were blue breath from the trees. . . .

Cleotha was blinded by a dazzling light in the distance, ahead of them, on the road.

It was a ball of diamond-brilliant light.

It danced, and shook, and quivered above the road far, far ahead. It seemed to be travelling between the pine trees on either side of the road, and somewhat above the road, and it was like nothing she had ever seen before. It was the most magic and exquisite thing she had ever seen, and wildly, even hopefully as a child is hopeful when there is a chance and a need for something miraculous to happen, she tried to explain it to herself. It could be a star in the daytime, shaking and quivering and travelling ahead of them, as if to lead them. It was their guide. It was shaped like a small cloud, but it was made of shine, and dazzle, and quiver. She held her breath for fear it should vanish, but it did not, and she wondered if the others in the car were smitten with the glory of it as she was.

It was brighter than the sun, whiter; it challenged the daytime, and obscured everything near it by its blaze of flashing and dancing light.

It was almost as if she had approached perfect innocence through her misery, and were enabled to receive portents that might not be visible to anyone else. She closed her eyes for a moment.

But the road curved, and everything travelling on it took the curve too, and the trembling pool of diamond-light ahead lost its liquid splendor, and turned into the tin signs on the back of a huge oil truck which was toiling over the mountain, trailing its links of chain behind.

When Clee looked again, the star above the road was gone. The road and the angle of the sun to the mountaintop and the two cars climbing upward had lost their harmony to produce the miracle. She saw the red oil truck, and simply saw it, and said to herself that the sun might have reflected off the big tin signs on the back of it. But she didn't believe it, for she was not thinking, but rather dreaming; fearful of awakening. . . .

The high climb up this drive always made Miss Latcher's ears pop, and she had discovered once that to swallow often prevented the disagreeable sensation. So she swallowed. Nothing happened to her ears. But she continued to swallow, and feel her ears with her cloth-covered fingers, but what really troubled her now would not be downed, and it came into her mouth as a taste; she felt giddy — that was the altitude, of course — when they got down the other side, she would be all right.

What it was was perfectly clear to her, for that was part of having an education and a trained mind — the processes of thought often went right on once you started them going.

Below the facts of this small family, in the worst trouble it had ever known, lay the fact of envy in Arleen's breast.

It made her head swim to realize this. But she envied them their entanglement with one another, and the dues they paid each other in the humility of the duty they were performing on this ride, to the family burial ground at Weed. Here she sat riding with them, to come along and be of help to them, and she was no help. She was unable to swallow the lump of desire that rose in her throat, for life's uses, even such bitter ones as that of the Powers family today. It had been filling her gradually, all the way over on the trip, this feeling of jealousy and degradation.

Now it choked her and she knew she had tried too hard to put from her the thing that threatened her, which was the touch of life through anybody else. She said to herself that she must keep control of herself.

But Buddy turned around again, just then, slowly, as if he were a young male cat who just happened to be turning around to see what he could see, and he looked at his mother with his large eyes, so like his father's: pale petal-blue, with drops of light like the centers of cats' eyes, and dark lashes. He had a solemn look, when he saw his mother's face, and he prayed her silently to acknowledge him. If she didn't, why, he was still alone. He would never again feel safe about running off to the highway to watch the scrapers work, or the huge Diesel oil tankers go by, or the cars with strange license plates — of which he had already counted thirty-two different kinds, his collection, as he called it. So if she didn't see him, why, what might he find when he came back home at times like those, when he went off for a little while just to play?

They were climbing down the other side of the ridge now. In a few minutes they would be riding into Weed. The sights as they approached were like images of awakening to Cleotha. Her heart began to hurt when she saw them. She recognized the tall iron smokestack of the sawmill. It showed above the trees down on the slope ahead of them. There was a stone house which had been abandoned even when she was a girl at home here, and its windows and doors standing open always seemed to her to depict a face with an expression of dismay. The car dropped farther down — they were making that last long curve of the road to the left — and now the town stood visible, with the sunlight resting on so many of the unpainted houses and turning their weathered gray to a dark silver. Surely they must be ready for them, these houses: all had been talked over by now. They could all mention that they knew Cleotha as a little girl.

She lifted her head.

There were claims upon her.

Buddy was looking at her soberly, trying to predict to himself how she would *be*. He was ready to echo with his own small face whatever her face would show him.

Miss Latcher was watching the two of them. Her heart was racing in her breast.

The car slowed up. Now Cleotha could not look out the windows at the wandering earthen street, and the places alongside it. They would have to drive right through town, to the hillside on the other side.

"Mumma?" asked the boy softly.

Cleotha winked both her eyes at him, and smiled, and leaned toward him a trifle.

And then he blushed, his eyes swam with happiness, and he smiled back at her, and his face poured forth such radiance that Miss Latcher took one look at him, and with a choke, burst into tears.

She wept into her hands, her gloves were moistened, her square shoulders rose to her ears, and she was overwhelmed by what the mother had been able to do for the boy. She shook her head and made long gasping sobs. Her sense of betrayal was not lessened by the awareness that she was weeping for herself.

Cleotha leaned across to her, and took her hand, and murmured to her. She comforted her, gently.

"Hush, honey, you'll be all right. Don't you cry, now. Don't you think about us. We're almost there, and it'll soon be over. God knows you were mighty sweet to come along and be with us. Hush, now, Arleen, you'll have Buddy crying too."

But the boy was simply watching the teacher, in whom the person he knew so well every day in school had broken up, leaving an unfamiliar likeness. It was like seeing a reflection in a pond, and then throwing a stone in. The reflection disappeared in ripples of something else.

Arleen could not stop.

The sound of her 'ooping made Jodey furious. He looked into the rear-view mirror and saw his wife patting her and comforting her. Cleotha looked so white and strained that he was frightened, and he said out, without turning around: "Arleen, you cut that out, you shut up, now. I won't have you wearin' down Clee, God damn it, you quit it!"

But this rage, which arose from a sense of justice, made Arleen feel guiltier than ever; and she laid her head against the car window, and her sobs drummed her brow bitterly on the glass.

"Hush," whispered Cleotha, but she could do no more, for they were arriving at the hillside, and the car was coming to a stop. They must awaken from this journey, and come out onto the ground, and begin to toil their way up the yellow hill, where the people were waiting. Over the ground grew yellow grass that was turning to green. It was like velvet, showing dark or light, according to the breeze and the golden afternoon sunlight. It was a generous hill, curving easily and gradually as it rose. Beyond it was only the sky, for the mountains faced it from behind the road. It was called Schoolhouse Hill, and at one time, the whole thing had belonged to Cleotha's father; and before there was any schoolhouse crowning its noble swell of earth, the departed members of his family had been buried halfway up the gentle climb.

Jodey helped her out of the car, and he tried to talk to her with his holding fingers. He felt her trembling, and she shook her head at him. Then she began to walk up there, slowly. He leaned into the car and took the covered box in his arms, and followed her. Miss Latcher was out of the car on her side, hiding from them, her back turned, while she used her handkerchief and positively clenched herself back into control of her thoughts and sobs. When she saw that they weren't waiting for her, she hurried, and in humility, reached for Buddy's hand to hold it for him as they walked. He let her have it, and he marched, watching his father, whose hair was blowing in the wind and sunshine. From behind, Jodey looked like just a kid. . . .

And now for Cleotha her visions on the journey appeared to have some value, and for a little while longer, when she needed it most, the sense of being in blind communion with life was granted her, at the little graveside where all those kind friends were gathered on the slow slope up of the hill on the summit of which was the schoolhouse of her girlhood.

It was afternoon, and they were all kneeling toward the upward rise, and Judge Crittenden was reading the prayer book.

Everything left them but a sense of their worship, in the present.

And a boy, a late scholar, is coming down the hill from the school, the sunlight edging him; and his wonder at what the people kneeling there are doing is, to Cleotha, the most memorable thing she is to look upon today; for she has resumed the life of her infant daughter, whom they are burying, and on whose behalf, something rejoices in life anyway, as if to ask the mother whether love itself is not ever-living. And she watches the boy come discreetly down the hill, trying to keep away from them, but large-eyed with a hunger *to know* which claims all acts of life, for him, and for those who will be with him later; and his respectful curiosity about those kneeling mourners, the edge of sunlight along him as he walks away from the sun and down the hill, is of all those things she saw and rejoiced in, the most beautiful; and at that, her breast is full, with the heaviness of a baby at it, and not for grief alone, but for praise.

"I believe, I believe!" her heart cries out in her, as if she were holding the peach stone of her eager girlhood in her woman's hand.

She puts her face into her hands, and weeps, and they all move closer to her. Familiar as it is, the spirit has had a new discovery....

Jodey then felt that she had returned to them all; and he stopped seeing, and just remembered, what happened yesterday; and his love for his wife was confirmed as something he would never be able to measure for himself or prove to her in words.

Haircut

I GOT another barber that comes over from Carterville and helps me out Saturdays, but the rest of the time I can get along all right alone. You can see for yourself that this ain't no New York City and besides that, the most of the boys works all day and don't have no leisure to drop in here and get themselves prettied up.

You're a newcomer, ain't you, I thought I hadn't seen you round before. I hope you like it good enough to stay. As I say, we ain't no New York City or Chicago, but we have pretty good times. Not as good, though, since Jim Kendall got killed. When he was alive, him and Hod Meyers used to keep this town in an uproar. I bet they was more laughin' done here than any town its size in America.

Jim was comical, and Hod was pretty near a match for him. Since Jim's gone, Hod tries to hold his end up just the same as ever, but it's tough goin' when you ain't got nobody to kind of work with.

They used to be plenty fun in here Saturdays. This place is jam-packed Saturdays, from four o'clock on. Jim and Hod would show up right after their supper, round six o'clock. Jim would set himself down in that big chair, nearest the blue spittoon. Whoever had been settin' in that chair, why they'd get up when Jim come in and give it to him.

"You'd of thought it was a reserved seat like they have sometimes in a theayter. Hod would generally always stand or walk up and down, or some Saturdays, of course, he'd be settin' in this chair part of the time, gettin' a haircut.

Well, Jim would set there a w'ile without openin' his mouth only to spit, and then finally he'd say to me, "Whitey" — my right name, that is, my right first name, is Dick, but everybody round here calls me Whitey — Jim would say, "Whitey, your nose looks like a rosebud tonight. You must of been drinkin' some of your aw de cologne."

So I'd say, "No, Jim, but you look like you'd been drinkin' somethin' of that kind or somethin' worse."

Jim would have to laugh at that, but then he'd speak up and say, "No, I ain't had nothin' to drink, but that ain't sayin' I wouldn't like somethin'. I wouldn't even mind if it was wood alcohol."

Then Hod Meyers would say, "Neither would your wife." That would set everybody to laughin' because Jim and his wife wasn't on very good terms. She'd of divorced him only they wasn't no chance to get alimony and she didn't have no way to take care of herself and the kids. She couldn't never understand Jim. He *was* kind of rough, but a good fella at heart.

Him and Hod had all kinds of sport with Milt Sheppard. I don't suppose you've seen Milt. Well, he's got an Adam's apple that looks more like a mushmelon. So I'd be shavin' Milt and when I'd start to shave down here on his neck, Hod would holler, "Hey, Whitey, wait a minute! Before you cut into it, let's make up a pool and see who can guess closest to the number of seeds."

And Jim would say, "If Milt hadn't of been so hoggish, he'd of ordered a half a cantaloupe, instead of a whole one and it might not of stuck in his throat."

All the boys would roar at this and Milt himself would force a smile, though the joke was on him. Jim certainly was a card!

There's his shavin' mug, settin' on the shelf, right next to Charley Vail's. "Charles M. Vail." That's the druggist. He comes in regular for his shave, three times a week. And Jim's is the cup next to

Charley's. "James H. Kendall." Jim won't need no shavin' mug no more, but I'll leave it there just the same for old time's sake. Jim certainly was a character!

Years ago, Jim used to travel for a canned goods concern over in Carterville. They sold canned goods. Jim had the whole northern half of the state and was on the road five days out of every week. He'd drop in here Saturdays and tell his experiences for that week. It was rich.

I guess he paid more attention to playin' jokes than makin' sales. Finally the concern let him out and he come right home here and told everybody he'd been fired instead of sayin' he'd resigned like most fellas would of.

It was a Saturday and the shop was full and Jim got up out of that chair and says, "Gentlemen, I got an important announcement to make. I been fired from my job."

Well, they asked him if he was in earnest and he said he was and nobody could think of nothin' to say till Jim finally broke the ice himself. He says, "I been sellin' canned goods and now I'm canned goods myself."

You see, the concern he'd been workin' for was a factory that made canned goods. Over in Carterville. And now Jim said he was canned himself. He was certainly a card!

Jim had a great trick that he used to play w'ile he was travelin'. For instance, he'd be ridin' on a train and they'd come to some little town like, well, like, we'll say, like Benton. Jim would look out the train window and read the signs on the stores.

For instance, they'd be a sign, "Henry Smith, Dry Goods." Well, Jim would write down the name and the name of the town and when he got to wherever he was goin' he'd mail back a postal card to Henry Smith at Benton and not sign no name to it, but he'd write on the card, well, somethin' like "Ask your wife about that book agent that spent the afternoon last week," or "Ask your missus who kept her from gettin' lonesome the last time you was in Carterville." And he'd sign the card, "A Friend."

Of course, he never knew what really come of none of these jokes, but he could picture what *probably* happened and that was enough.

Jim didn't work very steady after he lost his position with the Carterville people. What he did earn, doin' odd jobs round town, why he spent pretty near all of it on gin and his family might of starved if the stores hadn't of carried them along. Jim's wife tried her hand at dressmakin', but they ain't nobody goin' to get rich makin' dresses in this town.

As I say, she'd of divorced Jim, only she seen that she couldn't support herself and the kids and she was always hopin' that some day Jim would cut out his habits and give her more than two or three dollars a week.

They was a time when she would go to whoever he was workin' for and ask them to give her his wages, but after she done this once or twice, he beat her to it by borrowin' most of his pay in advance. He told it all round town, how he had outfoxed his missus. He certainly was a caution!

But he wasn't satisfied with just outwittin' her. He was sore the way she had acted, tryin' to grab off his pay. And he made up his mind he'd get even. Well, he waited till Evans's Circus was advertised to come to town. Then he told his wife and two kiddies that he was goin' to take them to the circus. The day of the circus, he told them he would get the tickets and meet them outside the entrance to the tent.

Well, he didn't have no intention of bein' there or buyin' tickets or nothin'. He got full of gin and laid round Wright's poolroom all day. His wife and the kids waited and waited and of course he didn't show up. His wife didn't have a dime with her, or nowhere else, I guess. So she finally had to tell the kids it was all off and they cried like they wasn't never goin' to stop.

Well, it seems, w'ile they was cryin', Doc Stair came along and he asked what was the matter, but Mrs. Kendall was stubborn and wouldn't tell him, but the kids told him and he insisted on takin' them and their mother in the show. Jim found this out afterwards and it was one reason why he had it in for Doc Stair.

Doc Stair come here about a year and a half ago. He's a mighty handsome young fella and his clothes always look like he has them made to order. He goes to Detroit two or three times a year and w'ile

he's there he must have a tailor take his measure and then make him
a suit to order. They cost pretty near twice as much, but they fit a
whole lot better than if you just bought them in a store.

For a w'ile everybody was wonderin' why a young doctor like Doc
Stair should come to a town like this where we already got old Doc
Gamble and Doc Foote that's both been here for years and all the
practice in town was always divided between the two of them.

Then there was a story got round that Doc Stair's gal had throwed
him over, a gal up in the Northern Peninsula somewheres, and the
reason he come here was to hide himself away and forget it. He
said himself that he thought they wasn't nothin' like general practice
in a place like ours to fit a man to be a good all-round doctor. And
that's why he'd came.

Anyways, it wasn't long before he was makin' enough to live on,
though they tell me that he never dunned nobody for what they
owed him, and the folks here certainly has got the owin' habit, even
in my business. If I had all that was comin' to me for just shaves
alone, I could go to Carterville and put up at the Mercer for a week
and see a different picture every night. For instance, they's old George
Purdy — but I guess I shouldn't ought to be gossipin'.

Well, last year, our coroner died, died of the flu. Ken Beatty, that
was his name. He was the coroner. So they had to chose another
man to be coroner in his place and they picked Doc Stair. He laughed
at first and said he didn't want it, but they made him take it. It ain't
no job that anybody would fight for and what a man makes out of
it in a year would just about buy seeds for their garden. Doc's the
kind, though, that can't say no to nothin' if you keep at him long
enough.

But I was goin' to tell you about a poor boy we got here in town
— Paul Dickson. He fell out of a tree when he was about ten years
old. Lit on his head and it done somethin' to him and he ain't never
been right. No harm in him, but just silly. Jim Kendall used to call
him cuckoo; that's a name Jim had for anybody that was off their
head, only he called people's head their bean. That was another of
his gags, callin' head bean and callin' crazy people cuckoo. Only poor
Paul ain't crazy, but just silly.

You can imagine that Jim used to have all kinds of fun with Paul.

He'd send him to the White Front Garage for a left-handed monkey wrench. Of course they ain't no such thing as a left-handed monkey wrench.

And once we had a kind of fair here and they was a baseball game between the fats and the leans and before the game started Jim called Paul over and sent him way down to Shrader's hardware store to get a key for the pitcher's box.

They wasn't nothin' in the way of gags that Jim couldn't think up, when he put his mind to it.

Poor Paul was always kind of suspicious of people, maybe on account of how Jim had kept foolin' him. Paul wouldn't have much to do with anybody only his own mother and Doc Stair and a girl here in town named Julie Gregg. That is, she ain't a girl no more, but pretty near thirty or over.

When Doc first come to town, Paul seemed to feel like here was a real friend and he hung round Doc's office most of the w'ile; the only time he wasn't there was when he'd go home to eat or sleep or when he seen Julie Gregg doin' her shoppin'.

When he looked out Doc's window and seen her, he'd run downstairs and join her and tag along with her to the different stores. The poor boy was crazy about Julie and she always treated him mighty nice and made him feel like he was welcome, though of course it wasn't nothin' but pity on her side.

Doc done all he could to improve Paul's mind and he told me once that he really thought the boy was gettin' better, that they was times when he was as bright and sensible as anybody else.

But I was goin' to tell you about Julie Gregg. Old Man Gregg was in the lumber business, but got to drinkin' and lost the most of his money and when he died, he didn't leave nothin' but the house and just enough insurance for the girl to skimp along on.

Her mother was a kind of a half invalid and didn't hardly ever leave the house. Julie wanted to sell the place and move somewheres else after the old man died, but the mother said she was born here and would die here. It was tough on Julie, as the young people round this town — well, she's too good for them.

She's been away to school and Chicago and New York and different places and they ain't no subject she can't talk on, where you take the rest of the young folks here and you mention anything to them outside of Gloria Swanson or Tommy Meighan and they think you're delirious. Did you see Gloria in *Wages of Virtue?* You missed somethin'!

Well, Doc Stair hadn't been here more than a week when he come in one day to get shaved and I recognized who he was as he had been pointed out to me, so I told him about my old lady. She's been ailin' for a couple years and either Doc Gamble or Doc Foote, neither one, seemed to be helpin' her. So he said he would come out and see her, but if she was able to get out herself, it would be better to bring her to his office where he could make a complete examination.

So I took her to his office and w'ile I was waitin' for her in the reception room, in come Julie Gregg. When somebody comes in Doc Stair's office, they's a bell that rings in his inside office so as he can tell they's somebody to see him.

So he left my old lady inside and come out to the front office and that's the first time him and Julie met and I guess it was what they call love at first sight. But it wasn't fifty-fifty. This young fella was the slickest lookin' fella she'd ever seen in this town and she went wild over him. To him she was just a young lady that wanted to see the doctor.

She'd came on about the same business I had. Her mother had been doctorin' for years with Doc Gamble and Doc Foote and without no results. So she'd heard they was a new doc in town and decided to give him a try. He promised to call and see her mother that same day.

I said a minute ago that it was love at first sight on her part. I'm not only judgin' by how she acted afterwards but how she looked at him that first day in his office. I ain't no mind reader, but it was wrote all over her face that she was gone.

Now Jim Kendall, besides bein' a jokesmith and a pretty good drinker, well, Jim was quite a lady-killer. I guess he run pretty wild durin' the time he was on the road for them Carterville people, and besides that, he'd had a couple little affairs of the heart right here in town. As I say, his wife could of divorced him, only she couldn't.

But Jim was like the majority of men, and women, too, I guess. He wanted what he couldn't get. He wanted Julie Gregg and worked his head off tryin' to land her. Only he'd of said bean instead of head.

Well, Jim's habits and his jokes didn't appeal to Julie and of course he was a married man, so he didn't have no more chance than, well, than a rabbit. That's an expression of Jim's himself. When somebody didn't have no chance to get elected or somethin', Jim would always say they didn't have no more chance than a rabbit.

He didn't make no bones about how he felt. Right in here, more than once, in front of the whole crowd, he said he was stuck on Julie and anybody that could get her for him was welcome to his house and his wife and kids included. But she wouldn't have nothin' to do with him; wouldn't even speak to him on the street. He finally seen he wasn't gettin' nowheres with his usual line so he decided to try the rough stuff. He went right up to her house one evenin' and when she opened the door he forced his way in and grabbed her. But she broke loose and before he could stop her, she run in the next room and locked the door and phoned to Joe Barnes. Joe's the marshal. Jim could hear who she was phonin' to and he beat it before Joe got there.

Joe was an old friend of Julie's pa. Joe went to Jim the next day and told him what would happen if he ever done it again.

I don't know how the news of this little affair leaked out. Chances is that Joe Barnes told his wife and she told somebody else's wife and they told their husband. Anyways, it did leak out and Hod Meyers had the nerve to kid Jim about it, right here in this shop. Jim didn't deny nothin' and kind of laughed it off and said for us all to wait; that lots of people had tried to make a monkey out of him, but he always got even.

Meanw'ile everybody in town was wise to Julie's bein' wild mad over the Doc. I don't suppose she had any idear how her face changed when him and her was together; of course she couldn't of, or she'd of kept away from him. And she didn't know that we was all noticin' how many times she made excuses to go up to his office or pass it on the other side of the street and look up in his window to see if he was there. I felt sorry for her and so did most other people.

Hod Meyers kept rubbin' it into Jim about how the Doc had cut him out. Jim didn't pay no attention to the kiddin' and you could see he was plannin' one of his jokes.

One trick Jim had was the knack of changin' his voice. He could make you think he was a girl talkin' and he could mimic any man's voice. To show you how good he was along this line, I'll tell you the joke he played on me once.

You know, in most towns of any size, when a man is dead and needs a shave, why the barber that shaves him soaks him five dollars for the job; that is, he don't soak *him,* but whoever ordered the shave. I just charge three dollars because personally I don't mind much shavin' a dead person. They lay a whole lot stiller than live customers. The only thing is that you don't feel like talkin' to them and you get kind of lonesome.

Well, about the coldest day we ever had here, two years ago last winter, the phone rang at the house w'ile I was home to dinner and I answered the phone and it was a woman's voice and she said she was Mrs. John Scott and her husband was dead and would I come out and shave him.

Old John had always been a good customer of mine. But they live seven miles out in the country, on the Streeter road. Still I didn't see how I could say no.

So I said I would be there, but would have to come in a jitney and it might cost three or four dollars besides the price of the shave. So she, or the voice, it said that was all right, so I got Frank Abbot to drive me out to the place and when I got there, who should open the door but old John himself! He wasn't no more dead than, well, than a rabbit.

It didn't take no private detective to figure out who had played me this little joke. Nobody could of thought it up but Jim Kendall. He certainly was a card!

I tell you this incident just to show you how he could disguise his voice and make you believe it was somebody else talkin'. I'd of swore it was Mrs. Scott had called me. Anyways, some woman.

Well, Jim waited till he had Doc Stair's voice down pat; then he went after revenge.

He called Julie up on a night when he knew Doc was over in Carterville. She never questioned but what it was Doc's voice. Jim said he must see her that night; he couldn't wait no longer to tell her somethin'. She was all excited and told him to come to the house. But he said he was expectin' an important long distance call and wouldn't she please forget her manners for once and come to his office. He said they couldn't nothin' hurt her and nobody would see her and he just *must* talk to her a little w'ile. Well, poor Julie fell for it.

Doc always keeps a night light in his office, so it looked to Julie like they was somebody there.

Meanw'ile Jim Kendall had went to Wright's poolroom, where they was a whole gang amusin' themselves. The most of them had drank plenty of gin, and they was a rough bunch even when sober. They was always strong for Jim's jokes and when he told them to come with him and see some fun they give up their card games and pool games and followed along.

Doc's office is on the second floor. Right outside his door they's a flight of stairs leadin' to the floor above. Jim and his gang hid in the dark behind these stairs.

Well, Julie come up to Doc's door and rung the bell and they was nothin' doin'. She rung it seven or eight times. Then she tried the door and found it locked. Then Jim made some kind of a noise and she heard it and waited a minute, and then she says, "Is that you, Ralph?" Ralph is Doc's first name.

They was no answer and it must of come to her all of a sudden that she'd been bunked. She pretty near fell downstairs and the whole gang after her. They chased her all the way home, hollerin', "Is that you, Ralph?" and "Oh Ralphie, dear, is that you?" Jim says he couldn't holler it himself, as he was laughin' too hard.

Poor Julie! She didn't show up here on Main Street for a long, long time afterward.

And of course Jim and his gang told everybody in town, everybody but Doc Stair. They was scared to tell him, and he might of never knowed only for Paul Dickson. The poor cuckoo, as Jim called him, he was here in the shop one night when Jim was still gloatin' yet over what he'd done to Julie. And Paul took in as much of it as he could understand and he run to Doc with the story.

It's a cinch Doc went up in the air and swore he'd make Jim suffer.

But it was a kind of a delicate thing, because if it got out that he had beat Jim up, Julie was bound to hear of it and then she'd know that Doc knew and of course knowin' that he knew would make it worse for her than ever. He was goin' to do somethin', but it took a lot of figurin'.

Well, it was a couple days later when Jim was here in the shop again, and so was the cuckoo. Jim was goin' duck-shootin' the next day and had come in lookin' for Hod Meyers to go with him. I happened to know that Hod had went over to Carterville and wouldn't be home till the end of the week. So Jim said he hated to go alone and he guessed he would call it off. Then poor Paul spoke up and said if Jim would take him he would go along. Jim thought a w'ile and then he said, well, he guessed a half-wit was better than nothin'.

I suppose he was plottin' to get Paul out in the boat and play some joke on him, like pushin' him in the water. Anyways, he said Paul could go. He asked him had he ever shot a duck and Paul said no, he'd never even had a gun in his hands. So Jim said he could set in the boat and watch him and if he behaved himself, he might lend him his gun for a couple of shots. They made a date to meet in the mornin' and that's the last I seen of Jim alive.

Next mornin', I hadn't been open more than ten minutes when Doc Stair come in. He looked kind of nervous. He asked me had I seen Paul Dickson. I said no, but I knew where he was, out duck-shootin' with Jim Kendall. So Doc says that's what he had heard, and he couldn't understand it because Paul had told him he wouldn't never have no more to do with Jim as long as he lived.

He said Paul had told him about the joke Jim had played on Julie. He said Paul had asked him what he thought of the joke and the Doc had told him that anybody that would do a thing like that ought not to be let live.

I said it had been a kind of a raw thing, but Jim just couldn't resist no kind of a joke, no matter how raw. I said I thought he was all right at heart, but just bubblin' over with mischief. Doc turned and walked out.

At noon he got a phone call from old John Scott. The lake where Jim and Paul had went shootin' is on John's place. Paul had come runnin' up to the house a few minutes before and said they'd been an accident. Jim had shot a few ducks and then give the gun to Paul and told him to try his luck. Paul hadn't never handled a gun and he was nervous. He was shakin' so hard that he couldn't control the gun. He let fire and Jim sunk back in the boat, dead.

Doc Stair, bein' the coroner, jumped in Frank Abbot's flivver and rushed out to Scott's farm. Paul and old John was down on the shore of the lake. Paul had rowed the boat to shore, but they'd left the body in it, waitin' for Doc to come.

Doc examined the body and said they might as well fetch it back to town. They was no use leavin' it there or callin' a jury, as it was a plain case of accidental shootin'.

Personally I wouldn't never leave a person shoot a gun in the same boat I was unless I was sure they knew somethin' about guns. Jim was a sucker to leave a new beginner have his gun, let alone a half-wit. It probably served Jim right, what he got. But still we miss him round here. He certainly was a card!

Comb it wet or dry?

ALBERT MALTZ

Man on a Road

AT ABOUT four in the afternoon I crossed the bridge at Gauley,
West Virginia, and turned the sharp curve leading into the tunnel
under the railroad bridge. I had been over this road once before and
knew what to expect — by the time I entered the tunnel I had my
car down to about ten miles an hour. But even at that speed I came
closer to running a man down than I ever have before. This is how
it happened.

The patched macadam road had been soaked through by an all-
day rain and now it was as slick as ice. In addition, it was quite dark
— a black sky and a steady, swishing rain made driving impossible
without headlights. As I entered the tunnel a big cream-colored
truck swung fast around the curve on the other side. The curve was
so sharp that his headlights had given me no warning. The tunnel
was short and narrow, just about passing space for two cars, and before I knew it he was in front of me with his big front wheels over
on my side of the road.

I jammed on my brakes. Even at ten miles an hour my car

194

skidded, first toward the truck and then, as I wrenched on the wheel, in toward the wall. There it stalled. The truck swung around hard, scraped my fender and passed through the tunnel about an inch away from me. I could see the tense face of the young driver with the tight bulge of tobacco in his cheek and his eyes glued on the road. I remember saying to myself that I hoped he'd swallow that tobacco and go choke himself.

I started my car and shifted into first. It was then I saw for the first time that a man was standing in front of my car about a foot away from the inside wheel. It was a shock to see him there. "For Chrissakes," I said.

My first thought was that he had walked into the tunnel after my car had stalled. I was certain he hadn't been in there before. Then I noticed that he was standing profile to me with his hand held up in the hitchhiker's gesture. If he had walked into that tunnel, he'd be facing me — he wouldn't be standing sideways looking at the opposite wall. Obviously I had just missed knocking him down and obviously he didn't know it. He didn't even know I was there.

It made me run weak inside. I had a picture of a man lying crushed under a wheel with me standing over him knowing it was my car.

I called out to him "Hey!" He didn't answer me. I called louder. He didn't even turn his head. He stood there, fixed, his hand up in the air, his thumb jutting out. It scared me. It was like a story by Bierce where the ghost of a man pops out of the air to take up his lonely post on a dark country road.

My horn is a good loud, raucous one and I knew that the tunnel would redouble the sound. I slapped my hand down on that little black button and pressed as hard as I could. That man was either going to jump or else prove that he was a ghost.

Well, he wasn't a ghost — but he didn't jump, either. And it wasn't because he was deaf. He heard that horn all right.

He was like a man in a deep sleep. The horn seemed to awaken him only by degrees, as though his whole consciousness had been sunk in deep recess within himself. He turned his head slowly and looked at me. He was a big man, about thirty-five with a heavy-featured face — an ordinary face with a big fleshy nose and a large mouth. The face didn't say much. I wouldn't have called it kind or brutal or intelligent or stupid. It was just the face of a big man, wet with rain, looking at me with eyes that seemed to have a glaze over them. Except for the eyes you see faces like that going into the pit at six in the morning or coming out of a steel mill or foundry where heavy work is done. I couldn't understand that glazed quality in his eyes. It wasn't the glassy stare of a drunken man or the wild, mad glare I saw once in the eyes of a woman in a fit of violence. I could only think of a man I once knew who had died of cancer. Over his eyes in the last days there was the same dull glaze, a far-away, absent look as though behind the blank outward film there was a secret flow of past events on which his mind was focused. It was this same look that I saw in the man on the road.

When at last he heard my horn, the man stepped very deliberately around the front of my car and came toward the inside door. The least I expected was that he would show surprise at an auto so dangerously close to him. But there was no emotion to him whatsoever. He walked slowly, deliberately, as though he had been expecting me and then bent his head down to see under the top of my car.

"Kin yuh give me a lift, friend?" he asked me.

I saw his big horse teeth chipped at the ends and stained brown by tobacco. His voice was high-pitched and nasal with the slurred, lilting drawl of the Deep South. In West Virginia few of the town-folk seem to speak that way. I judged he had been raised in the mountains.

I looked at his clothes — an old cap, a new blue work shirt and dark trousers, all soaked through with rain. They didn't tell me much.

I must have been occupied with my thoughts about him for some time, because he asked me again.

"Ahm goin' to Weston," he said. "Are you a-goin' thataway?"

As he said this, I looked into his eyes. The glaze had disappeared and now they were just ordinary eyes, brown and moist.

I didn't know what to reply. I didn't really want to take him in — the episode had unnerved me and I wanted to get away from the tunnel and from him too. But I saw him looking at me with a patient, almost humble glance. The rain was streaked on his face and he stood there asking for a ride and waiting in simple concentration for my answer. I was ashamed to tell him "no." Besides, I was curious.

"Climb in," I said.

He sat down beside me, placing a brown paper package on his lap. We started out of the tunnel.

From Gauley to Weston is about a hundred miles of as difficult mountain driving as I know — a five-mile climb to the top of a hill, then five miles down and then up another. The road twists like a snake on the run and for a good deal of it there is a jagged cliff on one side and a drop of a thousand feet or more on the other. The rain and the small rocks crumbling from the mountainsides and littering up the road made it very slow going. But in the four hours or so that it took for the trip, I don't think my companion spoke to me half a dozen times.

I tried often to get him to talk. It was not that he wouldn't talk, it was rather that he didn't seem to hear me — as though as soon as he had spoken, he would slip down into that deep, secret recess within himself. He sat like a man dulled by morphine. My conversation, the rattle of the old car, the steady pour of rain were all a distant buzz — the meaningless outside world that could not quite pierce the shell in which he seemed to be living.

As soon as we had started, I asked him how long he had been in the tunnel.

"Ah don't know," he replied. "A good tahm, ah reckon."

"What were you standing there for — to keep out of the rain?"

He didn't answer. I asked him again, speaking very loudly. He turned his head to me.

"Excuse me, friend," he said, "did you say somethin'?"

"Yes," I answered. "Do you know I almost ran you over back in that tunnel?"

"No-o," he said. He spoke the word in that breathy way that is typical of mountain speech.

"Didn't you hear me yell to you?"

"No-o." He paused. "Ah reckon ah was thinkin'."

Ah reckon you were, I thought to myself.

"What's the matter, are you hard of hearing?" I asked him.

"No-o," he said, and turned his head away looking out front at the road.

I kept right after him. I didn't want him to go off again. I wanted somehow to get him to talk.

"Looking for work?"

"Yessuh."

He seemed to speak with an effort. It was not a difficulty of speech, it was something behind, in his mind, in his will to speak. It was as though he couldn't keep the touch between his world and mine. Yet when he did answer me, he spoke directly and coherently. I didn't know what to make of it. When he first came into the car I had been a little frightened. Now I only felt terribly curious and a little sorry.

"Do you have a trade?" I was glad to come to that question. You know a good deal about a man when you know what line of work he follows and it always leads to further conversation.

"Ah ginerally follows the mines," he said.

Now, I thought, we're getting somewhere.

But just then we hit a stretch of unpaved road where the mud was thick and the ruts were hard to follow. I had to stop talking and watch what I was doing. And when we came to paved road again, I had lost him.

I tried again to make him talk. It was no use. He didn't even hear me. Then, finally, his silence shamed me. He was a man lost somewhere within his own soul, only asking to be left alone. I felt wrong to keep thrusting at his privacy.

So for about four hours we drove in silence. For me those hours were almost unendurable. I have never seen such rigidity in a human being. He sat straight up in the car, his outward eye fixed on the road in front, his inward eye seeing nothing. He didn't know I was in the car, he didn't know he was in the car at all, he didn't feel the rain that kept sloshing in on him through the rent in the side curtains. He sat like a slab of moulded rock and only from his breathing could I be sure that he was alive. His breathing was heavy.

Only once in that long trip did he change his posture. That was when he was seized with a fit of coughing. It was a fierce, hacking cough that shook his big body from side to side and doubled him over like a child with the whooping cough. He was trying to cough something up — I could hear the phlegm in his chest — but he couldn't succeed. Inside him there was an ugly, scraping sound as though cold metal were being rubbed on the bone of his ribs, and he kept spitting and shaking his head.

It took almost three minutes for the fit to subside. Then he turned around to me and said, "Excuse me, friend." That was all. He was quiet again.

I felt awful. There were times when I wanted to stop the car and tell him to get out. I made up a dozen good excuses for cutting the trip short. But I couldn't do it. I was consumed by a curiosity to know what was wrong with the man. I hoped that before we parted, perhaps even as he got out of the car, he would tell me what it was or say something that would give me a clue.

I thought of the cough and wondered if it were T.B. I thought of cases of sleeping sickness I had seen and of a boxer who was punch-drunk. But none of these things seemed to fit. Nothing physical seemed to explain this dark, terrible silence, this intense, all-exclusive absorption within himself.

Hour after hour of rain and darkness!

Once we passed the slate dump of a mine. The rain had made the surface burst into flames and the blue and red patches flickering in a kind of witch glow on a hill of black seemed to attract my companion. He turned his head to look at it, but he didn't speak, and I said nothing.

And again the silence and rain! Occasionally a mine tipple with the cold, drear smoke smell of the dump and the oil lamps in the broken-down shacks where the miners live. Then the black road again and the shapeless bulk of the mountains.

We reached Weston at about eight o'clock. I was tired and chilled and hungry. I stopped in front of a café and turned to the man.

"Ah reckon this is hit," he said.

"Yes," I answered. I was surprised. I had not expected him to know that we have arrived. Then I tried a final plunge. "Will you have a cup of coffee with me?"

"Yes," he replied, "thank you, friend."

The "thank you" told me a lot. I knew from the way he said it that he wanted the coffee, but couldn't pay for it; that he had taken my offer to be one of hospitality and was grateful. I was happy I had asked him.

We went inside. For the first time since I had come upon him in the tunnel, he seemed human. He didn't talk, but he didn't slip inside himself either. He just sat down at the counter and waited for his coffee. When it came, he drank it slowly, holding the cup in both hands as though to warm them.

When he had finished, I asked him if he wouldn't like a sandwich. He turned around to me and smiled. It was a very gentle, a very patient smile. His big, lumpy face seemed to light up with it and become understanding and sweet and gentle.

The smile shook me all through. It didn't warm me — it made me feel sick inside. It was like watching a corpse begin to stir. I wanted to cry out "My God, you poor man!"

Then he spoke to me. His face retained that smile and I could see the big horse teeth stained with tobacco.

"You've bin right nice to me, friend, an' ah do appreciate it."

"That's all right," I mumbled.

He kept looking at me. I knew he was going to say something else and I was afraid of it.

"Would yuh do me a faveh?"

"Yes," I said.

He spoke softly. "Ah've got a letter here that ah done writ to mah woman, but ah can't write very good. Would you-all be kind enough to write it ovah for me so it'd be proper like?"

"Yes," I said, "I'd be glad to."

"Ah kin tell you-all know how to write real well," he said, and smiled.

"Yes."

He opened his blue shirt. Under his thick woolen underwear there was a sheet of paper fastened by a safety pin. He handed it to me. It was moist and warm and the damp odor of wet cloth and the slightly sour odor of his flesh clung to it.

I asked the counterman for a sheet of paper. He brought me one.

This is the letter I copied. I put it down here in his own script.

    My dere wife —
i am awritin this yere leta to tell you somethin i did not tell you
afore i lef frum home. There is a cause to wy i am not able to get
me any job at the mines. i told you hit was frum work abein slack.
But this haint so.
    Hit comes frum the time the mine was shut down an i worked
in the tunel nere Gauley Bridge where the govinment is turnin
the river inside the mounten. The mine supers say they wont hire
any men war worked in thet tunel.
    Hit all comes frum thet rock thet we all had to dril. Thet rock
was silica and hit was most all of hit glass. The powder frum this
glass has got into the lungs of all the men war worked in thet tunel
thru their breathin. And this has given to all of us a sickness. The
doctors writ it down for me. Hit is silicosis. Hit makes the lungs to
git all scab like and then it stops the breathin.
    Bein as our hom is a good peece frum town you aint heerd
about Tom Prescott and Hansy McCulloh having died two days
back. But wen i heerd this i went to see the doctor.
    The doctor say i hev got me that sickness like Tom Prescott and
thet is the reason wy i am coughin sometime. My lungs is agittin
scab like. There is in all ova a hondred men war have this death
sickness frum the tunel. It is a turible plague becus the doctor says
this wud not be so if the company had gave us masks to ware an
put a right fan sistem in the tunel.
    So i am agoin away becus the doctor says i will be dead in about
fore months.
    i figger on gettin some work maybe in other parts. i will send you
all my money till i caint work no mohr.
    i did not want i should be a burdin upon you all at hum. So thet
is wy i hev gone away.
    i think wen you doan here frum me no mohr you orter go to your
grandmaws up in the mountens at Kilney Run. You kin live there
an she will take keer of you and the young one.
    i hope you will be well and keep the young one out of the
mines. Doan let him work there.
    Doan think hard on me for agoin away and doan feel bad. but

wen the young one is agrowed up you tell him wat the company
has done to me.

i reckon after a bit you shud try to git you anotha man. You are
a young woman yit.

Your loving husband
JACK PITCKETT

When I handed him the copy of his letter, he read it over. It took
him a long time. Finally he folded it up and pinned it to his under-
shirt. His big, lumpy face was sweet and gentle. "Thank you,
friend," he said. Then, very softly, with his head hanging a little —
"Ahm feelin' bad about this a-happenin' t'me. Mah wife was a good
woman." He paused. And then, as though talking to himself, so low
I could hardly hear it, "Ahm feelin' right bad."

As he said this, I looked into his face. Slowly the life was going
out of his eyes. It seemed to recede and go deep into the sockets like
the flame of a candle going into the night. Over the eyeballs came
that dull glaze. I had lost him. He sat deep within himself in his
sorrowful, dark absorption.

That was all. We sat together. In me there was only mute emotion — pity and love for him, and a cold, deep hatred for what had
killed him.

Presently he arose. He did not speak. Nor did I. I saw his thick,
broad back in the blue work shirt as he stood by the door. Then he
moved out into the darkness and rain.

J. F. POWERS

Prince of Darkness

I. MORNING

I SHOULD'VE KNOWN you'd be eating breakfast, Father. But I was at your Mass and I said to myself that must be Father Burner. Then I stayed a few minutes after Mass to make my thanksgiving."

"Fine," Father Burner said. "Breakfast?"

"Had it, Father, thanking you all the same. It's the regret of my life that I can't be a daily communicant. Doctor forbids it. 'Fast every day and see how long you last,' he tells me. But I do make it to Mass."

"Fine. You say you live in Father Desmond's parish?"

"Yes, Father. And sometimes I think Father Desmond does too much. All the societies to look after. Plus the Scouts and the Legion. Of course Father Kells being so elderly and all . . ."

"We're all busy these days."

"It's the poor parish priest's day that's never done, I always say, Father, not meaning to slight the ladies, God love 'em."

Father Burner's sausage fingers, spelling his impatience over and over, worked up sweat in the folds of the napkin which he kept in view to provoke an early departure. "About this matter you say Father Desmond thought I might be interested in —"

"The Plan, Father." Mr. Tracy lifted his seersucker trousers by the crease, crossed his shining two-tone shoes and rolled warmly forward. "Father . . ."

Father Burner met his look briefly. He was wary of the fatherers. A backslider he could handle, it was the old story, but a red-hot believer, especially a talkative one, could be a devilish nuisance. This kind might be driven away only by prayer and fasting, and he was not adept at either.

"I guess security's one thing we're all after."

Father Burner grunted. Mr. Tracy was too familiar to suit him. He liked his parishioners to be retiring, dumb or frightened. There were too many references made to the priest's hard lot. Not so many poor souls as all that passed away in the wee hours, nor was there so much bad weather to brave. Mr. Tracy's heart bled for priests. That in itself was a suspicious thing in a layman. It all led up to the Plan.

"Here's the Plan, Father . . ." Father Burner watched his eye peel down to naked intimacy. Then, half listening, he gazed about the room. He hated it too. A fabulous brown rummage of encylopedias, world globes, maps, phonographs, holy pictures, mirrors, crucifixes, tropical fish and too much furniture. The room reproduced the world in exact scale, all wonders and horrors seemingly, less land than water. From the faded precipices of the walls photographs viewed each other for the most part genially across time. Three popes, successively thinner, raised hands to bless their departed painters. The world globes simpered in the shadows, heavy-headed idiot boys, listening. A bird in a blacked-out cage scratched among its offal. An anomalous buddha peeked beyond his dusty umbilicus at the trampled figures in the rug. The fish swam on, the mirrors and encyclopedias turned in upon themselves, the earless boys heard everything and understood nothing. Father Burner put his big black shoe on a moth and sent dust flecks crowding up a shaft of sunlight to the distant ceiling.

"Say you pay in $22.50 every month, can be paid semi-annually or as you please, policy matures in twenty years and pays you $35.67 a month for twenty years or as long as you live. That's the deal for you, Father. It beats the deal Father Desmond's got, although he's got a darned good one, and I hope he keeps it up. But we've gone ahead in the last few years, Father. Utilities are sounder, bonds are more secure and this new legislation protects you one hundred per cent."

"You say Ed — Father Desmond — has the Plan?"

"Oh, indeed, Father." Mr. Tracy had to laugh. "I hope you don't think I'm trying to high-pressure you, Father. It's not just a piece of business with me, the Plan."

"No?"

"No. You see, it's more or less a pet project of mine. Hardly make a cent on it. Looking out after the fathers, you might say, so they'll maybe look out after me — spiritually. I call it heavenly life insurance."

Slightly repelled, Father Burner nodded.

"Not a few priests that I've sold the Plan to remember me at the altar daily. I guess prayer's one thing we can all use. Anyway it's why I take a hand in putting boys through seminary."

With that Mr. Tracy shed his happy anonymity and drew executive markings for Father Burner. He became the one and only Thomas Nash Tracy — T.N.T. It was impossible to read the papers and not know a few things about T.N.T. He was in small loans and insurance. His company's advertising smothered the town and country: everybody knew the slogan T.N.T. spells Security. He figured in any financial drive undertaken by the diocese, was caught by photographers in orphanages and sat at the heavy end of the table at communion breakfasts. Hundreds of nuns, thanks to his thoughtfulness, ate capon on Christmas Day and a few priests of the right sort received baskets of Scotch. He was a B.C.L., a Big Catholic Layman, and now Father Burner could see why. Father Burner's countenance softened at this intelligence and T.N.T. proceeded with more assurance.

"And don't call it charity, Father. Insurance, as I said, is a better name for it. I have a little money, Father, which makes it possible." He tuned his voice down to a whisper. "You might say I'm moderately wealthy." He looked sharply at Father Burner, not sure of his man. "But I'm told there isn't any crime in that."

"I believe you need not fear for your soul on that account."

"Glad to hear it from you, a priest, Father. Oft times it's thrown up to me." He came to terms with reality, smiling. "I wasn't always so well off myself, so I can understand the temptation to knock the other fellow."

"Fine."

"But that's still not to say that water's not wet or that names don't hurt sometimes, whatever the bard said to the contrary."

"What bard?"

" 'Sticks and stones —' "

"Oh."

"If this were a matter of Faith and Morals, Father, I'd be the one to sit back and let you do the talking. But it's a case of common sense, Father, and I think I can safely say if you listen to me you'll not lose by it in the long run."

"It could be."

"May I ask you a personal question, Father?"

Father Burner searched T.N.T.'s face. "Go ahead, Mr. Tracy."

"Do you bank, Father?"

"*Bank?* Oh, bank — no. Why?"

"Let's admit it, Father," T.N.T. coaxed, frankly amused. "Priests as a class are an improvident lot — our records show it — and you're no exception. But that, I think, explains the glory of the Church down through the ages."

"The Church is divine," Father Burner corrected. "And the concept of poverty isn't exactly foreign to Christianity or even to the priesthood."

"Exactly," T.N.T. agreed, pinked. "But think of the future, Father."

Nowadays when Father Burner thought of the future it required a firm act of imagination. As a seminarian twenty years ago, it had all been plain: ordination, roughly ten years as a curate somewhere (he was not the kind to be sent to Rome for further study), a church of his own to follow, the fruitful years, then retirement, pastor emeritus, with assistants doing the spade work, leaving the fine touches to him, still a hearty old man very much alive. It was not an uncommon hope and in fact all around him it had materialized for his friends. But for him it was only a bad memory growing worse. He was the desperate assistant now, the angry functionary aging in the outer office. One day he would wake up and find himself old, as the morning finds itself covered with snow. The future had assumed the forgotten character of a dream, so that he could not be sure that he had ever truly had one.

T.N.T. talked on and Father Burner felt a mist generating on his forehead. He tore his damp hands apart and put the napkin aside. Yes, yes, it was true a priest received miserably little, but then that was the whole idea. He did not comment, dreading T.N.T.'s foaming compassion, to be spat upon with charity. Yes as a matter of fact, it would be easier to face old age with something more to draw upon than what the ecclesiastical authorities deemed sufficient and would provide. Also, as T.N.T. pointed out, one never knew when he might come down with an expensive illness. T.N.T., despite himself, had something. . . . The Plan, in itself, was not bad. He must not reject the olive branch because it came by buzzard. But still Father Burner was a little bothered by the idea of a priest feathering his nest. Why? In other problems he was never the one to take the ascetic interpretation.

"You must be between thirty-five and forty, Father."

"I'll never see forty again."

"I'd never believe it from anyone else. You sure don't look it, Father."

"Maybe not. But I feel it."

"Worries, Father. And one big one is the future, Father. You'll get to be fifty, sixty, seventy — and what have you got? — not a penny saved. You look around and say to yourself — where did it go?"

T.N.T. had the trained voice of the good and faithful servant, supple from many such dealings. And still from time to time a faint draught of contempt seemed to pass through it which had something to do with his eyes. Here, Father Burner thought, was the latest thing in simony, unnecessary, inspired from without, participated in spiritlessly by the priest who must yet suffer the brunt of the blame and ultimately do the penance. Father Burner felt mysteriously purchasable. He was involved in an exchange of confidence which impoverished him mortally. In T.N.T. he sensed free will in its senility or the infinite capacity for equating evil with good — or with nothing, the same thing, only easier. Here was one more word in the history of the worm's progress, another wave on the dry flood that kept rising, the constant aggrandizement of decay. In the end it must touch the world and everything at the heart. Father Burner felt weak from a nameless loss.

"I think I can do us both a service, Father."

"I don't say you can't." Father Burner rose quickly. "I'll have to think about it, Mr. Tracy."

"To be sure, Father." He produced a glossy circular. "Just let me leave this literature with you."

Father Burner, leading him to the door, prevented further talk by reading the circular. It was printed in a churchy type, all purple and gold, a dummy leaf from a medieval hymnal, and entitled, "A Silver Lining in the Sky." It was evidently meant for clergymen only, though not necessarily priests, as Father Burner could instantly see from its general tone.

"Very interesting," he said.

"My business phone is right on the back, Father. But if you'd rather call me at my home some night — "

"No thanks, Mr. Tracy."

"Allow me to repeat, Father, this isn't just business with me."

"I understand." He opened the door too soon for T.N.T. "Glad to have met you."

"Glad to have met you, Father."

Father Burner went back to the table. The coffee needed warming up and the butter had vanished into the toast. "Mary," he called. Then he heard them come gabbing into the rectory, Quinlan and his friend Keefe, also newly ordained.

They were hardly inside the dining room before he was explaining how he came to be eating breakfast so late — so late, see? — not *still.*

"You protest too much, Father," Quinlan said. "The Angelic Doctor himself weighed three hundred pounds and I'll wager he didn't get it all from prayer and fasting."

"A pituitary condition," Keefe interjected, faltering. "Don't you think?"

"Yah, yah, Father, you'll wager" — Father Burner, eyes malignant, leaned on his knife, the blade bowing out bright and buttery beneath his fist — "and I'll wager you'll be the first saint to reach heaven with a flannel mouth!" Rising from the table, he shook Keefe's hand, which was damp from his pocket, and experienced a surge of strength, the fat man's contempt and envy for the thin man. He thought he might break Keefe's hand off at the wrist without drawing a drop of blood.

Quinlan stood aside, six inches or more below them, gazing up, as at two impossibly heroic figures in a hotel mural. Reading the caption under them, he mused, "Father Burner meets Father Keefe."

"I've heard about you, Father," Keefe said, plying him with a warmth beyond his means.

"Bound to be the case in a diocese as overstocked with magpies as this one." Father Burner threw a fresh napkin at a plate. "But be seated, Father Keefe." Keefe, yes, he had seen him before, a nobody in a crowd, some affair . . . the K.C. barbecue, the Youth Center? No, probably not, not Keefe, who was obviously not the type, too crabbed and introversive for Catholic Action. "I suppose," he said, "you've heard the latest definition of Catholic Action — the interference of the laity with the inactivity of the hierarchy."

"Very good," O'Keefe said uneasily.

Quinlan yanked off his collar and churned his neck up and down to get circulation. "Dean in the house? No? Good." He pitched the collar at one of the candles on the buffet for a ringer. "That turkey we met coming out the front door — think I've seen his face somewhere."

"Thomas Nash Tracy," Keefe said. "I thought you knew."

"The prominent lay priest and usurer?"

Keefe coughed. "They say he's done a lot of good."

Quinlan spoke to Father Burner: "Did you take out a policy, Father?"

"One of the sixth-graders threw a rock through his windshield," Father Burner said. "He was very nice about it."

"Muldoon or Ciesniewski?"

"A new kid. Public school transfer." Father Burner patted the napkin to his chin. "Not that I see anything wrong with insurance."

Quinlan laughed. "Let Walter tell you what happened to him a few days ago. Go ahead, Walter," he said to Keefe.

"Oh, that." Keefe fidgeted and seemingly against his better judgment began. "I had a little accident — was it Wednesday it rained so? I had the misfortune to skid into a fellow parked on Fairmount. Dented his fender." Keefe stopped and then, as though impelled by the memory of it, went on. "The fellow came raging out of his car at me. I thought there'd be serious trouble. Then he must have seen I was a priest, the way he calmed down, I mean. I had a funny feeling it wasn't because he was a Catholic or anything like that. As a matter of fact he wore a Masonic button." Keefe laughed. "I guess he saw I was a priest . . . ergo knew I'd have insurance."

"Take nothing for your journey, neither staff, nor scrip," Quinlan said, "words taken from today's gospel."

Father Burner spoke in a level tone: "Not that I *still* see anything wrong with insurance. It's awfully easy," he continued, hating himself for talking such drivel, "to make too much of little things." With Quinlan around he played the conservative; among the real right-handers he was the enfant terrible. He operated on the principle of discord at any cost. He did not know why. It was a habit. Perhaps it had something to do with being overweight.

Arranging the Dean's chair, which had arms, for himself, Quinlan sank into it, giving Keefe the Irish whisper, "Grace, Father."

Keefe addressed the usual words to God concerning the gifts they were about to receive. During the prayer Father Burner stopped chewing and did not reach for anything. He noted once more that Quinlan crossed himself sloppily enough to be a bishop.

Keefe nervously cleared the entire length of his throat. "It's a beautiful church you have here at Saint Patrick's, Father." A lukewarm light appeared in his eyes, flickered, sputtered out, leaving them blank and blue. His endless fingers felt for his receding chin in the onslaught of silence.

"I have?" Father Burner turned his spoon abasingly to his bosom. "*Me?*" He jabbed at the grapefruit before him, his second, demolishing its perfect rose window. "I don't know why it is the Irish without exception are always laying personal claim to church property.

The Dean is forever saying *my* church, *my* school, *my* furnace. . . ."

"I'm sorry, Father." Keefe said, flushing. "And I'll confess I did think he virtually built Saint Patrick's."

"Out of the slime of the earth, I know. A common error." With sudden, unabated displeasure Father Burner recalled how the Dean, one of the last of the old brick-and-mortar pastors, had built the church, school, sisters' house and rectory, and had named the whole thing through the lavish pretense of a popular contest. Opposed bitterly by Polish, German and Italian minorities, he had effected a compromise between their bad taste (Saint Stanislaus, Saint Boniface, Saint Anthony) and his own better judgment in the choice of Saint Patrick's.

Quinlan, snorting, blurted: "Well, he did build it, didn't he?"

Father Burner smiled at them from the other world. "Only, if you please, in a manner of speaking."

"True," Keefe murmured humbly.

"Nuts," Quinlan said. "It's hard for me to see God in a few buildings paid for by the funds of the faithful and put up by a mick contractor. A burning bush, yes."

Father Burner, lips parched to speak an unsummonable cruelty, settled for a smouldering aside to the kitchen. "Mary, more eggs here."

A stuffed moose of a woman with a tabbycat face charged in on swollen feet. She stood wavering in shoes sliced fiercely for corns. With the back of her hand she wiped some cream from the fuzz ringing her baby-pink mouth. Her hair poked through a broken net like stunted antlers. Father Burner pointed to the empty platter.

"Eggs," he said.

"Eggs!" she cried, tumbling her eyes like great blue dice among them. She seized up the platter and carried it whirling with grease into the kitchen.

Father Burner put aside the grapefruit. He smiled and spoke calmly. "I'll have to let the Dean know, Father, how much you like *his* plant."

"Do, Father. A beautiful church . . . 'a poem in stone' — was it Ruskin?"

"Ruskin? Stones of Venice," Father Burner grumbled. "*Sesame and Lilies,* I know ... but I never cared for his *style.*" He passed the knife lovingly over the pancakes on his plate and watched the butter bubble at the pores. "So much sweetness, so much light, I'm afraid, made Jack a dull boy."

Quinlan slapped all his pockets. "Pencil and paper, quick!"

"And yet . . ." Keefe cocked his long head, brow fretted, and complained to his upturned hands. "Don't understand how he stayed outside the Church." He glanced up hopefully. "I wonder if Chesterton gives us a clue."

Father Burner, deaf to such precious speculation, said: "In the nineteenth century Francis Thompson was the only limey worth his salt. It's true." He quartered the pancakes. "Of course, Newman."

"Hopkins has some good things."

"Good — yes, if you like jabberwocky and jebbies! I don't care for either." He dispatched a look of indictment at Quinlan.

"What a pity," Quinlan murmured, "Oliver Wendell couldn't be at table this morning."

"No, Father, you can have your Hopkins, you and Father Quinlan here. Include me out, as Sam Goldwyn says. Poetry, I'll take my poetry the way I take my liquor, neat."

Mary brought in the platter oozing with bacon and eggs.

"Good for you, Mary," Quinlan said. "I'll pray for you."

"Thank you, Father," Mary said.

Quinlan dipped the platter with a trace of obeisance to Father Burner.

"No thanks."

Quinlan scooped up the coffeepot in a fearsome rush and held it high at Father Burner, his arm so atremble the lid rattled dangerously. "Sure and will you be about having a sup of coffee now, Father?"

"Not now. And do you mind not playing the wild Irish wit so early in the day, Father?"

"That I don't. *But a relentless fate pursuing good Father Quinlan, he was thrown in among hardened clerics where but for the grace of God that saintly priest, so little understood so much maligned . . .*" Quinlan poured two cups and passed one to Keefe. "For yourself, Father."

Father Burner nudged the toast to Keefe. "Father Quinlan, that saintly priest, models his life after the Rover Boys, particularly Sam, the fun-loving one."

Quinlan dealt himself a mighty mea culpa.

Father Burner grimaced, the flesh rising in sweet concentric tiers around his mouth, and said in a tone both entrusting and ennobling Keefe with his confidence. "The syrup, if you please, Father." Keefe passed the silver pitcher which was running at the mouth. Father Burner reimmersed the doughy remains on his plate until the butter began to float around the edges as in a moat. He felt them both watching the butter. Regretting that he had not foreseen this attraction, he cast about in his mind for something to divert them and found the morning sun coming in too strongly. He got up and pulled down the shade. He returned to his place and settled himself in such a way that a new chapter was indicated. "Don't believe I know where you're located, Father."

"Saint Jerome's," Keefe said. "Monsignor Fiedler's."

"One of those P.N. places, eh? Is the Boss sorry he ever started it? I know some of them are."

Keefe's lips popped apart. "I don't quite understand."

Quinlan prompted: "P.N. — Perpetual Novena."

"Oh, I never heard him say."

"You wouldn't, of course. But I know a lot of them that are." Father Burner stuck a morsel on his fork and swirled it against the tide of syrup. "It's a real problem all right. I was all out for a P.N. here during the depression. Thought it might help. The Dean was against it."

"I can tell you this," Keefe said. "Attendance was down from what it used to be until the casualties began to come in. Now it's going up."

"I was just going to say the war ought to take the place of the depression." Father Burner fell silent. "Terrible thing, war. Hard to know what to do about it. I tried to sell the Dean the idea of a victory altar. You've seen them. Vigil lights — "

"At a dollar a throw," Quinlan said.

"Vigil lights in the form of a V, names of the men in the service and all that. But even that, I guess — Well, like I said, I tried . . . "

"Yes, it is hard," Keefe said.

"God, the Home and the Flag," Quinlan said. "The poets don't make the wars."

Father Burner ignored that. "Lately, though, I can't say how I feel about P.N.'s. Admit I'm not so strong for them as I was once. Ought to be some way of terminating them, you know, but then they wouldn't be perpetual, would they?"

"No, they wouldn't," Keefe said.

"Of course the term itself, perpetual novena, is preposterous, a solecism. Possibly dispensation lies in that direction, I'm not theologian enough to say. Fortunately it's not a problem we have to decide." He laid his knife and fork across the plate. "Many are the consolations of the lowly curate. No decisions, no money worries."

"We still have to count the sugar," Quinlan said. "And put up the card tables."

"Reminds me," Father Burner said earnestly. "Father Desmond at Assumption was telling me they've got a new machine does all that."

"Puts up card tables?" Quinlan inquired.

"Counts the collection, wraps the silver," Father Burner explained. "so it's all ready for the bank. Mean to mention it to the Dean, if I can catch him right."

"I'm afraid, Father, he knows about it already."

Father Burner regarded Quinlan sceptically. "Does? I suppose he's against it."

"I heard him tell the salesman that's what he had his assistants for."

"Assistant, Father, not assistants. You count the collection, not me. I was only thinking of you."

"I was only quoting him, Father. *Sic.* Sorry."

"Not at all. I haven't forgotten the days I had to do it. It's a job has to be done and nothing to be ashamed of. Wouldn't you say, Father Keefe?"

"I daresay that's true."

Quinlan, with Father Burner still molesting him with his eyes, poured out a glass of water and drank it all. "I still think we would do with a lot less calculating. I notice the only time we get rid of the parish paper is when the new lists are published — the official standings. Of course it's a lousy sheet anyway."

Father Burner, as editor of the paper, replied: "Yes, yes, Father. We all know how easy it is to be wrathful or fastidious about these things — or whatever the hell it is you are. And we all know there *are* abuses. But contributing to the support of the Church is still one of her commandments."

"Peace, Père," Quinlan said.

"Figures don't lie."

"Somebody was telling me just last night that figures do lie. He looked a lot like you."

Father Burner found his cigarettes and shuffled a couple half out of the pack. He eyed Quinlan and the cigarettes as though it were as simple to discipline the one as to smoke the others. "For some reason, Father, you're damned fond of those particular figures."

Keefe stirred. "Which particular figures, Father?"

"It's the figures put out by the Cardinal of Toledo on how many made their Easter duty last year." Father Burner offered Keefe a cigarette. "I discussed the whole thing with Father Quinlan last night. It's the latest thesis. Have a cigarette?"

"No, thanks," Keefe said.

"So you don't smoke?" Father Burner looked from Keefe to Quinlan, blacklisting them together. He held the cigarette hesitantly at his lips. "It's all right, isn't it?" He laughed and touched off the match with his thumbnail.

"His Eminence," Quinlan said, "reports only fifteen per cent of the women and five per cent of the men made their Easter duty last year."

"So that's only three times as many women as men," Father Burner said with buried gaiety. "Certainly to be expected in any Latin country."

"But fifteen per cent, Father! And five per cent! Just think of it!" Keefe glanced up at the ceiling and at the souvenir plates on the moulding, as though to see inscribed along with scenes from the Columbian Exposition the day and hour the end of the world would begin. He finally stared deep into the goldfish tank in the window.

Father Burner ploughed up the silence, talking with a mouthful of smoke. "All right, all right, I'll say what I said in the first place. There's something wrong with the figures. A country as overwhelmingly Catholic as Spain!" He sniffed, pursed his lips, and said: "Pooh!"

"Yes," Keefe said, still balking. "But it *is* disturbing, Father Burner."

"Sure it's disturbing, Father Keefe. *Lots* of things *are.*"

A big faded goldfish paused to stare through the glass at them and then with a single lob of its tail slipped into a dark green corner.

Quinlan said, "Father Burner belongs to the school that's always seeing a great renascence of faith in the offing. The hour before dawn and all that. Tell it to Rotary on Tuesday, Father."

Father Burner countered with a frosty pink smile. "What would I ever do without you, Father? If you're trying to say I'm a dreadful optimist, you're right and I don't mind at all. I am — proud of it!"

Ascending to his feet, he went to the right side of the buffet, took down the card index to parishioners and returned with it to his place. He pushed his dishes aside and began to sort out the deadheads to be called on personally by him or Quinlan. The Dean, like all pastors, he reflected, left the dirty work to the assistants. "Why doesn't he pull them," he snapped, tearing up a card, "when they kick off? Can't very well forward them to the next world. Say, how many Gradys live at 909 South Vine? Here's Anna, Catherine, Clement, Gerald, Harvey, James A., James F. — which James is the one they call Bum?"

"James F.," Quinlan said. "Can't you tell from the take? The other James works."

"John, Margaret, Matthew — that's ten, no eleven. Here's Dennis out of place. Patrick, Rita and William — fourteen of them, no birth control there, and they all give. Except Bum. Nice account otherwise. Can't we find Bum a job? What's it with him, drink?"

Now he came to Maple Street. These cards were the remains of little Father Vicci's work among the magdalens. Ann Mason, Estelle Rogers, May Miller, Billie Starr. The names had the generic ring.

Great givers when they gave — Christmas, $25.00; Easter, $20.00; Propagation of the Faith, $10.00; Catholic University, $10.00 — but not much since Father Vicci was exiled to the sticks. He put Maple Street aside for a thorough sifting.

The doorbell rang. Father Burner leaned around in his chair. "Mary." The doorbell rang again. Father Burner bellowed. "Mary!"

Quinlan pushed his chair away from the table. "I'll get it."

Father Burner blocked him. "Oh, I'll get it! Hell of a bell! Why does he have a bell like that!" Father Burner opened the door to a middle-aged woman whose name he had forgotten or never known. "Good morning," he said. "Will you step in?"

She stayed where she was and said, "Father, it's about the servicemen's flag in church. My son Stanley — you know him — "

Father Burner, who did not know him, half nodded. "Yes, how is Stanley?" He gazed over her shoulder at the lawn, at the dandelions turning into poppies before his eyes.

"You know he was drafted last October, Father, and I been watching that flag you got in church ever since and it's still the same, five hundred thirty-six stars. I thought you said you put a star up for all them that's gone in the service, Father."

Now the poppies were dandelions again. He could afford to be firm with her. "We can't spend all our time putting up stars. Sometimes we fall behind. Besides, a lot of the boys are being discharged."

"You mean there's just as many going in as coming out, so you don't have to change the flag?"

"Something like that."

"I see." He was sorry for her. They had run out of stars. He had tried to get the Dean to order some more, had even offered . . . and the Dean had said they could use up the gold ones first. When Father Burner had objected, telling him what it would mean, he had suggested that Father Burner apply for the curatorship of the armory.

"The Pastor will be glad to explain how it works the next time you see him."

"Well, Father, if that's the way it is . . . " She was fading down the steps. "I just thought I'd ask."

"That's right. There's no harm in asking. How's Stanley?"

"Fine, and thank you, Father, for your trouble."

"No trouble."

When he came back to the table they were talking about the junior clergymen's examinations which they would take for the first time next week. Father Burner interrupted. "The Dean conducts the history end of it, you know."

"I say!" Keefe said. "Any idea what we can expect?"

"You have nothing to fear. Nothing."

"Really?"

"Really. Last year, I remember, there were five questions and the last four depended on the first. So it was really only one question — if you knew it. I imagine you would've." He paused, making Keefe ask for it.

"Perhaps you can recall the question, Father?"

"Perfectly, Father. 'What event in the American history of the Church took place in 1541?' Father Burner, slumping in his chair, smirked at Keefe pondering for likely martyrs and church legislation. He imagined him skipping among the tomes and statuary of his mind, winnowing dates and little-known facts like mad, only at last to emerge dusty and downcast. Father Burner sat up with a jerk and assaulted the table with the flat of his hand. "Time's up. Answer: 'De Soto sailed up the Mississippi.'"

Quinlan snorted. Keefe sat very still, incredulous, silent, utterly unable to digest the answer, finally croaking, "How odd." Father Burner saw in him the boy whose marks in school had always been a consolation to his parents.

"So you don't have to worry, Father. No sense in preparing for it. Take in a couple of movies instead. And cheer up! The Dean's been examining the junior clergy for twenty-five years and nobody ever passed history yet. You wouldn't want to be the first one."

Father Burner said grace and made the sign of the cross with slow distinction. "And, Father," he said, standing, extending his hand to Keefe, who also rose, "I'm glad to have met you." He withdrew his hand before Keefe was through with it and stood against the table knocking toast crumbs onto his plate. "Ever play any golf? No? Well, come and see us for conversation then. You don't have anything against talking, do you?"

"Well, of course, Father, I . . . "

Father Burner gave Keefe's arm a rousing clutch. "Do that!"

"I will, Father. It's been a pleasure."

"Speaking of pleasure," Father Burner said, tossing Quinlan a stack of cards, "I've picked out a few lost sheep for you to see on Maple Street, Father."

II. NOON

He hung his best black trousers on a hanger in the closet and took down another pair, also black. He tossed them out behind him and they fell patched at the cuffs and baggy across his unmade bed. His old suede jacket, following, slid dumpily to the floor. He stood gaping in his clerical vest and undershorts, knees knocking and pimply, thinking . . . what else? His aviator's helmet. He felt all the hooks blindly in the darkness. It was not there. "Oh, hell!" he groaned, sinking to his knees. He pawed among the old shoes and boxes and wrapping paper and string that he was always going to need. Under his golf bag he found it. So Mary had cleaned yesterday.

There was also a golf ball unknown to him, a Royal Bomber, with one small hickey in it. Father Desmond, he remembered, had received a box of Royal Bombers from a thoughtful parishioner. He stuck the helmet on his balding head to get it out of the way and took the putter from the bag. He dropped the ball at the door of the closet. Taking his own eccentric stance — a perversion of what the pro recommended and a dozen books on the subject — he putted the ball across the room at a dirty collar lying against the bookcase. A thready place in the carpet caused the ball to jump the collar and to loose a pamphlet from the top of the bookcase. He restored the pamphlet — Pius XI on "Atheistic Communism" — and poked the ball back to the door of the closet. Then, allowing for the carpet, he drove the ball straight, *click,* through the collar, *clop.* Still had his old putting eye. And his irons had always been steady if not exactly crashing. It was his woods, the tee shots, that ruined his game. He'd give a lot to be able to hit his woods properly, not to dub his drives, if only on the first tee — where there was always a crowd (mixed).

At one time or another he had played every hole at the country club in par or less. Put all those pars and birdies together, adding in the only two eagles he'd ever had, and you had the winning round in the state open, write-ups and action shots in the papers — photo shows Rev, Ernest "Boomer" Burner, jar-shattering padre, blasting out of a trap. He needed only practice perhaps and at his earliest opportunity he would entice some of the eighth-grade boys over into the park to shag balls. He sank one more for good measure, winning a buck from Ed Desmond who would have bet against it, and put the club away.

Crossing the room for his trousers he noticed himself in the mirror with the helmet on and got a mild surprise. He scratched a little hair down from underneath the helmet to offset the egg effect. He searched his eyes in the mirror for a sign of ill health. He walked away from the mirror, as though done with it, only to wheel sharply so as to see himself as others saw him, front and profile, not wanting to catch his eye, just to see himself. . . .

Out of the top drawer of the dresser he drew a clean white silk handkerchief and wiped the shine from his nose. He chased his eyes over into the corner of the mirror and saw nothing. Then, succumbing to his original intention, he knotted the handkerchief at the crown of the helmet and completed the transformation of time and place and person by humming, vibrato, "Jeannine, I dream of lilac time," remembering the old movie. He saw himself over his shoulder in the mirror a sad war ace. It reminded him that his name was not Burner, but Boerner, an impediment removed at the outset of the first world war by his father. In a way he resented the old man for it. They had laughed at the seminary; the war, except as theory, hardly entered there. In perverse homage to the old Boerner, to which he now affixed a proud "von," he dropped the fair-minded American look he had and faced the mirror sneering, scar-cheeked and black of heart, the flying Junker who might have been. "Himmelkreuzdonnerwetter! When you hear the word 'culture,'" he snarled, hearing it in German, "reach for your revolver!"

Reluctantly he pulled on his black trousers, falling across the bed to do so, as though felled, legs heaving up like howitzers.

He lay still for a moment, panting, and then let the innerspring mattress bounce him to his feet, a fighter coming off the ropes. He stood looking out the window, buckling his belt, and then down at the buckle, chins kneading softly with the effort, and was pleased to see that he was holding his own on the belt, still a good half inch away from last winter's highwater mark.

At the sound of high heels approaching on the front walk below, he turned firmly away from the window and considered for the first time since he posted it on the wall the prayer for priests sent him by a candle concern. "Remember, O most compassionate God, that they are but weak and frail human beings. Stir up in them the grace of their vocation which is in them by the imposition of the Bishop's hands. Keep them close to Thee, lest the enemy prevail against them, so that they may never do anything in the slightest degree unworthy of their sublime . . . " His eyes raced through the prayer and out the window. . . .

He was suddenly inspired to write another letter to the Archbishop. He sat down at his desk, slipped a piece of paper into his portable, dated it with the saint's day it was, and wrote, "Your Excellency: Thinking my letter of some months ago may have gone amiss, or perhaps due to the press of business —" He ripped the paper from the portable and typed the same thing on a fresh sheet until he came to "business," using instead " "affairs of the church." He went on to signify — it was considered all right to "signify," but to resignify? — that he was still of the humble opinion that he needed a change of location and had decided, since he believed himself ready for a parish of his own, a rural one might be best, all things considered (by which he meant easier to get). He, unlike some priests of urban upbringing and experience, would have no objection to the country. He begged to be graced with an early reply. That line, for all its seeming docility, was full of dynamite and ought to break the episcopal silence into which the first letter had dissolved. This was a much stronger job. He thought it better for two reasons: the Archbishop was supposed to like outspoken people, or, that being only more propaganda talked up by the sycophants, then it ought to bring a reply which would reveal once and for all his prospects. Long overdue for the routine promotion, he had a just cause. He addressed the letter and placed it in his coat. He went to the bathroom. When he came back he put on the coat, picked up the suede jacket and helmet, looked around for something he might have forgot, a book of chances, a box of Sunday envelopes to be delivered, some copy for the printer, but there was nothing. He lit a cigarette at the door and not caring to throw the match on the floor or look for the ashtray, which was out of sight again, he dropped it in the empty holy water font.

Downstairs he paused at the telephone in the hall, scribbled "Airport" on the message pad, thought of crossing it out or tearing off the page, but since it was dated he let it stand and added "Visiting the sick," signing his initials, E.B.

He went through the wicker basket for mail. A card from the Book-of-the-Month Club. So it was going to be another war book selection this month. Well, they knew what they could do with it. He wished the Club would wake up and select some dandies, as they had in the past. He thought of *Studs Lonigan* — there was a book, the best thing since the Bible.

An oblique curve in the road: perfect, wheels parallel with the center line. So many drivers took a curve like that way over on the other fellow's side. Father Burner touched the lighter on the dashboard to his cigarette and plunged his hams deeper into the cushions. A cloud of smoke whirled about the little Saint Christopher garroted from the ceiling. Father Burner tugged viciously at both knees, loosening the binding black cloth, easing the seat. Now that he was in open country he wanted to enjoy the scenery — God's majesty. How about a sermon that would liken the things in the landscape to the people in a church? All different, all the same handiwork of God. Moral: it is right and meet for rocks to be rocks, trees to be trees, pigs to be pigs, but — and here the small gesture that says so much — what did that mean that men, created in the image and likeness of God, should be? And what — He thrust the sermon out of mind, tired of it. He relaxed, as before an open fireplace, the weight of dogma off his shoulders. Then he grabbed at his knees again, cursing. Did the tailor skimp on the cloth because of the ecclesiastical discount?

A billboard inquired — "Pimples?" Yes, he had a few, but he blamed them on the climate, the humidity. Awfully hard for a priest to transfer out of a diocese. He remembered the plan he had never gone through with. Would it work after all? Would another doctor recommend a change? Why? He would only want to know why, like the last bastard. Just a slight case of obesity, Reverend. Knew he was a non-Catholic when he said Reverend. Couldn't trust a Catholic one. Some of them were thicker than thieves with the clergy. Wouldn't want to be known as a malingerer, along with everything else.

Another billboard — "Need Cash? See T.N.T."

Rain. He knew it. No flying for him today. One more day between him and a pilot's license. Thirteen hours yet and it might have been twelve. Raining so, and with no flying, the world seemed to him . . . a valley of tears. He would drive on past the airport for a hamburger. If he had known, he would have brought along one of the eighth-grade boys. They were always bragging among themselves about how many he had bought them, keeping score. One of them, the Cannon kid, had got too serious from the hamburgers When he said he was "contemplating the priesthood!" Father Burner, wanting to spare him the terrible thing a false vocation could be, had told him to take up aviation instead. He could not forget the boy's reply: *But couldn't I be a priest like you, Father?*

On the other hand, he was glad to be out driving alone. Never had got the bang out of playing with the kids a priest in this country was supposed to. The failure of the Tom Playfair tradition. He hated most sports. Ed Desmond was a sight at a ball game. Running up and down base lines, giving the umpires hell, busting all the buttons off his cassock. Assumption rectory smelled like a locker room from all the equipment. Poor Ed.

The rain drummed on the engine hood. The windshield wiper sliced back and forth, reminding him a little of a guillotine. Yes, if he had to, he would die for the Faith.

From here to the hamburger place it was asphalt and slicker than concrete. Careful. Slick. Asphalt. Remembered . . . Quinlan coming into his room one afternoon last winter when it was snowing, the idiot, prating:

> *Here were decent godless people:*
> *Their only monument the asphalt road*
> *And a thousand lost golf balls . . .*

That was Quinlan for you, always spouting against the status quo without having anything better to offer. Told him that. Told him golfers, funny as it might seem to some people, have souls and who's to save them? John Bosco worked wonders in taverns, which was not to say Father Burner thought he was a saint, but rather only that he was not too proud to meet souls halfway wherever it might be, in the confessional or on the fairways. Saint Ernest Burner, Help of Golfers, Pray for Us! (Quinlan's came back.) Quinlan gave him a pain. Keefe, now that he knew what he was like, ditto. Non-smokers, Jansenists. First fervor is false fervor. They would cool. He would not judge them, however.

He slowed down and executed a sweeping turn into the parking lot reserved for patrons of the hamburger. He honked his horn his way, three shorts and a long — victory. She would see his car or know his honk and bring out two hamburgers, medium well, onions, pickle, relish, tomato, catsup, his way.

She came out now, carrying an umbrella, holding it ostensibly more over the hamburgers than herself. He took the tray from her. She waited dumbly, her eyes at a level with his collar.

"What's to drink?"

"We got pop, milk, coffee . . . " Here she faltered, as he knew she would, washing her hands of what recurrent revelation, rather than experience, told her was to follow.

"A nice cold bottle of beer." Delivered of the fatal words, Father Burner bit into the smoking hamburger. The woman turned sorrowfully away. He put her down again for native Protestant stock.

When she returned, sheltering the bottle under the umbrella, Father Burner had to smile at her not letting pious scruples interfere with business, another fruit of the so-called Reformation. Watch that smile, he warned himself, or she'll take it for carnal. He received the bottle from her hands. For all his familiarity with the type, he was uneasy. Her lowered eyes informed him of his guilt.

Was he immoderate? Who on earth could say? *In dubiis libertas,* not? He recalled his first church supper at Saint Patrick's, a mother bringing her child to the Dean's table. She's going to be confirmed next month, Monsignor. Indeed? Then tell me, young lady, what are the seven capital sins? Pride, Covetousness . . . Lust, Anger. Uh. The child's mother, one of those Irish females built like a robin, worried to death, lips silently forming the other sins for her daughter. Go ahead, dear. Envy. Proceed, child. Yes, Monsignor. Oh . . . Sloth.

To be sure. That's six. One more. And . . . uh. Fear of the Lord, perhaps? Meekness? Hey, Monsignor, ain't them the Divine Counsels! The Dean, smiling, looking at Father Burner's plate, covered with chicken bones, at his stomach, fighting his vest, and for a second into the child's eyes, slipping her the seventh sin. *Gluttony,* Monsignor! The Dean gave her a coin for her trouble. She stood awkwardly in front of Father Burner, lingering, twisting her gaze from his plate to his stomach, to his eyes, finally quacking, Oh Fawther!

Now he began to brood upon his failure as a priest. There was no sense in applying the consolations of an anchorite to himself. He wanted to know one thing: when would he get a pastorate? When would he make the great metamorphosis from assistant to pastor, from mouse to rat, as the saying went? He was forty-three, four times transferred, seventeen years an ordained priest, a curate yet and only. He was the only one of his class still without a parish. The only one . . . and in his pocket, three days unopened, was another letter from his mother, kept waiting all these years, who was to have been his housekeeper. He could not bear to warm up her expectations again.

Be a chaplain? That would take him away from it all and there was the possibility of meeting a remote and glorious death carrying the Holy Eucharist to a dying soldier. It would take something like that to make him come out even, but then that too, he knew in a corner of his heart, would be only exterior justification for him, a last bid for public approbation, a short cut to nothing. And the chaplain's job, it was whispered, could be an ordeal both ignominious and tragic. It would be just his luck to draw an assignment in the rehabilitation center, racking pool balls and repairing ping-pong bats for the boys — the apostolic game-room attendant and toastmaster. Sure, Sarge, I'll lay you even money the Sox make it three straight in Philly and spot you a run a game to boot. You win, I lose a carton of Chesters — I win, you go to Mass every day for a week! Hard-headed holiness. . . .

There was the painful matter of the appointment to Saint Patrick's. The Dean, an irremovable pastor, and the Archbishop had argued over funds and the cemetery association. And the Archbishop, losing though he won, took his revenge, it was rumored, by appointing

Father Burner as the Dean's assistant. It was their second encounter. In the first days of his succession, the Archbishop heard that the Dean always said a green Mass on Saint Patrick's Day, thus setting the rubrics at nought. Furious, he summoned the Dean into his presence, but stymied by the total strangeness of him and his great age, he had talked of something else. The Dean took a different view of his narrow escape, which is what the chancery office gossips called it, and now every year, on repeating the error, he would say to the uneasy man, "Sure and nobody ever crashed the gates of hell for the wearing of the green." (Otherwise it was not often he did something to delight the hearts of the professional Irish.)

In the Dean's presence Father Burner often had the sensation of confusion, a feeling that someone besides them stood listening in the room. To free himself he would say things he neither meant nor believed. The Dean would take the other side and then . . . there they were again. The Dean's position in these bouts was roughly that of the old saints famous for their faculty of smelling sins and Father Burner played the rôle of the one smelled. It was no contest. If the Archbishop could find no words for the Dean there was nothing he might do. He might continue to peck away at a few stray foibles behind the Dean's back. He might point out how familiar the Dean was with the Protestant clergy about town. He did. It suited his occasional orthodoxy (reserved mostly to confound his critics and other much worse, like Quinlan, whom he suspected of having him under observation for humorous purposes) to disapprove of all such questionable ties, as though the Dean were entertaining heresy or at least felt kindly toward this new "interfaith" nonsense so dear to the reformed Jews and freshwater sects. It was very small game, however. And the merest brush with the Dean might bring any one of a hundred embarrassing occasions back to life, and it was easy for him to burn all over again.

When he got his dark room rigged up in the rectory the Dean had come snooping around and inquired without staying for an answer if the making of tintypes demanded that a man shun the light to the extent Father Burner appeared to. Now and again, hearkening back to this episode, the Dean referred to him as the Prince of Darkness. It did not end there. The title caught on all over the diocese. It was not the only one he had.

In reviewing a new historical work for a national Catholic magazine, he had attempted to get back at two Jesuits he knew in town,
calling attention to certain tendencies — he meant nothing so gross
as "order pride" — which, if not necessarily characteristic of any
religious congregation within the Church, were still too often to be
seen in any long view of history (which the book at hand did not
pretend to take), and whereas the secular clergy, *per se,* had much
to answer for, was it not true, though certainly not through any
superior virtue, nor even as a consequence of their secularity — indeed he would be a fool to dream that such orders as those founded,
for instance, by Saint Benedict, Saint Francis and Saint Dominic
(Saint Ignatius was not instanced) were without their place in the
heart of the Church, even today, when perhaps . . .

Anyway "secular" turned up once as "circular" in the review. The
local Jesuits, writing in to the magazine as a group of innocent by-
standers, made many subtle plays upon the unfortunate "circular"
and its possible application to the person of the reviewer (they explained, enabled them to indulge in such conceivably dangerous
whimsy). But the direction of his utterances, they thought, seemed
clear, and they regretted more than they could say that the editors of
an otherwise distinguished journal had found space for them, especially in wartime, or perhaps they did not rightly comprehend the
course — was it something new? — set upon by the editors and if
so . . .

So Father Burner was also known as "the circular priest" and he
had not reviewed anything since for that magazine.

The mark of the true priest was heavy on the Dean. The mark was
on Quinlan, it was on Keefe. It was on every priest he could think
of, including a few on the bum and his good friend and bad companion Father Desmond. But it was not on him, not properly. They,
the others, were stained with it beyond all disguise or disfigurement
— indelibly, as indeed Holy Orders by its sacramental nature must
stain, for keeps in this world and the one to come. "Thou are a priest
forever." With him, however, it was something else and less, a mask
or badge which he could and did remove at will, a temporal part
to be played, almost only a doctor's or lawyer's. They, the others,
would be lost in any persecution. The mark would doom them. But
he, if that *dies irae* ever came — and it was every plump seminarian's

apple-cheeked dream — could pass as the most harmless and useful of humans, a mailman, a bus rider, a husband. But would he? No. They would see. I, he would say, appearing unsought before the judging rabble, am a priest, of the order of Melchisedech. Take me. I am ready. *Deo gratias.*

Father Burner got out the money to pay and honked his horn. The woman, coming for the bottle and tray, took his money without acknowledging the tip. She stood aside, the bottle held gingerly between offended fingers, final illustration of her lambishness, and watched him drive away. Father Burner, applying a cloven foot to the pedal, gave it the gas. He sensed the woman hoping in her simple heart to see him wreck the car and meet instant death in an unpostponed act of God.

Under the steadying influence of his stomach thrust against the wheel, the car proceeded while he searched himself for a cigarette. He passed a hitchhiker, saw him fade out of view in the mirror overhead, gesticulate wetly in the distance. Was the son of a gun thumbing his nose? Anti-clericalism. But pray that your flight be not in the winter . . . No, wrong text; he would not run away.

The road skirted a tourist village. He wondered who stayed in those places and seemed to remember a story in one of the religion scandal sheets . . . ILLICIT LOVE in steaming red type.

A billboard cried out, "Get in the scrap and — get in the scrap!" Some of this advertising, he thought, was pretty slick. Put out probably by big New York and Chicago agencies with crack men on their staffs, fellows who had studied at *Time.* How would it be to write advertising? He knew a few things about layout and type faces from editing the parish paper. He had read somewhere about the best men of our time being in advertising, the air corps of business. There was room for better taste in the Catholic magazines, for someone with a name in the secular field to step in and drive out the money-changers with their trusses, corn cures, non-tangle rosary beads and crosses that glow in the dark. It was a thought.

Coming into the city limits, he glanced at his watch, but neglected to notice the time. The new gold strap got his eye. The watch itself, a priceless pyx, held the hour (time is money) sacred, like a host.

He had chosen it for an ordination gift rather than the usual chalice. It took the kind of courage he had to go against the grain there.

"I'm a dirty stinker!" Father Desmond flung his arms out hard against the mattress. His fists opened on the sheet, hungry for the spikes, meek and ready. "I'm a dirty stinker, Ernest!"

Father Burner, seated deep in a red leather chair at the sick man's bedside, crossed his legs forcefully. "Now don't take on so, Father."

"Don't call me 'Father'!" Father Desmond's eyes fluttered open momentarily, but closed again on the reality of it all. "I don't deserve it. I'm a disgrace to the priesthood! I am not worthy. Lord, Lord, I am not worthy!"

A nurse entered and stuck a thermometer in Father Desmond's mouth.

Father Burner smiled at the nurse. He lit a cigarette and wondered if she understood. The chart probably bore the diagnosis "pneumonia," but if she had been a nurse very long she would know all about that. She released Father Desmond's wrist and recorded his pulse on her pad. She took the thermometer and left the room.

Father Desmond surged up in bed and flopped, turning with a wrench of the covers, on his stomach. He lay gasping like a fish out of water. Father Burner could smell it on his breath yet.

"Do you want to go to confession?"

"No! I'm not ready for it. I want to remember this time!"

"Oh, all right." It was funny, if a little tiresome, the way the Irish could exaggerate a situation. They all had access to the same two or three emotions. They all played the same battered barrel organ handed down through generations. Dying, fighting, talking, drinking, praying . . . wakes, wars, politics, pubs, church. The fates were decimated and hamstrung among them. They loved monotony.

Father Desmond, doing the poor soul uttering his last words in italics, said: "We make too good a thing out of confession, Ernest! Ever think of that, Ernest?" He wagged a nicotined finger. Some of his self-contempt seemed to overshoot its mark and include Father Burner.

Father Burner honked his lips — plutt! "Hire a hall, Ed." Father Desmond clawed a rosary out from under his pillow.

Father Burner left.

He put the car in the garage. On the way to his room he passed voices in the Dean's office.

"Father Burner!" the Dean called through the door.

Father Burner stayed in the hallway, only peeping in, indicating numerous commitments elsewhere. Quinlan and Keefe were with the Dean.

"Apparently, Father, you failed to kill yourself." Then, for Keefe, the Dean said: "Father Burner fulfils the dream of the American hierarchy and the principle of historical localization. He's been up in his flying machine all morning."

"I didn't go up." Sullenness came and went in his voice. "It rained." He shuffled one foot, about to leave, when the Dean's left eyebrow wriggled up, warning, holding him.

"I don't believe you've had the pleasure." The Dean gave Keefe to Father Burner. "Father Keefe, sir, went through school with Father Quinlan — from the grades through the priesthood." The Dean described an arc with his breviary, dripping with ribbons, to show the passing years. Father Burner nodded.

"Well?" The Dean frowned at Father Burner. "Has the cat got your tongue, sir? Why don't you be about greeting Father O'Keefe — or Keefe is it?"

"Keefe," Keefe said.

Father Burner, caught in the old amber of his inadequacy, stepped over and shook Keefe's hand once.

Quinlan stood by and let the drama play itself out.

Keefe, smiling a curious mixture more anxiety than amusement, said: "It's a pleasure, Father."

"Same here," Father Burner said.

"Well, good day, sirs!" The Dean cracked open his breviary and began to read, lips twitching.

Father Burner waited for them in the hall. Before he could explain that he thought too much of the Dean not to humor him and that besides the old fool was out of his head, the Dean proclaimed after them: "The Chancery phoned, Father Burner. You will hear confessions there tonight. I suppose one of those Cathedral jokers lost his faculties."

Yes, Father Burner knew, it was common procedure all right for the Archbishop to confer promotions by private interview, but every time a priest got called to the Cathedral it did not mean simply that. Many received sermons and it was most likely now someone was needed to hear confessions. And still Father Burner, feeling his pocket, was glad he had not remembered to mail the letter. He would not bother to speak to Quinlan and Keefe now.

III. NIGHT

"And for your penance say five Our Fathers and five Hail Marys and pray for my intention. And now make a good act of contrition. *Misereatur tui omnipotens Deus dimissis peccatis tuis . . .* " Father Burner swept out into the current of the prayer, stroking strongly in Latin, while the penitent, a miserable boy coming into puberty, paddled as fast as he could along the shore in English.

Finishing first, Father Burner waited for the boy to conclude. When, breathless, he did, Father Burner anointed the air and shot a whisper, "God bless you," kicking the window shut with the heel of his hand, ejecting the boy, an ear of corn, shucked clean, into the world again. There was nobody on the other side of the confessional, so Father Burner turned on the signal light. A spider drowsy in his web, drugged with heat and sins, he sat waiting for the next one to be hurled into his presence by guilt ruddy ripe, as with the boy, or, as with the old ladies who come early and stay late, by the spiritual famine of their lives or simply the desire to tell secrets in the dark.

He held his wrist in such a way as to see the sweat gleaming in the hairs. He looked at his watch. He had been at it since seven and now it was after nine. If there were no more kneeling in his section of the Cathedral at nine-thirty he could close up and have a cigarette. He was too weary to read his Office, though he had the Little Hours, Vespers and Compline still to go. It was the last minutes in the confessional that got him — the insensible end of the excursion that begins with so many sinewy sensations and good intentions to look sharp at the landscape. In the last minutes how many priests, would-be surgeons of the soul, ended as blacksmiths, hammering out absolution anyway?

A few of the Cathedral familiars still drifted around the floor. They were day and night in the shadows praying. Meeting one of them, Father Burner always wanted to get away. They were collectors of priests' blessings in a day when most priests felt ashamed to raise their hands to God outside the ceremonies. Their respect for a priest was fanatic, that of the unworldly, the martyrs, for an emissary of heaven. They were so desperately disposed to death that the manner of dying was their greatest concern. But Father Burner had an idea there were more dull pretenders than saints among them. They inspired no unearthly feelings in him, as true sanctity was supposed to, and he felt it was all right not to like them. They spoke of God, the Blessed Virgin, of miracles, cures and visitations, as of people and items in the news, which was annoying. The Cathedral, because of its location, described by brokers as exclusive, was not so much frequented by these wretches as it would have been if more convenient to the slums. But nevertheless a few came there, like the diarrheic pigeons, also a scandal to the neighborhood, and would not go away. Father Burner, from his glancing contact with them, had concluded that body odor is the real odor of sanctity.

Through the grating now Father Burner saw the young Vicar General stop a little distance up the aisle and speak to a couple of people who were possible prospects for Father Burner. "Anyone desiring to go to confession should do so at once. In a few minutes the priests will be gone from the confessionals." He crossed to the other side of the Cathedral.

Father Burner did not like to compare his career with the Vicar General's. The Archbishop had taken the Vicar General, a younger man than Father Burner by at least fifteen years, direct from the seminary. After a period of trial as Chancellor, he was raised to his present eminence — for reasons much pondered by the clergy and more difficult to discern than those obviously accounted for by intelligence, appearance and, post facto, the loyalty consequent upon his selection over many older and possibly abler men. It was a medieval act of preference, a slap in the face to the monsignori, a rebuke to the principle of advancement by years applied elsewhere. The Vicar General had the quality of inscrutability in an ideal measure. He did not seem at all given to gossip or conspiracy or even to that owlish secrecy peculiar to secretaries and so exasperating to others. He had possibly no enemies and certainly no intimates. In time he would be a bishop unless, as was breathed wherever the Cloth gathered over food and drink, he really was "troubled with sanctity," which might lead to anything else, the cloister or insanity.

The Vicar General appeared at the door of Father Burner's compartment. "The Archbishop will see you, Father, before you leave tonight." He went up the aisle, genuflected before the main altar, opened as a gate one of the host of brass angels surrounding the sanctuary, and entered the sacristies.

Before he would let hope have its way with him, Father Burner sought to recast the expression on the Vicar General's face. He could recall nothing significant. Very probably there had been nothing to see. Then, with a rush, he permitted himself to think this was his lucky day. Already he was formulating the way he would let the news out, providing he decided not to keep it a secret for a time. He might do that. It would be delicious to go about his business until the very last minute, to savour the old aggravations and feel none of the sting, to receive the old quips and smiles with good grace and know them to be toothless. The news, once out, would fly through the diocese. Hear about Burner at Saint Pat's, Tom? Finally landed himself a parish. Yeah, I just had it from McKenna. So I guess the A.B. wasn't so sore at the Round One after all. Well, he's just ornery enough to make a go of it.

Father Burner, earlier in the evening, had smoked a cigarette with one of the younger priests attached to the Cathedral (a classmate of Quinlan's but not half the prig), stalling, hoping someone would come and say the Archbishop wanted to see him. When nothing happened except the usual small talk and introductions to a couple of missionaries stopping over, he had given up hope easily. He had seen the basis for his expectations as folly once more. It did not bother him after the fact was certain. He was amenable to any kind of finality. He had a light heart for a . . . an American of German descent. And his hopes rose higher each time with less cause. He was a ball that bounced up only. He had kept faith. And now — his just reward.

A little surprised he had not thought of her first, he admitted his mother into the new order of things. He wanted to open the letter from her, still in his coat, and late as it was send her a wire, which would do her more good than a night's sleep. He thought of himself back in her kitchen, home from the sem for the holidays, a bruiser in a tight black suit, his feet heavy on the oven door. She was fussing at the stove and he was promising her a porcelain one as big as a house after he got his parish. But he let her know, kidding on the square, that he would be running things at the rectory. It would not be the old story of the priest taking orders from his housekeeper, even if she was his mother (seminarians, from winter evenings of shooting the bull, knew only too well the pitfalls of parish life), or as with Ed Desmond a few years ago when his father was still living with him, the old man losing his marbles one by one, butting in when people came for advice and instructions, finally coming to believe he was the one to say Mass in his son's absence, no need to get a strange priest in, and sneaking into the box to hear confessions the day before they took him away.

He would be gentle with his mother, however, even if she talked too much, as he recalled she did the last time he saw her. She was well preserved and strong for her age and ought to be able to keep the house up. Once involved in the social life of the parish she could be a valuable agent in coping with any lay opposition, which was too often the case when a new priest took over.

He resolved to show no nervousness before the Archbishop. A trifle surprised, yes — the Archbishop must have his due — but not overly affected by good fortune. If questioned, he would display a lot of easy confidence not unaccompanied by a touch of humility, a phrase or two like "God willing," or "with the help of Almighty God and your prayers, Your Excellency." He would also not forget to look the part, reliable, casual, cool, an iceberg, only the tip of his true worth showing.

At precisely nine-thirty Father Burner picked up his breviary and backed out of the stall. But then there was the scuff of a foot and the tap of one of the confessional doors closing and then, to tell him the last penitent was a woman, the scent of apple blossoms. He turned off the light, saying Damn! to himself, and sat down again inside. He threw back the partition and led off, "Yes?" He placed his hand alongside his head and listened, looking down into the deeper darkness of his cassock sleeve.

"I . . ."

"Yes?" At the heart of the apple blossoms another scent bloomed: gin and vermouth.

"Bless me, Father, I . . . have sinned."

Father Burner knew this kind. They would always wait until the last moment. How they managed to get themselves into church at all, and then into the confessional, was a mystery. Sometimes liquor thawed them out. This one was evidently young, nubile. He had a feeling it was going to be adultery. He guessed it was — and up to him to get her underway.

"How long since your last confession?"

"I don't know . . . "

"Have you been away from the Church?"

"Yes."

"Are you married?"

"Yes."

"To a Catholic?"

"No."

"Protestant?"

"No."

"Jew?"

"No."

"Atheist?"

"No — nothing."

"Were you married by a priest?"

"Yes."

"How long ago was that?"

"Four years."

"Any children?"

"No."

"Practice birth control?"

"Yes, sometimes."

"Don't you know it's a crime against nature and the Church forbids it?"

"Yes."

"Don't you know that France fell because of birth control?"

"No."

"Well, it did. Was it your husband's fault?"

"You mean — the birth control?"

"Yes."

"Not wholly."

"And you've been away from the Church ever since your marriage?"

"Yes."

"Now you see why the Church is against mixed marriages. All right, go on. What else?"

"I don't know . . . "

"Is that what you came to confess?"

"No. Yes. I'm sorry, I'm afraid that's all."

"Do you have a problem?"

"I think that's all Father."

"Remember, it is your obligation, and not mine, to examine your conscience. The task of instructing persons with regard to these delicate matters — I refer to the connubial relationship — is not an easy one. Nevertheless, since there is a grave obligation imposed by God, it cannot be shirked.. If you have a problem — "

"I don't have a *problem.*"

"Remember, God never commands what is impossible and so if you make use of the sacraments regularly you have every reason to be confident that you will be able to overcome this evil successfully, with His help. I hope this is all clear to you."

"All clear."

"Then if you are heartily sorry for your sins for your penance say the rosary daily for one week and remember it is the law of the Church that you attend Mass on Sundays and holy days and receive the sacraments at least once a year. It's better to receive them often. Ask your pastor about birth control if it's still not clear to you. Or read a Catholic book on the subject. And now make a good act of contrition . . . "

Father Burner climbed the three flights of narrow stairs. He waited a moment in silence, catching his breath. He knocked on the door and was suddenly afraid its density prevented him from being heard and that he might be found standing there like a fool or a spy. But to knock again, if heard the first time, would seem importunate.

"Come in, Father."

At the other end of the long study the Archbishop sat behind an ebony desk. Father Burner waited before him as though expecting not to be asked to sit down. The only light in the room, a lamp on the desk, was so set that it kept the Archbishop's face in the dark, fell with a gentle sparkle upon his pectoral cross and was absorbed all around by the fabric of the piped cloth he wore. Father Burner's eyes came to rest upon the Archbishop's freckled hand, ringed, square and healthy.

"Be seated, Father."

"Thank you, Your Excellency."

"Oh, sit in this chair, Father." There were two chairs. Father Burner changed to the soft one. He had a suspicion that in choosing the other one he had fallen into a silly trap, that it was a game the Archbishop played with his visitors: the innocent ones, seeing no issue, would take the soft chair, because handier; the guilty would go a step out of their way to take the hard one. "I called Saint Patrick's this morning, Father, but you were . . . out."

"I was visiting Father Desmond, Your Excellency."

"Father Desmond . . . "

"He's in the hospital."

"I know. Friend of his, are you, Father?"

"No, Your Excellency. Well" — Father Burner waited for the cock to crow the third time — "yes, I *know* the man." At once he regretted the scriptural complexion of the words and wondered if it were possible for the Archbishop not to be thinking of the earlier betrayal.

"It was good of you to visit Father Desmond, especially since you are not close to him. I hope he is better, Father."

"He is, Your Excellency."

The Archbishop got up and went across the room to a cabinet. "Will you have a little glass of wine, Father?"

"No. No, thanks, Your Excellency." Immediately he realized it could be another trap and, if so, he was caught again.

"Then I'll have a drop . . . *solus*." The Archbishop poured a glass and brought it back to the desk. "A little wine for the stomach's sake, Father."

Father Burner, not sure what he was expected to say to that, nodded gravely and said, "Yes, Your Excellency." He had seen that the Archbishop wore carpet slippers and that they had holes in both toes.

"But perhaps you've read Saint Bernard, Father, and recall where he says we priests remember well enough the apostolic counsel to use wine, but overlook the adjective 'little.' "

"I must confess I haven't read Saint Bernard lately, Your Excellency." Father Burner believed this was somehow in his favor. "Since seminary, in fact."

"Not all priests, Father, have need of him. A hard saint . . . for hardened sinners. What is your estimate of Saint Paul?"

Father Burner felt familiar ground under his feet at last. There were the Pauline and Petrine factions — a futile business, he thought — but he knew where the Archbishop stood and exclaimed: "One of the greatest — "

"Really! So many young men today consider him . . . a bore. It's always the deep-breathing ones, I notice. They say he cuts it too fine."

"I've never thought so, Your Excellency."

"Indeed? Well, it's a question I like to ask my priests. Perhaps you knew that."

"No, I didn't, Your Excellency."

"So much the better then . . . but I see you appraising the melodeon, Father. Are you musical?'

"Not at all, Your Excellency. Violin lessons as a child." Father Burner laughed quickly, as though it were nothing.

"But you didn't go on with them?"

"No, Your Excellency." He did not mean it to sound as sad as it came out.

"What a pity."

"No great loss, Your Excellency."

"You are too . . . modest, Father. But perhaps the violin was not your instrument."

"I guess it wasn't, Your Excellency." Father Burner laughed out too loud.

"And you have the choir at Saint Patrick's, Father?"

"Not this year, Your Excellency. Father Quinlan has it."

"Now I recall . . . "

"Yes." So far as he was concerned, and there were plenty of others who thought so too, Quinlan had played hell with the choir, canning all the women, some of them members for fifteen and twenty years, a couple even longer and practically living for it, and none of them as bad as Quinlan said. The liturgical stuff that Quinlan tried to pull off was all right in monasteries, where they had the time to train for it, but in a parish it sounded stodgy to ears used to the radio and split up the activity along sexual lines, which was really old hat in the modern world. The Dean liked it though. He called it "honest" and eulogized the men from the pulpit — not a sign that he heard how they brayed and whinnied and just gave out or failed to start — and each time it happened ladies in the congregation were sick and upset for days afterward, for he inevitably ended by attacking women, pants, cocktails, communism, cigarettes and running around half naked. The women looked at the men in the choir, all pretty in surplices, and said to themselves they knew plenty about some of them and what they had done to some women.

"He's tried a little Gregorian, hasn't he — Father Quinlan?"

"Yes, Your Excellency," Father Burner said. "He has."

"Would you say it's been a success — or perhaps I should ask you first if you care for Gregorian, Father."

"Oh, yes, Your Excellency. Very much."

"Many, I know, don't . . . I've been told our chant sounds like a wild bull in a red barn of consumptives coughing into a bottle, but I will have it in the Cathedral, Father. Other places, I am aware, have done well with . . . light opera."

Father Burner frowned.

"We are told the people prefer and understand it. But at the risk of seeming reactionary, a fate my office prevents me from escaping in any event, I say we spend more time listening to the voice of the people than is good for either it or us. We have been too generous with our ears, Father. We have handed over our tongues also. When they are restored to us I wonder if we shall not find our ears more itching than before and our tongues more tied than ever."

Father Burner nodded in the affirmative.

"We are now entering the whale's tail, Father. We must go back the way we came in." The Archbishop lifted the lid of the humidor on the desk. "Will you smoke, Father?"

"No, thanks, Your Excellency."

The Archbishop let the lid drop. "Today there are few saints, fewer sinners and everybody is already saved. We are all heroes in search of an underdog. As for villains, the classic kind with no illusions about themselves, they are . . . extinct. The very devil, for instance, where the devil is the devil today, Father?"

Father Burner, as the Archbishop continued to look at him, bit his lips for the answer, secretly injured that he should be expected to know, bewildered even as the children he toyed with in catechism.

The Archbishop smiled, but Father Burner was not sure at what, whether at him or what had been said. "Did you see, Father, where our brother Bishop Buckles said Hitler remains the one power on earth against the Church?"

Yes, Father Burner remembered seeing it in the paper; it was the sort of thing that kept Quinlan talking for days. "I did, Your Excellency."

"Alas, poor Buckles! He's a better croquet player than that." The Archbishop's hands unclasped suddenly and fell upon his memo pad. He tore off about a week and seemed to feel better for it. His hands, with no hint of violence about them now, came together again. "We look hard to the right and left, Father. It is rather to the center, I think, we should look, to ourselves, the devil in us."

Father Burner knew the cue for humility when he heard it. "Yes, Your Excellency."

With his chubby fingers the Archbishop made a steeple that was more like a dome. His eyes were reading the memo. "For instance, Father, I sometimes appear at banquets — when they can't line up a good foreign correspondent — banquets at which the poor are never present and at which I am unfailingly confronted by someone exceedingly well off who is moved to inform me that 'religion' is a great consolation to him. Opium, rather, I always think, perhaps wrongfully and borrowing a word from one of our late competitors, which is most imprudent of me, a bishop."

The Archbishop opened a drawer and drew out a sheet of paper and an envelope. "Yes, the rich have souls," he said softly, answering an imaginary objection which happened to be Father Burner's.

"But if they had Christ they would not be themselves, that is to say, rich."

"Very true, Your Excellency," Father Burner said.

The Archbishop faced sideways to use an old typewriter. "And likewise, lest we forget, we would not be ourselves, that is to say — what? For we square the circle beautifully in almost every country on earth. We bring neither peace nor a sword. The rich give us money. We give them consolation and make of the eye of the needle a gate. Together we try to reduce the Church, the Bride of Christ, to a streetwalker." The Archbishop rattled the paper, Father Burner's future, into place and rolled it crookedly into the typewriter. "Unfortunately for us, it doesn't end there. The penance will not be shared so equitably. Your Christian name, Father, is — ?"

"Ernest, Your Excellency."

The Archbishop typed several words and stopped, looking over at Father Burner. "I can't call to mind a single Saint Ernest, Father. Can you help me?"

"There were two, I believe, Your Excellency, but Butler leaves them out of his *Lives*."

"They would be German saints, Father?'

"Yes, Your Excellency. There was one an abbot and the other an archbishop."

"If Butler had been Irish, as the name has come to indicate, I'd say that's an Irishman for you, Father. He does not forget to include a power of Irish saints." The Archbishop was Irish himself. Father Burner begged to differ with him, believing here was a wrong deliberately set up for him to right. "I am not Irish myself, Your Excellency, but some of my best friends are."

"Tut, tut, Father. Such tolerance will be the death of you." The Archbishop, typing a few words, removed the paper, signed it and placed it in the envelope. He got up and took down a book from the shelves. He flipped it open, glanced through several pages and returned it to its place. "No Ernests in Baring-Gould either. Well, Father, it looks as if you have a clear field."

The Archbishop came from behind the desk and Father Burner, knowing the interview was over, rose. The Archbishop handed him the envelope. Father Burner stuffed it hastily in his pocket and knelt, the really important thing, to kiss the Archbishop's ring and receive his blessing. They walked together toward the door.

"Do you care for pictures, Father?"

"Oh, yes, Your Excellency."

The Archbishop, touching him lightly on the arm, stopped before a reproduction of Raphael's Sistine Madonna. "There is a good peasant woman, Father, and a nice fat baby." Father Burner nodded his appreciation. "She could be Our Blessed Mother, Father, though I doubt it. There is no question about the baby. He is not Christ." The Archbishop moved to another picture. "Rembrandt had the right idea, Father. See the gentleman pushing Christ up on the cross? That is Rembrandt, a self portrait." Father Burner thought of some of the stories about the Archbishop, that he slept on a cot, stood in line with people sometimes to go to confession, that he fasted on alternate days the year round. Father Burner was thankful for such men as the Archbishop. "But here is Christ, Father." This time it was a glassy-eyed Christ whose head lay against the rough wood of the cross he was carrying. "That is Christ, Father. The Greek painted Our Saviour."

The Archbishop opened the door for Father Burner, saying, "And, Father, you will please not open the envelope until after your Mass tomorrow."

Father Burner went swiftly down the stairs. Before he got into his car he looked up at the Cathedral. He could scarcely see the cross glowing on the dome. It seemed as far away as the stars. The cross needed a brighter light or the dome ought to be painted gold and lit up like the state capital, so people would see it. He drove a couple of blocks down the street, pulled up to the curb, opened the envelope, which had not been sealed, and read: "You will report on August 8 to the Reverend Michael Furlong, to begin your duties on that day as his assistant. I trust that in your new appointment you will find not peace but a sword."

WILLIAM SAROYAN

Resurrection of a Life

Everything begins with inhale and exhale, and never ends, moment after moment, yourself inhaling, and exhaling, seeing, hearing, smelling, touching, tasting, moving, sleeping, waking, day after day and year after year, until it is now, this moment, the moment of your being, the last moment, which is saddest and most glorious. It is because we remember, and I remember myself having lived among dead moments, now deathless because of my remembrance, among people now dead, having been a part of the flux which is now only a remembrance, of myself and this earth, a street I was crossing and the people I saw walking in the opposite direction, automobiles going away from me. Saxons, Dorts, Maxwells, and the streetcars and trains, the horses and wagons, and myself, a small boy, crossing a street, alive somehow, going somewhere.

First he sold newspapers. It was because he wanted to do something, he himself, standing in the city, shouting about what was happening in the world. He used to shout so loud, and he used to need to shout so much, that he would forget he was supposed to be selling papers; he would get the idea that he was only supposed to shout, to make people understand what was going on. He used to go through the city like an alley cat, prowling all over the place, into saloons, upstairs into whore houses, into gambling joints, to see: their faces the faces of those who were alive with him on earth, and the expressions of their faces, and their forms, the faces of old whores, and the way they talked, and the smell of all the ugly places, and the drabness of all the old and rotting buildings, all of it, of his time and his life, a part of him. He prowled through the city, seeing and smelling, talking, shouting about the big news, inhaling and exhaling, blood moving to the rhythm of the sea, coming and going, to the shore of self and back again to selflessness, inhale and newness, exhale and new death, and the boy in the city, walking through it like an alley cat, shouting headlines.

It was all ugly, but his being there was splendid and not an ugliness. His hands would be black with the filth of the city and his face would be black with it, but it was splendid, himself alive and walking, of the events of the earth, from day to day, new headlines every day, new things happening.

In the summer it would be very hot and his body would thirst for the sweet fluids of melons, and he would long for the shade of thick leaves and the coolness of a quiet stream, but always he would be in the city, shouting. It was his place and he was the guy, and he wanted the city to be the way it was, if that was the way. He would figure it out somehow. He used to stare at the rich people sitting at tables in hightone restaurants eating dishes of ice cream, electric fans making breezes for them, and he used to watch them ignoring the city, not going out to it and being of it, and it used to make him mad. Pigs, he used to say, having everything you want, having everything. What do you know of this place? What do you know of me, seeing this place with a clean eye, any of you? And he used to go, in the summer, to the Crystal Bar, and there he would study the fat man who slept in a chair all summer, a mountain of somebody, a man with a face and substance that lived, who slept all day every summer day, dreaming what? This fat man, three hundred pounds? What did he dream, sitting in the saloon, in the corner, not playing poker or pinochle like the other men, only sleeping and sometimes brushing the flies from his fat face? What was there for him to dream, anyway, with a body like that, and what was hidden beneath the fat of that body, what grace or gracelessness? He used to go into the saloon and spit on the floor like the men did and secretly watch the fat man sleeping, trying to figure it out. Him alive, too? he used to ask. That great big sleeping thing alive? Like myself?

In the winter he wouldn't see the fat man. It would be only in the summer. The fat man was like the hot sun, very near everything, of everything, sleeping, flies on his big nose. In the winter it would be cold and there would be much rain. The rain would fall over him and his clothes would be wet, but he would never get out of the rain, and he would go on prowling around in the city, looking for whatever it was that was there and that nobody else was trying to see, and he would go in and out of all the ugly places to see how it was with the faces of the people when it rained, how the rain changed the expressions of their faces. His body would be wet with the rain, but he would go from one place to another, shouting headlines, telling the city about the things that were going on in the world.

I was this boy and he is dead now, but he will be prowling through the city when my body no longer makes a shadow upon the pavement, and if it is not this boy it will be another, myself again, another boy alive on earth, seeking the essential truth of the scene, seeking the static and precise beneath that which is in motion and which is imprecise.

The theatre stood in the city like another universe, and he entered its darkness, seeking there in the falsity of pictures of man in motion the truth of his own city, and of himself, and the truth of all living. He saw their eyes: *While London Sleeps.* He saw the thin emaciated hand of theft twitching toward crime: Jean Valjean. In the darkness the false universe unfolded itself before him and he say the phantoms of man going and coming, making quiet horrifying shadows: *The Cabinet of Dr. Caligari.* He saw the endless sea, smashing against rocks, birds flying, the great prairie and herds of horses, New York and greater mobs of men, monstrous trains, rolling ships, men marching to war, and a line of infantry charging another line of infantry: *The Birth of a Nation.* And sitting in the secrecy of the theatre he entered the houses of the rich, saw them, the male and the female, the high ceilings, the huge marble pillars, the fancy furniture, great bathrooms, tables loaded with food, rich people laughing and eating and drinking, and then secrecy again and a male seeking a female, and himself watching carefully to understand, one pursuing and the other fleeing, and he felt the lust of man mounting in him, desire for the loveliest of them, the universal lady of the firm white shoulders and the thick round thighs, desire for her, he himself, ten years old, in the darkness.

He is dead and deathless, staring at the magnification of the kiss, straining at the mad embrace of male and female, walking alone from the theatre, insane with the passion to live. And at school he could not bear them. Their shallowness was too much. Don't try to teach me. That was his attitude. Teach the idiots. Don't try to tell me anything. I am getting it direct, straight from the pit, the ugliness with the loveliness. Two times two is many million people all over the earth, lonely and shivering, groaning one at a time, trying to figure it out. Don't try to teach me. I'll figure it out for myself.

Daniel Boone? he said. Don't tell me. I knew him. Walking through Kentucky. He killed a bear. Lincoln? A big fellow walking alone, looking at things as if he pitied them, a face like the face of man. The whole countryside full of dead men, men he loved, and he himself alive. Don't ask me to memorize his speech. I know all about it, the way he stood, the way the words came from his being.

He used to get up before daybreak and walk to The San Joaquin Baking Company. It was good, the smell of freshly baked bread, and it was good to see the machine wrapping the loaves in wax paper. Chicken bread, he used to say, and the important man in the fine suit of clothes used to smile at him. The important man used to say, What kind of chickens you got at your house, kid? And the man would smile nicely so that there would be no insult, and he would never have to tell the man that he himself and his brother and sisters were eating the chicken bread. He would just stand by the bin, not saying anything, not asking for the best loaves, and the important man would understand, and he would pick out the best of the loaves and drop them into the sack the boy held open. If the man happened to drop a bad loaf into the sack the boy would say nothing, and a moment later the man would pick out the bad loaf and throw it back into the bin. Those chickens, he would say, they might not like that loaf. And the boy would say nothing. He would just smile. It was good bread, not too stale and sometimes very fresh, sometimes still warm, only it was bread that had fallen from the wrapping machine and couldn't be sold to rich people. It was made of the same dough, in the same ovens, only after the loaves fell they were called chicken bread and a whole sack full cost only a quarter. The important man never insulted. Maybe he himself had known hunger once, maybe as a boy he had known how it felt to be hungry for bread. He was very funny, always asking about the chickens. He knew there were no chickens, and he always picked out the best loaves.

Bread to eat, so that he could move through the city and shout. Bread to make him solid, to nourish his anger, to fill his substance with vigor that shouted at the earth. Bread to carry him to death and back again to life, inhaling, exhaling, keeping the inward flame alive. Chicken bread, he used to say, not feeling ashamed. We eat it. Sure, sure. It isn't good enough for the rich. There are many at our house. We eat every bit of it, all the crumbs. We do not mind a little dirt on the crust. We put all of it inside. A sack of chicken bread. We know we're poor. When the wind comes up our house shakes, but we don't tremble. We can eat the bread that isn't good enough for the rich. Throw in the loaves. It is too good for chickens. It is our life. Sure we eat it. We're not ashamed. We're living on the money we earn selling newspapers. The roof of our house leaks and we catch the water in pans, but we are all there, all of us alive, and the floor of our house sags when we walk over it, and it is full of crickets and spiders, but we are in the house, living there. We eat this bread that isn't good enough for the rich, this bread that you call chicken bread.

Walking, this boy vanished, and now it is myself, another, no longer the boy, and the moment is now this moment, of my remembrance. The fig tree he loved: of all graceful things it was the most graceful, and in the winter it stood leafless, dancing, sculptural whiteness dancing. In the spring the new leaves appeared on the fig tree and the hard green figs. The sun came closer and closer and the heat increased, and he climbed the tree, eating the soft fat figs, the flowering of the lovely white woman, his lips kissing.

But always he returned to the city, back again to the place of man, the street, the structure, the door and window, the hall, the roof and floor, back again to the corners of dark secrecy, where they were dribbling out their lives, back again to the movement of mobs, to beds and chairs and stoves, away from the tree, away from the meadow and the brook. The tree was of the other earth, the older and lovelier earth, solid and quiet and of godly grace, of earth and water and sky, and of the time that was before, ancient places, quietly in the sun, Rome and Athens and Cairo, the white fig tree dancing. He talked to the tree, his mouth clenched, pulling himself over its smooth sensuous limbs, to be of you, he said, to be of your time, to be there, in the old world, and to be here as well, to eat your fruit, to feel your strength, to move with you as you dance, myself, alone in the world, with you only, my tree, that in myself which is of thee.

Dead, dead, the tree and the boy, and yet everlastingly alive, the white tree moving slowly in dance, and the boy talking to it in unspoken, unspeakable language: you, loveliness of the earth, the street waits for me, the moment of my time calls me back, and there he was suddenly, running through the streets, shouting that ten thousand huns had been destroyed. Huns? he asked. What do you mean, huns? They are men, aren't they? And he saw the people of the city smiling and talking with pleasure about the good news. He himself appreciated the goodness of the news because it helped him sell his papers, but after the shouting was over and he was himself again, he used to think of ten thousand men smashed from life to violent death, one man at a time, each man himself as he, the boy, was himself, bleeding, screaming, weeping, remembering life as dying men remember it, wanting it, gasping for breath, to go on inhaling and exhaling, living and dying, by always living somehow, stunned horrified, ten thousand faces suddenly amazed at the monstrousness of the war, the beastliness of man, who could be so godly.

There were no words with which to articulate his rage. All that he could do was shout: but even now I cannot see the war as historians see it. Succeeding moments have carried the germ of myself to this face and form, the one of this moment, now, my being in this small room, alone, as always, remembering the boy, resurrecting him, and I cannot see the war as historians see it. Those clever fellows study all the facts and they see the war as a large thing, one of the biggest events in the legend of man, something general, involving multitudes. I see it as a large thing too, only I break it into small units of one at a time, and I see it as a large and monstrous thing for each man involved. I see the war as death in one form or another for men dressed as soldiers, and all the men who survived the war, including myself, I see as men who died with their brothers, dressed as soldiers.

There is no such thing as a soldier. I see death as a private event, the destruction of the universe in the brain and in the senses of one man, and I cannot see any man's death as a contributing factor in the success or failure of a military campaign. The boy had to shout what had happened. Whatever happened, he had to shout it, making the city know. *Ten thousand huns killed, ten thousand,* one at a time, one, two, three, four, inestimably many, ten thousand, alive, and then dead, killed, shot, mangled, ten thousand huns, ten thousand men. I blame the historians for the distortion. I remember the coming of the gas mask to the face of man, the proper grimace of horror for the nightmare we were performing, artfully expressing the monstrousness of the inward face of man, the most pertinent truth that emerged from the whole affair. To the boy who is dead this war was the international epilepsy in the body and soul of man which brought about the systematic destruction of one man at a time until millions of men were destroyed.

There he is suddenly in the street, running, and it is 1917, shouting the most recent crime of man, extra, extra, ten thousand huns killed, himself alive, inhaling, exhaling, *ten thousand, ten thousand,* all the ugly buildings solid, all the streets solid, the city unmoved by the crime, *ten thousand,* windows opening, doors opening, and the people of the city smiling about it, good, good, ten thousand, ten thousand of them killed, good, good. Johnny, get your gun, and another trainload of boys in uniform, going away, torn from home, from the roots of life, their tragic smiling, and the broken hearts, all things in the world broken. And the fat man, sleeping in a corner of the Crystal Bar, what of him? Sleeping there, somehow alive in spite of the lewd death in him, but never budging. Pig, he said, ten thousand huns killed, ten thousand men with solid bodies mangled to death. Does it mean nothing to you? Does it not disturb your fat dream? Boys with loves, men with wives and children. What have you, sleeping? They are all dead, all of them dead. Do you think you are alive? Do you dream you are alive? The fly on your nose is more alive than you.

Sunday would come, *O day of rest and gladness, O day of joy and light, O balm of care and sadness. Most beautiful, most bright,* and he would put on his best shirt and his best trousers, and he would try to comb his hair down, to be neat and clean, meeting God, and he would go to the small church and sit in the shadow of religion: in the beginning, the boy David felling the giant Goliath, beautiful Rebecca, mad Saul, Daniel among lions, Jesus talking quietly to the men, and in the boat shouting at them because they feared, angry at them because they had fear, calm yourselves, boys, calm yourselves, let the storm rage, let the boat sink, do you fear going to God? Ah that was lovely, that love of death was lovely, Jesus loving it: calm yourselves, boys, God damn you, calm yourselves, why are you afraid? *Still, still with thee, when purple morning breaketh, abide, abide, with me, fast falls the eventide,* ah lovely. He sat in the basement of the church, among his fellows, singing at the top of his voice. I do not believe, he said. I cannot believe. There cannot be a God. *Saviour, breathe an evening blessing, sun of my soul, begin, my tongue, some heavenly theme, begin, my tongue, begin, begin.* Lovely, lovely, but I cannot believe. The poor and the rich, those who deserve life and those who deserve death, and the ugliness everywhere. Where is God? Big ships sinking at sea, submarines, men in the water, cannon booming, machine guns, men dying, ten thousand, where? But our singing, *Joy to the world, the Lord is come. Let earth receive her King. Silent night, holy night. What grace, O Lord, my dear redeemer. Ride on, ride on, in majesty. Angels, roll the rock away; death, yield up thy mighty prey.*

No, he could not believe. He had seen for himself. It was there, in the city, all the godlessness, the eyes of the whores, the men at cards, the sleeping fat man, and the mad headlines, it was all there, unbelief, ungodliness, everywhere, all the world forgetting. How could he believe? But the music, so good and clean, so much of the best in man: *lift up, lift up your voices now. Lo, he comes with clouds descending once for favored sinners slain. Arise, my soul, arise, shake off thy guilty fears, O for a thousand tongues to sing. Like a river glorious, holy Bible, book divine, precious treasure, thou art mine.* And spat, right on the floor of the Crystal Bar. And into Collette's Rooms, over The Rex Drug Store, the men buttoning their clothes, ten thousand huns killed, madam. *Break thou the bread of life, dear Lord, to me, as thou didst break the loaves, beside the sea.* And spat, on the floor, watching the fat man snoring. Another ship sunk. The Marne. Ypres. Russia. Poland. Spat. *Art thou weary, art thou languid, art thou sore distressed?* Zeppelin over Paris. The fat man sleeping. *Haste, traveler, haste, the night comes on.* Spat. *The storm is gathering in the west.* Cannon. Hutt! two three, four! Hutt! two three, four, how many men marching, how many? Onward, onward, unChristian soldiers. *I was a wandering sheep.* Spat. *I did not love my home.* Your deal, Jim. Spat. *Take me, O my father, take me.* Collette, I adore you, ugly whore. Spat. *This holy bread, this holy wine. My God, is an hour so sweet?* Submarine plunging. Spat. *Take my life and let it be consecrated, Lord, to Thee.* Spat.

He sat in the basement of the little church, deep in the shadow of faith, and of no faith: I cannot believe, it is too monstrous: where is the God of whom they speak, where? *Your harps, ye trembling saints, down from the willows take.* Where? Cannon. *Lead, oh lead, lead kindly light, amid the encircling gloom.* Spat. *Jesus, Saviour, pilot me.* Airplane: spat: smash. *Guide me, O thou great Jehovah. Bread of heaven, bread of heaven, feed me till I want no more.* The universal lady of the dark theatre: thy lips, beloved, thy shoulders and thighs, thy sea-surging blood. The tree, black figs in sunlight. Spat. *Rock of ages, cleft for me, let me hide myself in thee.* Spat. *Let the water and the blood, from thy riven side which flowed, be of sin and double cure.* Lady your arm, your arm: spat. The mountain of flesh sleeping through the summer. Ten thousand huns killed.

Sunday would come, turning him from the outward world to the inward, to the secrecy of the past, endless as the future, back to Jesus, to God; *when the weary, seeking rest, to thy goodness flee;* back to the earliest quiet: *He leadeth me, O blessed thought.* But he did not believe. He could not believe. Jesus was a remarkable fellow: you couldn't figure him out. He had a sort of pious love of death. An heroic fellow. And as for God. Well, he could not believe.

But the songs he loved and he sang them with all his might: *hold thou my hand, O blessed nothingness. I walk with thee. Awake, my soul, stretch every nerve, and press with vigor on. Work, for the night is coming, work, for the day is done.* Spat. Right on the floor of the Crystal Bar. It is Sunday again: O blessed nothingness, we worship thee. Spat. And suddenly the sleeping fat man sneezes. Hallelujah. Amen. Spat. Sleep on, beloved, sleep, and take thy rest. (Pig, he said.) *Lay down thy head upon thy Saviour's breast.* We love thee well, but Jesus loves thee best. Jesus loves thee. For the Bible tells you so. Amen. The fat man sneezes. He could not believe and he could not disbelieve. Sense? There was none. But glory. There was an abundance of it. Everywhere. Madly everywhere. Those crazy birds vomiting song. Those vast trees, solid and quiet. And clouds. And sun. And night. And day. *It is not death to die,* he sang: *to leave this weary road, to be at home with God.* God? The same. Nothingness. Nowhere. Everywhere. The crazy glory, everywhere: Madam Collette's Rooms, all modern conveniences, including beds. Spat. *I know not, Oh I know not, what joys await us there.* Where? Heaven? No. Madam Collette's: In the church, the house of God, with such thoughts: the boy singing, remembering the city's lust.

Boom: Sunday morning: and the war still booming: after the singing he would go to the newspaper office and get his SPECIAL SUNDAY EXTRAS and run through the city with them, his hair combed for God, and he would shout the news: amen, *I gave my life for Jesus.* Oh yeah? Ten thousand huns killed, and I am the guy, inhaling, exhaling, running through the town, I myself, seeing, hearing, touching, shouting, smelling, singing, wanting, I, the guy, the latest of the whole lot, alive by the grace of God: ten thousand, two times ten million, by the grace of God dead, by His grace smashed, amen, extra, extra: five cents a copy, extra, ten thousand killed.

I was this boy who is now lost and buried in the succeeding forms of myself, and I am now of this last moment, of this small room, and the night hush, time going, time coming, and gone, and gone, and again coming, and myself here, breathing, this last moment, inhale, exhale, the boy dead and alive. All that I have learned is that we breathe, from moment to moment, now, always now, and then we remember, and we see the boy moving through a city that has become lost, among people who have become dead, alive among dead moments, crossing a street, the scene thus, or standing by the bread bin in the bakery, a sack of chicken bread please so that we can live and shout about it, and it begins nowhere and it ends nowhere, and all that I know is that we are somehow alive, all of us in the light, making shadows, the sun overhead, space all around us, inhaling, exhaling, the face and form of man everywhere, pleasure and pain, sanity and madness, over and over again, war and no war, and peace and no peace, the earth solid and unaware of us, unware of our cities, our dreams, unaware of this love I have for life, the love that was the boy's, unaware of all things, my going, my coming, the earth everlastingly itself, not of me, everlastingly precise, and the sea sullen with movement like my breathing, waves pounding the shore of myself, coming and going, and all that I know is that I am alive and glad to be, glad to be of this ugliness and this glory, somehow glad that I can remember, somehow remember the boy climbing the fig tree, unpraying but religious with joy, somehow of the earth, of the time of the earth, somehow everlastingly of life, nothingness, blessed or unblessed, somehow deathless like myself, timeless, glad, insanely glad to be here, and so it is true, there is no death, somehow there is no death, and can never be.

IRWIN SHAW

Search Through the Streets
of the City

W HEN HE FINALLY saw her he nearly failed to recognize
her. He walked behind her for a half-block, vaguely noticing that
the woman in front of him had long legs and was wearing a loose,
college-girlish linen coat and a plain brown felt hat. Suddenly something about the way she walked made him remember — the almost
affected rigidity of her back and straightness of throat and head, with
all the movement of walking flowing up to the hips and stopping
there, like Negro women in the South and Mexican and Spanish
women carrying baskets on their heads.

For a moment he watched her walk along Twelfth Street, on the
sunny side of the street, in front of the little tired gardens behind
which lay the quiet, pleasantly run-down old houses. Then he caught
up with her and touched her arm.

"Low heels," he said. "I never thought I'd live to see the day."

She looked around in surprise, then smiled widely and took his
arm. "Hello, Paul," she said. "I've gone in for health."

"Whenever I think of you," he said, "I think of the highest heels
in New York City."

"The old days," Harriet said. They walked slowly down the sunny street toward Sixth Avenue. "I was a frivolous creature."

"You still walk the same way. As though you ought to have a basket of laundry on your head."

"I practiced walking like that for six months. You'd be surprised how much attention I get walking into a room that way."

"I wouldn't be surprised," Paul said, looking at her. She had black hair and pale, clear skin and a long, full body, and her eyes were deep gray and always brilliant, even after she'd been drinking for three days in a row.

Harriet began to walk a little faster. "I'm going to Wanamaker's," she said. "There's a couple of things I have to buy. Where you going?"

"Wanamaker's," Paul said. "I've been dying to go to Wanamaker's for three years."

They walked in silence for a few moments, Harriet's arm in his.

"Casual," Paul said. "I bet to the naked eye we look casual as hell. How do you feel?"

Harriet took her arm away. "Casual."

"Oh. Then that's how I feel, too." Paul whistled a few bars of the "1812 Overture." He stopped and looked critically at her, and she stopped too and turned toward him, a slight, puzzled smile on her face. "What makes you dress that way?" he asked. "You look like Monday morning in Northampton."

"I just threw on whatever was nearest," Harriet said. "I'm just going to be out about an hour."

"You used to look like a nice big box of candy in your clothes." Paul took her arm and they started off again. "Viennese bonbons. Every indentation carefully exploited in silk and satin. Even if you were just going down to the corner for a pint of gin, you'd look like something that ought to be eaten for dessert. This is no improvement."

"A girl has different periods in clothes," Harriet said. "Like Picasso. And if I'd known I was going to meet you, I'd've dressed differently."

Paul patted her arm. "That's better." He eyed her obliquely as they walked — the familiar long face, the well-known wide mouth with always a little too much lipstick on it, the little teeth that made her face, when she smiled, look suddenly like a little girl's in Sunday school.

"You're getting skinny, Paul," Harriet said.

Paul nodded. "I'm as lean as a herring. I've been leading a fevered and ascetic life. What sort of life have you been leading?"

"I got married." Harriet paused a moment. "Did you hear I got married?"

"I heard," Paul said. "The last time we crossed Sixth Avenue together the 'L' was still up. I feel a nostalgic twinge for the Sixth Avenue 'L.'" They hurried as the light changed. "On the night of January 9, 1940," Paul said, holding her elbow until they had crossed the street, "you were not home."

"Possible," Harriet said. "I'm a big girl now. I go out at night."

"I happened to pass your house and I noticed that the light wasn't on." They turned down toward Ninth Street. "I remembered how hot you kept that apartment — like the dahlia greenhouse in the Botanical Garden."

"I have thin blood," Harriet said gravely. "Long years of inbreeding in Massachusetts."

"The nicest thing about you," Paul said, "was you never went to sleep."

"Every lady to her own virtue," Harriet said. "Some women're beautiful, some're smart. Me, I never went to sleep. The secret of my great popularity — "

Paul grinned. "Shut up."

Harriet smiled back at him and they chuckled together. "You know what I mean," he said. "Any time I called you up — two, three in the morning — you'd come right over, lively and bright-eyed, all the rouge and mascara in the right places — "

"In my youth," said Harriet, "I had great powers of resistance."

"In the morning we'd eat breakfast at Beethoven. The Masterwork Hour, WNYC. Beethoven, by special permission of His Honor the Mayor, from nine to ten." Paul closed his eyes for a moment. "The Little Flower, Mayor for Lovers."

Paul opened his eyes and looked at the half-strange, half-familiar woman walking lightly at his side. He remembered lying close to her, dreamily watching the few lights of the towers of the nighttime city framed by the big window of his bedroom against the black sky, and one night when she moved sleepily against him and rubbed the back of his neck where the hair was sticking up in sharp little bristles because he had had his hair cut that afternoon. Harriet had rubbed them the wrong way, smiling dreamily, without opening her eyes. "What a delicious thing a man is," she'd murmured. And she'd sighed, then chuckled a little and fallen asleep, her hand still on the clipped back of his neck. Paul smiled, remembering.

"You still laughing at my clothes?" Harriet asked.

"I remembered something I heard someplace," Paul said. "'What a delicious thing a man is.'"

Harriet looked at him coldly. "Who said that?"

Paul squinted suspiciously at her. "Oswald Spengler."

"Uh huh," Harriet said soberly. "It's a famous quotation."

"It's a well-turned phrase," said Paul.

"That's what I think, too." Harriet nodded and walked a little faster.

They passed the run-down bar where they'd sat afternoons all one winter, drinking Martinis and talking and talking and laughing so loud the people at the other tables would turn and smile. Paul waited for Harriet to say something about the place, but she didn't even seem to notice it. "There's Eddie Bar," Paul said.

"Uh huh." Harriet nodded.

"He's going to start making his Martinis with sherry when all the French vermouth runs out," Paul said.

"It sounds horrible." Harriet made a face.

"Is that all you have to say?" Paul said loudly, remembering the times he'd looked in to see if she was there.

"What do you want me to say?" Harriet looked honestly puzzled, but Paul had never known when she was lying to him or telling the truth anyway, and he hadn't improved in these two years, he discovered.

"I don't want you to say anything," he said. "I'll take you in and buy you a drink."

"No, thanks. I've really got to get to Wanamaker's and back home in a hurry. Give me a rain check."

"Yeah," Paul said sourly.

They turned into Ninth Street toward Fifth Avenue.

"I knew I'd meet you someplace, finally," Paul said. "I was curious to see what would happen."

Harriet didn't say anything. She was looking absently at the buildings across the street.

"Don't you ever talk any more?" Paul asked.

"What *did* happen?"

"Every once in a while," he began, "I meet some girl I used to know — "

"I bet the country's full of them," Harriet said.

"The country's full of everybody's ex-girls."

Harriet nodded. "I never thought of it that way, but you're right."

"Most of the time I think, Isn't she a nice, decent person? Isn't it wonderful I'm no longer attached to her? The first girl I ever had," Paul said, "is a policewoman now. She subdued a gangster single-handed in Coney Island last summer. Her mother won't let her go out of the house in her uniform. She's ashamed for the neighbors."

"Naturally," Harriet said.

"Another girl I used to know changed her name and danced in the Russian Ballet. I went to see her dance the other night. She has legs like a Fordham tackle. I used to think she was beautiful. I used to think you were beautiful, too."

"We were a handsome couple," Harriet said. "Except you always needed a shave. That electric razor — "

"I've given it up."

They were passing his old house now and he looked at the doorway and remembered all the times he and Harriet had gone in and come out, the rainy days and the early snowy mornings with the milkman's horse silent on the white street behind them. They stopped and looked at the old red house with the shabby shutters and the window on the fourth floor they had both looked out of time and time again to see what the weather was. Paul remembered the first time, on a winter's night, he and Harriet had gone through that door together.

"I was so damn polite," Paul said softly.

Harriet smiled. "You kept dropping the key and saying 'Lord, Lord' under your breath while you were looking for it."

"I was nervous. I wanted to make sure you knew exactly how matters stood. No illusions. Good friends, everybody understanding everybody else, another girl coming in from Detroit in six weeks — no claims on me, no claims on you . . ." Paul looked at the window on the fourth floor and smiled. "What a god-damn fool!"

"It's a nice, quiet street," Harriet said, looking up at the window on the fourth floor, too. She shook her head, took Paul's arm again. "I've got to get to Wanamaker's."

They started off.

"What're you buying at Wanamaker's?" Paul asked.

Harriet hesitated for a moment. "Nothing much. I'm looking at some baby clothes. I'm going to have a baby." They crowded over to one side to let a little woman with four dachshunds pass them in a busy tangle. "Isn't it funny — me with a baby?" Harriet smiled. "I lie around all day and try to imagine what it's going to be like. In between, I sleep and drink beer to nourish us. I've never had such a good time in all my life."

"Well," said Paul, "at least it'll keep your husband out of the Army."

"Maybe. He's a raging patriot."

"Good. When he's at Fort Dix I'll meet you in Washington Square Park when you take the baby out for an airing in its perambulator. I'll put on a policeman's uniform to make it proper. I'm not such a raging patriot."

"They'll get you anyway, won't they?"

"Sure. I'll send you my picture in a lieutenant's suit. From Bulgaria. I have a premonition I'm going to be called on to defend a strategic point in Bulgaria."

"How do you feel about it?" For the first time, Harriet looked squarely and searchingly at him.

Paul shrugged. "It's going to happen. It's all damned silly, but it isn't as silly now as it was ten years ago."

Suddenly Harriet laughed.

"What's so funny?" Paul demanded.

"My asking you how you felt about something. I never used to have a chance. You'd let me know how you felt about everything. Roosevelt, James Joyce, Jesus Christ, Gypsy Rose Lee, Matisse, Yoga, liquor, sex, and architecture —"

"I was full of opinions in those days." Paul smiled. "Lust and conversation. The firm foundations of civilized relations between the sexes."

He turned and looked back at the window on the fourth floor. "That was a nice apartment," he said softly. "Lust and conversation —"

"Come on, Paul," Harriet said. "Wanamaker's isn't going to stay open all night."

"You were the only girl I ever know I could sleep in the same bed with," Paul said.

"That's a hell of a thing to say to a girl." Harriet laughed. "Is that your notion of a compliment?"

Paul shrugged. "It's an irrelevant fact. Or a relevant fact. Is it polite to talk to a married lady this way?"

"No."

Paul walked along with her. "What do you think of when you look at me?" he asked.

"Nothing much," Harriet said.

"What're you lying about?"

"Nothing much," Harriet said.

"Don't you ever think, what in the name of God did I ever see in him?"

"No." Harriet began to walk faster.

"Should I tell you what I think of when I look at you?"

"No."

"I've been looking for you for two years," Paul said.

"My name's been in the telephone book." Harriet hurried even more, wrapping her coat tightly around her.

"I didn't realize I was looking for you until I saw you."

"Please, Paul —"

"I would walk along the street and I'd pass a bar we'd been in together and I'd go in and sit there even though I didn't want a drink, not knowing why I was sitting there. Now I know. I was waiting for you to come in. I didn't pass your house by accident."

"Look, Paul," Harriet pleaded. "It was a long time ago and it was fine and it ended — "

"I was wrong," Paul said. "Do you like hearing that? I was wrong. You know, I never did get married after all."

"I know," Harriet said. "Please shut up."

"I walk along Fifth Avenue and every time I pass Saint Patrick's I half look up to see if you're passing, because I met you that day right after you'd had a tooth pulled. And it was cold and you were walking along with the tears streaming from your eyes and your eyes red and that was the only time I ever met you by accident any place."

Harriet smiled. "That certainly sounds like a beautiful memory."

"Two years," Paul said. "I've gone out with a lot of girls in the last two years." He shrugged. "They've bored me and I've bored them. I keep looking at every woman who passes to see if it's you. All the girls I go out with bawl the hell out of me for it. I've been walking around, following girls with dark hair to see if it'll turn out to be you, and girls with a fur jacket like that old one you had, and girls that walk in that silly, beautiful way you walk. I've been searching the streets of the city for you for two years and this is the first time I've admitted it even to myself. That little Spanish joint we went the first time. Every time I pass it I remember everything — how many drinks we had and what the band played and what we said and the fat Cuban who kept winking at you from the bar and the very delicate way we landed up in my apartment . . ."

They were both walking swiftly now, Harriet holding her hands stiffly down at her sides.

"There is a particular, wonderful way you are joined together — "

"Paul, stop it!" Harriet's voice was flat but loud.

"Two years. In two years the edge should be dulled off things like that. Instead . . ." How can you make a mistake as big as that? Paul thought. How can you deliberately be as wrong as that? And no remedy. So long as you live, no remedy. He looked harshly at Harriet. Her face was set, as though she weren't listening to him and was intent only on getting across the street as quickly as possible. "How about you?" he asked. "Don't you remember?"

"I don't remember anything," she said. And then, suddenly, the tears sprang up in her eyes and streamed down the tight, distorted cheeks. "I don't remember a god-damn thing!" She wept. "I'm not going to Wanamaker's. I'm going home! Good-bye." She ran over to a cab that was parked at the corner and opened the door and sprang in. The cab spurted past Paul and he had a glimpse of Harriet sitting stiffly upright, the tears bitter and unheeded in her eyes.

He watched the cab go down Fifth Avenue until it turned. Then he turned the other way and started walking, thinking, I must move away from this neighborhood, I've lived here long enough.

JEAN STAFFORD

The Interior Castle

Pansy Vanneman, injured in an automobile accident, often woke up before dawn when the night noises of the hospital still came, in hushed hurry, through her half-open door. By day, when the nurses talked audibly with the internes, laughed without inhibition, and took no pains to soften their footsteps on the resounding composition floors, the routine of the hospital seemed as bland and commonplace as that of a bank or a factory. But in the dark hours, the whispering and the quickly stilled clatter of glasses and basins, the moans of patients whose morphine was wearing off, the soft squeak of a stretcher as it rolled past in its way from the emergency ward — these suggested agony and death. Thus, on the first morning, Pansy had faltered to consciousness long before daylight and had found herself in a ward from every bed of which, it seemed to her, came the bewildered protest of someone about to die. A caged light burned on the floor beside the bed next to hers. Her neighbor was dying and a priest was administering Extreme Unction. He was stout and elderly and he suffered from asthma so that the struggle of

263

his breathing, so close to her, was the basic pattern and all the other sounds were superimposed upon it. Two middle-aged men in overcoats knelt on the floor beside the high bed. In a foreign tongue, the half-gone woman babbled against the hissing and sighing of the Latin prayers. She prayed with her rosary as if it were a toy: she tried, and failed, to put it into her mouth.

Pansy felt horror, but she felt no pity. An hour or so later, when the white ceiling lights were turned on and everything — faces, counterpanes, and the hands that groped upon them — was transformed into a uniform gray sordor, the woman was wheeled away in her bed to die somewhere else, in privacy. Pansy did not quite take this in, although she stared for a long time at the new, empty bed that had replaced the other.

The next morning, when she again woke up before the light, this time in a private room, she recalled the woman with such sorrow that she might have been a friend. Simultaneously, she mourned the driver of the taxicab in which she had been injured, for he had died at about noon the day before. She had been told this as she lay on a stretcher in the corridor, waiting to be taken to the X-ray room; an interne, passing by, had paused and smiled down at her and had said, "Your cab-driver is dead. You are lucky."

Six weeks after the accident, she woke one morning just as daylight was showing on the windows as a murky smear. It was a minute or two before she realized why she was so reluctant to be awake, why her uneasiness amounted almost to alarm. Then she remembered that her nose was to be operated on today. She lay straight and motionless under the seersucker counterpane. Her blood-red eyes in her darned face stared through the window and saw a frozen river and leafless elm trees and a grizzled esplanade where dogs danced on the ends of leashes, their bundled-up owners stumbling after them, half blind with sleepiness and cold. Warm as the hospital room was, it did not prevent Pansy from knowing, as keenly as though she were one of the walkers, how very cold it was outside. Each twig of a nearby tree was stark. Cold red brick buildings nudged the low-lying sky which was pale and inert like a punctured sac.

In six weeks, the scene had varied little: there was promise in the skies neither of sun nor of snow; no red sunsets marked these days.

The tree could neither die nor leaf out again. Pansy could not remember another season in her life so constant, when the very minutes themselves were suffused with the winter pallor as they dropped from the moon-faced clock in the corridor. Likewise, her room accomplished no alterations from day to day. On the glass-topped bureau stood two potted plants telegraphed by faraway well-wishers. They did not fade, and if a leaf turned brown and fell, it soon was replaced; so did the blossoms renew themselves. The roots, like the skies and like the bare trees, seemed zealously determined to maintain a status quo. The bedside table, covered every day with a clean white towel, though the one removed was always immaculate, was furnished sparsely with a water glass, a bent drinking tube, a sweating pitcher, and a stack of paper handkerchiefs. There were a few letters in the drawer, a hairbrush, a pencil, and some postal cards on which, from time to time, she wrote brief messages to relatives and friends: "Dr. Nash says that my reflexes are shipshape (*sic*) and Dr. Rivers says the frontal fracture has all but healed and that the occipital is coming along nicely. Dr. Nicholas, the nose doctor, promises to operate as soon as Dr. Rivers gives him the go-ahead sign (*sic*)."

The bed itself was never rumpled. Once fretful and now convalescent, Miss Vanneman might have been expected to toss or turn the pillows or to unmoor the counterpane; but hour after hour and day after day she lay at full length and would not even suffer the nurses to raise the head-piece of the adjustable bed. So perfect and stubborn was her body's immobility that it was as if the room and the landscape, mortified by the ice, were extensions of herself. Her resolute quiescence and her disinclination to talk, the one seeming somehow to proceed from the other, resembled, so the nurses said, a final coma. And they observed, in pitying indignation, that she might as *well* be dead for all the interest she took in life. Amongst themselves they scolded her for what they thought a moral weakness: an automobile accident, no matter how serious, was not reason enough for anyone to give up the will to live or to be happy. She had not — to come down bluntly to the facts — had the decency to be grateful that it was the driver of the cab and not she who had died. (And how dreadfully the man had died!) She was twenty-five years old and she came from a distant city. These were really the only facts known about her. Evidently she had not been here long, for she had no visitors, a lack which was at first sadly moving to the nurses but which became to them a source of unreasonable annoyance: had anyone the right to live so one-dimensionally? It was impossible to laugh at her, for she said nothing absurd; her demands could not be complained of because they did not exist; she could not be hated for a sharp tongue nor for a supercilious one; she could not be admired for bravery or for wit or for interest in her fellow creatures. She was believed to be a frightful snob.

Pansy, for her part, took a secret and mischievous pleasure in the bewilderment of her attendants and the more they courted her with offers of magazines, cross-word puzzles, and a radio which she could rent from the hospital, the farther she retired from them into herself and into the world which she had created in her long hours here and which no one could even penetrate nor imagine. Sometimes she did not even answer the nurses' questions; as they rubbed her back with alcohol and steadily discoursed, she was as remote from them as if she were miles away. She did not think that she lived on a higher plane than that of the nurses and the doctors but that she lived on a different one and that at this particular time — this time of exploration and habituation — she had no extra strength to spend on making herself known to them. All she had been before and all the memories she might have brought out to disturb the monotony of, say, the morning bath, and all that the past meant to the future when she would leave the hospital, were of no present consequence to her. Not even in her thoughts did she employ more than a minimum of memory. And when she did remember, it was in flat pictures, rigorously independent of one another: she saw her thin, poetic mother who grew thinner and more poetic in her canvas deck chair at Saranac reading *Lalla Rookh*. She saw herself in an inappropriate pink hat drinking iced tea in a garden so oppressive with the smell of phlox that the tea itself tasted of it. She recalled an afternoon in autumn in Vermont when she had heard three dogs' voices in the north woods and she could tell, by the characteristic minor key struck three times at intervals, like bells from several churches, that they had treed something: the eastern sky was pink and the trees on the horizon looked like some eccentric vascular system meticulously drawn on colored paper.

What Pansy thought of all the time was her own brain. Not only the brain as the seat of consciousness, but the physical organ itself which she envisaged, romantically, now as a jewel, now as a flower, now as a light in a glass, now as an envelope of rosy vellum containing other envelopes, one within the other, diminishing infinitely. It was always pink and always fragile, always deeply interior and invaluable. She believed that she had reached the innermost chamber of knowledge and that perhaps her knowledge was the same as the saint's achievement of pure love. It was only convention, she thought, that made one say "sacred heart" and not "sacred brain."

Often, but never articulately, the color pink troubled her and the picture of herself in the wrong hat hung steadfastly before her mind's eye. None of the other girls had worn hats and since autumn had come early that year, they were dressed in green and rusty brown and dark yellow. Poor Pansy wore a white eyelet frock with a lacing of black ribbon around the square neck. When she came through the arch, overhung with bittersweet, and saw that they had not yet heard her, she almost turned back, but Mr. Oliver was there and she was in love with him. She was in love with him though he was ten years older than she and had never shown any interest in her beyond asking her once, quite fatuously but in an intimate voice, if the yodeling of the little boy who peddled clams did not make her wish to visit Switzerland. Actually, there was more to this question than met the eye, for some days later Pansy learned that Mr. Oliver, who was immensely rich, kept an apartment in Geneva. In the garden that day, he spoke to her only once. He said, "My dear, you look exactly like something out of Katherine Mansfield," and immediately turned and within her hearing asked Beatrice Sherburne to dine with him that night at the Country Club. Afterward, Pansy went down to the sea and threw the beautiful hat onto the full tide and saw it vanish in the wake of a trawler. Thereafter, when she heard the clam boy coming down the road, she locked the door and when the knocking had stopped and her mother called down from her chaise longue, "Who was it, dearie?" she replied, "A salesman."

It was only the fact that the hat had been pink that worried her. The rest of the memory was trivial, for she knew that she could never again love anything as ecstatically as she loved the spirit of Pansy Vanneman, enclosed within her head.

But her study was not without distraction, and she fought two adversaries: pain and Dr. Nicholas. Against Dr. Nicholas, she defended herself valorously and in fear; but pain, the pain, that is, that was independent of his instruments, she sometimes forced upon herself adventurously like a child scaring himself in a graveyard.

Dr. Nicholas greatly admired her crushed and splintered nose which he daily probed and peered at, exclaiming that he had never seen anything like it. His shapely hands ached for their knives; he was impatient with the skull-fracture man's cautious delay. He spoke of "our" nose and said "we" would be a new person when we could breathe again. His own nose, the trademark of his profession, was magnificent. Not even his own brilliant surgery could have improved upon it nor could a first-rate sculptor have duplicated its direct downward line which permitted only the least curvature inward toward the end; nor the thin-walled, perfectly matched nostrils. Miss Vanneman did not doubt his humaneness nor his talent — he was a celebrated man — but she questioned whether he had imagination. Immediately beyond the prongs of his speculum lay her treasure whose price he, no more than the nurses, could estimate. She believed he could not destroy it, but she feared that he might maim it: might leave a scratch on one of the brilliant facets of the jewel, bruise a petal of the flower, smudge the glass where the light burned, blot the envelopes, and that then she would die or would go mad. While she did not question that in either eventuality her brain would after a time redeem its original impeccability, she did not quite yet wish to enter upon either kind of eternity, for she was not certain that she could carry with her knowledge as well as its receptacle.

Blunderer that he was, Dr. Nicholas was an honorable enemy, not like the demon, pain, which skulked in a thousand guises within her head, and which often she recklessly willed to attack her and then drove back in terror. After the rout, sweat streamed from her face and soaked the neck of the coarse hospital shirt. To be sure, it came usually of its own accord, running like a wild fire through all the convulsions to fill with flame the small sockets and ravines and then, at last, to withdraw, leaving behind a throbbing and an echo. On these occasions, she was as helpless as a tree in a wind. But at the other times when, by closing her eyes and rolling up the eyeballs in such a way that she fancied she looked directly on the place where her brain was, the pain woke sluggishly and came toward her at a snail's pace. Then, bit by bit, it gained speed. Sometimes it faltered back, subsided altogether, and then it rushed like a tidal wave driven by a hurricane, lashing and roaring until she felt their bones must snap. Each cove, each narrow inlet, every living bay was flooded and the frail brain, a little hat-shaped boat, was washed from its mooring and set adrift. The skull was as vast as the world and the brain was as small as a seashell.

Then came calm weather and the safe journey home. She kept vigil for a while, though, and did not close her eyes, but gazing pacifically at the trees, conceived of the pain as the guardian of her treasure who would not let her see it; that was why she was handled so savagely whenever she turned her eyes inward. Once this watch was interrupted: by chance she looked into the corridor and saw a shaggy mop slink past the door, followed by a senile porter. A pair of ancient eyes, as rheumy as an old dog's, stared uncritically in at her and the toothless mouth formed a brutish word. She was so surprised that she immediately closed her eyes to shut out the shape of the word and the pain dug up the unmapped regions of her head with mattocks, ludicrously huge. It was the familiar pain, but this time, even as she endured it, she observed with detachment that its effect upon her was less than that of its contents, the by-products, for example, of temporal confusion and the bizarre misapplication of the style of one sensation to another. At the moment, for example, although her brain reiterated to her that *it* was being assailed, she was stroking her right wrist with her left hand as though to assuage the ache, long since dispelled, of the sprain in the joint. Some minutes after she had opened her eyes and left off soothing her wrist, she lay rigid experiencing the sequel to the pain, an ideal terror. For, as before on several occasions, she was overwhelmed with the knowledge that the pain had been consummated in the vessel of her mind and for the moment the vessel was unbeautiful: she thought, quailing, of those plastic folds as palpable as the fingers of locked hands containing in their very cells, their fissures, their repulsive hemispheres, the mind, the soul, the inscrutable intelligence.

The porter, then, like the pink hat and like her mother and the hounds' voices, loitered with her.

Dr. Nicholas came at nine o'clock to prepare her for the operation. With him came an entourage of white-frocked acolytes, and one of them wheeled in a wagon on which lay knives and scissors and pincers, cans of swabs and gauze. In the midst of these was a bowl of liquid whose rich purple color made it seem strange like the brew of an alchemist.

"All set?" he asked her, smiling. "A little nervous, what? I don't blame you. I've often said I'd rather lose an arm than have a submucuous resection." Pansy thought for a moment he was going to touch his nose. His approach to her was roundabout. He moved through the yellow light shed by the globe in the ceiling which gave his forehead a liquid gloss; he paused by the bureau and touched a blossom of the cyclamen; he looked out the window and said, to no one and to all, "I couldn't start my car this morning. Came in a cab." Then he came forward. As he came, he removed a speculum from the pocket of his short-sleeved coat and like a cat, inquiring of the nature of a surface with its paws, he put out his hand toward her and drew it back, gently murmuring, "You must not be afraid, my dear. There is no danger, you know. Do you think for a minute I would operate if there were?"

Dr. Nicholas, young, brilliant, and handsome, was an aristocrat, a husband, a father, a clubman, a Christian, a kind counselor, and a trustee of his school alumni association. Like many of the medical profession, even those whose specialty was centered on the organ of the basest sense, he interested himself in the psychology of his patients: in several instances, for example, he had found that severe attacks of sinusitis were coincident with emotional crises. Miss Vanneman more than ordinarily captured his fancy since her skull had been fractured and her behavior throughout had been so extraordinary that he felt he was observing at first hand some of the results of shock, that incommensurable element, which frequently were too subtle to see. There was, for example, the matter of her complete passivity during a lumbar puncture, reports of which were written down in her history and were enlarged upon for him by Dr. Rivers' interne who had been in charge. Except for a tremor in her throat and a deepening of pallor, there were no signs at all that she was aware of what was happening to her. She made no sound, did not close her eyes nor clench her fists. She had had several punctures; her only reaction had been to the very first one, the morning after she had been brought in. When the interne explained to her that he was going to drain off cerebro-spinal fluid which was pressing against her brain, she exclaimed, "My God!" but it was not an exclamation of fear. The young man had been unable to name what it was he had heard in her voice; he could only say that it had not been fear as he had observed it in other patients.

He wondered about her. There was no way of guessing whether she had always had a nature of so tolerant and undemanding a complexion. It gave him a melancholy pleasure to think that before her accident she had been high-spirited and loquacious; he was moved to think that perhaps she had been a beauty and that when she had first seen her face in the looking glass she had lost all joy in herself. It was very difficult to tell what the face had been, for it was so bruised and swollen, so hacked up and lopsided. The black stitches the length of the nose, across the saddle, across the cheekbone, showed that there would be unsightly scars. He had ventured once to give her the name of a plastic surgeon but she had only replied with a vague, refusing smile. He had hoisted a manly shoulder and said. "You're the doctor."

Much as he pondered, coming to no conclusions, about what went on inside that pitiable skull, he was, of course, far more interested in the nose, deranged so badly that it would require his topmost skill to restore its functions to it. He would be obliged not only to make a submucuous resection, a simple run-of-the-mill operation, but to remove the vomer, always a delicate task but further complicated in this case by the proximity of the bone to the frontal fracture line which conceivably was not entirely closed. If it were not and he operated too soon and if a cold germ then found its way into the opening, his patient would be carried off by meningitis in the twinkling of an eye. He wondered if she knew in what potential danger she lay; he desired to assure her that he had brought his craft to its nearest perfection and that she had nothing to fear of him, but feeling that she was perhaps both ignorant and unimaginative and that such consolation would create a fear rather than dispel one, he held his tongue and came nearer to the bed.

Watching him, Pansy could already feel the prongs of his pliers opening her nostrils for the insertion of his fine probers. The pain he caused her with his instruments was of a different kind from that she felt unaided: it was a naked, clean, and vivid pain which made her faint and ill and made her wish to die. Once she had fainted as he ruthlessly explored and after she was brought around, he continued until he had finished his investigation. The memory of this outrage had afterwards several times made her cry.

This morning she looked at him and listened to him with hatred. Fixing her eyes upon the middle of his high, protuberant brow, she imagined the clutter behind it and she despised its obtuse imperfection, the reason's oblique comprehension of itself. In his bland unawareness, this nobody, this nose-bigot, was about to play with fire and she wished him ill.

He said, "I can't blame you. No, I expect you're not looking forward to our little party. But I expect you'll be glad to be able to breathe again."

He stationed his lieutenants. The interne stood opposite him on the left side of the bed. The surgical nurse wheeled the wagon within easy reach of his hands and stood beside it. Another nurse stood at the foot of the bed. A third drew the shades at the windows and attached the blinding light which shone down on the patient hotly, and then she left the room, softly closing the door. Pansy stared at the silver ribbon tied in a great bow around the green crêpe paper of one of the flower pots. It made her realize for the first time that one of the days she had lain here had been Christmas, but she had no time to consider this strange and thrilling fact, for Dr. Nicholas was genially explaining his anaesthetic. He would soak packs of gauze in the purple fluid, a cocaine solution, and he would place them then in her nostrils, leaving them there for an hour. He warned her that the packing would be disagreeable (he did not say "painful") but that it would be well worth a few minutes of discomfort not to be in the least sick after the operation. He asked her if she were ready and when she nodded her head, he adjusted the mirror on his forehead and began.

At the first touch of his speculum, Pansy's fingers mechanically bent to the palms of her hands and she stiffened. He said, "A pack, Miss Kennedy," and Pansy closed her eyes. There was a rush of plunging pain as he drove the sodden gobbet of gauze high up her nose and something bitter burned in her throat so that she retched. The doctor paused a moment and the surgical nurse wiped her mouth. He returned to her with another pack, pushing it with his bodkin doggedly until it lodged against the first. Stop! Stop! cried all her nerves, wailing along the surface of her skin. The coats that covered them were torn off and they shuddered like naked people screaming, Stop! Stop! But Dr. Nicholas did not hear. Time and again he came back with a fresh pack and did not pause at all until one nostril was finished. She opened her eyes and saw him wipe the sweat off his forehead and saw the dark interne bending over her, fascinated. Miss Kennedy bathed her temples in ice water and Dr. Nicholas said, "There. It won't be much longer. I'll tell them to send you some coffee, though I'm afraid you won't be able to taste it. Ever drink coffee with chicory in it? I have no use for it."

She snatched at his irrelevancy and, though she had never tasted chicory, she said savagely, "I love it."

Dr. Nicholas chuckled. "De gustibus. Ready? A pack, Miss Kennedy."

The second nostril was harder to pack since the other side was now distended and the passage was anyhow much narrower, as narrow, he had once remarked, as that in the nose of an infant. In such pain as passed all language and even the farthest fetched analogies, she turned her eyes inward thinking that under the obscuring cloak of the surgeon's pain, she could see her brain without the knowledge of its keeper. But Dr. Nicholas and his aides would give her no peace.

They surrounded her with their murmuring and their foot-shuffling and the rustling of their starched uniforms, and her eyelids continually flew back in embarrassment and mistrust. She was claimed entirely by this present, meaningless pain and suddenly and sharply, she forgot what she had meant to do. She was aware of nothing but her ascent to the summit of something; what it was she did not know, whether it was a tower or a peak or Jacob's ladder. Now she was an abstract word, now she was a theorem of geometry, now she was a kite flying, a top spinning, a prism flashing, a kaleidoscope turning.

But none of the others in the room could see inside and when the surgeon was finished, the nurse at the foot of the bed said, "Now you must take a look in the mirror. It's simply too comical." And they all laughed intimately like old, fast friends. She smiled politely and looked at her reflection: over the gruesomely fattened snout, her scarlet eyes stared in fixed reproach upon the upturned lips, gray with bruises. But even in its smile of betrayal, the mouth itself was puzzled: it reminded her that something had been left behind, but she could not recall what it was. She was hollowed out and was as dry as a white bone.

They strapped her ankles to the operating table and put leather nooses round her wrists. Over her head was a mirror with a thousand facets in which she saw a thousand travesties of her face. At her right side was the table, shrouded in white, where lay the glittering blades of the many knives, thrusting out fitful rays of light. All the cloth was frosty; everything was white or silver and as cold as snow. Dr. Nicholas, a tall snowman with silver eyes and silver fingernails, came into the room soundlessly for he walked on layers and layers of snow which deadened his footsteps; behind him came the interne, a smaller snowman, less impressively proportioned. At the foot of the table, a snow figure put her frozen hands upon Pansy's helpless feet. The doctor plucked the packs from the cold, numb nose. His laugh was like a cry on a bitter, still night: "I will show you now," he called across the expanse of snow, "that you can feel nothing." The pincers bit at nothing, snapped at the air and cracked a nerveless icicle. Pansy called back and heard her own voice echo: "I feel nothing."

Here the walls were gray, not tan. Suddenly the face of the nurse at the foot of the table broke apart and Pansy first thought it was in grief. But it was a smile and she said, "Did you enjoy your coffee?" Down the gray corridors of the maze, the words rippled, ran like mice, birds, broken beads: Did you enjoy your coffee? your coffee? your coffee? Similarly once in another room that also had gray walls, the same voice had said, "Shall I give her some whiskey?" She was overcome with gratitude that this young woman (how pretty she was with her white hair and her white face and her china-blue eyes!) had been with her that first night and was with her now.

In the great stillness of the winter, the operation began. The knives carved snow. Pansy was happy She had been given a hypodermic just before they came to fetch her and she would have gone to sleep had she not enjoyed so much this trickery of Dr. Nicholas' whom now she tenderly loved.

There was a clock in the operating room and from time to time she looked at it. An hour passed. The snowman's face was melting; drops of water hung from his fine nose, but his silver eyes were as bright as ever. Her love was returned, she knew: he loved her nose exactly as she loved his knives. She looked at her face in the domed mirror and saw how the blood had streaked her lily-white cheeks and had stained her shroud. She returned to the private song: Did you enjoy your coffee, your coffee?

At the half-hour, a murmur, anguine, and slumbrous, came to her and only when she had repeated the words twice did they engrave their meaning upon her. Dr. Nicholas said, "Stand back now, nurse. I'm at this girl's brain and I don't want my elbow jogged." Instantly Pansy was alive. Her strapped ankles arched angrily; her wrists strained against their bracelets. She jerked her head and she felt the pain flare; she had made the knife slip.

"Be still!" cried the surgeon. "Be quiet, please!"

He had made her remember what it was she had lost when he had rammed his gauze into her nose: she bustled like a housewife to shut the door. She thought, I must hurry before the robbers come. It would be like the time Mother left the cellar door open and the robber came and took, of all things, the terrarium.

Dr. Nicholas was whispering to her. He said, in the voice of a lover, "If you can stand it five minutes more, I can perform the second operation now and you won't have to go through this again. What do you say?"

She did not reply. It took her several seconds to remember why it was her mother had set such store by the terrarium and then it came to her that the bishop's widow had brought her an erb from Palestine to put in it.

The interne said, "You don't want to have your nose packed again, do you?"

The surgical nurse said, "She's a good patient, isn't she, sir?"

"Never had a better," replied Dr. Nicholas. "But don't call me 'sir.' You must be a Canadian to call me 'sir.'"

The nurse at the foot of the bed said, "I'll order some more coffee for you."

"How about it, Miss Vanneman?" said the doctor. "Shall I go ahead?"

She debated. Once she had finally fled the hospital and fled Dr. Nicholas, nothing could compel her to come back. Still, she knew that the time would come when she could no longer live in seclusion, she must go into the world again and must be equipped to live in it; she banally acknowledged that she must be able to breathe. And finally, though the world to which she would return remained unreal, she gave the surgeon her permission.

He had now to penetrate regions that were not anaesthetized and this he told her frankly, but he said that there was no danger at all. He apologized for the slip of the tongue he had made: in point of fact, he had not been near her brain, it was only a figure of speech. He began. The knives ground and carved and curried and scoured the wounds they made; the scissors clipped hard gristle and the scalpels chipped off bone. It was as if a tangle of tiny nerves were being cut dexterously, one by one; the pain writhed spirally and came to her who was a pink bird and sat on the top of a cone. The pain was a pyramid made of a diamond; it was an intense light; it was the hottest fire, the coldest chill, the highest peak, the fastest force, the furthest reach, the newest time. It possessed nothing of her but its one infinitesimal scene: beyond the screen as thin as gossamer, the brain trembled for its life, hearing the knives hunting like wolves outside, sniffing and snapping. Mercy! Mercy! cried the scalpel nerves.

At last, miraculously, she turned her eyes inward tranquilly. Dr. Nicholas had said, "The worst is over. I am going to work on the floor of your nose," and at his signal she closed her eyes and this time and this time alone, she saw her brain lying in a shell-pink satin case. It was a pink pearl, no bigger than a needle's eye, but it was so beautiful and so pure that its smallness made no difference. Anyhow, as she watched, it grew. It grew larger and larger until it was an enormous bubble that contained the surgeon and the whole room within its rosy luster. In a long ago summer, she had often been absorbed by the spectacle of flocks of yellow birds that visited a cedar tree and she remembered that everything that summer had been some shade of yellow. One year of childhood, her mother had frequently taken her to have tea with an aged schoolmistress upon whose mantelpiece there was a herd of ivory elephants; that had been the white year. There was a green spring when early in April she had seen a grass snake on a boulder, but the very summer that followed was violet, for vetch took her mother's garden. She saw a swatch of blue tulle lying in a raffia basket on the front porch of Uncle Marion's brown house. Never before had the world been pink, whatever else it had been. Or had it been, one other time? She could not be sure and she did not care. Of one thing she was certain: never had the world enclosed her before and never had the quiet been so smooth.

For only a moment the busybodies left her to her ecstasy and then, impatient and gossiping, they forced their way inside, slashed at her resisting trance with questions and congratulations, with statements of facts and jokes. "Later," she said to them dumbly. "Later on, perhaps. I am busy now." But their voices would not go away. They touched her, too, washing her face with cloths so cold they stung, stroking her wrists with firm, antiseptic fingers. The surgeon, squeezing her arm with avuncular pride, said, "Good girl," as if she were a bright dog that had retrieved a bone. Her silent mind abused him: You are a thief, it said, you are a heartless vagabond and you should be put to death. But he was leaving, adjusting his coat with an air of vainglory, and the interne, abject with admiration, followed him from the operating room smiling like a silly boy.

Shortly after they took her back to her room, the weather changed, not for the better. Momentarily the sun emerged from its concealing murk, but in a few minutes the snow came with a wind that promised a blizzard. There was great pain, but since it could not serve her, she rejected it and she lay as if in a hammock in a pause of bitterness. She closed her eyes, shutting herself up within her treasureless head.

WILBUR DANIEL STEELE

How Beautiful With Shoes

By THE TIME the milking was finished, the sow, which had far-rowed the past week, was making such a row that the girl spilled a pint of warm milk down the trough lead to quiet the animal before taking the pail to the well house. Then in the quiet she heard a sound of hoofs on the bridge, where the road crossed the creek a hundred yards below the house, and she set the pail down on the ground beside her bare, barn-soiled feet. She picked it up again. She set it down. It was as if she calculated its weight.

That was what she was doing, as a matter of fact, setting off against its pull toward the well house the pull of that wagon team in the road, with little more of personal will or wish in the matter than has a wooden weathervane between two currents in the wind. And as with the vane, so with the wooden girl — the added behest of a whiplash cracking in the distance was enough; leaving the pail at the barn door, she set off in a deliberate, docile beeline through the cowyard, over the fence, and down in a diagonal across the farm's one tilled field toward the willow brake that walled the road

279

at the dip. And once under way, though her mother came to the kitchen door and called in her high, flat voice, "Amarantha, where you goin', Amarantha?" the girl went on apparently unmoved, as though she had been as deaf as the woman in the doorway; indeed, if there was emotion in her it was the purely sensuous one of feeling the clods of the furrows breaking softly between her toes. It was springtime in the mountains.

"Amarantha, why don't you answer me, Amarantha?"

For moments after the girl had disappeared beyond the willows the widow continued to call, unaware through long habit of how absurd it sounded, the name which that strange man her husband had put upon their daughter in one of his moods. Mrs. Doggett had been deaf so long she did not realize that nobody else ever thought of it for the broad-fleshed, slow-minded girl, but called her Mary, or even more simply, Mare.

Ruby Herter had stopped his team this side of the bridge, the mules' heads turned into the lane to his father's farm beyond the road. A big-barreled, heavy-limbed fellow with a square, sallow, not unhandsome face, he took out youth in ponderous gestures of masterfulness; it was like him to have cracked his whip above his animals' ears the moment before he pulled them to a halt. When he saw the girl getting over the fence under the willows he tongued the wad of tobacco out of his mouth into his palm, threw it away beyond the road, and drew a sleeve of his jumper across his lips.

"Don't run yourself out o'breath, Mare; I got all night."

"I was comin'." It sounded sullen only because it was matter of fact.

"Well, keep a-comin' and give us a smack." Hunched on the wagon seat, he remained motionless for some time after she had arrived at the hub, and when he stirred it was but to cut a fresh bit of tobacco, as if already he had forgotten why he threw the old one away. Having satisfied his humor, he unbent, climbed down, kissed her passive mouth, and hugged her up to him, roughly and loosely, his hands careless of contours. It was not out of the way; they were used to handling animals both of them; and it was spring. A slow warmth pervaded the girl, formless, nameless, almost impersonal.

Her betrothed pulled her head back by the braid of her yellow hair. He studied her face, his brows gathered and his chin out.

"Listen, Mare, you wouldn't leave nobody else hug and kiss you, dang you!"

She shook her head, without vehemence or anxiety.

"Who's that?" She harkened up the road. "Pull your team out," she added, as a Ford came in sight around the bend above the house, driven at speed. "Geddap!" she said to the mules herself.

But the car came to a halt near them, and one of the five men crowded in it called, "Come on, Ruby, climb in. They's a loony loose out o' Dayville Asylum, and they got him trailed over somewheres on Split Ridge, and Judge North phoned up to Slosson's store for ever'body come help circle him — come on, hop the runnin'-board!"

Ruby hesitated, an eye on his team.

"Scared, Ruby?" The driver raced his engine. "They say this boy's a killer."

"Mare, take the team in and tell Pa." The car was already moving when Ruby jumped it. A moment after it had sounded on the bridge it was out of sight.

"Amarantha, Amarantha, why don't you come, Amarantha?"

Returning from her errand, fifteen minutes later, Mare heard the plaint lifted in the twilight. The sun had dipped behind the back ridge, and though the sky was still bright with day, the dusk began to smoke up out of the plowed field like a ground fog. The girl had returned through it, got the milk, and started toward the well house before the widow saw her.

"Daughter, seems to me you might!" she expostulated without change of key. "Here's some young man friend o' yourn stopped to say howdy, and I been rackin' my lungs out after you. . . . Put that milk in the cool and come!"

Some young man friend? But there was no good to be got from puzzling. Mare poured the milk in the pan in the dark of the low house over the well, and as she came out, stooping, she saw a figure waiting for her, black in silhouette against the yellowing sky.

"Who are you?" she asked, a native timidity making her sound sulky.

" 'Amarantha!' " the fellow mused. "That's poetry." And she knew then that she did not know him.

She walked past, her arms straight down and her eyes front. Strangers always affected her with a kind of muscular terror simply by being strangers. So she gained the kitchen steps, aware by his tread that he followed. There, taking courage at the sight of her mother in the doorway, she turned on him, her eyes down at the level of his knees.

"Who are you and what d' y' want?"

He still mused. "Amarantha! Amarantha in Carolina! That makes me happy!"

Mare hazarded one upward look. She saw that he had red hair, brown eyes, and hollows under his cheekbones, and though the green sweater he wore on top of a gray overall was plainly not meant for him, sizes too large as far as girth went, yet he was built so long of limb that his wrists came inches out of the sleeves and made his big hands look even bigger.

Mrs. Doggett complained. "Why don't you introduce us, daughter?"

The girl opened her mouth and closed it again. Her mother, unaware that no sound had come out of it, smiled and nodded, evidently taking to the tall, homely fellow and tickled by the way he could not seem to get his eyes off her daughter. But the daughter saw none of it, all her attention centered upon the stranger's hands.

Restless, hard-fleshed, and chap-bitten, they were like a countryman's hands; but the fingers were longer than the ordinary, and slightly spatulate at their ends, and these ends were slowly and continuously at play among themselves.

The girl could not have explained how it came to her to be frightened and at the same time to be calm, for she was inept with words. It was simply that in an animal way she knew animals, knew them in health and ailing, and when they were ailing she knew by instinct, as her father had known, how to move so as not to fret them.

Her mother had gone in to light up; from beside the lampshelf she called back, "If he's aimin' to stay to supper you should've told me, Amarantha, though I guess there's plenty of the side-meat to go 'round, if you'll bring me in a few more turnips and potatoes, though it is late."

At the words the man's cheeks moved in and out. "I'm very hungry," he said.

Mare nodded deliberately. Deliberately, as if her mother could hear her, she said over her shoulder, "I'll go get the potatoes and turnips, Ma." While she spoke she was moving, slowly, softly, at first, toward the right of the yard, where the fence gave over into the field. Unluckily her mother spied her through the window.

"Amarantha, where *are* you goin'?"

"I'm goin' to get the potatoes and turnips." She neither raised her voice nor glanced back, but lengthened her stride. He won't hurt her, she said to herself. He won't hurt her; it's me, not her, she kept repeating, while she got over the fence and down into the shadow that lay more than ever like a fog on the field.

The desire to believe that it actually did hide her, the temptation to break from her rapid but orderly walk grew till she could no longer fight it. She saw the road willows only a dash ahead of her. She ran, her feet floundering among the furrows.

She neither heard nor saw him, but when she realized he was with her she knew he had been with her all the while. She stopped, and he stopped, and so they stood, with the dark open of the field all around. Glancing sidewise presently, she saw he was no longer looking at her with those strangely importunate brown eyes of his, but had raised them to the crest of the wooded ridge behind her.

By and by, "What does it make you think of?" he asked. And when she made no move to see, "Turn around and look!" he said, and though it was low and almost tender in its tone, she knew enough to turn.

A ray of the sunset hidden in the west struck through the tops of the topmost trees, far and small up there, a thin, bright hem.

"What does it make you think of, Amarantha? . . . Answer!"

"Fire," she made herself say.

"Or blood."

"Or blood, yeh. That's right, or blood." She had heard a Ford going up the road beyond the willows, and her attention was not on what she said.

The man soliloquized. "Fire and blood, both; spare one or the other, and where is beauty, the way the world is? It's an awful thing to have to carry, but Christ had it. Christ came with a sword. I love beauty, Amarantha. . . . I say, I love beauty!"

"Yeh, that's right, I hear." What she heard was the car stopping at the house.

"Not prettiness. Prettiness'll have to go with ugliness, because it's only ugliness trigged up. But beauty!" Now again he was looking at her. "Do you know how beautiful you are, Amarantha, 'Amarantha sweet and fair'?" Of a sudden, reaching behind her, he began to unravel the meshes of her hair braid, the long, flat-tipped fingers at once impatient and infinitely gentle. " 'Braid no more that shining hair!' "

Flat-faced Mare Dogget tried to see around those glowing eyes so near to hers, but wise in her instinct, did not try too hard. "Yeh," she temporized. "I mean, no, I mean."

"Amarantha, I've come a long, long way for you. Will you come away with me now?"

"Yeh — that is — in a minute I will, mister — yeh . . ."

"Because you want to, Amarantha? Because you love me as I love you? Answer!"

"Yeh — sure — uh . . . *Ruby!*"

The man tried to run, but there were six against him, coming up out of the dark that lay in the plowed ground. Mare stood where she was while they knocked him down and got a rope around him; after that she walked back toward the house with Ruby and Older Haskins, her father's cousin.

Ruby wiped his brow and felt of his muscles. "Gees, you're lucky we come, Mare. We're no more'n past the town, when they come hollerin' he'd broke over this way."

When they came to the fence the girl sat on the rail for a moment and rebraided her hair before she went into the house, where they were making her mother smell ammonia.

Lots of cars were coming. Judge North was coming, somebody said. When Mare heard this she went into her bedroom off the kitchen and got her shoes and put them on. They were brand-new two-dollar shoes with cloth tops, and she had only begun to break them in last Sunday; she wished afterwards she had put her stockings on too, for they would have eased the seams. Or else that she had put on the old button pair, even though the soles were worn through.

Judge North arrived. He thought first of taking the loony straight through to Dayville that night, but then decided to keep him in the lockup at the courthouse till morning and make the drive by day. Older Haskins stayed in, gentling Mrs. Doggett, while Ruby went out to help get the man into the Judge's sedan. Now that she had them on, Mare didn't like to take the shoes off till Older went; it might make him feel small, she thought.

Older Haskins had a lot of facts about the loony.

"His name's Humble Jewett," he told them. "They belong back in Breed County, all them Jewetts, and I don't reckon there's none of 'em that's not a mite unbalanced. He went to college though, worked his way, and he taught somethin' 'rother in some academy-school a spell, till he went off his head all of a sudden and took after folks with an axe. I remember it in the paper at the time. They give out one while how the Principal wasn't goin' to live, and there was others — there was a girl he tried to strangle. That was four-five year back."

Ruby came in guffawing. "Know the only thing they can get 'im to say, Mare? Only God thing he'll say is 'Amarantha, she's goin' with me.' . . . Mare!"

"Yeh, I know."

The cover of the kettle the girl was handling slid off the stove with a clatter. A sudden sick wave passed over her. She went out to the back, out into the air. It was not till now she knew how frightened she had been.

Ruby went home, but Older Haskins stayed to supper with them, and helped Mare do the dishes afterward; it was nearly nine when he left. The mother was already in bed, and Mare was about to sit down to get those shoes off her wretched feet at last, when she heard the cow carrying on up at the barn, lowing and kicking, and next minute the sow was in it with a horning note. It might be a fox passing by to get at the henhouse, or a weasel. Mare forgot her feet, took a broom handle they used in boiling clothes, opened the back door, and stepped out. Blinking the lamplight from her eyes, she peered up toward the outbuildings, and saw the gable end of the barn standing like a red arrow in the dark, and the top of a butternut tree beyond it drawn in skeleton traceries, and just then a cock crowed.

She went to the right corner of the house and saw where the light came from, ruddy above the woods down the valley. Returning into the house, she bent close to her mother's ear and shouted, "Somethin's a-fire down to the town, looks like," then went out again and up to the barn. "Soh! Soh!" she called in to the animals. She climbed up and stood on the top rail of the cow-pen fence, only to find she could not locate the flame even there.

Ten rods behind the buildings a mass of rock mounted higher than their ridgepoles, a chopped off buttress of the back ridge, covered with oak scrub and wild grapes and blackberries, whose thorny ropes the girl beat away from her skirt with the broom handle as she scrambled up in the wine-colored dark. Once at the top, and the brush held aside, she could see the tongue-tip of the conflagration half a mile away at the town. And she knew by the bearing of the two church steeples that it was the building where the lockup was that was burning.

There is a horror in knowing animals trapped in a fire, no matter what the animals.

"Oh, my God!" Mare said.

A car went down the road. Then there was a horse galloping. That would be Older Haskins probably. People were out at Ruby's father's farm; she could hear their voices raised. There must have been another car up from the other way, for lights wheeled and shouts were exchanged in the neighborhood of the bridge. Next thing she knew, Ruby was at the house below, looking for her probably.

He was telling her mother, Mrs. Doggett was not used to him, so he had to shout even louder than Mare had to.

"What y' reckon he done, the hellion! he broke the door and killed Lew Fyke and set the courthouse afire! . . . Where's Mare?"

Her mother would not know. Mare called. "Here, up the rock here."

She had better go down. Ruby would likely break his bones if he tried to climb the rock in the dark, not knowing the way. But the sight of the fire fascinated her simple spirit, the fearful element, more fearful than ever now, with the news. "Yes, I'm comin'," she called sulkily, hearing feet in the brush. "You wait; I'm comin'."

When she turned and saw it was Humble Jewett, right behind her among the branches, she opened her mouth to screech. She was not quick enough. Before a sound came out he got one hand over her face and the other around her body.

Mare had always thought she was strong, and the loony looked gangling, yet she was so easy for him that he need not hurt her. He made no haste and little noise as he carried her deeper into the undergrowth. Where the hill began to mount it was harder though.

Presently he set her on her feet. He let the hand that had been over her mouth slip down to her throat, where the broad-tipped fingers wound, tender as yearning, weightless as caress.

"I was afraid you'd scream before you knew who 'twas, Amarantha. But I didn't want to hurt your lips, dear heart, your lovely, quiet lips."

It was so dark under the trees she could hardly see him, but she felt his breath on her mouth, near to. But then, instead of kissing her, he said, "No! No!" took from her throat for an instant the hand that had held her mouth, kissed its palm, and put it back softly against her skin.

"Now, my love, let's go before they come."

She stood stock-still. Her mother's voice was to be heard in the distance, strident and meaningless. More cars were on the road. Nearer, around the rock, there were sounds of tramping and thrashing. Ruby fussed and cursed. He shouted, "Mare, dang you, where are you, Mare?" his voice harsh with uneasy anger. Now, if she aimed to do anything, was the time to do it. But there was neither breath nor power in her windpipe. It was as if those yearning fingers had paralyzed the muscles.

"Come!" The arm he put around her shivered against her shoulder blades. It was anger. "I hate killing. It's a dirty, ugly thing. It makes me sick." He gagged, judging by the sound. But then he ground his teeth. "Come away, my love!"

She found herself moving. Once when she broke a branch underfoot with an instinctive awkwardness he chided her. "Quiet, my heart, else they'll hear!" She made herself heavy. He thought she grew tired and bore more of her weight till he was breathing hard.

Men came up the hill. There must have been a dozen spread out, by the angle of their voices as they kept touch. Always Humble Jewett kept caressing Mare's throat with one hand; all she could do was hang back.

"You're tired and you're frightened," he said at last. "Get down here."

There were twigs in the dark, the overhang of a thicket of some sort. He thrust her in under this, and lay beside her on the bed of groundpine. The hand that was not in love with her throat reached across her; she felt the weight of its forearm on her shoulder and its fingers among the strands of her hair, eagerly, but tenderly, busy. Not once did he stop speaking, no louder than breathing, his lips to her ear.

"*'Amarantha sweet and fair — Ah, braid no more that shining hair . . .'*"

Mare had never heard of Lovelace, the poet; she thought the loony was just going on, hardly listened, got little sense. But the cadence of it added to the lethargy of all her flesh.

"*'Like a dew of golden thread — Most excellently ravelled . . .'*"

Voices loudened; feet came tramping; a pair went past not two rods away.

"*' . . . Do not then wind up the light — In ribbands, and o'ercloud in night . . .'*"

The search went on up the woods, men shouting to one another and beating the brush.

"*' . . . But shake your head and scatter day.'* I've never loved, Amarantha. They've tried me with prettiness, but prettiness is too cheap, yes, it's too cheap."

Mare was cold, and the coldness made her lazy. All she knew was that he talked on.

"But dogwood blowing in the spring isn't cheap. The earth of a field isn't cheap. Lots of times I've lain down and kissed the earth of a field, Amarantha. That's beauty, and a kiss for beauty." His breath moved up her cheek. He trembled violently. "No, no, not yet!" He got to his knees and pulled her by an arm. "We can go now."

They went back down the slope, but at an angle, so that when they came to the level they passed two hundred yards to the north of the house, and crossed the road there. More and more her walking was like sleepwalking, the feet numb in their shoes. Even where he had to let go of her, crossing the creek on stones, she stepped where he stepped with an obtuse docility. The voices of the searchers on the back ridge were small in distance when they began to climb the fence of Coward Hill, on the opposite side of the valley.

There is an old farm on top of Coward Hill, big hayfields as flat as tables. It had been half-past nine when Mare stood on the rock above the barn; it was toward midnight when Humble Jewett put aside the last branches of the woods and let her out on the height, and a half a moon had risen. And a wind blew there, tossing the withered tops of last year's grasses, and mists ran with the wind, and ragged shadows with the mists, and mares'-tails of clear moonlight among the shadows, so that now the boles of birches on the forest's edge beyond the fences were but opal blurs and now cut alabaster. It struck so cold against the girl's cold flesh, this wind, that another wind of shivers blew through her, and she put her hands over her face and eyes. But the madman stood with his eyes open and his mouth open, drinking the moonlight and the wet wind.

His voice, when he spoke at last, was thick in his throat.

"Get down on your knees." He got down on his and pulled her after. "And pray!"

Once in England a poet sang four lines. Four hundred years have forgotten his name, but they have remembered his lines. The daft man knelt upright, his face raised to the wild scud, his long wrists hanging to the dead grass. He began simply:

> *"O western wind, when wilt thou blow*
> *"That the small rain down can rain?"*

The Adam's apple was big in his bent throat. As simply he finished.

> *"Christ, that my love were in my arms*
> *"And I in my bed again!"*

Mare got up and ran. She ran without aim or feeling in the power of the wind. She told herself again that the mists would hide her from him, as she had done at dusk. And again, seeing that he ran at her shoulder, she knew he had been there all the while, making a race of it, flailing the air with his long arms for joy of play in the cloud of spring, throwing his knees high, leaping the moon-blue waves of the brown grass, shaking his bright hair; and her own hair was a weight behind her, lying level on the wind. Once a shape went bounding ahead of them for instants; she did not realize it was a fox till it was gone.

She never thought of stopping; she never thought of anything, except once, Oh, my God, I wish I had my shoes off! And what would have been the good in stopping or in turning another way, when it was only play? The man's ecstasy magnified his strength. When a snake fence came at them he took the top rail in flight, like a college hurdler, and seeing the girl hesitate and half turn as if to flee, he would have releaped it without touching a hand. But then she got a loom of buildings, climbed over quickly, before he should jump, and ran along the lane that ran with the fence.

Mare had never been up there, but she knew that the farm and the house belonged to a man named Wyker, a kind of cousin of Ruby Herter's, a violent, bearded old fellow who lived by himself. She could not believe her luck. When she had run half the distance and Jewett had not grabbed her, doubt grabbed her instead. "Oh, my God, go careful!" she told herself. "Go slow!" she implored herself, and stopped running, to walk.

Here was a misgiving the deeper in that it touched her special knowledge. She had never known an animal so far gone that its instincts failed it; a starving rat will scent the trap sooner than a fed one. Yet, after one glance at the house they approached, Jewett paid it no further attention, but walked with his eyes to the right, where the cloud had blown away, and wooded ridges, like black waves rimed with silver, ran down away toward the Valley of Virginia.

"I've never lived!" In his single cry there were two things, beatitude and pain.

Between the bigness of the falling world and his eyes the flag of her hair blew. He reached out and let it whip between his fingers. Mare was afraid it would break the spell then, and he would stop looking away and look at the house again. So she did something incredible; she spoke.

"It's a pretty — I mean — a beautiful view down that-a-way."

"God Almighty beautiful, to take your breath away. I knew I'd never loved, Beloved — " He caught a foot under the long end of one of the boards that covered the well and went down heavily on his hands and knees. It seemed to make no difference. "But I never knew I'd never lived," he finished in the same tone of strong rapture, quadruped in the grass, while Mare ran for the door and grabbed the latch.

When the latch would not give, she lost what little sense she had. She pounded with her fists. She cried with all her might: "Oh — hey — in there — hey — in there!" Then Jewett came and took her gently between his hands and drew her away, and then, though she was free, she stood in something like an awful embarrassment while he tried shouting.

"Hey! Friend! whoever you are, wake up and let my love and me come in!"

"No!" wailed the girl.

He grew peremptory. "Hey, wake up!" He tried the latch. He passed to full fury in a wink's time; he cursed, he kicked, he beat the door till Mare thought he would break his hands. Withdrawing, he ran at it with his shoulder; it burst at the latch, went slamming in, and left a black emptiness. His anger dissolved in a big laugh. Turning in time to catch her by a wrist, he cried joyously, "Come, my Sweet One!"

"No! No! Please — aw — listen. There ain't nobody there. He ain't to home. It wouldn't be right to go in anybody's house if they wasn't to home, you know that."

His laugh was blither than ever. He caught her high in his arms. "I'd do the same by his love and him if 'twas my house, I would." At the threshold he paused and thought. "That is, if she was the true love of his heart forever."

The room was the parlor. Moonlight slanted in at the door, and another shaft came through a window and fell across a sofa, its covering dilapidated, showing its wadding in places. The air was sour, but both of them were farm-bred.

"Don't, Amarantha!" His words were pleading in her ear. "Don't be so frightened."

He set her down on the sofa. As his hands let go of her they were shaking.

"But look, I'm frightened too." He knelt on the floor before her, reached out his hands, withdrew them. "See, I'm afraid to touch you." He mused, his eyes rounded. "Of all the ugly things there are, fear is the ugliest. And yet, see, it can be the very beautifulest. That's a strange queer thing."

The wind blew in and out of the room, bringing the thin, little bitter sweetness of new April at night. The moonlight that came across Mare's shoulders fell full upon his face, but hers it left dark, ringed by the aureole of her disordered hair.

"Why do you wear a halo, Love?" He thought about it. "Because

you're an angel, is that why?" The swift, untempered logic of the
mad led him to dismay. His hands came flying to hers, to make sure
they were of earth; and he touched her breast, her shoulders, and her
hair. Peace returned to his eyes as his fingers twined among the
strands.

" 'Thy hair is as a flock of goats that appear from Gilead . . .' "
He spoke like a man dreaming. " 'Thy temples are like a piece of
pomegranate within thy locks.' "

Mare never knew that he could not see her for the moonlight.

"Do you remember, Love?"

She dared not shake her head under his hand. "Yeh, I reckon," she
temporized.

"You remember how I sat at your feet, long ago, like this, and
made up a song? And all the poets in all the world have never made
one to touch it, have they, Love?"

"Ugh-ugh — never."

" 'How beautiful are thy feet with shoes . . .' Remember?"

"Oh, my God, what's he sayin' now?" she wailed to herself.

*" 'How beautiful are thy feet with shoes, O prince's daughter! the joints of
thy thighs are like jewels, the work of the hands of a cunning workman.
Thy navel is like a round goblet, which wanteth not liquor; thy belly is like
an heap of wheat set about with lilies.
Thy two breasts are like two young roes that are twins.' "*

Mare had not been to church since she was a little girl, when her
mother's black dress wore out. "No, no!" she wailed under her breath.
"You're awful to say such awful things." She might have shouted it;
nothing could have shaken the man now, rapt in the immortal,
passionate periods of Solomon's Song.

*" ' . . . now also thy breasts shall be as clusters of the vine, and the smell of
thy nose like apples.' "*

Hotness touched Mare's face for the first time. "Aw, no, don't talk
so!"

*" 'And the roof of thy mouth like the best wine for my beloved . . . causing
the lips of them that are asleep to speak.' "*

He had ended. His expression changed. Ecstasy gave place to

anger, love to hate. And Mare felt the change in the weight of the fingers in her hair.

"What do you mean, I mustn't say it like that?" But it was not to her his fury spoke, for he answered himself straightway. "Like poetry, Mr. Jewett; I won't have blasphemy around my school."

"Poetry. My God! if that isn't poetry — if that isn't music — " ... "It's Bible, Jewett. What you're paid to teach here is *literature.*"

"Doctor Ryeworth, you're the blasphemer and you're an ignorant man." ... "And your principal. And I won't have you going around reading sacred allegory like earthly love."

"Ryeworth, you're an old man, a dull man, a dirty man, and you'd be better dead."

Jewett's hands had slid down from Mare's head. "Then I went to put my fingers around his throat, so. But my stomach turned, and I didn't do it. I went to my room. I laughed all the way to my room. I sat in my room at my table and laughed. I laughed all afternoon and long after dark came. And then, about ten, somebody came and stood beside me in my room."

" 'Wherefore dost thou laugh, son?'

"Then I knew who He was, He was Christ.

" 'I was laughing about that dirty, ignorant, crazy old fool, Lord.

" 'Wherefore dost thou laugh?'

"I didn't laugh any more. He didn't say any more. I kneeled down, bowed my head.

" 'Thy will be done! Where is he, Lord?'

" 'Over at the girls' dormitory, waiting for Blossom Sinckley.'

"Brassy Blossom, dirty Blossom . . ."

It had come so suddenly it was nearly too late. Mare tore at his hands with hers, tried with all her strength to pull her neck away.

"Filthy Blossom! and him an old filthy man, Blossom! and you'll find him in Hell when you reach there, Blossom. . . ."

It was more the nearness of his face than the hurt of his hands that gave her power of fright to choke out three words.

"*I — ain't — Blossom!*"

Light ran in crooked veins. Through the veins she saw his face bewildered. His hands loosened. One fell down and hung; the other he lifted and put over his eyes, took it away again and looked at her.

"Amarantha!" His remorse was fearful to see. "What have I done!" His hands returned to hover over the hurts, ravening with pity, grief and tenderness. Tears fell down his cheeks. And with that, dammed desire broke its dam.

"Amarantha, my love, my dove, my beautiful love — "

"And I ain't Amarantha neither, I'm Mary! Mary, that's my name!"

She had no notion what she had done. He was like a crystal crucible that a chemist watches, changing hue in a wink with one adeptly added drop; but hers was not the chemist's eye. All she knew was that she felt light and free of him; all she could see of his face as he stood away above the moonlight were the whites of his eyes.

"Mary!" he muttered. A slight paroxysm shook his frame. So in the transparent crucible desire changed its hue. He retreated farther, stood in the dark by some tall piece of furniture. And still she could see the whites of his eyes.

"Mary! Mary Adorable!" A wonder was in him. "Mother of God."

Mare held her breath. She eyed the door, but it was too far. And already he came back to go on his knees before her, his shoulders so bowed and his face so lifted that it must have cracked his neck, she thought; all she could see on the face was pain.

"Mary Mother, I'm sick to my death. I'm so tired."

She had seen a dog like that, one she had loosed from a trap after it had been there three days, its caught leg half gnawed free. Something about the eyes.

"Mary Mother, take me in your arms . . ."

Once again her muscles tightened. But he made no move.

" . . . and give me sleep."

No, they were worse than the dog's eyes.

"Sleep, sleep! why won't they let me sleep? Haven't I done it all yet, Mother? Haven't I washed them yet of all their sins? I've drunk the cup that was given me; is there another? They've mocked me and reviled me, broken my brow with thorns and my hands with nails, and I've forgiven them, for they knew not what they did. Can't I go to sleep now, Mother?"

Mare could not have said why, but now she was more frightened than she had ever been. Her hands lay heavy on her knees, side by side, and she could not take them away when he bowed his head and rested his face upon them.

After a moment he said one thing more. "Take me down gently when you take me from the Tree."

Gradually the weight of his body came against her shins, and he slept.

The moon streak that entered by the eastern window crept north across the floor, thinner and thinner; the one that fell through the southern doorway traveled east and grew fat. For a while Mare's feet pained her terribly and her legs too. She dared not move them, though, and by and by they did not hurt so much.

A dozen times, moving her head slowly on her neck, she canvassed the shadows of the room for a weapon. Each time her eyes came back to a heavy earthenware pitcher on a stand some feet to the left of the sofa. It would have had flowers in it when Wyker's wife was alive; probably it had not been moved from its dust ring since she died. It would be a long grab, perhaps too long; still, it might be done if she had her hands.

To get her hands from under the sleeper's head was the task she set herself. She pulled first one, then the other, infinitesimally. She waited. Again she tugged a very, very little. The order of his breathing was not disturbed. But at the third trial he stirred.

"Gently! gently!" His own muttering waked him more. With some drowsy instinct of possession he threw one hand across her wrists, pinning them together between thumb and fingers. She kept dead quiet, shut her eyes, lengthened her breathing, as if she too slept.

There came a time when what was pretense grew a peril; strange as it was, she had to fight to keep her eyes open. She never knew whether or not she really napped. But something changed in the air, and she was wide awake again. The moonlight was fading on the doorsill, and the light that runs before dawn waxed in the window behind her head.

And then she heard a voice in the distance, lifted in maundering song. It was old man Wyker coming home after a night, and it was plain he had had some whiskey.

Now a new terror laid hold of Mare.

"Shut up, you fool you!" she wanted to shout. "Come quiet, quiet!" She might have chanced it now to throw the sleeper away from her and scramble and run, had his powers of strength and quickness not taken her simple imagination utterly in thrall.

Happily the singing stopped. What had occurred was that the farmer had espied the open door and, even befuddled as he was, wanted to know more about it quietly. He was so quiet that Mare had began to fear he had gone away. He had the squirrel-hunter's foot, and the first she knew of him was when she looked and saw his head in the doorway, his hard, soiled, whiskery face half upside-down with craning.

He had been to the town. Between drinks he had wandered in and out of the night's excitement; had even gone a short distance with one search party himself. Now he took in the situation in the room. He used his forefinger. First he held it to his lips. Next he pointed it with a jabbing motion at the sleeper. Then he tapped his own forehead and described wheels. Lastly, with his whole hand, he made pushing gestures, for Mare to wait. Then he vanished as silently as he had appeared.

The minutes dragged. The light in the east strengthened and turned rosy. Once she thought she heard a board creaking in another part of the house, and looked down sharply to see if the loony stirred. All she could see of his face was a temple with freckles on it and the sharp ridge of a cheekbone, but even from so little she knew how deeply and peacefully he slept. The door darkened. Wyker was there again. In one hand he carried something heavy; with the other he beckoned.

"Come jumpin'!" he said out loud.

Mare went jumping, but her cramped legs threw her down halfway to the sill; the rest of the distance she rolled and crawled. Just as she tumbled through the door it seemed as if the world had come to an end above her; two barrels of a shotgun discharged into a room make a noise. Afterwards all she could hear in there was something twisting and bumping on the floor boards. She got up and ran.

Mare's mother had gone to pieces; neighbor women put her to bed when Mare came home. They wanted to put Mare to bed, but she would not let them. She sat on the edge of her bed in her lean-to bedroom off the kitchen, just as she was, her hair down all over her shoulders and her shoes on, and stared away from them, at a place in the wallpaper.

"Yeh, I'll go myself. Lea' me be!"

The women exchanged quick glances, thinned their lips, and left her be. "God knows," was all they would answer to the questionings of those that had not gone in, "but she's gettin' herself to bed."

When the doctor came through he found her sitting just as she had been, still dressed, her hair down on her shoulders and her shoes on.

"What d' y' want?" she muttered and stared at the place in the wallpaper.

How could Doc Paradise say, when he did not know himself?

"I didn't know if you might be — might be feeling very smart, Mary."

"I'm all right. Lea' me be."

It was a heavy responsibility. Doc shouldered it. "No, it's all right," he said to the men in the road. Ruby Herter stood a little apart, chewing sullenly and looking another way. Doc raised his voice to make certain it carried. "Nope, nothing."

Ruby's ears got red, and he clamped his jaws. He knew he ought to go in and see Mare, but he was not going to do it while everybody hung around waiting to see if he would. A mule tied near him reached out and mouthed his sleeve in idle innocence; he wheeled and banged a fist against the side of the animal's head.

"Well, what d' y' aim to do 'bout it?" he challenged its owner.

He looked at the sun then. It was ten in the morning. "Hell, I got work!" he flared, and set off down the road for home. Doc looked at Judge North, and the Judge started after Ruby. But Ruby shook his head angrily. "Lea' me be!" He went on, and the Judge came back.

It got to be eleven and then noon. People began to say, "Like enough she'd be as thankful if the whole neighborhood wasn't camped here." But none went away.

As a matter of fact they were no bother to the girl. She never saw them. The only move she made was to bend her ankles over and rest her feet on the edge; her shoes hurt terribly and her feet knew it, though she did not. She sat all the while staring at that one figure in the wallpaper, and she never saw the figure.

Strange as the night had been, this day was stranger. Fright and physical pain are perishable things once they are gone. But while pain merely dulls and telescopes in memory and remains diluted pain, terror looked back upon has nothing of terror left. A gambling chance taken, at no matter what odds, and won was a sure thing since the world's beginning; perils come through safely were never perilous.

But what fright does do in retrospect is this — it heightens each sensuous recollection, like a hard, clear lacquer laid on wood, bringing out the color and grain of it vividly.

Last night Mare had lain stupid with fear on groundpine beneath a bush, loud footfalls and light whispers confused in her ear. Only now, in her room, did she smell the groundpine.

Only now did the conscious part of her brain begin to make words of the whispering.

"*Amarantha*," she remembered, "*Amarantha sweet and fair.*" That was as far as she could go for the moment, except that the rhyme with "fair" was "hair." But then a puzzle, held in abeyance, brought other words. She wondered what "ravel Ed" could mean. "*Most excellently ravell-ed.*" It was left to her mother to bring the end.

They gave up trying to keep her mother out at last. The poor woman's prostration took the form of fussiness.

"Good gracious, daughter, you look a sight. Them new shoes, half ruined; ain't your feet *dead?* And look at your hair, all tangled like a wild one!"

She got a comb.

"Be quiet, daughter; what's ailin' you. Don't shake your head!"

"'*But shake your head and scatter day.*'"

"What you say, Amarantha?" Mrs. Doggett held an ear down.

"Go 'way! Lea' me be!"

Her mother was hurt and left. And Mare ran, as she stared at the wallpaper.

"*Christ, that my love were in my arms . . .*"

Mare ran. She ran through a wind white with moonlight and wet with "the small rain." And the wind she ran through, it ran through her, and made her shiver as she ran. And the man beside her leaped high over the waves of the dead grasses and gathered the wind in his arms, and her hair was heavy and his was tossing, and a little fox ran before them across the top of the world. And the world spread down around in waves of black and silver, more immense than she had ever known the world could be, and more beautiful.

"*God Almighty beautiful, to take your breath away!*"

Mare wondered, and she was not used to wondering. "Is it only crazy folks ever run like that and talk that way?"

She no longer ran; she walked; for her breath was gone. And there was some other reason, some other reason. Oh, yes, it was because her feet were hurting her. So, at last, and roundabout, her shoes had made contact with her brain.

Bending over the side of the bed, she loosened one of them mechanically. She pulled it half off. But then she looked down at it sharply, and she pulled it on again.

"How beautiful . . ."

Color overspread her face in a slow wave.

"How beautiful are thy feet with shoes . . ."

"Is it only crazy folks ever say such things?"

"O prince's daughter!"

"Or call you that?"

By and by there was a knock at the door. It opened, and Ruby Herter came in.

"Hello, Mare old girl!" His face was red. He scowled and kicked at the floor. "I'd 'a' been over sooner, except we got a mule down sick." He looked at his dumb betrothed. "Come on, cheer up, forget it! He won't scare you no more, not that boy, not what's left o' him. What you lookin' at, sourface? Ain't you glad to see me?"

Mare quit looking at the wallpaper and looked at the floor.

"Yeh," she said.

"That's more like it, babe." He came and sat beside her, reached down behind her and gave her a spank. "Come on, give us a kiss, babe!" He wiped his mouth on his jumper sleeve, a good farmer's sleeve, spotted with milking. He put his hands on her; he was used to handling animals. "Hey, you, warm up a little; reckon I'm goin' to do all the lovin'?"

"Ruby, lea' me be!"

"What!"

She was up, twisting. He was up, purple.

"What's ailin' of you, Mare? What you bawlin' about?"

"Nothin' — only go 'way!"

She pushed him to the door and through it with all her strength, and closed it in his face, and stood with her weight against it, crying, "Go 'way! Go 'way! Lea' me be!"

WALLACE STEGNER

The Women on the Wall

THE CORNER WINDOW of the study overlooked a lawn, and beyond that a sunken lane between high pines, and beyond the lane a point of land with the old beach club buildings at one end and a stone wall around its tip. Beyond the point, through the cypresses and eucalyptuses, Mr. Palmer could see the Pacific, misty blue, belted between shore and horizon with a band of brown kelp.

Writing every morning in his study, making over his old notebooks into a coherent account of his years on the Galapagos, Mr. Palmer could glance up from his careful longhand and catch occasional glimpses, as a traveler might glance out of the window of a moving train. And in spite of the rather special atmosphere of the point, caused by the fact that until the past year it had been a club, there was something homey and neighborly and pleasant about the place that Mr. Palmer liked. There were children, for one thing, and dogs drifting up and down, and the occasional skirr of an automobile starting in the quiet, the diminishing sound of tires on asphalt, the distant racket of a boy being a machine-gun with his mouth.

Mr. Palmer had been away from the States a long time; he found the noises on the point familiar and nostalgic and reassuring in this time of war, and felt as if he had come home. Though California differed considerably from his old home in Ohio, he fell naturally and gratefully into its procession of morning and afternoon, its neighborhood routines, the pleasant breathing of its tides. When anything outside broke in upon his writing, it was generally a commonplace and familiar thing; Mr. Palmer looked up and took pleasure in the interruption.

One thing he could be sure of seeing, every morning but Sunday. The section was outside the city limits, and mail was delivered to a battery of mailboxes where the sunken lane joined the street. The mail arrived at about eleven; about ten-thirty the women from the beach club apartments began to gather on the stone wall. Below the wall was the beach, where the tides leaned in all the way from Iwo and Okinawa. Above it was the row of boxes where as regularly as the tide the mail carrier came in a gray car and deposited postmarked flotsam from half a world away.

Sometimes Mr. Palmer used to pause in his writing and speculate on what these women thought of when they looked out across the gumdrop blue water and the brown kelp and remembered that across this uninterrupted ocean their husbands fought and perhaps bled and possibly died, that in those far islands it was already tomorrow, that the green water breaking against the white foot of the beach might hold in suspension minute quantities of the blood shed into it thousands of miles away, that the Japan current, swinging in a great circle up under the Aleutians and back down the American coast, might as easily bear the mingled blood or the floating relics of a loved one lost as it could bear the glass balls of Japanese netfloats that it sometimes washed ashore.

Watching the women, with their dogs and children, waiting patiently on the stone wall for that most urgent of all gods, that Mercury in the gray uniform, Mr. Palmer thought a good deal about Penelope on the rocky isle of Ithaca above the wine-dark sea. He got a little sentimental about these women. Sometimes he was almost frightened by the air of patient, withdrawn seriousness they wore as they waited, and the unsmiling alacrity with which they rose and crowded around the mailman when he came. And when the mail was late, and one or two of them sat out on the wall until eleven-thirty, twelve, sometimes twelve-thirty, Mr. Palmer could hardly bear it at all.

Waiting, Mr. Palmer reflected, must cause a person to remove to a separate and private world. Like sleep or insanity, waiting must have the faculty of making the real unreal and remote. It seemed to Mr. Palmer pathetic and somehow thrilling that these women should have followed their men to the very brink of the west, and should remain here now with their eyes still westward, patiently and faithfully suspending their own normal lives until the return of their husbands. Without knowing any of the women, Mr. Palmer respected and admired them. They did not invite his pity. Penelope was as competent for her waiting as Ulysses was for his wars and wiles.

Mr. Palmer had been working in his new house hardly a week before he found himself putting on his jacket about eleven and going out to join the women.

He knew them all by sight, just from looking out the window. The red-haired woman with the little boy was sitting on the wall nearest him. Next was the thin girl who always wore a bathing suit and went barefooted. Next was the dark-haired one, five or six months pregnant. And next to her was the florid, quick, wren-like woman with the little girl about five. Their faces all turned as Mr. Palmer came up.

"Good morning," he said.

The red-haired woman's plain, serious, freckled face acknowledged him, and she murmured good morning. The girl in the bathing suit had turned to look off over the ocean, and Mr. Palmer felt that she had not made any reply. The pregnant girl and the woman with the little girl both nodded.

The old man put his hands on his knees, rounded his mouth and eyes, and bent to look at the little boy hanging to the red-haired woman's hand. "Well!" he said. "Hi, young fella!"

The child stared at him, crowding against his mother's legs. The mother said nothing, and rather than push first acquaintance too far, Mr. Palmer walked on along the wall.

As he glanced at the thin girl, he met her eyes, so full of cold hostility that for a moment he was shocked. He had intended to sit down in the middle of the wall, but her look sent him on further, to sit between the pregnant girl and the wren-like woman.

"These beautiful mornings!" Mr. Palmer said, sitting down with a sigh.

The wren-like woman nodded, the pregnant one regarded him with quiet ox-eyes.

"This is quite a ritual, waiting for the mail," Mr. Palmer said. He pointed to the gable of his house across the lane. "I see you from my window over there, congregating on the wall here every morning."

The wren-like woman looked at him rather oddly, then leaped to prevent her daughter from putting out the eyes of the long-suffering setter she was mauling. The pregnant girl smiled a slow, soft smile. Over her shoulder Mr. Palmer saw the thin girl hitch herself up and sit on her hands. The expression on her face said that she knew very well why Mr. Palmer had come down and butted in, and why he watched from his window.

"The sun's so warm out here," the pregnant girl said. "It's a way of killing part of the morning, sitting out here."

"A very good way," Mr. Palmer said. He smoothed the creases in his trousers, finding speech a little difficult. From the shelter of his mother's legs the two-year-old boy down the wall stared at him solemnly. Then the wren-like woman hopped off the wall and dusted her skirt.

"Here he is!" she said.

They all started across the mouth of the lane, and for some reason, as they waited for the mailman to sort and deliver, Mr. Palmer felt that his first introduction hadn't taken him very far. In a way, as he thought it over, he respected the women for that, too. They were living without their husbands, and had to be careful. After all, Penelope had many suitors. But he could not quite get over wanting to spank the thin girl on her almost exposed backside, and he couldn't shake the sensation of having wandered by mistake into the ladies' room.

After that, without feeling that he knew them at all, he respected them and respected their right to privacy. Waiting, after all, put you in an exclusive club. No outsider had any more right on that wall than he had in the company of a bomber crew. But Mr. Palmer felt that he could at least watch from his window; and at the mailboxes he could, almost by osmosis, pick up a little more information.

The red-haired woman's name was Kendall. Her husband was an army captain, a doctor. The thin girl, Mrs. Fisher, got regular letters bearing a Marine Corps return. The husband of Mrs. Corson, the wren-like woman, commanded a flotilla of minesweepers in the western Pacific. Of the pregnant girl, Mrs. Vaughn, Mr. Palmer learned little. She got few letters, and none with any postmarks that told anything.

From his study window Mr. Palmer went on observing them benignly and making additions to his notes on the profession of waiting. Though the women differed sharply one from another, they seemed to Mr. Palmer to have one thing in common: they were all quiet, peaceful, faithful to the times and seasons of their vigil, almost like convalescents in a hospital. They made no protests or outcries; they merely lived at a reduced tempo, as if pulse rate and respiration rate and metabolic rate and blood pressure were all tuned down. Mr. Palmer had a notion how it might be. Sometimes when he awoke very quietly in the night he could feel how quietly and slowly and regularly his heart was pumping, how slow and regular his breathing was, how he lay there mute and cool and inert with everything turned down to idling speed, his old body taking care of itself. And when he woke that way he had a curious feeling that he was waiting for something.

Every morning at ten-thirty, as regular as sun and tide, Mrs. Kendall came out of the beach club apartments and walked across the point, leading her little boy by the hand. She had the child tuned down, too, apparently. He never, to Mr. Palmer's knowledge, ran or yelled or cried or made a fuss, but walked quietly beside his mother, and sat with her on the big stump until five minutes to eleven, and then walked with her across to the end of the stone wall. About that time the other women began to gather, until all four of them were there in a quiet, uncommunicative row.

Only once in all that drowsy spring was there any breaking of the pattern. That was one Monday after Mr. Palmer had been away for the weekend. When he strolled out at mailtime he found the women not sitting on the wall, but standing in a nervous conversational group. They opened to let him in, for once accepting him silently among them, and he found that the thin girl had moved out suddenly the day before: the Saturday mail had brought word that her husband had gone down in flames over the Marianas.

The news depressed Mr. Palmer in curious ways. It depressed him to see the women shaken from their phlegmatic routine, because the moment they were so shaken they revealed the raw fear under their quiet. And it depressed him that the thin girl's husband had been killed. That tragedy should come to a woman he personally felt to be a snob, a fool, a vain and inconsequent chit, seemed to him sad and incongruous and even exasperating. As long as she was one of the company of Penelopes, Mr. Palmer had refused to dislike her. The moment she made demands upon his pity he disliked her very much.

After that sudden blow, as if a hawk had struck among the quiet birds on the wall, Mr. Palmer found it less pleasant to watch the slow, heavy-bodied walking of Mrs. Kendall, her child always tight by the hand, from apartment to stump to wall. Unless spoken to, she never spoke. She wore gingham dresses that were utterly out of place in the white sun above the white beach. She was plain, unattractive, patient, the most remote, the most tuned-down, the quietest and saddest and most patient and most exasperating of the Penelopes. She too began to make wry demands on Mr. Palmer's pity, and he found himself almost disliking her. He was guilty of a little prayer that Mrs. Kendall's husband would be spared, so that his pity would not have to go any further than it did.

Then one morning Mr. Palmer became aware of another kind of interruption on the point. Somebody there had apparently bought a new dog. Whoever had acquired it must have fed it, though Mr. Palmer never saw anyone do so, and must have exercised it, though he never saw that either. All he saw was that the dog, a half-grown cocker, was tied to the end of a rose trellis in the clubhouse yard. And all he heard, for two solid days, was the uproar the dog made.

It did not like being tied up. It barked, and after a while its voice would break into a kind of hysterical howling mixed with shuddering diminuendo groans. Nobody ever came and told it to be still, or took care of it, or let it loose. It stayed there and yanked on the rope and chewed at the trellis post and barked and howled and groaned until Mr. Palmer's teeth were on edge and he was tempted to call the Humane Society.

Actually he didn't, because on the third morning the noise had stopped and as he came into his study to begin working he saw that the dog was gone. Mrs. Corson was sitting in a lawn chair under one of the cypresses, and her daughter was digging in the sandpile. There was no sign either of Mrs. Kendall or Mrs. Vaughn. The owner of the house was raking leaves on the lawn above the seawall.

Mr. Palmer looked at his watch. It was nine-thirty. On an impulse he slipped on a jacket and went down and out across the lawn and down across the lane and up the other side past the trellis. Where the dog had lain the ground was strewn with chewed green splinters.

Mrs. Corson looked up from her chair. Her cheeks were painted with a patchwork of tiny ruddy veins, and her eyes looked as if she hadn't slept. They had a stary blankness like blind eyes, and Mr. Palmer noticed that the pupils were dilated, even in the bright light. She took a towel and a pack of cigarettes and a bar of coco-butter off the chair next to her.

"Good morning," she said in her husky voice. "Sit down." "Thank you," Mr. Palmer said. He let himself down into the steeply slanting wooden chair and adjusted the knees of his slacks. "It *is* a good morning," he said slyly. "So quiet."

Mrs. Corson's thin neck jerked upward and backward in a curious gesture. Her throaty laughter was loud and unrestrained, and the eyes she turned on Mr. Palmer were red with mirth.

"That damned dog," she said. "Wasn't that something?"

"I thought I'd go crazy," Mr. Palmer said. "Whose dog was it, anyway?"

Mrs. Corson's rather withered, red-nailed hand, with a big diamond and a wedding ring on the fourth finger, reached down and picked up the cigarettes. The hand trembled as it held the pack out.

"No thank you," he said.

Mrs. Corson took one. "It was Mrs. Kendall's dog," she said. "She took it back."

"Thank God!" said Mr. Palmer.

Her hands nervous with the matchbox in her lap, Mrs. Corson sat and smoked. Mr. Palmer saw that her lips, under the lipstick, were chapped, and that there was a dried, almost leathery look to her tanned and freckled skin.

He slid deeper into the chair and looked out over the water, calm as a lake, the long light swells breaking below him with a quiet, lulling swish. Up the coast heavier surf was breaking farther out. Its noise came like a pulsating tremble on the air, hardly a sound at all. Everything tuned down, Mr. Palmer was thinking. Even the lowest frequency of waves on the beach. Even the ocean waited.

"I should think you'd bless your stars, having a place like this to wait in," he said.

One of Mrs. Corson's eyebrows bent. She shot him a sideward look.

"Think of the women who are waiting in boardinghouse rooms," Mr. Palmer said, a little irritated at her manner. "Think of the ones who are working and leaving their children in nurseries."

"Oh, sure," Mrs. Corson said. "It's fine for Anne, with the beach and yard."

Mr. Palmer leaned on the arm of the chair and looked at her quizzically. He wished any of these women would ever put away their reticence and talk about their waiting, because that was where their life lay, that was where they had authority. "How long has your husband been gone?" he asked.

"Little over two years."

"That's a long time," Mr. Palmer said, thinking of Penelope and her wait. Ten years while the war went on at Troy, ten more years while Ulysses wandered through every peril in the Mediterranean, past Scylla and Charybdis and Circe and the Cyclops and the iron terrors of Hades and the soft temptations of Nausicaa. But that was poetry. Twenty years was too much. Two, in all conscience, was enough.

"I shouldn't kick," the woman said. "Mrs. Kendall's husband has been gone for over three."

"I've noticed her," Mr. Palmer said. "She seems rather sad and repressed."

For a moment Mrs. Corson's eyes, slightly bloodshot, the pupils dilated darkly, were fixed questioningly on Mr. Palmer's. Then the woman shook herself almost as a dog does. "I guess," she said. She rose with a nervous snap and glanced at her watch. From the sand-pile the little girl called, "Is it time, Mommy?"

"I guess so," Mrs. Corson said. She laid the back of her hand across her eyes and made a face.

"I'll be getting along," Mr. Palmer said.

"I was just taking Anne down for her pony ride. Why don't you ride down with us?"

"Well . . ."

"Come on," Mrs. Corson said. "We'll be back in less than an hour."

The child ran ahead of them and opened the car doors, down in the widened part of the lane. As Mr. Palmer helped Mrs. Corson in she turned her face a little, and he smelled the stale alcohol on her breath. Obviously Mrs. Corson had been drinking the night before, and obviously she was a little hung over.

But my Lord, why not? he said to himself. Two years of waiting, nothing to do but sit and watch and do nothing and be patient. He didn't like Mrs. Corson any less for occasional drinking. She was higher-strung than either Mrs. Vaughn or Mrs. Kendall. You could almost lift up the cover board and pluck her nerves like the strings of a piano. Even so, she played the game well. He liked her.

At the pony track Anne raced down the fenced runway at a pink fluttering gallop, and Mr. Palmer and Mrs. Corson, following more slowly, found her debating between a black and a pinto pony.

"Okay," the man in charge said. "Which'll it be today, young lady?"

"I don't know," the girl said. Her forehead wrinkled. "Mommy, which do you think?"

"I don't care, hon," her mother said. "Either one is nice."

Pretty, her blonde braids hanging in front and framing her odd pre-Raphaelite face, Anne stood indecisive. She turned her eyes up to Mr. Palmer speculatively. "The black one's nice," she said, "but so's the . . ."

"Oh, Anne," her mother said. "For heaven's sake make up your mind."

"Well . . . the black one, then," Anne said. She reached out a hand and touched the pony's nose, pulling her fingers back sharply and looking up at her mother with a smile that Mr. Palmer found himself almost yearning over. She was a pretty, dainty little child, no mistake.

"You're a nitwit," her mother said. "Hop on, so we can get back for the mailman."

The attendant swung her up, but with one leg over the saddle Anne kicked and screamed to get down. "I've changed my mind," she said. "Not this one, the pinto one."

The attendant put her up on the pinto and Mrs. Corson, her chapped lips trembling, said, "Another outburst like that and you won't get on any, you little . . . !"

The pony started, led by the attendant who rocked on one thick-soled shoe. For a moment Mrs. Corson and Mr. Palmer stood in the sun under the sign that said "Pony Rides, 10 Cents, 12 for $1.00." They were, Mr. Palmer noticed, in the Mexican part of town. Small houses, some of them almost shacks, with geraniums climbing all over them, strung out along the street. Down on the corner beyond the car was a tavern with a dusty tin sign. Mrs. Corson unsnapped her purse and fished out a wadded bill and held it vaguely in her hand, looking off up the street past the track and the pinto pony and the pink little huddle on its back and the attendant rocking along ahead on his one thick shoe.

"I wonder," she said. "Would you do me a favor?"

"Anything."

"Would you stay here five minutes while I go to the store? Just keep an eye on her?"

"Of course," he said. "I'd be glad to go to the store for you, if you'd like."

"No," she said. "No, I'd better get it." She put the crumpled bill into his hand. "Let her have all the rides she wants. I'll be back in a few minutes."

Mr. Palmer settled himself on a chair against the stable wall and waited. When Anne and the attendant got back he waved the bill at them. "Want another ride?"

"Yes!" Anne said. Her hands were clenched tightly in the pony's mane, and her eyes danced and her mouth was a little open. The attendant turned and started down the track again. "Run!" Anne cried to him. "Make him run!"

The crippled hostler broke into a clumsy hop-skip-and-jump for a few yards, pulling the pony into a trot. The girl screamed with delight. Mr. Palmer yawned, tapped his mouth, smiled a little as he smelled the powder-and-perfume smell on the dollar bill, yawned again. Say what you would, it was decent of the woman to come out with a hangover and take her child to the pony track. She must feel pretty rocky, if her eyes were any criterion.

He waited for some time. Anne finished a second ride, took a third, finished that and had a fourth. The attendant was sweating a little. From the fence along the sidewalk two Negro children and a handful of little Mexicans watched. "How about it?" Mr. Palmer said. "Want another?"

She nodded, shaken with giggles and sudden shyness when she looked around and found her mother gone.

"Sure you're not getting sore?" Mr. Palmer patted his haunch suggestively.

She shook her head.

"Okay," the hostler said. "Here we go again, then."

At the end of the fifth ride Anne let herself be lifted off. The hostler went inside and sat down, the pony joined its companion at the rail, cocked its hip and tipped its right hoof and closed its eyes. Anne climbed up into Mr. Palmer's lap.

"Where's Mommy?"

"She went to buy something."

"Darn her," Anne said. "She does that all the time. She better hurry up, it's getting mail time."

"Don't you like to miss the mail?"

"Sometimes there's packages and things from Daddy," Anne said. "I got a grass skirt once."

Mr. Palmer rounded his mouth and eyes. "You must like your daddy."

"I do. Mommy doesn't, though."

"What?"

"Mommy gets mad," Anne said. "She thinks Daddy could have

had shore duty a long time ago, he's had so much combat, but she says he likes the Navy better than home. He's a commander."

"Yes, I know," Mr. Palmer said. He looked up the street, beginning to be fretful. The fact that the woman spent her whole life waiting shouldn't make her quite so callous to how long she kept other people waiting. "We are going to miss the mailman if your mommy doesn't hurry," he said.

Anne jumped off his lap and puckered her lips like her mother. "And today's a package!"

Mr. Palmer raised his eyebrows. "How do you know?"

"The fortune teller told Mommy."

"I see," the old man said. "Does your mother go to fortune tellers often?"

"Every Saturday," Anne said. "I went with her once. You know what she said? And it came true, too."

Mr. Palmer saw the girl's mother coming down the sidewalk, and stood up. "Here comes Mommy," he said. "We'd better meet her at the car."

"She said we'd get good news, and right away Daddy was promoted," Anne said. "And she said we'd get a package, and that week we got *three!*"

Mrs. Corson was out of breath. In the bright sun her eyes burned with a curious sightless brilliance. The smell of alcohol on her was fresher and stronger.

"I'm sorry," she said as she got in. "I met a friend, and it was so hot we stopped for a beer."

On the open highway, going back home, she stepped down hard on the throttle, and her fingers kept clasping and unclasping the wheel. Her body seemed possessed of electric energy. She radiated something, she gave off sparks. Her eyes, with the immense dark pupils and suffused whites, were almost scary.

When they pulled up in front of Mr. Palmer's gate, opposite the mail boxes, the little red flags on some of the boxes were still up. On the stone wall sat Mrs. Kendall, her son Tommy, and the pregnant girl, Mrs. Vaughn. "Late again," Mrs. Corson said. "Damn that man."

"Can I play, Mommy?" Anne said.

"Okay." As the child climbed out, the mother said, "Don't get into any fixes with Tommy. Remember what I told you."

"I will," Anne said. Her setter came up and she stopped to pull its ears.

Her mother's face went pinched and mean. "And stop abusing that dog!" she said.

Mr. Palmer hesitated. He was beginning to feel uncomfortable, and he thought of the pages he might have filled that morning, and the hour that still remained before noon. But Mrs. Corson was leaning back with the back of her hand across her eyes. Through the windshield Mr. Palmer could see the two women and the child on the wall, like a multiple Patience on a monument. When he looked back at Mrs. Corson he saw that she too was watching them between her fingers. Quite suddenly she began to laugh.

She laughed for a good minute, not loudly but with curious violence, her whole body shaking. She dabbed her eyes and caught her breath and shook her head and tried to speak. Mr. Palmer attended uneasily, wanting to be gone.

"Lord," Mrs. Corson said finally. "Look at 'em. Vultures on a limb. Me too. Three mama vultures and one baby vulture."

"You're a little hard on yourself," Mr. Palmer said, smiling. "And Anne, I'd hardly call her a vulture."

"I didn't include her," Mrs. Corson said. She turned her hot red eyes on him. "She's got sense enough to run and play, and I hope I've got sense enough to let her."

"Well, but little Tommy . . ."

"Hasn't had his hand out of Mama's since they came here," Mrs. Corson said. "Did you ever see him play with anybody?"

Mr. Palmer confessed that he hadn't, now that he thought of it.

"Because if you ever do," Mrs. Corson said, "call out all the preachers. It'll be Christ come the second time. Honest to God, sometimes that woman . . ."

Bending forward, Mr. Palmer could see Mrs. Kendall smoothing the blue sweater around her son's waist. "I've wondered about her," he said, and stopped. Mrs. Corson had started to laugh again.

When she had finished her spasm of tight, violent mirth, she said, "It isn't her child, you know."

"No?" he said, surprised. "She takes such care of it."

"You're not kidding," Mrs. Corson said. "She won't let him play with Anne. Anne's too dirty. She digs in the ground and stuff. Seven months we've lived in the same house, and those kids haven't played together once. Can you imagine that?"

"No," Mr. Palmer confessed. "I can't."

"She adopted it when it was six months old," Mrs. Corson said. "She tells us all it's a love-child." Her laugh began again, a continuous, hiccoughy chuckle. "Never lets go its hand," she said. "Won't let him play with anybody. Wipes him off like an heirloom. And brags around he's a love-child. My God!"

With her thin, freckled arm along the door and her lips puckered, she fell silent. "Love-child!" she said at last. "Did you ever look at her flat face? It's the last place love would ever settle on."

"Perhaps that explains," Mr. Palmer said uncomfortably. "She's childless, she's unattractive. She pours all that frustrated affection out on this child."

Mrs. Corson twisted to look almost incredulously into his face. "Of course," she said. Her alcoholic breath puffed at him "Of course. But why toot it up as a love-child?" she said harshly. "What does she think my child is, for God's sake? How does she think babies are made?"

"Well, but there's that old superstition," Mr. Palmer said. He moved his hand sideward. "Children born of passion, you know — they're supposed to be more beautiful . . ."

"And doesn't that tell you anything about her?" Mrs. Corson said. "Doesn't that show you that she never thought of passion in the same world with her husband? She has to go outside herself for any passion, there's none in her."

"Yes," Mr. Palmer said. "Well, of course one can speculate, but one hardly knows . . ."

"And that damned dog," Mrs. Corson said. "Tommy can't play with other kids. They're too dirty. So she gets a dog. Dogs are cleaner than Anne, see? So she buys her child this nice germless dog, and then ties him up and won't let him loose. So the dog howls his head off, and we all go nuts. Finally we told her we couldn't stand it, why didn't she let it loose and let it run. But she said it might run away, and Tommy loved it so she didn't want to take a chance on losing the pup. So I finally called the Society for the Prevention of Cruelty to Animals, and they told her either to give it regular running and exercise or take it back. She took it back last night, and now she hates me."

As she talked, saliva had gathered in the corner of her mouth. She sucked it in and turned her head away, looking out on the street. "Lord God," she said. "So it goes, so it goes."

Through the windshield Mr. Palmer watched the quiet women on the wall, the quiet, well-behaved child. Anne was romping with the setter around the big stump, twenty feet beyond, and the little boy was watching her. It was a peaceful, and windless morning steeped in sun. The mingled smell of pines and low tide drifted across the street, and was replaced by the pervading faint fragrance of Ceanothus, blooming in shades of blue and white along Mr. Palmer's walk.

"I'm amazed," he said. "She seems so quiet and relaxed and plain."

"That's another thing," Mrs. Corson said. "She's a cover-yourself-up girl, too. Remember Margy Fisher, whose husband was killed a few weeks ago? You know why she never wore anything but a bathing suit? Because this old biddy was always after her about showing herself."

"Well, it's certainly a revelation," Mr. Palmer said. "I see you all from my window, you know, and it seems like a kind of symphony of waiting, all quiet and harmonious. The pregnant girl, too — going on with the slow inevitable business of life while her husband's gone, the rhythm of the generations unchanged. I've enjoyed the whole thing, like a pageant, you know."

"Your window isn't a very good peekhole," Mrs. Corson said dryly.

"Mm?"

"Hope's husband was killed at Dieppe," said Mrs. Corson.

For a moment Mr. Palmer did not catch on. At first he felt only a flash of pity as he remembered the girl's big steady brown eyes, her still, rather sad face, her air of pliant gentleness. Then the words Mrs. Corson had spoken began to take effect. Dieppe — almost three years ago. And the girl six months pregnant.

He wished Mrs. Corson would quit drumming her red nails on the car door. She was really in a state this morning, nervous as a cat. But that poor girl, sitting over there with all that bottled up inside of her, the fear and uncertainty growing as fast as the child in her womb grew . . .

"Some naval lieutenant," Mrs. Corson said. "He's right in the middle of the fighting, gunnery officer on a destroyer. You ought to hear Hope when she gets scared he'll never come back and make a decent woman of her."

"I'd not like to," Mr. Palmer said, and shook his head. Across the lane the placid scene had not changed, except that Mrs. Kendall had let Tommy toddle fifteen feet out from the wall, where he was picking up clusters of dry pine needles and throwing them into the air.

The figures were very clean, sharp-edged in the clear air against the blue backdrop of sea. An Attic grace informed all of them: the girl stooping above the long-eared red setter, the child with his hands in the air, tossing brown needles in a shower, the curving seated forms of the women on the wall. To Mr. Palmer's momentarily tranced eyes they seemed to freeze in attitudes of flowing motion like figures on a vase, cameo-clear in the clear air under the noble trees, with the quiet ocean of their watchfulness stretching blue to the misty edge. Like figures on a Grecian urn they curved in high relief against the white moulding of the wall, and a drift of indescribable melancholy washed across the point and pricked goosepimples on Mr. Palmer's arms. "It's sad," he said, opening the door and stepping down. "The whole thing is very sad."

With the intention of leaving he put his hand on the door and pushed it shut, thinking that he did not want to stay longer and hear Mrs. Corson's bitter tongue and watch the women on the wall. Their waiting now, with the momentary trance broken and the momentary lovely frozen group dispersed in motion, seemed to him a monstrous aberration, their patience a deathly apathy, their hope an obscene selfdelusion.

He was filled with a sense of the loveliness of the white paper and the cleanly sharpened pencils, the notebooks and the quiet and the sense of purpose that waited in his study. Most of all the sense of purpose, the thing to be done that would have an ending and a result.

"It's been very pleasant," he said automatically. At that moment there came a yowl from the point.

He turned. Apparently Anne, romping with the dog, had bumped

Tommy and knocked him down. He sat among the pine needles in his blue play suit and squalled, and Mrs. Kendall came swiftly out from the wall and took Anne by the arm, shaking her.

"You careless child!" she said. "Watch what you're doing."

Instantly Mrs. Corson was out of the car. Mr. Palmer saw her start for the point, her lips puckered, and was reminded of some mechanical toy tightly wound and tearing erratically around a room giving off sparks of ratchety noise. When she was twenty feet from Mrs. Kendall she shouted hoarsely, "Let go of that child!"

Mrs. Kendall's heavy gingham body turned. Her plain face, the mouth stiff with anger, confronted Mrs. Corson. Her hand still held Anne's arm. "It's possible to train children . . ." she said.

"Yes, and it's possible to mistreat them," Mrs. Corson said. "Let go of her."

For a moment neither moved. Then Mrs. Corson's hands darted down, caught Mrs. Kendall's wrist, and tore her hold from Anne's arm. Even across the lane, fifty feet away, Mr. Palmer could see the white fury in their faces as they confronted each other.

"If I had the bringing up of that child . . . !" Mrs. Kendall said. "I'd . . ."

"You'd tie her to your apron strings like you've tied your own," Mrs. Corson said. "Like you tie up a dog and expect it to get used to three feet of space. My God, a child's a little animal. He's got to run!"

"And knock other children down, I suppose."

"O my God!" Mrs. Corson said, and turned her thin face skyward as if to ask God to witness. She was shaking all over. Mr. Palmer could see the trembling of her dress. "Listen!" she said, "I don't know what's the matter with you, and why you can't stand nakedness, and why you think a bastard child is something holier than a legitimate one, and why you hang on to that child as if he was worth his weight in diamonds. But you keep your claws off mine, and if your little bastard can't get out of the way, you can just . . ."

Mrs. Kendall's face was convulsed. She raised both hands above her head, stuttering for words. From the side the pregnant girl slipped in quietly, and Mr. Palmer, rooted uneasily across the lane, heard her quiet voice. "You're beginning to draw a crowd," she said. "For the love of mike, turn it down."

Mrs. Corson swung on her. Her trembling had become an ecstasy. When she spoke she chewed loudly on her words, mangling them almost beyond recognition. "You keep out of this, you pregnant bitch," she said. "Any time I want advice on how to raise love-children, I'll come to you too, but right now I haven't got any love-children, and I'm raising what I've got my own way."

A window had gone up in the house next to Mr. Palmer's, and three boys were drifting curiously down the street, their pants sagging with the weight of armament they carried. Without hesitating more than a moment, Mr. Palmer crossed the street and cut them off. "I think you'd better beat it," he said, and pushed his hands in the air as if shooing chickens. The boys stopped and eyed him suspiciously, then began edging around the side. It was clear that in any contest of speed, agility, endurance, or anything else Mr. Palmer was no match for them. He put his hand in his pocket and pulled out some change. The boys stopped. Behind him Mr. Palmer heard the saw-edged voice of Mrs. Corson. "I'm not the kind of person that'll stand it, by God! If you want to . . ."

"Here," Mr. Palmer said. "Here's a quarter apiece if you light out and forget anything you saw."

"Okay!" they said, and stepped up one by one and got their quarters and retreated, their heads together and their armed hips clanking together and their faces turning once, together, to stare back at the arguing women on the point. Up the street Mr. Palmer saw a woman and three small children standing in the road craning. Mrs. Corson's voice carried for half a mile.

In the hope that his own presence would bring her to reason, Mr. Palmer walked across the lane. Mrs. Corson's puckered, furious face was thrust into Mrs. Kendall's, and she was saying, "Just tell me to my face I don't raise my child right! Go on, tell me so. Tell me what you told Margy, that Anne's too dirty for your bastard to play with. Tell me, I dare you, and I'll tear your tongue out!"

Mr. Palmer found himself standing next to Mrs. Vaughn. He glanced at her once and shook his head and cleared his throat. Mrs. Corson continued to glare into the pale flat face before her. When Mrs. Kendall turned heavily and walked toward the wall, the wren-like woman skipped nimbly around her and confronted her from the other side. "You've got a lot of things to criticize in me!" she said.

Her voice, suddenly, was so hoarse it was hardly more than a whisper. "Let's hear you say them to my face. I've heard them behind my back too long. Let's hear you say them!"

"Couldn't we get her into the house?" Mr. Palmer said to the pregnant girl. "She'll raise the whole neighborhood."

"Let her disgrace herself," Mrs. Vaughn said, and shrugged.

"But you don't understand," Mr. Palmer said. "She had a beer or so downtown, and I think that, that and the heat . . ."

The girl looked at him with wide brown eyes in which doubt and contempt and something like mirth moved like shadows on water. "I guess *you* don't understand," she said. "She isn't drunk. She's hopped."

"Hopped?"

"I thought you went downtown with her."

"I did."

"Did she leave you at the pony track?"

"Yes, for a few minutes."

"She goes to a joint down there," Mrs. Vaughn said. "Fortune telling in the front, goofballs and reefers in the rear. She's a sucker for all three."

"Goofballs?" Mr. Palmer said. "Reefers?"

"Phenobarb," Mrs. Vaughn said. "Marijuana. Anything. She doesn't care, long as she gets high. She's high as a kite now. Didn't you notice her eyes?"

Mrs. Kendall had got her boy by the hand. She was heavily ignoring Mrs. Corson. Now she lifted the child in her arms and turned sideways, like a cow ducking to the side to slip around a herder, and headed for the stone wall. Mrs. Corson whipped around her flanks, first on one side, then on the other, her hoarse whisper a continuing horror in Mr. Palmer's ears.

"What I ought to do," Mrs. Corson said, "is forbid Anne to even speak to that bastard of yours."

Mrs. Kendall bent and put the child on the ground and stood up. "Don't you call him that!" she shouted. "Oh, you vulgar, vicious, drunken, depraved woman! Leave me alone! Leave me alone, can't you?"

She burst into passionate tears. For a moment Mr. Palmer was terrified that they would come to blows and have to be pulled apart. He started forward, intending to take Mrs. Corson by the arm and lead her, forcefully if necessary, to the house. This disgraceful exhibition had gone on long enough. But the pregnant girl was ahead of him.

Mr. Palmer caught his cue. He put out his hand to Anne, and walked her down across the mouth of the lane. He did not look back, but his ears were sharp for a renewal of the cat-fight. None came. By the time the man in gray had distributed the papers and magazines to all the battery of boxes, and was unstrapping the pack of letters, Mr. Palmer was aware without turning that both Mrs. Corson and Mrs. Kendall were in the background by the gray car, waiting quietly.

Dawn of Remembered Spring

B<small>E</small> CAREFUL, Shan," Mom said. "I'm afraid if you wade that creek that a water moccasin will bite you."

"All right, Mom."

"You know what happened to Roy Deer last Sunday!"

"Yes, Mom!"

"He's nigh at the point of death," she said. "I'm going over there now to see him. His leg's swelled hard as a rock and it's turned black as black-oak bark. They're not looking for Roy to live until midnight tonight."

"All water moccasins ought to be killed, hadn't they, Mom?"

"Yes, they're pizen things, but you can't kill them," Mom said. "They're in all of these creeks around here. There's so many of them we can't kill 'em all."

Mom stood at the foot-log that crossed the creek in front of our house. Her white apron was starched stiff; I heard it rustle when Mom put her hand in the little pocket in the right upper corner to get tobacco crumbs for her pipe. Mom wore her slat bonnet that shaded her sun-tanned face — a bonnet with strings that came under her chin and tied in a bowknot.

"I feel uneasy," Mom said as she filled her long-stemmed clay-stone pipe with bright-burley crumbs, tamped them down with her index finger, and struck a match on the rough bark of an apple tree that grew on the creek bank by the foot-log.

"Don't feel uneasy about me," I said.

"But I do," Mom said. "Your pa out groundhog huntin' and I'll be away at Deers' — nobody at home but you, and so many pizen snakes around this house."

Mom blew a cloud of blue smoke from her pipe. She walked across the foot-log — her long clean dress sweeping the weed stubble where Pa had mown the weeds along the path with a scythe so we could leave the house without getting our legs wet by the dew-covered weeds.

When Mom walked out of sight around the turn of the pasture hill and the trail of smoke that she left behind her had disappeared into the light blue April air, I crossed the garden fence at the wild-plum thicket.

Everybody gone, I thought. I am left alone. I'll do as I please. A water moccasin bit Roy Deer but a water moccasin will never bite me. I'll get me a club from this wild-plum thicket and I'll wade up the creek killing water moccasins.

There was a dead wild-plum sprout standing among the thicket of living sprouts. It was about the size of a tobacco stick. I stepped out of my path into the wild-plum thicket. Barefooted, I walked among the wild-plum thorns. I uprooted the dead wild-plum sprout. There was a bulge on it where roots had once been — now the roots had rotted in the earth. It was like a maul with this big bulge on the end of it. It would be good to hit water moccasins with.

The mules played in the pasture. It was Sunday — their day of rest. And the mules knew it. This was Sunday and it was my day of rest. It was my one day of freedom, too, when Mom and Pa were gone and I was left alone. I would like to be a man now, I thought, I'd love to plow the mules, run a farm, and kill snakes. A water moccasin bit Roy Deer but one would never bite me.

The bright sunlight of April played over the green Kentucky hills.

Sunlight fell onto the creek of blue water that twisted like a crawling snake around the high bluffs, and between the high rocks. In many places dwarf willows, horseweeds, iron weeds, and wild grapevines shut away the sunlight and the creek waters stood in quiet pool puddles. These little puddles under the shade of weeds, vines, and willows were the places where the water moccasins lived.

I rolled my overall legs above my knees so I wouldn't wet them and Mom wouldn't know I'd been wading the creek. I started wading up the creek toward the head of the hollow. I carried my wild-plum club across my shoulder with both hands gripped tightly around the small end of it. I was ready to maul the first water moccasin I saw.

"One of you old water moccasins bit Roy Deer," I said bravely, clinching my grip tighter around my club, "but you won't bite me."

As I waded the cool creek waters, my bare feet touched gravel on the creek bottom. When I touched a wet water-soaked stick on the bottom of the creek bed, I'd think it was a snake and I'd jump. I'd wade into banks of quicksand. I'd sink into the sand above my knees. It was hard to pull my legs out of this quicksand and when I pulled them out they'd be covered with thin quicky mud that the next puddle of water would wash away.

A water moccasin, I said to myself. I was scared to look at him. He was wrapped around a willow that was bent over the creek. He was sleeping in the sun. I slipped toward him quietly — step by step — with my club drawn over my shoulder. Soon as I got close enough to reach him, I came over my shoulder with the club. I hit the water moccasin a powerful blow that mashed its head flat against the willow. It fell dead into the water. I picked it up by the tail and threw it upon the bank.

One gone, I said to myself.

The water was warm around my feet and legs. The sharp-edged gravels hurt the bottoms of my feet but the soft sand soothed them. Butterflies swarmed over my head and around me — alighting on the wild pink phlox that grew in clusters along the creek bank. Wild honeybees, bumblebees, and butterflies worked on the elder blossoms, the shoe-make blossoms and the beet-red finger-long blossoms of the ironweed and the whitish pink-covered smart-weed blossoms. Birds sang among the willows and flew up and down the creek with four-winged snakefeeders in their bills.

This is what I like to do, I thought. I love to kill snakes. I'm not afraid of snakes. I laughed to think how afraid of snakes Mom was — how she struck a potato-digger tine through a big rusty-golden copperhead's skin just enough to pin him to the earth and hold him so he couldn't get under our floor. He fought the potato-digger handle until Pa came home from work and killed him. Where he'd thrown poison over the ground it killed the weeds and weeds didn't grow on this spot again for four years.

Once when Mom was making my bed upstairs, she heard a noise of something running behind the paper that was pasted over the cracks between the logs — the paper split and a house snake six feet long fell onto the floor with a mouse in his mouth. Mom killed him with a bed slat. She called me once to bring her a goose-neck hoe upstairs quickly. I ran upstairs and killed two cow snakes restin' on the wall plate. And Pa killed twenty-eight copperheads out of a two-acre oat field in the hollow above the house one spring season.

"Snakes — snakes," Mom used to say, "are goin' to run us out'n this Hollow."

"It's because these woods ain't been burnt out in years," Pa'd always answer. "Back when I's a boy the old people burnt the woods out every spring to kill the snakes. Got so anymore there ain't enough good timber for a board tree and people have had to quit burning up the good timber. Snakes are about to take the woods again."

I thought about the snakes Pa had killed in the cornfield and the tobacco patch and how nearly copperheads had come to biting me and how I'd always seen the snake in time to cut his head off with a hoe or get out of his way. I thought of the times I had heard a rattle-snake's warning and how I'd run when I hadn't seen the snake. As I thought these thoughts, plop, a big water moccasin fell from the creek bank into a puddle of water.

"I'll get you," I said. "You can't fool me! You can't stand muddy water."

I stirred the water until it was muddy with my wild-plum club.

I waited for the water moccasin to stick his head above the water. Where wild ferns dipped down from the bank's edge and touched the water, I saw the snake's head rise slowly above the water — watchin' me with his lidless eyes. I swung sidewise with my club like batting at a ball. I couldn't swing over my shoulder, for there were willow limbs above my head.

I surely got him, I thought. I waited to see. Soon, something like milk spread over the water. "I got 'im." I raked in the water with my club and lifted from the bottom of the creek bed a water moccasin long as my club. It was longer than I was tall. I threw him upon the bank and moved slowly up the creek — looking on every drift, stump, log, and sunny spot. I looked for a snake's head along the edges of the creek bank where ferns dipped over and touched the water.

I waded up the creek all day killing water moccasins. If one were asleep on the bank, I slipped upon him quietly as a cat. I mauled him with the big end of my wild-plum club. I killed him in sleep. He never knew what struck him. If a brush caught the end of my club and caused me to miss and let the snake get into a puddle of water, I muddied the water and waited for him to stick his head above the water. When he stuck his head above the water, I got him. Not one water moccasin got away from me. It was four o'clock when I stepped from the creek onto the bank. I'd killed fifty-three water moccasins.

Water moccasins are not half as dangerous as turtles, I thought. A water moccasin can't bite you under the water for he gets his mouth full of water. A turtle can bite you under water, and when one bites you he won't let loose until it thunders, unless you cut his head off. I'd been afraid of turtles all day because I didn't have a knife in my pocket to cut one's head off if it grabbed my foot and held it.

When I left the creek, I was afraid of the snakes I'd killed. I didn't throw my club away. I gripped the club until my hands hurt. I looked below my path, above my path, and in front of me. When I saw a stick on the ground, I thought it was a snake. I eased up to it quietly as a cat trying to catch a bird. I was ready to hit it with my club.

What will Mom think when I tell her I've killed fifty-three water moccasins? I thought. A water moccasin bit Roy Deer but one's not going to bite me. I paid the snakes back for biting him. It was good enough for them. Roy wasn't bothering the water moccasin that bit him. He was just crossing the creek at the foot-log and it jumped from the grass and bit him.

Shadows lengthened from the tall trees. The Hollow was deep and the creek flowed softly in the cool recesses of evening shadows. There was one patch of sunlight. It was upon the steep broomsedge-covered bluff above the path.

"Snakes," I cried, "snakes a-fightin' and they're not water moccasins! They're copperheads!"

They were wrapped around each other. Their lidless eyes looked into each other's eyes. Their hard lips touched each other's lips. They did not move. They did not pay any attention to me. They looked at one another.

I'll kill 'em, I thought, if they don't kill one another in this fight.

I stood in the path with my club ready. I had heard snakes fought each other but I'd never seen them fight.

"What're you lookin' at, Shan?" Uncle Alf Skinner asked. He walked up the path with a cane in his hand.

"Snakes a-fightin'."

"Snakes a-fightin'?"

"Yes."

"I never saw it in my life."

"I'll kill 'em both if they don't finish the fight," I said. "I'll club 'em to death."

"Snakes a-fightin', Shan," he shouted, "you are too young to know! It's snakes in love! Snakes in love! Don't kill 'em — just keep your eye on 'em until I bring Martha over here! She's never seen snakes in love!"

Uncle Alf ran around the turn of the hill. He brought Aunt Martha back with him. She was carrying a basket of greens on her arm and the case knife that she'd been cutting greens with in her hand.

"See 'em, Martha," Uncle Alf said. "Look up there in that broomedge!"

"I'll declare," she said. "I've lived all my life and I never saw this. I've wondered about snakes!"

She stood with a smile on her wrinkled lips. Uncle Alf stood with a wide smile on his deep-lined face. I looked at them and wondered why they looked at these copperheads and smiled. Uncle Alf looked at Aunt Martha. They smiled at each other.

"Shan! Shan!" I heard Mom calling.

"I'm here," I shouted.

"Where've you been?" she asked as she turned around the bend of the hill with a switch in her hand.

"Be quiet, Sall," Uncle Alf said. "Come here and look for yourself!"

"What is it?" Mom asked.

"Snakes in love," Uncle Alf said.

Mom was mad. "Shan, I feel like limbing you," she said. "I've hunted every place for you! Where've you been?"

"Killin' snakes," I answered.

"Roy Deer is dead," she said. "That's how dangerous it is to fool with snakes."

"I paid the snakes back for him," I said. "I've killed fifty-three water moccasins!"

"Look, Sall!"

"Yes, Alf, I see," Mom said.

Mom threw her switch on the ground. Her eyes were wide apart. The frowns left her face.

"It's the first time I ever saw anything like this," Mom said. "Shan, you go tell your pa to come and look at this."

I was glad to do anything for Mom. I was afraid of her switch. When I brought Pa back to the sunny bank where the copperheads were loving, Art and Sadie Baker were there and Tom and Ethel Riggs — and there were a lot of strangers there. They were looking at the copperheads wrapped around each other with their eyes looking into each other's eyes and their hard lips touching each other's lips.

"You hurry to the house, Shan," Pa said, "and cut your stove wood for tonight."

"I'd like to kill these copperheads," I said.

"Why?" Pa asked.

"Fightin'," I said.

Uncle Alf and Aunt Martha laughed as I walked down the path carrying my club. It was something — I didn't know what — all the crowd watching the snakes were smiling. Their faces were made over new. The snakes had done something to them. Their wrinkled faces were as bright as the spring sunlight on the bluff; their eyes were shiny as the creek was in the noonday sunlight. And they laughed and talked to one another. I heard their laughter grow fainter as I walked down the path toward the house. Their laughter was louder than the wild honeybees I had heard swarming over the shoe-make, alderberry, and wild phlox blossoms along the creek.

A Wife of Nashville

THE LOVELLS' old cook Sarah had quit to get married in the spring, and they didn't have anybody else for a long time —for several months, that is. It was during the depression, and when a servant quit, people in Nashville (and even people out at Thornton, where the Lovells came from) tried to see how long they could go before they got another. All through the summer, there would be knocks on the Lovell's front door or on the wooden porch floor, by the steps. And when one of the children or their mother went to the door, some Negro man or woman would be standing there, smiling and holding out a piece of paper. A recommendation it was supposed to be, but the illegible note scribbled with a blunt lead pencil was something no white person could have written if he had tried. If Helen Ruth, the children's mother, went to the door, she always talked awhile to whoever it was, but she hardly ever even looked at the note held out to her. She would give a piece of advice or say to meet her around at the back door for a handout. If one of the boys — there were three Lovell boys, and no girls — went to the door, he always brought the note in to Helen Ruth, unless John R., their father, was at home, sick with his back ailment. Helen Ruth would shake her head and say to tell whoever it was to go away, go away! "Tell him to go back home," she said once to the oldest boy, who was standing in the sun-parlor doorway with a smudged scrap of paper in his hand. "Tell him if he had any sense, he never would have left the country."

"He's probably not from the country, Mother."

"They're all from the country," Helen Ruth said. "When they knock on the porch floor like that, they're bound to be from the country, and they're better off at home, where somebody cares some-thing about them. I don't care anything about them any more than you do."

But one morning Helen Ruth hired a cheerful-looking and rather plump, light-complexioned young Negro girl named Jess McGehee, who had come knocking on the front-porch floor just as the others had. Helen Ruth talked to her at the front door for a while; then she told her to come around to the kitchen, and they talked there for nearly an hour. Jess stayed to fix lunch and supper, and after she had been there a few days, the family didn't know how they had ever got along without her.

In fact, Jess got on so well with the Lovells that Helen Ruth even decided to let her come and live on the place, a privilege she had never before allowed a servant of hers. Together, she and Jess moved all of John R.'s junk — a grass duck-hunting outfit, two mounted stags' heads, an outboard motor, and so on — from the little room above the garage into the attic of the house. John R. lent Jess the money for the down payment on a "suit" of furniture, and Jess moved in. "You would never know she was out there," Helen Ruth told her friends. "There is never any rumpus. And her room! It's as clean as yours or mine."

Jess worked for them for eight years. John R. got so one of his favorite remarks was "The honeymoon is over, but this is the real thing this time." Then he would go on about what he called Helen Ruth's "earlier affairs." The last one before Jess was Sarah, who quit to get married and go to Chicago at the age of sixty-eight.

She was with them for six years and was famous for her pies and her banana dishes. Before Sarah, there was Carrie. Carrie had been with them when the two younger boys were born, and it was she who had once tried to persuade Helen Ruth not to go to the hospital but to let her act as midwife. She had quit them after five years, to become an undertaker. And before Carrie there was Jane Blakemore, the very first of them all, whom John R. and Helen Ruth had brought with them from Thornton to Nashville when they married. She lasted less than three years; she quit soon after John R., Jr., was born, because, she said, the baby made her nervous.

"It's an honorable record," John R. would say. "Each of them was better than the one before, and each one stayed with us longer. It proves that experience is the best teacher."

Jess's eight years were the years when the boys were growing up; the boys were children when she came, and when she left them, the youngest, little Robbie, had learned to drive the car. In a sense, it was Jess who taught all three boys to drive. She didn't give them their first lessons, of course, because, like Helen Ruth, she had never sat at the wheel of an automobile in her life. She had not ridden in a car more than half a dozen times when she came to the Lovells, but just by chance, one day, she was in the car when John R. let John R. Jr., take the wheel. The car would jerk and lunge forward every time the boy shifted gears, and his father said, "Keep your mind on what you're doing."

"I am," John R., Jr., said, "but it just does that. What makes it do it?"

"Think!" John R. said. "Think! . . . *Think!*"

"I *am* thinking, but what makes it do it?"

Suddenly, Jess learned forward from the back seat and said, "You letting the clutch out too fast, honey."

Both father and son were so surprised they could not help laughing. They laughed harder, of course because what Jess said was true. And Jess laughed with them. When they had driven another block, they reached a boulevard stop, and in the process of putting on the brake John R., Jr., killed the engine and then flooded the motor. His father shouted, "Well, let it rest! We're just stuck here for about twenty minutes!"

Jess, who was seated with one arm around a big bag of groceries, began to laugh again. "Turn off the key," she said. "Press down on the starter a spell. Then torectly you turn on the key and she'll start."

John R. looked over his shoulder at her, not smiling but not frowning, either. Presently, he gave the order "Try it."

"Try what *Jess said?*" John R., Jr., asked.

"Try what Jess said."

The boy tried it, and in a moment he was racing the motor and grinning at his father. When they had got safely across the boulevard, John R. turned around to Jess again. He asked in a quiet, almost humble manner — the same manner he used when describing the pains in his back to Helen Ruth — where she had learned these things about an automobile. "Law," she said, "I learned them listening to my brother-in-law that drives a truck talk. I don't reckon I really know'm, but I can say them."

John R. was so impressed by the incident that he did not make it one of his stories. He told Helen Ruth about it, of course, and he mentioned it sometimes to his close friends when they were discussing "the good things" about Negroes. With his sons, he used it as an example of how much you can learn by listening to other people talk, and after that day he would permit John R., Jr., to go for drives in the car without him provided Jess went along in his place. Later on, when the other boys got old enough to drive, there were periods when he turned their instruction over to Jess. Helen Ruth even talked of learning to drive, herself, with the aid of Jess.

But it never came to more than talk with Helen Ruth, though John R. encouraged her, saying he thought driving was perhaps a serious strain on his back. She talked about it for several months, but in the end she said that the time had passed when she could learn new skills. When John R. tried to encourage her in the idea, she would sometimes look out one of the sun-parlor windows toward the street and think of how much she had once wanted to learn to drive. But that had been long ago, right after they were married, in the days when John R. had owned a little Ford coupé. John R. was on the road for the Standard Candy Company then, and during most of the week she was alone in their apartment at the old Vaux Hall. While he was away, John R. kept the coupé stored in a garage only two blocks east, on Broad Street; in those days travelling men still used the railroads, because Governor Peay hadn't yet paved Tennessee's highways. At that time, John R. had not believed in women's driving automobiles, and Helen Ruth had felt that he must be right about it; she had even made fun of women who went *whizzing* about town, blowing horns at every intersection. Yet in her heart she had longed to drive that coupé! Jane Blakemore was working for them then, and one day Jane had put Helen Ruth's longings into words. "Wouldn't it be dandy," she said, "if me and you clomb in that car one of these weekdays and toured out to Thornton to see all the folks — white and black?"

But without a moment's hesitation Helen Ruth gave the answer that she knew John R. would have given. "Now, think what you're saying, Jane!" she said. "Wouldn't we be a fool-looking pair pulling into the square at Thornton? *Think* about it. What if we should have a flat tire when we got out about as far as Nine Mile Hill? Who would change it? *You* certainly couldn't! Jane Blakemore, I don't think you use your head about anything!"

That was the way Helen Ruth had talked to Jane on more occasions than one. She was a plain-spoken woman, and she never spoke plainer to anyone that she did to Jane Blakemore during the days when they were shut up together in that apartment at the Vaux Hall. Since Jane was from Thornton and knew how plain-spoken all Helen Ruth's family were, she paid little attention to the way Helen Ruth talked to her. She would smile, or else sneer, and go on with her work of cooking and cleaning. Sometimes she would rebel and speak just as plainly as Helen Ruth did. When Helen Ruth decided to introduce butter plates to their table, Jane said, "I ain't never heard tell of no butter dishes."

Helen Ruth raised her eyebrow. "That's because you are an ignoramus from Thornton, Tennessee," she said.

"I'm ignoramus enough to know ain't no need in nastying up all them dishes for me to wash."

Helen Ruth had, however, made Jane Blakemore learn to use butter plates and had made her keep the kitchen scrubbed and the other rooms of the apartment dusted and polished and in such perfect order that even John R. had noticed it when he came on weekends. Sometimes he had said, "You drive yourself too hard, Helen Ruth."

Jess McGehee was as eager and quick to learn new things as Jane Blakemore had been unwilling and slow. She would even put finger bowls on the breakfast table when there was grapefruit. And how she did spoil the three boys about their food! There were mornings when she cooked eggs for each of them in a different way while John R. sat and shook his head in disgust at the way she pampered the boys. John R.'s "condition" in his back kept him at home a lot of the time during the eight years Jess was with them. He had long since left off travelling for the candy company; soon after the first baby came, he had opened an insurance agency of his own.

When Jane Blakemore left them and Helen Ruth hired Carrie (after fifteen or twenty interviews with other applicants), she had had to warn Carrie that John R.'s hours might be very irregular, because he was in business for himself and wasn't able merely to punch a time clock and quit when the day ended. "He's an onsurance man, ain't he?" Carrie had asked and had showed by the light in her eyes how favorable impressed she was. "I know about him," she had said. "He's a life-onsurance man, and that's the best kind to have."

At that moment, Helen Ruth thought perhaps she had made a mistake in Carrie. "I don't like my servant to discuss my husband's business," she said.

"No'm!" Carrie said with enthusiasm. "No, *ma'am!*" Helen Ruth was satisfied, but often afterward she told herself that her first suspicion had been right. Carrie was nosy and prying and morbid — and she gossiped with other people's servants. Her curiosity and her gossiping were especially trying for Helen Ruth during her and John R.'s brief separation. They had actually separated for nearly two months right after Kenneth, the middle boy, was born. Helen Ruth had gone to her father's house at Thornton, taking the two babies and Carrie with her. The boys never knew about the trouble between their parents, of course, until Kenneth pried it out of his mother after they were all grown, and at the time people in Nashville and Thornton were not perfectly sure that it was a real separation. Helen Ruth had tried to tell herself that perhaps Carrie didn't know it was a real separation. But she was never able to deny completely the significance of Carrie's behavior while they were at Thornton. Carrie's whole disposition had seemed to change the afternoon they left Nashville. Up till then, she had been a moody, shifty, rather loud-mouthed brown woman, full of darky compliments for white folks and of gratuitous promises of extra services she seldom rendered. But at Thornton she had put the old family servants to shame with her industriousness and her respectful, unassuming manner. "You don't find them like Carrie in Thornton any more," Helen Ruth's mother said. "The good ones all go to Nashville or Memphis." But Helen Ruth, sitting by an upstairs window one afternoon, saw her mother's cook and Carrie sauntering toward the back gate to meet a caller. She saw Carrie being introduced and then she recognized the caller as Jane Blakemore. Presently the cook returned to the kitchen and Helen Ruth saw Carrie and Jane enter the servants' house in the corner of the yard. During the hour that they visited there, Helen Ruth sat quietly by the window in the room with her two babies. It seemed to her the most terrible hour of her separation from John R. When Carrie and Jane reappeared on the stoop of the servants' house and Carrie was walking with Jane to the gate, there was no longer any doubt in Helen Ruth's mind but that she would return to her husband, and return without any complaints or stipulations. During that hour she had tried to imagine exactly what things the black Jane and the brown Carrie were talking about, or, rather, *how* and in what terms they were talking about the things they must be talking about. In her mind, she reviewed the sort of difficulties she had had with Jane and the sort she had with Carrie and tried to imagine what defense they would make for themselves — Jane for her laziness and contrariness, Carrie for her usual shiftiness and negligence. Would they blame her for these failings of theirs? Or would they blandly pass over their own failings and find fault with her for things that she was not even aware of, or that she could not help and could not begin to set right? Had she really misused these women, either the black one or the brown one? It seemed to her then that she had so little in life that she was entitled to the satisfaction of keeping an orderly house and to the luxury of efficient help. There was too much else she had not had — an "else" nameless to her, yet sorely missed — for her to be denied these small satisfactions. As she sat alone with her two babies in the old nursery and thought of the two servants gossiping about her, she became an object of pity to herself. And presently John R., wherever he might be at that moment — in his office or at the club or, more likely, on a hunting or fishing trip somewhere — became an object of pity, too. And her two babies, one in his crib and the other playing on the carpet with a string of spools, were objects of pity. Even Carrie, standing alone by the gate after Jane had gone, seemed a lone and pitiful figure.

A few days later, Helen Ruth and Carrie and the two babies returned to Nashville.

In Nashville, Carrie was herself again; everything was done in her old slipshod fashion. Except during that interval at Thornton, Carrie was never known to perform any task to Helen Ruth's complete satisfaction. Hardly a meal came to the table without the soup or the dessert or some important sauce having been forgotten; almost every week something important was left out of the laundry; during a general cleaning the upper sashes of two or three windows were invariably left unwashed. Yet never in her entire five years did Carrie answer back or admit an unwillingness to do the most menial or the most nonessential piece of work. In fact, one of her most exasperating pronouncements was "You are exactly right," which was often followed by a lengthy description of how she would do the thing from then on, or an explanation of how it happened that she had forgotten to do it. Not only that, she would often undertake to explain to Helen Ruth, Helen Ruth's reason for wanting it done. "You are exactly right, and I know how you mean. You want them drapes shut at night so it can seem like we're living in a house out in the Belle Meade instead of this here Vox Hall flat, and some fool might be able to look in from the yard."

"Never mind the reasons, Carrie," was Helen Ruth's usual answer. But her answers were not always so gentle — not when Carrie suggested that she have the second baby at home with Carrie acting as midwife, not when Carrie spoke to her about having the third baby circumcised. And the day that Helen Ruth began packing her things to go to Thornton, she was certain that Carrie would speak out of turn with some personal advice. That would have been more than she could bear, and she was prepared to dismiss Carrie from her service and make the trip alone. But neither then nor afterward did Carrie give any real evidence of understanding the reasons for the trip to Thornton.

In fact, it was not until long afterward, when Carrie had quit them to become an undertaker, that Helen Ruth felt that Carrie's gossip with other Nashville servants had, by accident, played a part in her separation from John R. She and John R. had talked of separation and a divorce more than once during the first two years they were married, in the era of Jane Blakemore. It was not that any quarrelling led to this talk but that each accused the other of being dissatisfied with their marriage. When John R. came in from travelling, on a weekend or in the middle of the week — he was sometimes gone only two or three days at a time — he would find Helen Ruth sitting alone in the living room, without a book or even a deck of cards to amuse herself with, dressed perhaps in something new her mother had sent her, waiting for him. She would rise from her chair to greet him, and he would smile in frank admiration of the tall, graceful figure and of the countenance whose features seemed always composed, and softened by her hair, which was beginning to be gray even at the time of their marriage. But he had not come home many times before Helen Ruth was greeting him not with smiles but with tears. At first, he had been touched, but soon he began to complain that she was unhappy. He asked her why she did not see something of other people while he was away — the wives of his business and hunting friends, or some of the other Thornton girls who were married and living in Nashville. She replied that she did see them occasionally but that she was not the sort of woman who enjoyed having a lot of women friends. Besides, she was perfectly happy with her present life; it was only that she believed that he must be unhappy and that he no longer enjoyed her company. She understood that he had to be away most of the week, but even when he was in town, she saw very little of him. When he was not at his office, he was fishing out on Duck River or was off to a hunt up at Gallatin. And at night he either took her to parties with those hunting people, with whom she had nothing in common, or piled up on the bed after supper and slept. All of this indicated that he was not happy being married to her, she said, and so they talked a good deal about separating.

After the first baby came, there was no such talk for a long time — not until after the second baby. After the first baby came, Helen Ruth felt that their marriage must be made to last, regardless of her or John R.'s happiness. Besides, it was at that time that one of John R.'s

hunting friends — a rich man named Rufus Brantley — had secured
the insurance agency for him, and almost before John R. opened his
office, he had sold policies to other hunting friends of his, among
whom were the very richest men in Nashville. "Among the wealthiest
in the whole South, for that matter," said John R. For a while, he was
at home more than he had ever been before. But soon, when his
business was established, he began to attend more and more meets
and trials, all over Tennessee and Alabama and Kentucky. He even
owned horses and dogs, which he kept at his friends' stables and
kennels. And then his friends began to take him on trips to distant
parts of the country. It seemed that when he was not deep-sea fishing
in the Gulf, he was deer hunting in the State of Maine. Helen Ruth
did sometimes go with him to the local horse shows, but one night,
at the Spring Horse Show, she had told Mrs. Brantley that she had a
new machine, and Mrs. Brantley had thought she meant an automobile, instead of a sewing machine. That, somehow, had been the last
straw. She would never go out with "people like the Brantleys" after
that. She was pregnant again before the first baby was a year old,
and this soon became her excuse for going nowhere in the evening.
The women she did visit with very occasionally in the daytime were
those she had known as girls in Thornton, women whose husbands
were bank tellers and office managers and were barely acquainted
with John R. Lovell.

After the second baby came, Helen Ruth saw these women more
frequently. She began to feel a restlessness that she could not explain
in herself. There were days when she could not stay at home. With
Carrie and the two babies, she would traipse about town, on foot or
by streetcar, to points she had not visited since she was a little girl
and was in Nashville with her parents to attend the State Fair or the
Centennial. She went to the Capitol, to Centennial Park and the
Parthenon, and even out to the Glendale Zoo. Once, with Nancy
Lowder and Lucy Parkes, two of her old Thornton friends, she made
an excursion to Cousin Mamie Lovell's farm, which was several miles
beyond the town of Franklin. They went by the electric interurban
to Franklin, and from there they took a taxi to the farm. Cousin
Mamie's husband had been a second cousin of John R.'s father, and
it was a connection the Thornton Lovells had once been very proud

to claim. But for a generation this branch of the family had been in decline. Major Lovell had been a prominent lawyer in Franklin and had been in politics, but when he died, he left his family "almost penniless." His boys had not gone to college; since the farm was supposed to have been exhausted, they did not try to farm it but clerked in stores in Franklin. There was said to be a prosperous son-in-law in St. Louis, but the daughter was dead and Cousin Mamie was reported to have once called her son-in-law a parvenu to his face. Helen Ruth and her friends made the excursion because they wanted to see the house, which was one of the finest old houses in the county and full of antiques.

But Cousin Mamie didn't even let them inside the house. It was a hot summer day, and she had all the blinds closed and the whole L-shaped house shut up tight, so that it would be bearable at night. She received them on the long ell porch. Later, they moved their chairs out under a tree in the yard, where Cousin Mamie's cook brought them a pitcher of iced tea. While they were chatting under the tree that afternoon, they covered all the usual topics that are dealt with when talking to an old lady one doesn't know very well — the old times and the new times, mutual friends and family connections, country living and city living, and always, of course, the lot of woman as it relates to each topic.

"Where are you and John R. living?" Cousin Mamie asked Helen Ruth.

"We're still at the Vaux Hall, Cousin Mamie."

"I'd suppose the trains would be pretty bad for noise there, that close to the depot."

"They're pretty bad in the summer."

"I'd suppose you had a place out from town, seeing how often John R.'s name's in the paper as master of hounds here and horse judge there!"

"That's John R.'s life," Helen Ruth said, "not mine."

"He runs with a fine pack, I must say," said Cousin Mamie.

Nancy Lowder and Lucy Parkes nodded and smiled, Lucy said, "The swells of Narville, Miss Mamie."

But Cousin Mamie said, "There was a day when they weren't the swells. Forty years ago, people like Major Lovell didn't know people like the Brantleys. I think the Brantleys quarried limestone, to begin with. I guess it don't matter, though, for when I was a girl in upper East Tennessee, people said the Lovells started as land speculators hereabouts and at Memphis. But I don't blame you for not wanting to fool with Brantleys, Helen Ruth."

"John R. and I each live our own life, Cousin Mamie."

"Helen Ruth is a woman with a mind of her own, Miss Mamie," Nancy Lowder said. "It's too bad more marriages can't be like theirs, each living their own life. Everyone admires it as a real achievement."

And Lucy Parkes said, "Because a woman's husband hunts is no reason for her to hunt, any more than because a man's wife sews is any reason for him to sew."

"Indeed not," Cousin Mamie said, actually paying little attention to what Lucy and Nancy were saying. Presently, she continued her own train of thought. "Names like Brantley and Partee and Havemyer didn't mean a thing in this state even thirty years ago."

What Lucy and Nancy said about her marriage that day left Helen Ruth in a sort of daze and at the same time made her see her situation more clearly. She had never discussed her marriage with anybody, and hearing it described so matter-of-factly by these two women made her understand for the first time what a special sort of marriage it was and how unhappy she was in it. At the time, John R. was away on a fishing trip to Tellico Plains. She did not see him again before she took the babies and Carrie to Thornton. She sent a note to his office saying that she would return when he decided to devote his time to his wife and children instead of to his hounds and horses. While she was at Thornton, her letters from John R. made no mention of her note. He wrote about his business, about his hounds and horses, about the weather, and he always urged her to hurry home as soon as she had seen everybody and had a good visit. Meanwhile, he had a room at the Hermitage Club.

When Helen Ruth returned to Nashville, their life went on as before. A year later, the third boy, Robbie, was born, and John R. bought a large bungalow on Sixteenth Avenue, not too far from the Tarbox School, where they planned to send the boys. Carrie was with them for three years after the separation, and though her work did not improve, Helen Ruth found herself making excuses for her. She began to attribute Carrie's garrulity to "a certain sort of bashfulness, or the Negro equivalent of bashfulness." And with the three small boys, and the yard to keep, too, there was so much more for Carrie to do than there had been before! Despite the excuses she made for her, Helen Ruth could see that Carrie was plainly getting worse about everything and that she now seemed to take pleasure in lying about the smallest, most unimportant things. But Helen Ruth found it harder to confront Carrie with her lies or to reprimand her in any way.

During the last months before Carrie quit, she would talk sometimes about the nightwork she did for a Negro undertaker. To make Helen Ruth smile, she would report things she had heard about the mourners. Her job, Carrie always said, was to sweep the parlors after the funeral and to fold up the chairs. It was only when she finally gave notice to Helen Ruth that she told her what she professed was the truth. She explained that during all those months she had been learning to embalm. "Before you can get a certificate," she said, "you has to handle a bad accident, a sickness, a case of old age, a drowning, a burning, and a half-grown child or less. I been waiting on the child till last night, but now I'll be getting my certificate."

Helen Ruth would not even let Carrie go to the basement to get her hat and coat. "You send somebody for them," she said. "But *you,* you get off these premises, Carrie!" She was sincerely outraged by what Carrie had told her, and when she looked at Carrie's hands, she was filled with new horror. But something kept her from saying all the things that one normally said to a worthless, lying servant who had been guilty of one final outrage. *"Leave,* Carrie!" she said, consciously restraining herself. *"Leave* this place!" Carrie went out the kitchen door and down the driveway to the street, bareheaded, coatless, and wearing her kitchen slippers.

After Carrie, there was old Sarah, who stayed with them for six years and then quit them to get married and go to Chicago. Sarah was too old to do heavy work even when she first came, and before she had been there a week, John R. had been asked to help move the sideboard and to bring the ladder up from the basement. He said it seemed that every minute he was in the house, he was lifting or moving something that was too much for Sarah. Helen Ruth replied that perhaps she should hire a Negro man to help in the house and look after the yard. But John R. said no, he was only joking, he thought Sarah far and away the best cook they had ever had, and besides business conditions didn't look too good and it was no time to be taking on more help. But he would always add he did not understand why Helen Ruth babied Sarah so. "From the first moment old Sarah set foot in this house, Helen Ruth has babied her," he would say to people in Helen Ruth's presence.

Sarah could neither read nor write. Even so, it took her only a short while to learn all Helen Ruth's special recipes and how to cook everything the way the Lovells liked it. For two weeks, Helen Ruth stayed in the kitchen with Sarah, reading to her from *How We Cook in Tennessee* and giving detailed instructions for every meal. It was during that time that her great sympathy for Sarah developed. Sarah was completely unashamed of her illiteracy, and it was this that first impressed Helen Ruth. She admired Sarah for having no false pride and for showing no resentment of her mistress's impatience. She observed Sarah's kindness with the children. And she learned from Sarah about Sarah's religious convictions and about her long, unhappy marriage to a Negro named Morse Wilkins, who had finally left her and gone up North.

While Sarah was working for them, John R. and Helen Ruth lived the life that Helen Ruth had heard her friends describe to John R.'s Cousin Mamie. It was not until after Sarah had come that Helen Ruth, recalling the afternoon at Cousin Mamie's, identified Lucy Parkes' words about a wife's sewing and a husband's hunting as the very answer she had once given to some of Carrie's impertinent prying. That afternoon, the remark had certainly sounded familiar, but she had been too concerned with her own decision to leave her husband to concentrate upon anything so trivial. And after their reconciliation she tried not to dwell on the things that had led her to leave John R. Their reconciliation, whatever it meant to John R., meant to her the acceptance of certain mysteries — the mystery of his love of hunting, of his attraction to rich people, of his desire to maintain a family and home of which he saw so little, of his attachment to her, and of her own devotion to him. Her babies were now growing into little boys. She felt that there was much to be thankful for, not the least of which was a servant as fond of her and of her children as Sarah was. Sarah's affection for the three little boys often reminded Helen Ruth how lonely Sarah's life must be.

One day, when she had watched Sarah carefully wrapping up little Robbie in his winter play clothes before he went out to play in the snow, she said, "You love children so much, Sarah, didn't you ever have any of your own?"

Sarah, who was a yellow-skinned woman with face and arms covered with brown freckles, turned her gray eyes and fixed them solemnly on Helen Ruth. "Why, I had the cutest little baby you ever did see," she said, "and Morse went and killed it."

"Morse *killed* your baby?"

"He rolled over on it in his drunk sleep and smothered it in the bed."

After that, Helen Ruth would never even listen to Sarah when she talked about Morse, and she began to feel a hatred toward any and all of the men who came to take Sarah home at night. Generally, these men were the one subject Sarah did not discuss with Helen Ruth, and their presence in Sarah's life was the only serious complaint Helen Ruth made against her. They would come sometimes as early as four in the afternoon and wait on the back porch for Sarah to get through. She knew that Sarah was living with first one and then another of them, but when she told John R. she was going to put her foot down on it, he forbade her to do so. And so through nearly six years she tolerated this weakness of Sarah's. But one morning in the late spring Sarah told her that Morse Wilkins had returned from up North and that she had taken him back as her husband. Helen Ruth could not find anything to say for a moment, but after studying the large diamond on her engagement ring for a while she said, "My servant's private life is her own affair, but I give you warning now, Sarah, I want to see no more of your men friends — Morse or *any other* — on this place again."

From that time, she saw no more men on the place until Morse himself came, in a drunken rage, in the middle of a summer's day. Helen Ruth had been expecting something of the sort to happen. Sarah had been late to work several times during the preceding three weeks. She had come one morning with a dark bruise on her cheek and said she had fallen getting off the streetcar. Twice, Helen Ruth had found Sarah on her knees, praying, in the kitchen. The day Helen Ruth heard the racket at the back-porch door, she knew at once that it was Morse. She got up from her sewing machine and went directly to the kitchen. Sarah was on the back porch, and Morse was outside the screen door of the porch, which was hooked on the inside. He was a little man, shrivelled up, baldheaded, not more than five feet tall, and of a complexion very much like Sarah's. Over his white shirt he wore a dark sleeveless sweater. "You come on home," he was saying as he shook the screen door.

Helen Ruth stepped to the kitchen door. "Is that her?" Morse asked Sarah, motioning his head toward Helen Ruth.

When Sarah turned her face around, her complexion seemed several shades lighter than Morse's. "I got to go," she said to Helen Ruth.

"No, Sarah, *he's* got to go. But *you* don't."

"He's gonna leave me again."

"That's the best thing that could happen to you, Sarah."

Sarah said nothing, and Morse began shaking the door again.

"Is he drunk, Sarah?" Helen Ruth asked.

"He's so drunk I don't know how he find his way here."

Helen Ruth went out onto the porch. "Now, you get off this place, and quick about it," she said to Morse.

He shook the screen door again. "You didn't make me come here, Mrs. Lovellel, and you can't make me leave, Mrs. Lovellel."

"I can't make you leave," Helen Ruth said at once, "but there's a bluecoat down on the corner who can."

Suddenly Sarah dropped to her knees and began praying. Her lips moved silently, and gradually she let her forehead come to rest on the top of the rickety vegetable bin. Morse looked at her through the screen, putting his face right against the wire. "Sarah," he said, "you come on home. You better come on now if you think I be there."

Sarah got up off her knees.

"I'm going to phone the police," Helen Ruth said, pretending to move toward the kitchen.

Morse left the door and staggered backward toward the driveway. "Come on, Sarah," he shouted.

"I got to go," Sarah said.

"I won't let you go, Sarah!"

"She can't make you stay!" Morse shouted. "You better come on if you coming!"

"It will be the worst thing you ever did in your life, Sarah," said Helen Ruth. "And if you go with him, you can't ever come back here. He'll kill you someday, too — the way he did your baby."

Sarah was on her knees again, and Morse was out of sight but still shouting as he went down the driveway. Suddenly, Sarah was on her feet. She ran into the kitchen and on through the house to the front porch.

Helen Ruth followed, calling her back. She found Sarah on the front porch waving to Morse, who was halfway down the block, running in a zigzag down the middle of the street, still shouting at the top of his voice. Sarah cried out to him, "Morse! Morse!"

"Sarah!" Helen Ruth said.

"Morse!" Sarah cried again, and then she began mumbling words that Helen Ruth could not quite understand at the time. Afterward, going over it in her mind, Helen Ruth realized that what Sarah had been mumbling was "If I don't see you no more on this earth, Morse, I'll see you in Glory."

Sarah was with the Lovells for four more months, and then one night she called up on the telephone and asked John R., Jr., to tell his mother that she was going to get married to a man named Racecar and they were leaving for Chicago in the morning.

Jess McGehee came to them during the depression. Even before Sarah left the Lovells, John R. had had to give up all of his "activities" and devote his entire time to selling insurance. Rufus Brantley had shot himself through the head while cleaning a gun at his hunting lodge, and most of John R.'s other hunting friends were no longer rich men. The changes in their life had come so swiftly that Helen Ruth did not realize for a while what they meant in her relationship with John R. It seemed as though she woke up one day and discovered that she was not married to the same man. She found herself spending all her evenings playing Russian bank with a man who had no interest in anything but his home, his wife, and his three boys. Every night, he would give a brief summary of the things that had happened at his office or on his calls, and then he would ask her and the boys for an account of everything they had done that day.

He took an interest in the house and the yard, and he and the boys made a lily pool in the back yard, and singlehanded he screened in the entire front porch. Sometimes he took the whole family to Thornton for a weekend, and he and Helen Ruth never missed the family reunions there in September.

In a sense, these were the happiest years of their married life. John R.'s business got worse and worse, of course, but since part of their savings were in the bank at Thornton that did not fail, they never had any serious money worries. Regardless of their savings, however, John R.'s loss of income and his having to give up his friends and his hunting wrought very real, if only temporary, changes in him. There were occasions when he would sit quietly and listen to his family's talk without correcting them or pointing out how foolish they were. He gave up saying "Think!" to the boys, and instead would say, "Now, let's see if we can't reason this thing out." He could never bring himself to ask for any sympathy from Helen Ruth for his various losses, but as it was during this time that he suffered so from the ailment in his back (he and Helen Ruth slept with boards under their mattress for ten years), the sympathy he got for his physical pain was more than sufficient. All in all, it was a happy period in their life, and in addition to their general family happiness they had Jess.

Jess not only cooked and cleaned, she planned the meals, did the marketing, and washed everything, from handkerchiefs and socks to heavy woollen blankets. When the boys began to go to dances, she even learned to launder their dress shirts. There was nothing she would not do for the boys or for John R. or for Helen Ruth. The way she idealized the family became the basis for most of the "Negro jokes" told by the Lovells during those years. In her room, she had a picture of the family, in a group beside the lily pool, taken with her own box Brownie; she had tacked it and also a picture of each of them on the wall above her washstand. In her scrapbook she had pasted every old snapshot and photograph that Helen Ruth would part with, as well as old newspaper pictures of John R. on horseback or with a record-breaking fish he had caught. She had even begged from Helen Ruth an extra copy of the newspaper notice of their wedding.

Jess talked to the family a good deal at mealtime, but only when they addressed her first and showed that they wanted her to talk. Her remarks were mostly about things that related to the Lovells. She told a sad story about a "very loving white couple" from Brownsville, her home town, who had been drowned in each other's arms when their car rolled off the end of a river ferry. The point of the story was that those two people were the same fine, loving sort of couple that John R. and Helen Ruth were. All three of the boys made good grades in school, and every month Jess would copy their grades in her scrapbook, which she periodically passed around for the family to appreciate. When Kenneth began to write stories and articles for his high-school paper, she would always borrow the paper overnight; soon it came out that she was copying everything he wrote onto the big yellow pages of her scrapbook.

After three or four years, John R. began to say that he thought Jess would be with them always and that they would see the day when the boys' children would call her "Mammy." Helen Ruth said that she would like to agree with him about that, but actually she worried, because Jess seemed to have no life of her own, which wasn't at all natural. John R. agreed that they should make her take a holiday now and then. Every summer, they would pack Jess off to Brownsville for a week's visit with her kinfolks, but she was always back in her room over the garage within two or three days; she said that her people fought and quarrelled so much that she didn't care for them. Outside her life with the Lovells, she had only one interest and only one friend. Her interest was the movies, and her friend was "the Mary who works for Mrs. Dunbar." Jess and Mary went to the movies together as often as three or four times a week, and on Sunday afternoons Mary came to see Jess or Jess went to see Mary, who lived over the Dunbars' garage. Jess always took along her scrapbook and her most recent movie magazines. She and Mary swapped movie magazines, and it was apparent from Jess's talk on Monday mornings that they also swapped eulogies of their white families.

Sometimes Helen Ruth would see Mrs. Dunbar downtown or at a P.T.A. meeting; they would discuss their cooks and smile over the reports that each had received of the other's family. "I understand that your boys are all growing into very handsome men," Mrs. Dunbar

said once, and she told Helen Ruth that Jess was currently comparing one of the boys — Mrs. Dunbar didn't know which one — to
Neil Hamilton, and that she was comparing Helen Ruth to Irene
Rich, and John R. to Edmund Lowe. As the boys got older, they
began to resent the amount of authority over them — though it was
small — that Jess had been allowed by their parents and were embarrassed if anyone said Jess had taught them to drive the car. When
John R., Jr., began at the University, he made his mother promise
not to let Jess know what grades he received, and none of the boys
would let Jess take snapshots of them any more. Their mother tried
to comfort Jess by saying that the boys were only going through a
phase and that it would pass in time. One day, she even said this in
the presence of Robbie, who promptly reported it to the older boys,
and it ended with John R., Jr., complaining to his father that their
mother ought not to make fun of them to Jess. His father laughed
at him but later told Helen Ruth that he thought she was making
a mistake.

She didn't make the same mistake again, but though Jess never gave
any real sign of her feelings' being hurt, Helen Ruth was always
conscious of how the boys were growing away from their good-
natured servant. By the time Robbie was sixteen, they had long since
ceased to have any personal conversation with Jess, and nothing
would have induced Robbie to submit to taking drives with her but
the knowledge that his father would not allow him to use the car
on dates until he had had months of driving practice. Once, when
Robbie and Jess returned from a drive, Jess reported, with a grin,
that not a word had passed between them during the entire hour and
a half. Helen Ruth only shook her head sadly. But the next day she
bought Jess a new bedside radio.

The radio was the subject of much banter among the boys and
their father. John R. said Helen Ruth had chosen the period of hard
times and the depression to become more generous with her servant
than she had ever been before in her life. They recalled other presents
she had given Jess recently, and from that time on they teased her
regularly about how she spoiled Jess. John R. said that if Jess had had
his back trouble, Helen Ruth would have retired her at double pay
and nursed her with twice the care that he received. The boys teased

her by saying that at Christmas time she reversed the custom of shopping for the servant at the ten-cent stores and for the family at the department stores.

Yet as long as Jess was with them, they all agreed that she was the best help they had ever had. They said that, and then there would be a silence, during which they were probably thinking about the summer morning just before the war when Jess received a telephone call.

When the telephone rang that morning, Helen Ruth and John R. and the boys had just sat down to breakfast. As usual in the summer-time, they were eating at the big drop-leaf table in the sun parlor. Jess had set the coffee urn by Helen Ruth's place and was starting from the room when the telephone rang. Helen Ruth, supposing the call was for a member of the family, and seeing that Jess lingered in the dorway, said for her to answer it there in the sun parlor instead of running to the telephone in the back hall.

Jess answered it, announcing whose residence it was in a voice so like Helen Ruth's that it made the boys grin. For a moment, everyone at the table kept silent. They waited for Jess's eyes to single out one of them. John R., Jr., and Kenneth even put down their grapefruit spoons. But the moment Jess picked up the instrument, she fixed her eyes on the potted fern on the window seat across the room. At once her nostrils began to twitch, her lower lip fell open, and it seemed only by an act of will that she was twice able to say "Yes, ma'am," in answer to the small, metallic voice.

When she had replaced the telephone on its cradle, she turned quickly away and started into the dining room. But Helen Ruth stopped her. "Jess," she asked, her voice full of courtesy, "was the call for you?"

Jess stopped, and they all saw her hands go to her face. Without turning around, she leaned against the door-jamb and began sobbing aloud. Helen Ruth jumped up from the table, saying: "Jess, honey what *is* the matter?" John R. and the boys stood up, too.

"It was a telegram for me — from Brownsville."

Helen Ruth took her in her arms. "Is someone dead?"

Between sobs, Jess answered, "My little brother — our baby

brother —the only one of 'em I cared for." Then her sobs became more violent.

Helen Ruth motioned for John R. to move the morning paper from the big wicker chair, and she led Jess in that direction. But Jess would not sit down, and she could not be pulled away from Helen Ruth. She held fast to her, and Helen Ruth continued to pat her gently on the back and to try to console her with gentle words. Finally, she said, "Jess, you must go to Brownsville. Maybe there's been some mistake. Maybe he's not dead. But you must go, anyway."

Presently, Jess did sit in the chair, and dried her eyes on Helen Ruth's napkin. The boys shook their heads sympathetically and John R. said she certainly must get to Brownsville. She agreed, and said she believed there was a bus at ten that she would try to catch. Helen Ruth patted her hand, telling her to go along to her room when she felt like it, and said that *she* would finish getting breakfast.

"I want to go by to see Mary first," Jess said, "so I better make haste." She stood up, forcing a grateful smile. Then she burst into tears again and threw her arms about Helen Ruth, mumbling, "Oh God! Oh, God!" The three boys and their father saw tears come into Helen Ruth's eyes, and through her tears Helen Ruth saw a change come over their faces. It hardly seemed possible that so similar a change could reflect four men's individual feelings. She concluded that her own emotion, and probably the actual tears in her eyes, had made her imagine the change, and when Jess now pulled away and hurried off to her room, Helen Ruth's tears had dried and she could see no evidence of the change she had imagined in her husband's and her sons' faces.

While Jess was in her room preparing to leave, they finished breakfast. Then Helen Ruth began clearing the table, putting the dishes on the teacart. She had said little while they were eating, but in her mind she was all the while going over something that she knew she must tell her family. As she absent-mindedly stacked the dishes, her lips even moved silently over the simple words she would use in telling them. She knew that they were watching her, and when Robbie offered to take Jess to the bus station, she knew that the change she had seen in their faces had been an expression of sympathy for *her* as well as of an eagerness to put this whole episode behind them. "I'll take Jess to her bus," he said.

But Helen Ruth answered, in the casual tone she had been preparing to use, that she thought it probably wouldn't be the thing to do.

"Why, what do you mean, Helen Ruth?" John R. asked her.

"It was very touching, Mother," Kenneth said in his new, manly voice, "the way she clung to you." He, too, wanted to express sympathy, but he also seemed to want to distract his mother from answering his father's question.

At that moment, Jess passed under the sun-parlor windows, walking down the driveway, carrying two large suitcases. Helen Ruth watched her until she reached the sidewalk. Then, very quietly, she announced to her family that Jess had no baby brother and had never had one. "Jess and Mary are leaving for California. They think they're going to find themselves jobs out there."

"You knew that right along?" John R. asked.

"I knew it right along."

"Did she know you did, Helen Ruth?" he asked. His voice had in it the the sternness he used when questioning the boys about something.

"No, John R., she did not. I didn't learn it from her."

"Well, I don't believe it's so," he said. "Why, I don't believe that for a minute. Her carrying on was too real."

"They're going to California. They've already got their two tickets. Mrs. Dunbar got wind of it somehow, by accident, from Mrs. Lon Thompson's cook, and she called me on Monday. They've saved their money and they're going."

"And you let Jess get away with all that crying stuff just now?" John R. said.

Helen Ruth put her hands on the handle bar of the teacart. She pushed the cart a little way over the tile floor but stopped when he repeated his question. It wasn't to answer his question that she stopped, however. "Oh, my dears!" she said, addressing her whole family. Then it was a long time before she said anything more. John R. and the three boys remained seated at the table, and while Helen Ruth gazed past them and toward the front window of the sun parlor, they sat silent and still, as though they were in a picture.

What could she say to them, she kept asking herself. And each time she asked the question, she received for answer some different memory of seemingly unrelated things out of the past twenty years of her life. These things presented themselves as answers to her question, and each of them seemed satisfactory to her. But how little sense it would make to her husband and her grown sons, she reflected, if she should suddenly begin telking them about the long hours she had spent waiting in that apartment at the Vaux Hall while John R. was on the road for the Standard Candy Company, and in the same breath should tell them about how plainly she used to talk to Jane Blakemore and how Jane pretented that the baby made her nervous and went back to Thornton. Or suppose she should abruptly remind John R. of how ill at ease the wives of his hunting friends used to make her feel and how she had later driven Sarah's worthless husband out of the yard, threatening to call a bluecoat. What if she should suddenly say that because a woman's husband hunts, there is no reason for *her* to hunt, any more than because a man's wife sews, there is reason for him to sew. She felt that she would be willing to say anything at all, no matter how cruel or absurd it was, if it would make them understand that everything that happened in life only reflected in some way the loneliness of people. She was ready to tell them about sitting in the old nursery at Thornton and waiting for Carrie and Jane Blakemore to come out of the cabin in the yard. If it would make them see what she had been so long in learning to see, she would even talk at last about the "so much else" that had been missing from her life and that she had not been able to name, and about the foolish mysteries she had so nobly accepted upon her reconciliation with John R. To her, these things were all one now; they were her loneliness, the loneliness from which everybody, knowingly or unknowingly, suffered. But she knew that her husband and her sons did not recognize her loneliness or Jess's or their own. She turned her eyes from the window to look at their faces around the table, and it was strange to see that they were still thinking in the most personal and particular terms of how they had been deceived by a servant, the ignorant granddaughter of an ignorant slave, a Negro woman from Brownsville who was crazy about the movies and who would soon be riding a bus, mile after mile, on her way to Hollywood, where she might find the friendly faces of the real Neil Hamilton and the real Irene Rich. It was with effort that Helen Ruth thought again of Jess's departure and the problem of offering an explanation to her family. At least, she said patiently, "My dears, don't you see how it was for Jess? How else can they tell us anything when there is such a gulf?" After a moment she said, "How can I make you understand this?"

Her husband and her three sons sat staring at her, their big hands, all so alike, resting on the breakfast table, their faces stamped with identical expressions, not of wonder but of incredulity. Helen Ruth was still holding firmly to the handle of the teacart. She pushed it slowly and carefully over the doorsill and into the dining room, dark and cool as an underground cavern, and spotlessly clean, the way Jess McGehee had left it.

JAMES THURBER

The Catbird Seat

MR. MARTIN bought the pack of Camels on Monday night in the most crowded cigar store on Broadway. It was theatre time and seven or eight men were buying cigarettes. The clerk didn't even glance at Mr. Martin, who put the pack in his overcoat pocket and went out. If any of the staff at F & S had seen him buy the cigarettes, they would have been astonished, for it was generally known that Mr. Martin did not smoke, and never had. No one saw him.

It was just a week to the day since Mr. Martin had decided to rub out Mrs. Ulgine Barrows. The term "rub out" pleased him because it suggested nothing more than the correction of an error — in this case an error of Mr. Fitweiler. Mr. Martin had spent each night of the past week working out his plan and examining it. As he walked home now he went over it again. For the hundredth time he resented the element of imprecision, the margin of guesswork that entered into the business. The project as he had worked it out was casual and bold, the risks were considerable. Something might go wrong anywhere along the line. And therein lay the cunning of his scheme. No one would ever see in it the cautious, painstaking hand of Erwin Martin, head of the filing department at F & S, of whom Mr. Fitweiler had once said, "Man is fallible but Martin isn't." No one would see his hand, that is, unless it were caught in the act.

Sitting in his apartment, drinking a glass of milk, Mr. Martin reviewed his case against Mrs. Ulgine Barrows, as he had every night for seven nights. He began at the beginning. Her quacking voice and braying laugh had first profaned the halls of F & S on March 7, 1941 (Mr. Martin had a head for dates). Old Roberts, the personnel chief, had introduced her as the newly appointed special adviser to the president of the firm, Mr. Fitweiler. The woman had appalled Mr. Martin instantly, but he hadn't shown it. He had given her his dry hand, a look of studious concentration, and a faint smile. "Well," she had said, looking at the papers on his desk, "are you lifting the oxcart out of the ditch?" As Mr. Martin recalled that moment, over his milk, he squirmed slightly. He must keep his mind on her crimes as a special adviser, not on her peccadillos as a personality. This he found difficult to do, in spite of entering an objection and sustaining it. The faults of the woman as a woman kept chattering on in his mind like an unruly witness. She had, for almost two years now, baited him. In the halls, in the elevator, even in his own office, into which she romped now and then like a circus horse, she was constantly shouting these silly questions at him. "Are you lifting the oxcart out of the ditch? Are you tearing up the pea patch? Are you hollering down the rain barrel? Are you scraping the bottom of the pickle barrel? Are you sitting in the catbird seat?"

It was Joey Hart, one of Mr. Martin's two assistants, who had explained what the gibberish meant. "She must be a Dodger fan," he had said. "Red Barber announces the Dodger games over the radio and he uses those expressions — picked 'em up down South." Joey had gone on to explain one or two. "Tearing up the pea patch" meant going on a rampage; "sitting in the catbird seat" meant sitting pretty, like a batter with three balls and no strikes on him. Mr. Martin dismissed all this with an effort. It had been annoying, it had driven him near to distraction, but he was too solid a man to be moved to murder by anything so childish. It was fortunate, he reflected as he passed on to the important charges against Mrs. Barrows, that he had stood up under it so well. He had maintained always an outward appearance of polite tolerance. "Why, I even believe you like the woman," Miss Paird, his other assistant, had once said to him. He had simply smiled.

A gavel rapped in Mr. Martin's mind and the case proper was resumed. Mrs. Ulgine Barrows stood charged with willful, blatant, and persistent attempts to destroy the efficiency and system of F & S. It was competent, material, and relevant to review her advent and rise to power. Mr. Martin had got the story from Miss Paird, who seemed always able to find things out. According to her, Mrs. Barrows had met Mr. Fitweiler at a party, where she had rescued him from the embraces of a powerfully built drunken man who had mistaken the president of F & S for a famous Middle Western football coach. She had led him to a sofa and somehow worked upon him a monstrous magic. The aging gentleman had jumped to the conclusion there and then that this was a woman of singular attainments, equipped to bring out the best in him and in the firm. A week later he had introduced her into F & S as his special adviser. On that day confusion got its foot in the door. After Miss Tyson, Mr. Brundage, and Mr. Bartlett had been fired and Mr. Munson had taken his hat and stalked out, mailing in his resignation later, old Roberts had been emboldened to speak to Mr. Fitweiler. He mentioned that Mr. Munson's department had been "a little disrupted" and hadn't they perhaps better resume the old system there? Mr. Fitweiler had said certainly not. He had the greatest faith in Mrs. Barrows' ideas. "They require a little seasoning, a little seasoning, is all," he had added. Mr. Roberts had given it up. Mr. Martin reviewed in detail all the changes wrought by Mrs. Barrows. She had begun chipping at the cornices of the firm's edifice and now she was swinging at the foundation stones with a pickaxe.

Mr. Martin came now, in his summing up, to the afternoon of Monday, November 2, 1942 — just one week ago. On that day, at 3 P.M., Mrs. Barrows had bounced into his office. "Boo!" she had yelled. "Are you scraping the bottom of the pickle barrel?" Mr. Martin had looked at her from under his green eyeshade, saying nothing. She had begun to wander about the office, taking it in with her great popping eyes. "Do you really need *all* these filing cabinets?"

she demanded suddenly. Mr. Martin's heart had jumped. "Each of these files," he had said, keeping his voice even, "plays an indispensable part in the system of F & S." She had brayed at him, "Well, don't tear up the pea patch!" and gone to the door. From there she had bawled, "But you sure have got a lot of fine scrap in here!" Mr. Martin could no longer doubt that the finger was on his beloved department. Her pickaxe was on the upswing, poised for the first blow. It had not come yet; he had received no blue memo from the enchanted Mr. Fitweiler bearing nonsensical instructions deriving from the obscene woman. But there was no doubt in Mr. Martin's mind that one would be forthcoming. He must act quickly. Already a precious week had gone by. Mr. Martin stood up in his living room, still holding his milk glass. Gentlemen of the jury, he said to himself, I demand the death penalty for this horrible person.

The next day Mr. Martin followed his routine, as usual. He polished his glasses more often and once sharpened an already sharp pencil, but not even Miss Paird noticed. Only once did he catch sight of his victim; she swept past him in the hall with a patronizing "Hi!" At five-thirty he walked home, as usual, and had a glass of milk, as usual. He had never drunk anything stronger in his life — unless you could count ginger ale. The late Sam Schlosser, the S of F & S, had praised Mr. Martin at a staff meeting several years before for his temperate habits. "Our most efficient worker neither drinks nor smokes," he had said. "The results speak for themselves." Mr. Fitweiler had sat by, nodding approval.

Mr. Martin was still thinking about that red-letter day as he walked over to the Schrafft's on Fifth Avenue near Forty-Sixth Street. He got there, as he always did, at eight o'clock. He finished his dinner and the financial page of the *Sun* at a quarter to nine, as he always did. It was his custom after dinner to take a walk. This time he walked down Fifth Avenue at a casual pace. His gloved hands felt moist and warm, his forehead cold. He transferred the Camels from his overcoat to a jacket pocket. He wondered, as he did so, if they did not represent an unnecessary note of strain. Mrs. Barrows smoked only Luckies. It was his idea to puff a few puffs on a Camel (after the rubbing-out), stub it out in the ashtray holding her lipstick-stained Luckies, and thus drag a small red herring across the trail. Perhaps it was not a good idea. It would take time. He might even choke, too loudly.

Mr. Martin had never seen the house on West Twelfth Street where Mrs. Barrows lived, but he had a clear enough picture of it. Fortunately, she had bragged to everybody about her ducky first-floor apartment in the perfectly darling three-story red-brick. There could be no doorman or other attendants; just the tenants of the second and third floors. As he walked along, Mr. Martin realized that he would get there before nine-thirty. He had considered walking north on Fifth Avenue from Schrafft's to a point from which it would take him until ten o'clock to reach the house. At that hour people were less likely to be coming in or going out. But the procedure would have an awkward loop in the straight thread of his casualness, and he had abandoned it. It was impossible to figure when people would be entering or leaving the house, anyway. There was a great risk at any hour. If he ran into anbody, he would simply have to place the rubbing-out of Ulgine Barrows in the inactive file forever. The same thing would hold true if there were someone in her apartment. In that case he would just say that he had been passing by, recognized her charming house, and thought to drop in.

It was eighteen minutes after nine when Mr. Martin turned into Twelfth Street. A man passed him, and a man and a woman, talking. There was no one within fifty paces when he came to the house, half-way down the block. He was up the steps and in the small vestibule in no time, pressing the bell under the card that said "Mrs. Ulgine Barrows." When the clicking in the lock started, he jumped forward against the door. He got inside fast, closing the door behind him. A bulb in a lantern hung from the hall ceiling on a chain seemed to give a monstrously bright light. There was nobody on the stair, which went up ahead of him along the left wall. A door opened down the hall in the wall on the right. He went toward it swiftly, on tip-toe.

"Well, for God's sake, look who's here!" bawled Mrs. Barrows, and her braying laugh rang out like the report of a shotgun. He rushed past her like a football tackle, bumping her. "Hey, quit shoving!" she said, closing the door behind them. They were in her living room, which seemed to Mr. Martin to be lighted by a hundred lamps. "What's after you?" she said. "You're as jumpy as a goat." He found he was unable to speak. His heart was wheezing in his throat. "I — yes," he finally brought out. She was jabbering and laughing as she started to help him off with his coat. "No, no," he said. "I'll put it here." He took it off and put it on a chair near the door. "Your hat and gloves, too," she said. "You're in a lady's house." He put his hat on top of the coat. Mrs. Barrows seemed larger than he had thought. He kept his gloves on. "I was passing by," he said. "I recognized — is there anyone here?" She laughed louder than ever. "No," she said, "we're all alone. You're as white as a sheet, you funny man. Whatever *has* come over you? I'll mix you a toddy." She started toward a door across the room. "Scotch-and-soda be all right? But say, you don't drink, do you?" She turned and gave him her amused look. Mr. Martin pulled himself together. "Scotch-and-soda will be all right," he heard himself say. He could hear her laughing in the kitchen.

Mr. Martin looked quickly around the living room for the weapon. He had counted on finding one there. There were andirons and a poker and something in a corner that loked like an Indian club. None of them would do. It couldn't be that way. He began to pace around. He came to a desk. On it lay a metal paper knife with an ornate handle. Would it be sharp enough? He reached for it and knocked over a small brass jar. Stamps spilled out of it and it fell to the floor with a clatter. "Hey," Mrs. Barrows yelled from the kitchen, "are you tearing up the pea patch?" Mr. Martin gave a strange laugh. Picking up the knife, he tried its point against his left wrist. It was blunt. It wouldn't do.

When Mrs. Barrows reappeared, carrying two highballs, Mr. Martin, standing there with his gloves on, became acutely conscious of the fantasy he had wrought. Cigarettes in his pocket, a drink prepared for him — it was all too grossly improbable. It was more than that; it was impossible. Somewhere in the back of his mind a vague idea stirred, sprouted. "For heaven's sake, take off those gloves," said Mrs. Barrows. "I always wear them in the house," said Mr. Martin. The idea began to bloom, strange and wonderful. She put the glasses on a coffee table in front of a sofa and sat on the sofa. "Come over here, you odd little man," she said. Mr. Martin went over and sat beside her. It was difficult getting a cigarette out of the pack of Camels, but he managed it. She held a match for him, laughing. "Well," she said, handing him his drink, "this is perfectly marvellous. You with a drink and a cigarette."

Mr. Martin puffed, not too awkwardly, and took a gulp of the highball. "I drink and smoke all the time," he said. He clinked his glass against hers. "Here's nuts to that old windbag, Fitweiler," he said, and gulped again. The stuff tasted awful, but he made no grimace. "Really, Mr. Martin," she said, her voice and posture changing, "you are insulting our employer." Mrs. Barrows was now all special adviser to the president. "I am preparing a bomb," said Mr. Martin, "which will blow the old goat higher than hell." He had only had a little of the drink, which was not strong. It couldn't be that. "Do you take dope or something?" Mrs. Barrows asked coldly. "Heroin," said Mr. Martin. "I'll be coked to the gills when I bump that old buzzard off." "Mr. Martin!" she shouted, getting to her feet. "That will be all of that. You must go at once." Mr. Martin took another swallow of his drink. He tapped his cigarette out in the ashtray and put the pack of Camels on the coffee table. Then he got up. She stood glaring at him. He walked over and put on his hat and coat. "Not a word about this," he said, and laid an index finger against his lips. All Mrs. Barrows could bring out was "Really!" Mr. Martin put his hand on the doorknob. "I'm sitting in the catbird seat," he said. He stuck his tongue out at her and left. Nobody saw him go.

Mr. Martin got to his apartment, walking, well before eleven. No one saw him go in. He had two glasses of milk after brushing his teeth, and he felt elated. It wasn't tipsiness, because he hadn't been tipsy. Anyway, the walk had worn off all effects of the whiskey. He got in bed and read a magazine for a while. He was asleep before midnight.

Mr. Martin got to the office at eight-thirty the next morning, as usual. At a quarter to nine, Ulgine Barrows, who had never before arrived at work before ten, swept into his office. "I'm reporting to

Mr. Fitweiler now!" she shouted. "If he turns you over to the police, it's no more than you deserve!" Mr. Martin gave her a look of shocked surprise. "I beg your pardon?" he said. Mrs. Barrows snorted and bounced out of the room, leaving Miss Paird and Joey Hart staring after her. "What's the matter with that old devil now?" asked Miss Paird. "I have no idea," said Mr. Martin, resuming his work. The other two looked at him and then at each other. Miss Paird got up and went out. She walked slowly past the closed door of Mr. Fitweiler's office. Mrs. Barrows was yelling inside, but she was not braying. Miss Paird could not hear what the woman was saying. She went back to her desk.

Forty-five minutes later, Mrs. Barrows left the president's office and went into her own, shutting the door. It wasn't until half an hour later that Mr. Fitweiler sent for Mr. Martin. The head of the filing department, neat, quiet, attentive, stood in front of the old man's desk. Mr. Fitweiler was pale and nervous. He took his glasses off and twiddled them. He made a small, bruffing sound in his throat. "Martin," he said, "you have been with us more than twenty years." "Twenty-two, sir," said Mr. Martin. "In that time," pursued the president, "your work and your — uh — manner have been exemplary." "I trust so, sir," said Mr. Martin. "I have understood, Martin," said Mr. Fitweiler, "that you have never taken a drink or smoked." "That is correct, sir," said Mr. Martin. "Ah, yes." Mr. Fitweiler polished his glasses. "You may describe what you did after leaving the office yesterday, Martin," he said. Mr. Martin allowed less than a second for his bewildered pause. "Certainly, sir," he said. "I walked home. Then I went to Schrafft's for dinner. Afterward I walked home again. I went to bed early, sir, and read a magazine for a while. I was asleep before eleven." "Ah, yes," said Mr. Fitweiler again. He was silent for a moment, searching for the proper words to say to the head of the filing department. "Mrs. Barrows," he said finally, "Mrs. Barrows has worked hard, Martin, very hard. It grieves me to report that she has suffered a severe breakdown. It has taken the form of a persecution complex accompanied by distressing hallucinations." "I am very sorry, sir," said Mr. Martin. "Mrs. Barrows is under the delusion," continued Mr. Fitweiler, "that you visited her last evening and behaved yourself in an — uh — unseemly manner."

He raised his hand to silence Mr. Martin's little pained outcry. "It is the nature of these psychological diseases," Mr. Fitweiler said, "to fix upon the least likely and most innocent party as the — uh — source of persecution. These matters are not for the lay mind to grasp, Martin. I've just had my psychiatrist, Doctor Fitch, on the phone. He would not, of course, commit himself, but he made enough generalizations to substantiate my suspicions. I suggested to Mrs. Barrows, when she had completed her — uh — story to me this morning, that she visit Doctor Fitch, for I suspected a condition at once. She flew, I regret to say, into a rage, and demanded — uh — requested that I call you on the carpet. You may not know, Martin, but Mrs. Barrows had planned a reorganization of your department — subject to my approval, of course, subject to my approval. This brought you, rather than anyone else, to her mind — but again that is a phenomenon for Doctor Fitch and not for us. So, Martin, I am afraid Mrs. Barrows' usefulness here is at an end." "I am dreadfully sorry, sir," said Mr. Martin.

It was at this point that the door to the office blew open with the suddenness of a gas-main explosion and Mrs. Barrows catapulted through it. "Is the little rat denying it?" she screamed. "He can't get away with that!" Mr. Martin got up and moved discreetly to a point beside Mr. Fitweiler's chair. "You drank and smoked at my apartment," she bawled at Mr. Martin, "and you know it! You called Mr. Fitweiler an old windbag and said you were going to blow him up when you got coked to the gills on your heroin!" She stopped yelling to catch her breath and a new glint came into her popping eyes. "If you weren't such a drab, ordinary little man," she said, "I'd think you'd planned it all. Sticking your tongue out, saying you were sitting in the catbird seat, because you thought no one would believe me when I told it! My God, it's really too perfect!" She brayed loudly and hysterically, and the fury was on her again. She glared at Mr. Fitweiler. "Can't you see how he has tricked us, you old fool? Can't you see his little game?" But Mr. Fitweiler had been surreptitiously pressing all the buttons under the top of his desk and employees of F & S began pouring into the room. "Stockton," said Mr. Fitweiler, "you and Fishbein will take Mrs. Barrows to her home. Mrs. Powell, you will go with them." Stockton, who had played a little football in high school, blocked Mrs. Barrows as she made for Mr. Martin. It took him and Fishbein together to force her out of the door into the hall, crowded with stenographers and office boys. She was still screaming imprecations at Mr. Martin, tangled and contradictory imprecations. The hubbub finally died out down the corridor.

"I regret that this has happened," said Mr. Fitweiler. "I shall ask you to dismiss it from your mind, Martin. "Yes, sir," said Mr. Martin, anticipating his chief's "That will be all" by moving to the door. "I will dismiss it." He went out and shut the door, and his step was light and quick in the hall. When he entered his department he had slowed down to his customary gait, and he walked quietly across the room to the W20 file, wearing a look of studious concentration.

EUDORA WELTY

A Curtain of Green

Every DAY, on summer in Larkin's Hill, it rained a little. The rain was a regular thing, and would come about two o'clock in the afternoon.

One day, almost as late as five o'clock, the sun was still shining. It seemed almost to spin in a tiny groove in the polished sky, and down below, in the trees along the street and in the rows of flower gardens in the town, every leaf reflected the sun from a hardness like a mirror-surface. Nearly all the women sat at the windows of their houses, fanning and sighing, waiting for the rain.

Mrs. Larkin's garden was a large, densely grown plot running downhill behind the small white house where she lived alone since the death of her husband. The sun and the rain of that summer had not discouraged her from working there daily. Now the intense sun like a tweezers picked out her clumsy, slight figure in its old pair of men's overalls rolled up at the sleeves and trousers, separated it from the thick leaves and made it look strange and yellow as she worked with a hoe — overvigorous, disreputable, and heedless.

Within its border of hedge, like a wall, and visible only from the upstairs windows of the neighbors, this slanting, tangled garden, more and more overabundant and confusing, must have become so familiar to Mrs. Larkin that she might be unable, by now to conceive of any other place. Since the accident in which her husband was killed, she had never once been seen anywhere else. Every morning she might be observed walking slowly, rather timidly, out of the white house, wearing a pair of the untidy overalls, often with her hair streaming and almost matted where she had neglected to comb it. She would wander about for a little while at first, uncertainly, deep among the plants and wet with their dew, and yet not quite putting out her hand to touch anything. And then a sort of sturdiness would possess her — stabilize her; she would stand still for a moment as if a blindfold had been removed; and then she would kneel in the flowers and begin to work.

She worked without stopping, almost invisibly, submerged all day among the thick, irregular, sloping beds of plants. The servant would call her at dinnertime, and she would obey; but it was not until it was completely dark that she would truthfully give up her labor and with a drooping, submissive walk appear at the house, slowly opening the small low door at the back. Even the rain would bring only a pause to her; she would move to the shelter of the pear tree, which in mid-April hung heavily almost to the ground in brilliant full leaf, in the center of the garden.

It might seem as if the extreme fertility of her garden were at once a preoccupation and challenge to Mrs. Larkin. Only by ceaseless activity could she cope with the rich blackness of this soil. Only by cutting, separating, thinning, and tying back in the clumps of flowers and bushes and vines could she have kept them from overreaching their boundaries and multiplying out of all reason. The daily summer rains could only increase her vigilance and her already excessive energy. And yet, Mrs. Larkin rarely cut, separated, tied back. . . . To a certain extent, she seemed not to seek for order, but to allow an overflowering, as if she consciously ventured now a little further, a little deeper, into her life in the garden.

She planted every kind of flower that she could find or order from a catalogue — planted thickly and hastily, without stopping to think, without any regard for the ideas that her neighbors might elect in their club as to what constituted an appropriate vista, or an effect of restfulness, or even harmony of color. Just to what end Mrs. Larkin worked so strenuously in her garden, her neighbors could not see. She certainly never sent a single one of her fine flowers to any of them. And if she thought of *beauty* at all (they regarded her stained overalls, now almost of a color with the leaves), she certainly did not strive for it in her garden. It was impossible to enjoy looking at such a place; to the neighbors gazing down from their upstairs windows, it had the appearance of a sort of jungle, in which the slight, heedless form of its owner daily lost itself.

At first, after the death of Mr. Larkin — for whose father, after all, the town had been named — they had called upon the widow with decent frequency; but she had not appreciated it, they said to one another. Now, occasionally, they looked down from their bedroom windows as they brushed studiously at their hair in the morning; they found her place in her garden, as they might have run their fingers toward a city in a map of a foreign country, located her from their distance almost in curiosity, and then forgot her.

Early that morning they had heard whistling in the Larkin garden. They had recognized Jamey's tune, and had seen him kneeling in the flowers at Mrs. Larkin's side. He was only the colored boy who worked in the neighborhood by the day. Even Jamey, it was said, Mrs. Larkin would tolerate only now and then. . . .

Throughout the afternoon she had raised her head at intervals to see how fast he was getting along in his transplanting. She had not let him wait until after the rain to do it. She was busy with the hoe, clearing one of the last patches of uncultivated ground for some new shrubs. She bent under the sunlight, chopping in blunt, rapid, tireless strokes. Once she raised her head far back to stare at the flashing sky. Her eyes were dull and puckered, as if from long impatience or bewilderment. Her mouth was a sharp line. People said she never spoke.

But memory tightened about her easily, without any prelude of warning or even despair. She would see promptly, as if a curtain had been jerked quite unceremoniously away from a little scene, the front porch of the white house, the shady street in front, and the blue automobile in which her husband approached, driving home from work. It was a summer day, a day from the summer before. In the freedom of gaily turning her head, a motion she was now forced by memory to repeat as she hoed the ground, she could see again the tree that was going to fall. There had been no warning. But there was the enormous tree, the fragrant chinaberry tree, suddenly tilting, dark and slow like a cloud, leaning down to her husband. From her place on the front porch she had spoken in a soft voice to him, never so intimate as at that moment, "You can't be killed." But the tree had fallen, had struck the car exactly so as to crush him to death. She had waited there on the porch for a time afterwards, not moving at all — in a sort of recollection — as if to reach under and bring out from obliteration her protective words, and to try them once again. . . . so as to change the whole happening. It was an accident that was incredible, when her love for her husband was keeping him safe.

She continued to hoe the black ground, to beat down the juicy weeds. Presently she became aware that hers was the only motion to continue in the whole slackened place. There was no wind at all now. The cries of the birds had hushed. The sun seemed clamped to the side of the sky. Everything had stopped once again; the stillness had mesmerized the stems of the plants, and all the leaves went suddenly into thickness. The shadow of the pear tree, in the center of the garden, lay callous on the ground. Across the yard, Jamey knelt motionless.

"Jamey!" she called angrily.

But her voice hardly carried in the dense garden. She felt all at once terrified, as though her loneliness had been pointed out by some outside force whose finger parted the hedge. She drew her hand for an instant to her breast. An obscure fluttering there frightened her, as though the force babbled to her, The bird that flies within your heart could not divide this cloudy air. . . . She stared without expression at the garden. She clung to the hoe again, and stared across the green leaves toward Jamey.

A look of docility in the Negro's back as he knelt in the flowers began to infuriate her. She started to walk toward him, dragging the hoe vaguely through the flowers behind her. She forced herself to look at him, and noticed him closely for the first time — the way he looked like a child. As he turned his head a little to one side and negligently stirred the dirt with his yellow finger, she saw, with a sort of helpless suspicion and hunger, a soft, rather deprecating smile on his face; he was lost in some impossible dream of his own while he transplanted the zinnia shoots. He was not even whistling; even that sound was gone.

She walked nearer to him — he must have been deaf! — almost stealthily bearing down upon his laxity and his absorption, as if that glimpse of the side of his face, that turned-away smile, were a teasing, innocent, flickering, and beautiful vision — some mirage to her strained and wandering eyes.

Yet a feeling of stricture, of a responding hopelessness almost approaching ferocity, grew with alarming quickness about her. When she was directly behind him she stood quite still for a moment, in the queer, sheathed manner she had before beginning her gardening in the morning. Then she raised the hoe above her head; the clumsy sleeves fell back, exposing the thin, unsunburned whiteness of her arms, the shocking fact of their youth.

She gripped the handle tightly, tightly, as though convinced that the wood of the handle could feel, and that all her strength could indent its surface with pain. The head of Jamey, bent there below her, seemed witless, terrifying, wonderful, almost inaccessible to her, and yet in its explicit nearness meant surely for destruction, with its clustered hot woolly hair, its intricate glistening ears, its small brown branching streams of sweat, the bowed head holding so obviously and so deafly its ridiculous dream.

Such a head she could strike off, intentionally, so deeply did she know, from the effect of a man's danger and death, its cause in oblivion; and so helpless was she, too helpless to defy the workings of accident, of life and death, of unaccountability. . . . Life and death, she thought, gripping the heavy hoe, life and death, which now meant nothing to her, but which she was compelled to continue to wield with both her hands, ceaselessly, asking, Was it not possible to compensate? to punish? to protest? Pale darkness turned for a moment through the sunlight, like a narrow leaf blown through the garden in a wind.

At that moment, the rain came. The first drop touched her unraised arm. Small, close sounds and coolness touched her.

Sighing, Mrs. Larkin lowered the hoe to the ground and laid it carefully among the growing plants. She stood still where she was, close to Jamey, and listened to the rain falling. It was so gentle. It was so full — the sound of the end of waiting.

In the light from the rain, different from sunlight, everything appeared to gleam unreflecting from within itself, in its quiet arcade of identity. The green of the small zinnia shoots was very pure, almost burning. One by one, as the rain reached them, all the individual little plants shone out, and then the branching vines. The pear tree gave a soft rushing noise, like the wings of a bird alighting. She could sense behind her, as if a lamp were lighted in the night, the signal-like whiteness of the house. Then Jamey, as if in the shock of realizing the rain had come, turned his full face toward her, questions and delight intensifying his smile, gathering up his aroused, stretching body. He stammered some disconnected words, shyly.

She did not answer Jamey or move at all. She would not feel anything now except the rain falling. She listened for its scattered soft drops between Jamey's words, its quiet touching of the spears of the iris leaves, and a clear sound like a bell as it began to fall in a pitcher the cook had set on the doorstep.

Finally, Jamey stood there quietly, as if waiting for his money, with his hand trying to brush his confusion away from before his face. The rain fell steadily. A wind of deep wet fragrance beat against her.

Then as if it had swelled and broken over a daily levee, tenderness tore and spun through her sagging body.

It has come, she thought senselessly, her head lifting and her eyes looking without understanding at the sky which had begun to move, to fold nearer in softening, dissolving clouds. It was almost dark. Soon the loud and gentle night of rain would come. It would pound upon the steep roof of the white house. Within, she would lie in her bed and hear the rain. On and on it would fall, beat and fall. The day's work would be over in the garden. She would lie in bed, her arms tired at her sides and in motionless peace: against that which was inexhaustible, there was no defense.

Then Mrs. Larken sank in one motion down into the flowers and lay there, fainting and streaked with rain. Her face was fully up-turned, down among the plants, with the hair beaten away from her forehead and her open eyes closing at once when the rain touched them. Slowly her lips began to part. She seemed to move slightly, in the petulant adjustment of a sleeper.

Jamey ran jumping and crouching about her, drawing in his breath alternately at the flowers breaking under his feet and at the shapeless, passive figure on the ground. Then he became quiet, and stood back at a little distance and looked in awe at her unknowing face, white and rested under its bombardment. He remembered how something had filled him with stillness when he felt her standing there behind him looking down at him, and he would not have turned around at that moment for anything in the world. He remembered the oblivious crash of the windows next door being shut when the rain started. . . . But now, in this unseen place, it was he who stood looking at Mrs. Larkin.

In a horrified, piteous, beseeching voice he began to call her name until she stirred.

"Miss Lark'! Miss Lark'!"

Then he jumped nimbly to his feet and ran out of the garden.